PENGUIN BOOKS

A Year and a Day

Isabelle Broom was born in Cambridge nine days before the 1980s began and studied Media Arts at the University of West London before starting a career first in local newspapers and then as a junior sub-editor at *heat* magazine. She travelled through Europe during her gap year and went to live on the Greek island of Zakynthos for an unforgettable and life-shaping six months after completing her degree. Since then, she has travelled to Canada, Sri Lanka, Sicily, New York, LA, the Canary Islands, Spain and lots more of Greece, but her wanderlust was reined in when she met Max, a fluffy little Bolognese puppy desperate for a home. When she's not writing novels set in far-flung locations, Isabelle spends her time being the Book Reviews Editor at *heat* magazine and walking her beloved dog round the parks of north London.

You can follow her on Twitter @Isabelle_Broom or find her on Facebook under Isabelle Broom Author.

A Year and a Day

ISABELLE BROOM

PENGUIN BOOKS

PENGUIN BOOKS

UK | USA | Canada | Ireland | Australia
India | New Zealand | South Africa

Penguin Books is part of the Penguin Random House group of companies
whose addresses can be found at global.penguinrandomhouse.com.

First published 2016
001

Set in 12.5/14.75pt Garamond MT Std
Typeset by Palimpsest Book Production Limited,
Falkirk, Stirlingshire
Printed in Great Britain by Clays Ltd, St Ives plc

A CIP catalogue record for this book is available from the British Library

ISBN: 978–1–405–92533–4

www.greenpenguin.co.uk

For Sadie

Acknowledgements

I only went and wrote another novel! My first thanks must go to you, dearest reader, for picking up the book and coming on this journey with me. I really hope you enjoy it, and please feel free to come and chat to me about it on Twitter @Isabelle_Broom. I would dearly love to hear from you.

Hannah Ferguson – aka agent extraordinaire – what would I do without you? Your continued support, advice, enthusiasm, brilliance and hard work astonish me on a daily basis, and it's no exaggeration to say that I hold you responsible for making all my dreams come true, and then some. The team at Hardman & Swainson and the Marsh Agency are nothing short of legendary – Camilla and Fay, we got there in the end! Huge thanks and love to every single one of you.

Oh, Miss Kimberley Atkins of Penguin Michael Joseph, where do I even start? I know where, by telling you that you are the undisputed empress of all editors EVER. Thank you for your boundless energy, inexhaustible encouragement, truly masterful editing skills and total professionalism at all times. I don't think you'll ever know just how much I love and admire you. I honestly couldn't do any of this without you, so thank you. To Maxine Hitchcock, Claire Bush, Jenny Platt, Sarah Bance, Emma Brown and everyone at Penguin who worked towards getting this book baby out into the world – you are all amazing! Jess Hart, you've done it again with this cover, lady. I'm in absolute awe of your talents.

Being an author is without a doubt the best of all jobs, not least because it all takes place in a world populated by all the very best people. I'd like to thank my author chums Katie Marsh, Stella Newman, Paige Toon, Ali Harris, Giovanna Fletcher, Rosie Walsh, Kirsty Greenwood, Cesca Major, Cressida McLaughlin, Lisa Dickenson, Jo Thomas, Miranda Dickinson, Milly Johnson, Louise Candlish, Penny Parkes, Hannah Beckerman, Dani Atkins, Kate Eberlen, Fanny Blake, Katie Fforde, Adele Parks, Tasmina Perry, Victoria Fox, Jennifer Barclay, Dorothy Koomson, Rosanna Ley, Julie Cohen, Rowan Coleman, Lindsey Kelk and Victoria Walters for all their love, advice and support. You are all wonderful, brilliant and gorgeous. Massive thanks must also go to Claire 'Frosty' Frost, Francesca Brown, Francesca Russell, Georgina Moore, Ben Willis, Sophie Ransom, Jenny Stallard, Nina Pottell, Sara-Jade Virtue, Fran Gough, Anne Cater, Sharon Wilden, Vicki Bowles, Linda Hill and Effrosyni Moschoudi, and to all the other bloggers, book fans and readers who take the time to post reviews. It's thanks to you that novels find their way under the noses of new people, which is what it's all about.

Oh, and I mustn't forget to thank my Book Angel, Annette Hannah, firstly for letting me pinch her name for one of the characters in this book, but even more importantly for making me giggle like a drunken Muttley whenever I see her.

To my *heat* family, both past and present, you are all

amazing. Thanks so much for all the support you've given me and for being generally hilarious on a daily basis. We will always have each other, no matter what.

I feel extremely lucky to have such epic friends, and if I could list every single one of you here then I would, but paper is apparently really expensive. Tchuh! I do, however, want to thank my beautiful, bold, brilliant and blooming hilarious best friend Sadie Davies, without whom life would lose so much incomparable fun and adventure. Thanks also to Ian Lawton, who has the biggest heart and best laugh of anyone I know, and to Tom Harding, Dominic Morgan, Ewan Bishop, Sarah Holmes, Corrie Heale, Jamie Green, Matt Hurrell, Lisa Howells, Daniel Tang, Alex Holbrook, Charlotte McKeggie, Vicky Zimmerman, Molly Haynes, Mark Tamsett, Lindsey Perkins, Richard Perry, Jonathan Paul Gunson, the KMC Massive – aka Tamsin Carroll and Gemma Courage – and my uni crew, Ranjit Dhillon, Colette Berry, Sarah Beddingfield, Chad Higgins, Jim Morris, Carrie Wallder and Sue Pigott. You are all legends.

To my family, this is where I run out of words. What is there to say except thank you for always being there and for championing me from the rooftops. Mum, from that big blue notebook you bought me to write stories in aged six, to the present day, when you stay awake all night to read the first drafts of my novels: you've always been my rock, my best friend and my inspiration. I do ALL of it for you, every single last word.

The snow started as night fell and with it came the silence. That magical, almost ethereal quiet that always seems to accompany the gently falling flakes, as if all the inhabitants of the world had paused just to admire their beauty.

One person, however, was not moved by the snow – nor was she watching it. Standing by the wall on the edge of the bridge, the cobbles wet beneath the soles of her shoes and her breath clearly visible in the sharp, still air, she found herself drawn instead to the dark mass of water below.

What would it feel like to plunge straight down into it? she wondered. Would the river impale her with its icy fingers, would she cough and splutter and flail her arms above her head, or would she feel nothing but a sense of relief? The latter option was deliciously tempting. These past few days had been so exhausting, and she was weary. Weary of the confusion, weary of the uncertainty and weary of the pain.

She heard the clock begin to strike and closed her eyes, the individual chimes rattling her insides with their unintended finality: a countdown to hopelessness, a symphony of despair. The snow was falling even harder now and it was becoming difficult to see through her tears.

Just one step up, a leg swung over, a final gasp of air and then a single jump. It could all be over in less than a minute.

High above the bridge and past clouds bloated with snow, the moon sat snug and proud in the sky. From up here the world was merely a coloured penny in an ocean of blackness, a bright pebble of life and love and sadness and joy. Back on the bridge, the moonlight was everywhere, illuminating the statues and making the patches of rubbed gold gleam blue in the darkness. Still the snow fell.

The clock had chimed for the final time and with it came the realisation. She took a deep breath and steadied her hands against the stone wall, preparing to support herself as she climbed up. But as her foot left the ground, she heard a shout.

It was him. He had come.

I

Megan screwed her jeans up into a ball and lobbed them as hard as she could across the room. They hit the wall with a disappointingly quiet thump and slid forlornly to the floor, landing on top of the three shirts and five pairs of knickers she had already thrown.

Packing was something she'd always been good at, a fact she was quite smug about. Those neatly rolled clothes, socks stuffed into shoes, toiletries decanted into miniature bottles and a careful amount of space left over for any purchases made while away.

This time, however, she was having a hell of a job.

Just what did you pack for a trip you're taking with a friend who is a man, but definitely not your significant other? A man you kissed once when drunk ages ago, but who you don't want to kiss again. A man who has invited you along on a trip to Prague on a purely platonic basis, but who is most definitely single. A man who you will have to spend some serious one-on-one time with over the next five days. A man who you will even have to share a bed with.

It was a bit weird.

Megan had refused to listen when her friends told her it would all end in tears. Hell, even her own mother had issued a word of warning.

'I don't want the poor boy getting hurt,' she'd said. Typical Mum.

Megan had waved aside their concerns, telling them that it was fine. Ollie knew that the stupid kiss had been a one-off, and that they were just good friends.

But still – weird.

Should she pack her black dress with the great cleavage? It looked nice on her and she liked wearing it, but would Ollie think it was a sign that she wanted him to notice her? Would she lead him on without even meaning to? And what about pyjamas? If she brought the new satin set with the lace trim, would he take them as a green light and assume she fancied a friendly fumble under the covers? But her only other alternative was the grotty T-shirt and shorts combo that had been festering away in her chest of drawers since university. She didn't want Ollie to think she was a gross old tramp either. It was a problem.

Vest tops that had once been so innocuous now reeked of suggestion, jeans that had fitted well across the bum had all of a sudden become slutty, and as for her underwear selection . . . she didn't even know where to start with that heap of provocative red flags to a sex-mad bull. It was no good, she was going to have to go to the most boring clothes shop in London and buy a sample wardrobe of the plainest and least offensive garments they had. Great.

Megan's phone vibrated in her pocket. A message from Ollie:

> Hope you're all packed.
> Looking forward to tomorrow.
> Pints at the airport at 6 a.m.,
> right? You're buying x

Oh God, he'd added a kiss. It had started already.

She chewed her lip as she mulled over her reply, finally settling for:

> Packed hours ago, you div.
> And YOU'RE buying.

No kiss for him, oh no.

Sighing, Megan abandoned the sheer hopelessness that was her packing and picked up her camera instead. Immediately she felt calmer. She loved feeling the weight of it in her hands, the texture of the casing beneath her practised fingers, the gentle click as she shifted the lens into position, and the surge of pleasure as she finally pressed the shutter down and captured her image. A snapshot of a moment, a memory saved forever, the view of the world as she saw it. Nothing made Megan happier than taking photos, and she knew photography would always be her first love. Not a man, not her friends, not even – her brain frowned momentarily – her family could compete. This camera was as much a part of Megan as her limbs, skin, hair and soul, and just holding it now, in the midst of a pile of rejected clothes, she felt comforted.

When Ollie had revealed that he'd be teaching his class of eight-year-olds about Prague next term, he had asked Megan if she'd accompany him on a fact-finding trip during a teacher training week. As his non-official photographer, Megan had done extensive research on the place before making her decision – and it looked absolutely magical. All those cobbled streets and statues, not to mention the beautiful Vltava River, which ran right through the heart of the city. Prague was also packed with architectural treats, some dating back to before the thirteenth century, and Megan felt the hairs stand up on her arms with anticipation whenever she thought about it.

She was so sure that the trip was going to inspire her that she had finally chewed up her nerves, spat them out, and booked herself a May exhibition space along the South Bank here in London. It was to be her first big showcase in the capital and, with Christmas only a few weeks away now, she was cutting it quite fine, time-wise – but that's how she preferred to work. Setting deadlines, writing lists, nagging herself to get up and get out, do something with her day, achieve something, anything – that was Megan all over.

Her phone was vibrating again.

> Just thought – should we
> travel to the airport together?
> Taxi from mine? x

Megan put her camera down and groaned. She only had herself to blame for agreeing to flights that departed at such an ungodly hour, but she didn't want to add to her sleep deprivation by trekking all the way over to Ollie's at five a.m. And he'd added another kiss.

Come to mine – it's easier. Megan pressed send and waited, watching as the message registered as delivered. As she suspected, it didn't take Ollie long to reply.

> OK boss xx

TWO KISSES?

Megan spent the rest of her afternoon procrastinating. Having firmly decided that it was totally absurd to buy boring clothes that she'd never wear again, she packed, then repacked her case, then deliberated for twenty whole minutes over whether or not to bother shaving her legs. By the time she was cleaned, preened, packed and settling down in front of the TV with a glass of red wine in hand, it was almost ten o'clock. If Ollie was coming round at five in the morning, she had better try to get some sleep soon, although there was only half a bottle of red left. No point in leaving any dregs if she was going away for five days – that was just wasteful.

The sound of the doorbell almost made her lose what was in her glass.

'Bloody hell,' she muttered, picking up the baseball bat that she kept by the top of the stairs and wrapping her oversized cardigan tighter around her body. Megan had lived in North London for over ten years now and never in that time had she been mugged, attacked or otherwise burgled, but a girl living on her own could never be too careful.

'Who's there?' she yelled through the door.

She heard a low chuckle, before Ollie's familiar voice replied: 'The man of your wildest dreams.'

Megan lowered her bat and opened the door a crack, glaring at her bespectacled friend through the gap.

'You're a bit early, don't you think?'

'What do you mean?' Ollie had the grace to look momentarily confused, and Megan realised now that there was a suitcase by his feet.

'I thought you were coming over in the morning.'

'What, trudge all the way over here from Putney at five in the morning? As if I was ever going to do that. I thought you meant me to come over tonight.'

He didn't look like he was lying, and Megan opened the door a fraction further.

'You'll have to sleep on the sofa,' she told him, trying not to care that she was wearing fluffy dog slippers and not a single scrap of make-up.

Ollie heaved his case over the threshold and Megan let him go up the stairs first. She told him it was because she needed to lock the door properly, but really she didn't want him staring at her bum on the way up. She'd caught him gawping at it once before, on an occasion where she had regrettably worn some very tight jeans, but she had no idea what he'd found so alluring. If she was going to pick one word to describe her bottom, it would be gargantuan.

'Help yourself to wine,' she told him when they were upstairs, already lamenting the extra glass she'd been planning to drink. Then again, she reminded herself, they could do all the drinking they liked over the next few days – Prague was famous for its beer halls.

As if reading her mind, Ollie proposed a toast to 'the first of many' when he clinked his glass against her own, and she allowed herself to smile at her friend for the first time. There were plenty of things she liked about Ollie: he was tall, he had lots of thick chestnut hair that he actually remembered to wash, he had a nice job that provided lots of funny anecdotes on an almost daily basis, he still spoke to his parents regularly and not under duress, he was funny, and he was one of the best, most loyal friends she'd ever had.

'Do you think this is going to be weird?'

She hadn't meant to say it, but she was glad she had

when Ollie merely grinned at her and placed a reassuring hand on her arm.

'Nah.' He shrugged. 'It'll be fun.'

He'd taken off his glasses because they'd steamed up, as they always did in her tropical front room. The radiator had broken years ago and was set permanently to super-high, but Megan, unlike any other poor soul who dared to enter her lair, had grown used to it.

Ollie's eyes were probably his best feature, she decided. They were a bright hazel colour and magnified most of the time by his specs. She, by contrast, had tiny eyes, and they were a rather uninspiring pavement shade of grey.

The silence that had inexplicably reared up was becoming uncomfortable, so Megan filled it by telling him about her plans for the new exhibition. She hadn't settled on a theme yet, she told him, but was hoping that Prague would give her all the inspiration she needed. What she didn't do, however, was explain exactly why this exhibition meant so much to her. That could wait for another day.

'It sounds great,' Ollie said, draining his wine and topping up both their glasses with the small amount that was left. He was always so supportive about her work – it was one of the reasons she liked having him around.

'We are doing something special for my birthday, though, right?' Ollie looked at her quizzically.

'Um . . .'

'I turned thirty-five a month ago, and I've yet to get so much as a card from you. Thirty-five is a milestone, you know. So I insist you take me to dinner at the classiest goulash joint in the whole of Prague.'

'You're an idiot,' she told him, wondering silently if she

had time to sneakily go online, find a restaurant in Prague and book them a table before their flight. She guessed that she probably didn't.

'I'm only teasing you.' He nudged her leg with his foot and she clocked his bright pink socks. 'How about another snog instead?'

Megan couldn't help it; she pulled a face.

'Ollie . . .' she began, but he held up a hand.

'I know, I know – we're friends and there's to be no funny business whatsoever. I promise I was only joking, Meg.'

She narrowed her eyes at his bemused expression.

'You're so easy to wind up,' Ollie told her, pushing his glasses up on his nose.

Megan was suddenly assailed by a memory of the first time they'd sat side by side on her sofa, having only met a few hours before. She had been buoyed up by wine in her system then too, but the outcome had been very different to this.

'Is it hot in here, or is it just me?' she murmured, looking up to find Ollie peering at her in amusement.

'You've gone all pink in the face, young lady,' he said, taking her glass out of her hand and draining it himself. 'Come on – time for bed. We've got a long day tomorrow.'

Megan forced herself to walk to the cupboard and fetch the spare bedding, which she dropped on the sofa next to him, waiting out in the hallway until she heard him start to undress.

This trip was clearly going to be weird, she realised. But then there was nothing Megan Spencer loved more than a challenge.

2

For a long time after her daughter hung up, Hope simply sat and stared into space. She supposed she ought to feel grateful that Annette hadn't actually slammed down the receiver, but then you couldn't really do that any more, could you? Not with everyone and their pet dog owning a mobile phone. It was far less dramatic to jab a screen with your finger than smash plastic against plastic and hear that satisfying ring of enraged silence, but the result was still the same: she felt as if her heart was breaking into pieces.

There was a bowl of fruit on the table in front of her, and Hope picked up one of the satsumas. It was an easy peeler, the kind you found in every supermarket in the run-up to Christmas, and this one was definitely past its best. The skin had started to harden, and when she squeezed it, Hope could feel the overripe fruit mushing unpleasantly inside.

It's just like me, she thought – outwardly tough, but mush underneath. Annette didn't agree, though – she'd said as much on the phone just a few minutes ago, accusing her mum of having no heart, of being selfish, of ruining her life.

Hope stood up abruptly and took the satsuma into the kitchen, where she tossed it into the bin. Reaching across the narrow space, she flicked on the kettle and readied a mug for tea, more out of habit than an actual desire to drink one.

She still felt a bit like a spare part in this flat. Back at home – well, back at the other house – she'd always had a job to do. Beds needing to be made, dinner to be cooked, laundry to be done. But here? Here there was just the two of them, and such a small amount of space.

But you chose this, she reminded herself, squeezing the teabag against the side of the mug. You couldn't have carried on the way things were.

Hope took her tea to the front window and peered down at the street below. A woman about the same age as her had just parked her car across the road by the post office, and was now trying to juggle a large stack of parcels wrapped in brown paper. Hope noted her neat, set curls and her smart coat, all buttoned up against the chilly December wind.

She wondered if the woman had got all dressed up just for this single errand, as Hope would once have done. For a while, she had channelled all her energy into looking her very best for just two hours a week, then slowly it became four, then six. Now she got up early every single morning to brush her hair and apply make-up. Today she was wearing a beautiful green dress with a plunging neckline – something she would once upon a time have saved for a special occasion, but now felt able to wear whenever she wanted.

She should really go out today, head over to the Arndale Centre and pick up some bits for Christmas, perhaps get her nails done and treat herself to a mulled wine at the open-air market. It would be a lot more fun with a friend, but she wasn't sure if any of them would even want to hear from her. It was so awkward, this sort of thing, and Hope didn't really blame them, but she did wince inwardly as an awful sense of loneliness crept through her.

The tea had gone cold, so Hope poured it down the sink then washed up the mug, dried it, and put it back in the cupboard. The clock above the draining board ticked round to eleven a.m., and Hope heard the front door downstairs open and close, followed by the sound of feet on the stairs.

He still gave her butterflies.

'Hello, gorgeous.'

Charlie crossed the living room and pulled Hope into his arms, kissing the tip of her nose and gazing into her eyes.

'I still can't believe you're here,' he said, his eyes never leaving hers.

Hope felt the wonderful warmth that had become so addictive ooze through her, as if the tips of Charlie's fingers were open faucets, affection pouring out from them into every part of her body, filling her up with love. When he took her in his arms like this, all the hurt and confusion that was plaguing her would miraculously melt away – it was no wonder that she could never get enough of him.

'Well, I am.' She smiled up at him.

Charlie kissed her again, on the lips this time. He was wearing a bright red woolly hat, which clashed with the pink of his cheeks.

Hope dipped her head and rested it shyly against his chest. It was ridiculous, really; a woman of her age being reduced to a blushing teenager.

Charlie was now looking at her like a teenage boy might if he'd just been given a year's subscription to *Playboy* magazine and a Manchester United season ticket. All he had to do was look at her like this, and Hope felt better about everything. If Charlie said that everything would be okay, then she believed him. It had always been that way between them right from the very first day they met. Finding Charlie had been like opening a window in a stuffy room – she had been drowning, and now she was floating free.

'I thought you had lessons all day?' she asked him now, rearranging the front of her dress where it had become entangled in the buttons of his coat. Charlie was a driving instructor – and a very in-demand one at that.

'Mr Ahmed cancelled at the last minute, but I wanted to pop back anyway,' he went on. 'I have a surprise for you.'

She pulled a face.

'Don't be like that.' He followed her into the kitchen, where she switched the kettle on again. 'We didn't get to celebrate your birthday properly, and I thought you could use a treat.'

Hope thought back to her birthday celebrations two months ago, when she had still been living in the other house. A horrible, stilted dinner with barely any conversation and even less joy. Even the cake had looked embarrassed to be there.

'What kind of treat are we talking about?' she asked.

'Wait here!'

The flat was so small that it only took Charlie a few seconds to dart across the landing into the bedroom and back, an envelope clutched in his hand, and his hat, which he still hadn't taken off, sitting at a very jaunty angle.

'Open it.'

Hope put down the teaspoon she'd been using to shovel sugar into Charlie's coffee – three heaps per cup, it was a wonder the man had any of his own teeth left – and slid a timid finger under the flap. There were two bits of folded paper inside, one detailing flights and the other a hotel booking.

'Prague?' she gasped, looking from the paper in her hands to him and back again.

'Please tell me you've never been?' he said, putting his hands together in mock prayer.

She shook her head. The only place other than the UK that Hope had ever been was Majorca. They had gone every year – same resort, same hotel, same unappetising buffet.

'I went a few years ago for Alan's son's stag,' he told her. 'We spent most of the time boozing, of course, but it looked like an amazing place. I've always wanted to go back and explore with someone special.'

'You are so sweet,' Hope smiled, feeling overwhelmed.

Charlie took a step forward and picked up her hands, the paper crinkling slightly beneath his fingers.

'I know these past few weeks have been hard for you,' he said, shaking his head as she went to disagree. 'It's okay to be sad, you know. I understand what a big upheaval all this has been. And all the stuff with Annette . . .' He tailed off as the mention of her name caused Hope's face to crumple.

'I just thought it would do you good to get out of Manchester for a few days. It will do both of us some good.'

Hope nodded mutely, unable to articulate the tumble of emotions she was feeling.

'This is so wonderful,' she managed at last, letting him pull her against his chest. 'Thank you.'

Charlie reached over her shoulder to retrieve his coffee and took a sip, grinning at her over the rim.

'I love seeing you smile,' he said. 'That's my job now, to make you smile like this, every single day.'

For so many years, Hope felt like she had barely smiled. Her grins were all reserved for when Annette came home from school, and later, work. Her friends used to encourage her to try harder, to be positive and start each day afresh, to forget the grievances she'd felt as she went to sleep the night before. And Hope had tried to be happy – she'd stood in front of the tiny mirror in the bathroom and smiled until her jaw ached – but it didn't work. In the end it just became easier to accept what was happening. Being fake was exhausting, and Hope didn't feel as if she had the energy to keep up the pretence. She had accepted that happiness wasn't something she would ever really feel again. And then she met Charlie.

'I am happy,' she told him now, forcing a note of warmth into her voice.

They smiled at each other as Charlie gulped down the last of his coffee and reached for his keys.

'What are you up to for the rest of the day?' he asked, pulling on his jacket.

Hope told him her shopping, nails and wine plan and he gave her a thumbs up.

'Treat yourself to something nice to wear in Prague,

too,' he told her. 'Something warm – I hear it's freezing over there.'

Hope waited for him to leave before she allowed herself to look again at the exciting bits of paper on the kitchen counter. Prague: a place she had never really even thought about before, but now, suddenly, somewhere she was going to experience with the man that she loved – the man that loved her.

She was going to make sure it was a trip that neither of them would ever forget.

3

'Hey, this is Robin – either I can't get to the phone right now, or I saw your number come up and assumed you were calling about PPI. If you are the latter, you'd better get used to this message, because it's the closest you're ever gonna get to me!'

Sophie ended her call and smiled, her ears warmed by the sound of her fiancé's voice on the recorded message. Typical Robin, always the joker. She felt a big explosion of love go off in her chest and affection swarmed deliciously inside her. Even after ten years, she still felt a thrill whenever she thought about him.

But this wouldn't do; she was supposed to be packing. Her train up to London left in a few hours and she hadn't even started. This time tomorrow, she would be in Prague. The thought made her smile all over again. It was their place, hers and Robin's – the place where it had all started and the place they always went back to. And there was no better time to visit than now, in the weeks leading up to Christmas, when the city was transformed by the falling snow into a scene straight from a fairy tale, all domed rooftops dusted white, glistening cobbles and crunchy frost. A time when you could scurry from one warm tavern to the next, sipping hot cups of mead sweetened with honey and gobbling up plate after plate of goulash and dumplings. It was just what they needed, and Sophie couldn't wait to be back there.

Reaching into the wardrobe to fetch her favourite dress, she caught sight of her battered old rucksack nestled in the far corner. It had fallen pretty much to pieces years ago now – which wasn't surprising given the number of miles it had travelled – but Sophie had never been able to bring herself to throw it away. The front was festooned with little fabric flags of the countries she had visited, all sewn on by Sophie herself during a long bus or train journey between one place and another. There was Germany, France, Italy, Spain, Russia, Chile, Australia, Canada, Bali, Thailand and many more, all of which held such wonderful memories. She and Robin had spent the best part of three years making their way around the world, doing whatever they had to in order to feed themselves and afford a roof over their heads. Some nights they found themselves with nothing, but those were often some of the best, because they inevitably led to a new adventure.

Once they were forced to spend three nights sleeping on a kind stranger's roof in Morocco, only to find out at five in the morning that it was the rainy season. Another time they had pitched a borrowed tent on what they thought was a patch of dry wasteland on the Greek island of Kos, only to be chased away in the dead of night by an enraged olive farmer wielding a pitchfork. Yep, they'd certainly had an eventful few years, herself and Robin.

It was a real credit to Prague that the Eastern European city had become the one place the two of them returned to every year without fail, even long after they'd hung up their respective tatty backpacks and settled down into life in Devon. Robin's family lived in Cornwall, but after a few months of commuting along the coast and back to see each other, Robin had taken the plunge and moved in with Sophie at her parents' sprawling farm, soon after winning his dream job as an instructor at the local surf school. Sophie knew it was a bit lame to still be living at home with your mum and dad at the age of twenty-eight, but the house was so big that it never felt overcrowded. If she and Robin fancied a night in alone, they simply stayed over in their side. And anyway, her parents loved Robin like a son-in-law right from the second they met him, so nobody felt as if they were stepping on anybody's toes.

Sophie drew the zip slowly round the edge of her case, listening with pleasure as the metal clipped neatly together. The unique sound of a zip being fastened always meant travel, which meant adventure, which to Sophie also meant happiness. She'd travelled an awful lot, but never tired of the experience. She loved everything about it, even the tedious airport queues and the wait at baggage reclaim.

It must be awful to have to travel as part of your job, she thought. To become so blasé about the process – fed up, even. To board a plane and not feel that tingle of excitement in the tips of your fingers as you fastened your seatbelt. To touch down in an amazing city such as New York or Shanghai or Moscow, and be thinking only about the meeting you have to attend and the sales figures you have to reach. How depressing.

Nope, working in your parents' farm shop might not be the most glamorous of jobs, but at least she still got to crouch in the starting gates of adventure, ready to set off at any minute.

Robin was an expert in sleeping on flights, a skill he'd

developed over the years they'd spent on the road. During those first few exquisite months after they met and began travelling together, Sophie had liked to watch him as he slept. She loved the way his full lips sagged open on one side of his face, and how his long, blond lashes almost reached his cheekbones. Sometimes he would twitch a little, or emit a small snuffle, and she would gaze at him in adoration, wondering what he was dreaming about and if she was part of it. She wanted not only to know his every waking thought, but also those he had while asleep. It wasn't that she was controlling or obsessive, more that she loved him so much that the conscious version wasn't enough to sate her appetite – she never stopped wanting more of him, and that had never changed.

Sophie picked up her phone and opened the weather app. As she had hoped, the weather in Prague over the next week was reliably freezing, with snow forecast a few days from now. It was a bit frustrating that Robin couldn't make the journey over there with her, but he would catch her up in a few days, and then they could celebrate their anniversary in style.

It was almost time to head to the station. Sophie looked at herself in the mirror as she shrugged her way into her coat. Her hair was so short that she looked like a boy from a distance – a young Prince Harry, according to her mum. Underneath this spiky ginger crop, Sophie's startlingly large and wide-set emerald eyes appeared even bigger than usual. They were Robin's most favourite thing about her, and he delighted in telling her how much she resembled an insect. He'd come up with the nickname 'Bug' just a few days after they first met, and had infuriatingly refused to drop it since. Sophie didn't really mind, but she was looking forward to being able to hide her eyes behind her fringe again. It had seemed like such a great idea at the time, cutting off all her hair.

Grimacing slightly and turning away from the mirror, Sophie reached over and snatched up the floppy knitted bobble hat that she'd made for Robin years before and jammed it down over her short back and sides. It was so big on her minuscule head that it looked more like a tea cosy than a chic winter accessory, but Sophie couldn't have cared less. She was the one heading to a cold country today, after all, so arguably she needed it more than Robin did. He wouldn't mind anyway – he always said that whatever was his was also hers.

The journey into London went without a hitch, and although it was weird not having her fiancé by her side for the first time in what felt like forever, Sophie felt proud that she'd managed to navigate the Underground system without losing her temper. It wasn't so much that it was confusing – quite the contrary, in fact – it was more the sheer number of people barging into her as if they owned the place. London had always made her squirm with revulsion – it wasn't a city she had any time for whatsoever, and she was glad that Robin felt the same way. Like her, he craved the outdoors and, being a surfer, the sea. To take Robin away from the ocean would be to sever the main reason he had for getting up in the morning. Well, the sea and Sophie, of course.

When she'd arrived at the cheap hotel next to Heathrow Airport and was sitting on the hard, narrow bed gazing out over the light-splattered horizon, Sophie called Robin and laughed at his voicemail recording yet again.

Her flight was first thing the next morning, but sleep was being an evasive little devil this evening. As she lay under the over-washed sheets, the thin pillow crackling uncomfortably under her head, Sophie allowed her thoughts to drift – as they always did nowadays when she couldn't seem to drop off – to the wedding.

They would have the reception at the farm, that much was certain. Silly to pay an extortionate fee to hire a venue when they had so much space freely available. Her dad would rope in the darts team from the pub to help get the marquee up, then she and her mum would enlist the help of their assorted friends and family to decorate the inside with fairy lights, flowers and bunting. They could hang up photos of herself and Robin, too, and people could write messages in a guest book. It would be charming and pretty and full of warmth.

In the evening, they'd light candles in a circle around the edge of the dance floor, and she and Robin would have their first waltz as husband and wife. People would cry and her dad would look fit to burst from pride. Then her mum would dance with Robin's dad, and they'd all joke and laugh together, until the sun came up over the distant hills.

At some point, she and Robin would sneak off and make their way down to the beach, where he would pick her up in her dress and swirl her around and around, kissing her over and over and calling her by her new married name, Mrs Palmer. Then they would sit on the wet sand, not caring about her dress or his suit, and use a stick to spell out their names. Sophie would add hearts and Robin would joke that she was a soppy idiot, and then they would kiss again, on and on and on until they were out of breath with love for one another.

As Sophie finally slipped away into slumber, a smile of contentment playing on her lips, her phone lit up on the bedside table. A face surrounded by blond hair flashed up on the screen as the handset vibrated quietly across the surface, but she didn't stir, lost as she was in the dreams of her future. Eventually, as the rain began and lashed at the window outside, the light from the phone went out.

4

'Well, that's a big bed.'

Megan looked sideways at Ollie.

'I bet Sherlock Holmes is holding tight to his sleuth crown with you around,' she drawled. He was right, though, it was a very big bed. And not only that, it was also a four-poster, with extravagant red and gold striped curtains and a matching bedspread – opulent didn't even begin to cover it. Megan cursed herself for allowing Ollie to pick the hotel and for not checking the place out in more detail when he'd emailed her the link. They'd crashed out together on her sofa and at various house parties in the six months since she'd met him, but sharing a bed in a hotel room felt different. It was more intimate somehow.

At the end of the bed, directly in front of where Megan and Ollie were standing awkwardly side by side, was a banquette upholstered in cream and gold satin. It matched the two chairs that were tucked neatly away underneath a small wooden table in the corner by the circular window, which was framed by yet more red and gold curtains. They were at the very top of the hotel, and the ceiling rose high above them into the eaves of the old building, exposed beams criss-crossing the white painted walls. It was stunning, if a little twee, and Megan felt her fingers itch for her camera.

Ollie had ventured into the bathroom, and she heard him emit a shout of laughter.

'There's a tub for two in here!' he called. 'And gold taps.'

Megan rolled her eyes. At least he was seeing the funny side. Their journey to the airport earlier that morning had gone without a hitch, the only awkward moment coming before they left her flat, when she'd bumped into him in the hallway wearing just his boxers and a sleepy grin. He didn't seem at all bothered by his near-nudity, but the mere sight of him had sent Megan scuttling back into her bedroom like a frightened woodlouse.

Once through security at the airport, Ollie insisted they get a pint of beer for breakfast. Apparently, the fact that it was seven in the morning did not matter – they were officially on 'holiday time', he told her, and that meant all the normal rules were now defunct.

'Oi, Spencer!' he'd barked, distracting her attention from the laminated menu she'd been examining. He'd produced a pack of playing cards from his bag and begun shuffling them on the table.

'There's another hour until take-off and I want to thrash you at Rummy at least twelve times before then.'

He had as well. Ollie was good at cards, just like he was good at most things, not least diffusing the awkward tension that had reared up like a stroppy horse as soon as they'd found themselves standing in front of this ridiculous bed. He was now merrily running himself a bath while shouting through that she should investigate the contents of the minibar.

It's only a bed, she told herself sternly, extracting a miniature bottle of vodka and splashing it into two plastic cups. It's no different to if you were here with a female friend, she added firmly, tipping in orange juice.

Ollie came to the bathroom door to collect his drink, again clad in just his boxers, and grinned at her.

'I'm going to go down to the bar,' she squeaked, rather than said, downing her vodka and orange in one and heading across the room to retrieve her bag.

Ollie laughed. 'I won't be far behind you – I can never resist a hotel bath, me. I'll meet you down there in a bit and we can go exploring, yeah?'

'Okay!'

She slammed the door behind her and leaned on it for a few seconds. This was going to be even weirder than she'd feared. What was Ollie thinking, prancing around in his pants like that? She wasn't one of his bloke mates, for God's sake!

It wasn't until she was in the lift heading downwards that Megan realised with an audible groan that she'd left her camera in the bedroom. She couldn't exactly go back and fetch it, not when her potentially-by-now-naked friend was roaming around like a tipsy peacock. She'd had half a plan to sneak out and explore the immediate area while he was in the tub, but there was little point if she couldn't take photos. The brief glimpses of Prague that she'd seen on the taxi ride over from the airport had whetted her appetite to an almost unbearable level. Ollie had better make this bath snappy.

Stomping resolutely into the hotel bar a few minutes later, Megan immediately noticed a couple snuggling at a table in the corner.

Wow, they really needed to get a room.

After ordering herself a coffee – definitely much needed after a morning of beer followed by the vodka she'd just necked – Megan retreated to the opposite corner of the room and chose a seat by the window. The décor in the bar wasn't quite as garish as in the bedroom upstairs, but there were still plenty of polished gold fixtures, an extremely large chandelier and an abundance of cushions, each with a gold tassel attached to the zip. A buzz in her pocket alerted her to the free Wi-Fi connection, but she couldn't be bothered to waste any time online – especially not when she had this view to gaze out at.

The hotel courtyard on the other side of the glass was covered with a thick layer of frost, but that only made it seem all the more magical. The ground sparkled as if dusted with glitter, and Megan could make out neat banks of sagging winter flowers alongside little pathways. Everything was paved in red and grey stone, and in the centre of the garden there was an ancient-looking fountain coughing out a feeble trickle of water.

If only she had her camera, she would have been able to capture the faint sunlight streaking through the surrounding trees, the way the dribbling water from the fountain had cut a ragged path through the frost, and the tantalising glimpse of Prague's famous red rooftops peeking over the wall from the street outside. It was so beautiful already, and they hadn't even left the hotel yet.

'Excuse me, are you here alone?'

Megan looked up with a jolt to find the woman from the other table standing in front of her. Her lipstick was smudged slightly where she'd been kissing her bald companion, but her eyes shone with kindness.

'No. I, er . . .' Megan hesitated for a second, suddenly unsure of how exactly to describe Ollie. 'I'm here with a friend. He's having a bath, the weirdo.'

The woman chuckled at this. 'Charlie, that's my boyfriend – he's gone up to have a shower. Men, eh? I just want to get outside and explore, don't you?'

'Yes! Oh my God, I totally agree. Have you seen the view out here – it's amazing!' Megan moved her chair aside so the woman could slip round and stand next to her. It was a full minute before she spoke again.

'It's like a proper fairy grotto,' the older woman said, her warm breath leaving a damp circle on the cold glass.

She was quite glamorous up close, Megan realised, taking in the neatly set ash-blonde curls, flattering black dress and perfect nails. She guessed the woman was probably around the same age as her mum, but she'd looked far younger from a distance. Only a faint spiderweb of lines around her eyes and mouth gave her away, and she'd done her best to cover these up with foundation.

'Have you been to Prague before?' the woman asked Megan now, turning to face her.

'Never.' Megan motioned that she should sit down. 'My friend is a teacher and he's doing a project with his pupils about Prague next year, so he wanted to check it out. I've just tagged along to take photos. How about you?'

'I haven't been before, no – and I didn't choose it. Charlie booked it all as a surprise. He got an online deal for a good price, but I won't even tell you what time we had to leave Manchester this morning.'

'That's men for you,' Megan said. 'Great at the romantic gestures, not so great with the important details. Have you two been together long?'

It was an innocent enough question, but the woman seemed to tense up a fraction before she answered, and fiddled with the stem of her wine glass.

'Not very long, no.' She glanced sideways at Megan. 'We're very much in the honeymoon stage, I guess.'

'I noticed!' Megan told her with a grin. 'I saw you two over in the corner.'

'Oh, God!' The woman blushed, but she was laughing, too.

'I'm Hope,' she added, offering Megan a perfectly manicured hand.

'Megan.'

They chatted for a while about the hotel – Hope had found her bedroom furnishings hilariously over the top as well – and about Megan's photography. Hope confessed that she didn't have a job at the moment, but that she was keen to find something part-time when she got back to Manchester.

'I get so bored rattling around at Charlie's,' she explained. Megan wondered why she was living with him if they'd only been together for a short time, but she was astute enough not to ask. Ollie was really taking his time, and just as she was wondering if she should head up and check that he hadn't actually drowned, Hope suggested another drink.

'We're allowed to, we're on holiday,' the older woman assured her as she returned from the bar, and Megan nodded along in agreement. She had never really been the type to make friends with total strangers in hotel bars before, but there was something irresistibly fun yet also motherly about Hope. She had real warmth to her, which reminded Megan of her own mum – albeit a far more polished version. Megan's mother was a stereotypical artist – she used a paintbrush to keep her wiry thatch of hair in a bun and dressed like a Victorian orphan most of the time – but she also had that unidentifiable mother-ness about her. She should really make more effort to see her mum – and her dad, too, thought Megan. They were actually pretty brilliant, even if they did keep trying to talk her into marrying Ollie.

'He's perfect for you. Such a nice boy, and so tall,' her mum had said, running a despairing hand into her hair and promptly getting it stuck. 'You don't want to end up with a grumpy hobbit like I did.'

'I heard that,' Megan's dad had intoned, peering over the top of his Sunday broadsheet with a scowl on his face. He couldn't really argue the point, though, given that he was only five foot six in his socks. Megan, who had inherited both his height and his ability to scowl like an absolute pro, had given her dad a sly thumbs up as soon as her mum turned back to her latest messy landscape.

Hope was talking about her daughter now. Apparently she'd just left home for the first time and moved in with her boyfriend – and she was only twenty-five. Megan had never lived with a boy, and nor was she planning to any time soon, much to the despair of her assorted friends and family. She was only thirty; there was still plenty of time for all that.

They were still chattering away when the door opened and a girl walked in. Megan and Hope both looked up, expecting to see their respective male companions, so they each watched as the tiny figure made her way silently over to the bar and ordered herself a tea. The barman was very friendly, and he started chatting to her, asking the normal questions such as how long she was staying and whether she'd been to the city before. Megan strained to hear her replies, but her voice must be as tiny as she was, because she could barely make out a word.

Once the girl had her drink, she turned and smiled briefly at Hope and Megan, before settling herself down at one of the other tables and taking out her phone.

'Should we ask her to join us, do you think?' Hope said. The second glass of wine had given her cheeks an attractive glow.

'I'm not sure,' Megan murmured. 'She looks like she's waiting for a call.'

It was true – the girl had put her mobile down on the table, but was staring at it intently. After a time, she took off her huge, floppy beanie hat and put it down next to her phone.

'That's a brave hairdo,' Hope breathed. 'You see so many girls with short hair these days. Mine was right down to my waist when I was her age.'

'It is very short,' Megan whispered back, feeling a bit guilty to be gossiping. 'I could never have my hair that short, but she's so pretty she gets away with it.'

As they were both watching the girl staring at her phone, Megan's own phone buzzed across the table with a message. It was Ollie:

> I wanted to bring your
> camera down for you, but
> there are about a million bits.
> Get up here and help me! x

Megan snorted with laughter. 'I have to go,' she told Hope, downing the dregs of her beer and picking up her bag.

She bounded back up to the fourth floor, taking two extravagantly carpeted stairs at a time, enjoying the sensation of excitement that was bubbling away in the bottom of her stomach like soup in a pan. Weirdness aside, she was in one of the most beautiful cities in the world with her camera and one of her most favourite people. Sometimes life was pretty good.

5

Sophie jabbed a finger at her phone and slipped it into her coat pocket. The frost-covered cobbles crunched under her boots, but it wasn't enough to distract her from the tears that were threatening to fall. She stopped, took a deep breath, then continued, keeping her eyes down.

It wasn't Robin's fault that he couldn't be here. She knew that. But this knowledge was doing little to comfort her. She'd thought it would be okay, being here without him. She thought she knew the place well enough to feel comforted by the surrounding buildings, so familiar and so magnificent, their multi-coloured facades peering down at her like a collection of kindly aunts.

It's only a few days, she told herself now. He would be here before she knew it.

Glancing upwards, she saw heavy clouds clustering together in the east and slyly crossed her fingers in a silent prayer for snow. Prague was beautiful at every time of year – she knew that for a fact, because she and Robin had visited in every season – but nothing made the city seem more magical than a thick coating of the white stuff. Even snow itself was quite magical, if she thought about it, each flake unique and intricate. If angels existed then Sophie liked to imagine that it was they who sat together up in the heavens, knitting together these beautiful frozen creations to shower down on the Earth. When she was a child, she used to try and catch them in her outstretched palm and memorise the pattern before it melted away.

Sophie's warm memory bubble was all of a sudden punctured by a shriek of delighted laughter. Peering through the groups of people who were heading into Prague's annual Christmas Market, she saw the woman who had been in the hotel bar earlier that morning, the one who had smiled at her so kindly. She was with a tall man wearing a red woolly hat and was laughing at something he was whispering in her ear. Like many others, they had most likely been lured over by the enticing smell of cinnamon, brandy and berries coming from a makeshift bar, and the cups of mulled wine in their gloved hands were sending up twists of curly steam into the freezing air.

For a minute, Sophie considered going over to join them. They looked so irresistibly happy that she couldn't help but yearn for a slice of it. However, when she took one tentative step towards them, the man bent his head and kissed the woman full on the mouth, and Sophie, feeling like she was intruding just by standing there, scuttled away.

It was past lunchtime now, but she didn't feel hungry. Not even the stalls offering enormous, sizzling vats of potatoes, sauerkraut, cheese and roasted pork could tempt her, nor could the huge *klobasy* sausages. One of her favourite photos of Robin was of him holding one of these massive treats up in front of his mouth, the two ends curled upwards like a big, meaty grin and splatters of spicy sauce dripping all down the front of his scarf. He was such a plonker sometimes, but he was her plonker.

There was music coming from somewhere and Sophie paused for a few seconds, trying to locate the source. There was always music playing in Prague, whether it was streaming out from one of the many bars or coming from a local band that had set up on the cobbles, a flat cap tossed on the ground in front of them to encourage tips from generous passers-by. She wondered if these musicians knew just how intrinsic they were to the beauty of this city, and how, by turning up every day and transforming one small corner of Prague, they made a home for themselves in the memories of so many.

Squeezed tight in the warming hug of her surroundings, her earlier melancholy put aside, Sophie headed towards her destination with a renewed energy. She'd known Prague wouldn't let her down. She had been silly to ever let the dark shadow of doubt cast its nasty hunched shoulders across her mind. Everything was going to be perfect, she could feel it – and now here she was, back in the very same spot she and Robin had first laid eyes on one another: the Charles Bridge.

Back then it really had been snowing, and Sophie was standing with her back to the passing train of pedestrians, staring out across the Vltava River towards Mala Strana, the south-west area of the city. The surface of the water was the colour of granite and the lights of the far bank had turned hazy amid the falling flakes. Sophie was captivated, and it was a good few minutes before she realised that someone had come to stand beside her.

'I love watching the snow, don't you?'

She turned to find a pair of blue eyes, a slightly large

nose turned red with the cold and a wide, smiling mouth, all of which were framed by messy blond hair escaping from a striped bobble hat.

'Who doesn't?' she replied, realising as she did so that this boy's smile was extremely contagious.

'My parents bloody hate it,' he told her, staring out across the water. 'My mum would move to Australia if she could – she's a total sun addict.'

He was English, that much was clear, and Sophie felt something begin to flutter deep inside her chest. She liked this boy.

'Australia's on my list, too,' she said, daring to look at him again. 'I'm doing Europe first, then hopefully the rest of the world.'

'A girl after my own heart,' he grinned, making her insides lurch like a fairground ride.

'Are you travelling as well?' she asked boldly, going bright red as he looked at her and nodded.

'Yep. All on my tod. How about you?'

Should she really tell a man she'd just met that she was travelling all by herself?

'Just me.'

There was a short silence as they stared at one another, each wondering if what they were feeling was real. Robin later told her that he'd known right then, right in that moment, that she was going to be by his side for the rest of their lives. He couldn't ever explain how he knew – he just did. Sophie, meanwhile, was simply thinking that she wanted to kiss this boy more than anything she'd ever wanted to do in her life. Whether or not that was the same thing, she didn't know, but what was instantly undeniable was the chemistry between them. It was as clear as the silhouettes of the Charles Bridge statues against the white sky, and they both knew it.

'I'm Robin,' was what he said next, offering her a hand encased in a stripy glove to match his hat.

'Sophie.' She took it and squeezed, feeling the warmth of his skin through the layers of knitted wool.

They stood there in the snow chatting for what felt to Sophie like forever, all about where they had already been and where they were going. She was thrilled to learn that his planned path around Europe was almost identical to her own, and that they had both been drawn to the same cities on the route.

'I want to see Venice, but I'm not as bothered about Florence,' he said. 'I like the more magical places, and I reckon Venice has that in abundance.'

He was right, of course, as they would both discover a few weeks later.

'I think every city has its magical parts,' she told him. 'You just have to be willing to go looking for them.'

'You're probably right,' he shrugged, never taking his eyes off her. 'It's a good thing I found you so early on in my trip. Now you can enlighten me at every step.'

He was being forward and cheeky and presumptuous and he knew it, but Sophie felt herself swell with happiness and excitement. This boy really wanted to spend time with her, and she found that she couldn't get enough of him. She was already wishing that she could turn back time somehow and meet him years before. They'd known each other for all of half an hour, but she already felt as if she'd been cheated out of potential time they could have spent together. If she could have pressed a button right then and there that would have taken them both back to infancy together, she would have done so without hesitation. She also knew full well that these thoughts were utterly ludicrous, but she felt giddy with the promise of him. Of them together.

'Shall we go and get a drink?' he asked eventually.

The bridge had become all but deserted as the snow had continued to fall, and it was now barely possible to see the river below them, let alone the surrounding landscape.

Sophie laughed as she realised what they must look like, standing there on the bridge as if they were the only people in the world, snow piling up on top of their hats and on their shoulders. It had been a good twenty minutes since she had been able to feel any of her fingers or toes, but she'd never felt so alert in her life, so aware of her body and of her own movements. It was as if Robin had flicked a switch inside her that had never been pressed before, and now she was coming alive, really alive, for the very first time.

They shuffled through the snow slowly, both aware that the slippery, uneven ground could claim them at any step, and Robin told her about his love of surfing.

'I should have guessed you were a surfer from your hair,' she told him when they reached a cosy-looking Irish pub and he pulled off his snow-drenched hat.

'And I guess that makes you a leprechaun, then, right?' he joked. 'Small and ginger!'

'Oi!' She aimed a playful swipe in his direction. Sophie had been lucky enough to attend a school where being ginger didn't automatically mean relentless teasing from the age of five to fifteen, but she was still slightly self-conscious of her fiery hair. There was no hiding when you were a redhead, no vanishing into the crowds as a brunette so easily could, and Sophie had reluctantly grown used to being looked at wherever she went.

'I'd rather be a merry little Irish fellow than someone who could have been in the cast of *Home and Away* in 1992.'

He laughed at that, and it was a lovely, proper belly laugh.

'Touché, Little Miss Sophie.' He nudged her with a casual arm. 'I'll let you win that one, but I'll warn you now, I'll be ready for the next one. I'm going to think up lots of clever retorts right now and keep them stored in my brain, just in case.'

'Do your worst!' she dared him, giving him the benefit of an amused side-eye.

Their huge tankards of beer arrived, a frothy head the size of a small country on the top of each, and they clinked their glasses together in celebration of having met one another.

'I feel like I've known you for years,' Robin told her an hour later. They were sitting side by side at the bar, and his thigh was pressed warmly against her own. 'Does that sound mad? It does, doesn't it? I'm not a crazy stalker, I promise.'

'Oh, shut up,' she giggled. 'You don't sound mad at all. In fact, I was just thinking the exact same thing myself. Does that make me some sort of mad bunny-boiler?'

'Yes,' he joked, lurching sideways to avoid another jab.

Sophie glared at him in mock outrage and reached for her beer. It was her third, and with every sip she was growing braver. All she wanted to do was climb across her own stool and on to his lap, wrap her legs around his waist and order him to kiss her right now. But of course she didn't.

She'd read about being undressed by someone's eyes in books before, but she'd never experienced it. Robin was looking at her with a hunger that was almost primal, but rather than feel intimidated, she felt content, as if this exact moment was the entire reason she had been born in the first place. She would try to describe it to him months later, when they lay, clammy limbs entwined, on the single mattress of a top bunk in a hostel in Athens. He would listen intently and nod along, tell her that he knew what she meant: being with her had always felt right. He felt like he was home.

Robin was a gentleman that first night and walked her back to her hostel before heading off to his own. Sophie couldn't help herself; she grabbed his hand as he made to turn away, suddenly fearful at the thought of never seeing him again. She was afraid that she'd wake up and discover that he had been nothing but a dream.

Robin looked down at his own hand clasped in both of hers and smiled. The snow had finally stopped, but the air around them had retained a frozen stillness that under usual circumstances would have left them both shivering from head to toe. Sophie found that she was shivering, but it was nothing to do with the temperature.

'Have breakfast with me tomorrow,' he said at last, raising her hand up towards his mouth as he did so and slowly easing off her glove with his fingers.

'Of course,' she murmured, watching her bare skin emerge and feeling her eyes widen and her legs tremble as he brought the tips of her fingers up to his lips. For a second he just breathed on them to warm them, making sure she could feel every tiny sensation, and then, so briefly she would later wonder if he had even done it at all, he kissed them.

'I know a place that does a mean apple strudel,' he said, dropping her limp hand and taking a step backwards. 'See you back here at nine?'

'I'll be here,' she managed, watching as he smiled at her one final time and turned to walk away. It was the last time they spent a night apart for months.

Sophie looked down to find that her fingers were gripping the edge of the bridge, the nails white against the cold stone. They had been back here so many times now, herself and Robin. The first time they'd returned he had even crouched down and kissed the ground, thanking it for being the place that he'd found her, that they'd found each other. Sophie remembered it now and laughed. He could be a livewire sometimes, but his exuberance was one of the many things she loved so much about him.

The clocks around the city were taking it in turns to strike the hour, but for the first time she didn't find their chiming a comfort. Shaking her head in an attempt to refocus her senses, Sophie found her eyes drawn upwards, towards the cluttered horizon that was dominated by Prague Castle. She never failed to be moved by the architecture here. She decided to buy herself a mulled wine and take a stroll through the streets of the Little Quarter.

Buoyed by her plan and with her spirits lifted by so many happy memories, she made her way along the cobbled pathway of the bridge and vanished into the crowds beyond.

6

'That is the biggest sausage I've ever seen in my life!'

'Wow. You really know how to make a man feel inadequate.'

Hope laughed and jabbed Charlie in the ribs. Hopefully the man selling the sausages didn't speak any English, but Hope noticed a glimmer in his eye and feared that he probably did.

'You know I wasn't referring to . . . to *that*,' she scolded, grinning as he put an arm around her waist. He'd barely let go of her since they'd arrived, and Hope had needed all her powers of persuasion to get him out of their hotel room.

'We could just stay here all day?' he'd suggested, sitting down on the edge of the bed in just his towel and beckoning for her to join him. Hope continued to be impressed by his energy – he was forty-eight and she was fifty, for crying out loud – but then she'd also been pleasantly surprised by her own sexual appetite being reawakened. She'd thought those years were long behind her, but she had been wrong.

'We could,' she told him, resisting the temptation to step into his embrace. 'But we are in a beautiful city, love. And I really want to see the Christmas Market. Megan, the girl I just met downstairs, she told me it's world famous.'

'Well, if it's a *famous* market . . .' Charlie grinned, getting to his feet. Hope watched him with affection as he strolled into the bathroom and closed the door.

Their trip over to Prague had all been so last-minute that Hope hadn't found time to read up on it, but skimming through the guidebook she'd picked up at the airport, she'd found the location of their hotel on the pull-out map inside and knew that they were only a few streets away from the famous Old Town Square.

'There's a clock in the square that was made in 1410,' she told Charlie as they stopped just inside the hotel entrance so he could button up his coat against the cold. 'So it's around the same age as me.'

'Don't be daft.' He bent down and kissed her affectionately. 'You're in the prime of your life – just like me.'

She let him take her hand and they made their way along the icy pavement, Hope gazing upwards at the surrounding buildings. It was all she could do to stop her mouth dropping open in awe. She knew from her guidebook that the architecture in Prague spanned over a thousand years, and represented every era from Gothic to Renaissance to Baroque to Art Nouveau. It reeked of history at every turn, and she was immediately captivated by the tall, proud houses, with their curved, ornamental balconies. There was a hint of music in the air, indistinguishable but undeniable, and Hope strained to pick out the individual notes.

As they rounded a corner and entered the Old Town Square, they were confronted by a riot of colour, not just from the lively Christmas Market sprawled across its centre, but from the far buildings, which were cream, red, pink and blue. The frost was not yet thick enough to mask the vibrant deep orange of the rooftops, and Hope felt her eyes widen as she spun around to take it all in.

'Oh, Charlie,' she mumbled, leaning against him. 'It's so beautiful.'

'Isn't it?' He looked proud. 'And this is just the start of it – there's lots more to explore. Do you really like it?'

He sounded almost nervous, and Hope wrapped her arms around his waist before answering. 'I love it.'

'Right then,' he said, rearranging his woolly hat. 'Now, I don't know about you, but I can smell mulled wine. Fancy one?'

She nodded. 'Yes, please.'

As they entered the market, however, Hope felt her euphoric mood begin to sag. Annette would absolutely love it here, and she felt suddenly guilty that she was here seeing it all without her daughter. In the past, they had done everything together: shopping, trips to the races, girly nights out. Now, however, Annette could barely stand to look at her.

They stopped beside a stall selling Christmas decorations and Hope picked up an angel. It had been carved from wood and was dressed in a beautiful white and gold tunic, its smiling features painted carefully into place. Picking up another one and holding them side by side, Hope realised that each face was different, each angel unique, and for some reason that made her want to cry.

'Are you all right?' Charlie asked, full of concern. He looked from her face to the ornaments in her hands. 'We can buy those, if you like?'

'It's not that.' She put them down. 'I was just thinking how much Annette would love it here . . .' She trailed off.

Of course he knew, she knew he did – but what could he do about it?

'I don't mean to sound ungrateful,' she told him quickly. 'It's just a mum thing. I'm just being stupid.'

'You could never be stupid.' He put a comforting arm around her shoulders. 'Why don't we go and get that drink, and then, when you're feeling better, maybe we can come back and buy one of these angels for Annette? She might like it.'

Hope thought privately that the hand-carved angels were far too beautiful to risk Annette throwing them hard against the nearest wall, but she nodded regardless. Charlie was doing everything he could to make her happy, so she really should try to cheer up.

They carried on through the market, finding the stall selling the huge sausages and crunching across the frosty cobbles past wooden carts selling all manner of trinkets and treats. Hope found her eyes drawn repeatedly to the huge Christmas tree in the middle of the square. It was festooned in blue and white lights, and the branches sagged under the weight of hundreds of glass baubles.

'We'll have to come back after dark,' she told Charlie as they made their way towards the smell of mulled wine. 'I bet it looks amazing around here with all these lights.'

'Anything you want,' he said, grabbing her arm and spinning her around in a clumsy pirouette.

'Steady on!' she gasped, narrowly avoiding a group of Japanese tourists.

'Let's dance!' he declared, holding out his hand.

She folded her arms.

Charlie's energy and sense of fun were two of the

things she loved most about him. It was his get-up-and-go attitude that made him so different to Dave. Hope couldn't remember ever seeing her ex-husband dance except at their wedding, and that had been under duress. She used to love how grown-up he was, how he'd rather cuddle up with her on the sofa than join his mates down the pub, but over time it had begun to frustrate her. Once Annette had turned eighteen and gained some independence, Hope had wanted to start going out more, to visit their friends or have them over for dinner, but Dave wasn't interested.

She reached the mulled wine stall first and ordered two cups, smiling at the rosy-cheeked man on the other side of the counter as she handed over her Czech korunas. Everyone here was so friendly, so ready to spring into action, as if nothing would be too much trouble. It made all the difference to the place.

'Are you okay?'

Charlie had caught up with her, concern etched all over his lovely face. She felt horrible now for refusing to dance.

'I promise I'll dance with you later,' she told him.

He took a large sip of his drink and smiled.

Hope had realised over the past few months that she had been asleep when she met Charlie. Not literally, of course – that would have been absurd, given that he was giving her a driving lesson at the time – but in every other sense. She felt no desire, she experienced little joy and all the fight had long since gone out of her. For years she had battled to find the right flint that would put the spark back into her marriage, until eventually she wondered if there had ever been one. There was just routine and habit and mutual comfort. It felt to Hope as if it was enough for

Dave to know she was there. Sometimes in the night he would even reach out for her, his ever-expanding gut pressing into the small of her back as he snaked an arm around her waist. How awful it had been to be that woman. A woman whose own husband could only bear to touch her when he was more or less unconscious. She didn't know who was more to blame, she only knew that there was no way back.

When everything had fallen apart and she'd been forced to tell Dave that she was leaving, he hadn't even looked that surprised. Perhaps he was relieved to see the back of her? There was no way of knowing, given that he wouldn't talk about it. Dave had always been a quiet soul, as closed to the world as a clam stuck fast to the side of a rock, and apparently no amount of her screaming and yelling could dislodge him. It was Annette she worried about now, not Dave.

Charlie had been reading the guidebook as she stared off into space, and he was now peering over her head as if trying to locate something.

'What are you looking for?' she asked, her voice coming out croaky from all the suppressed emotions.

'That clock you mentioned earlier,' he said, squinting into the distance. 'It says here that the best time to take a look is on the hour, and it's nearing that now. Shall we?'

'Yes!' she exclaimed, with far more enthusiasm than was strictly necessary. Anything to get her mind off her failed marriage.

She put her empty cup into a nearby bin and grabbed Charlie's hand.

'Come on, then, you gorgeous man – let's dance there.'

7

'There are giant babies crawling up the side of that tower.'

'What?' Ollie peered into the viewfinder of Megan's camera and laughed.

'So there are. That's weird.'

They were at the very top of the Old Town Hall Tower, which was situated in the corner of the square. Megan had reached the summit first because she refused to walk all the way up the steeply sloping walkway with Ollie, who was now panting and sweating beside her. Megan, being sensible and, if she was completely honest, a bit lazy, had determinedly taken the lift up instead.

The odd structure they were now gazing at looked from a distance like some sort of shuttle launcher. Three circular towers thrust upwards, punctuated not only by the rather sinister crawling babies, but also by sporadic pod-like floors. It was very futuristic in style and looked at odds with the centuries-old churches and monasteries which were jostling for space along the skyline.

'It's called the Zizkov TV Tower,' Megan said, letting her precious camera rest by its strap against her chest as she fingered through the pages of the guidebook.

'Why the babies?' Ollie asked.

'Ah, we have David Cerny to thank for those,' she told him. 'He's quite a famous Czech sculptor. I remember him now from when I did my art foundation course.

They were put up there temporarily in the year 2000, it says here, then brought back by popular demand a year later.'

'We should go!' Ollie was all enthusiasm. 'I want to see that baby – and those babies – up close.'

'I could probably take some great photos,' Megan agreed, but she wasn't quite as keen. The tower wasn't really what she had in mind for her upcoming exhibition. Megan's work was all about finding a connection between an image and an emotion, and there was nothing about the cold, clean lines of the tower that were drawing her in. She had, however, already snapped her way through at least a hundred photos, and all they'd done was walk from the hotel across the square. She'd been utterly captivated by the riot of colours at the Christmas Market, and Ollie got so bored waiting for her to finish taking pictures of the fairy lights against the grey afternoon sky that he'd chewed his way through two enormous sausages.

'I shouldn't have had that second sausage,' he said now, with a wounded expression. 'Eating that lot then coming all the way up here at speed was not the best idea I've ever had.'

'I told you to take the lift,' she said, jabbing him affectionately in his full stomach.

'Careful, woman!'

She pulled a face at him. 'Where to next?'

'Well . . .' Ollie pointed off to the south. 'There's Wenceslas Square and the National Museum that way, or we could head over the Charles Bridge . . .' he swung an arm over to the west, 'and visit the castle or the parks?'

Megan wiggled her freezing toes inside her boots and looked down. The red rooftops of the Christmas Market were spread out below them like burning embers and the warmth it exuded was too much to resist.

'Or we could get a mulled wine and just have a wander?' she suggested. Megan always found that you got the best from a place simply by exploring – and you discovered its true essence by taking the streets that nobody else was bothering with. She was enchanted by Prague's historic centre, but she also wanted to see the more secret side of the city, the parts that the people who lived here kept to themselves.

'Whatever you say.' Ollie smiled down at her. 'You're the boss.'

She was glad they were in agreement on that point.

Back at street level and with a warm and deliciously spicy wine in hand, they strolled slowly around the edge of the market, pausing every so often to examine one of the many stalls in more detail. Megan stopped Ollie at one selling a whole range of trinkets adorned with the image of the Astronomical Clock. She had read about it on the flight over and couldn't wait to see it in action.

'Remind me again what's going to happen,' Ollie asked ten minutes later. They were back at the Old Town Hall, the tower stretching high into the air and a solid hub of tourists surrounding them on every side. The Astronomical Clock was directly above them, its gold, blue and bright orange colours gleaming in the dusk.

'Just before the hour, that little skeleton up there,' she pointed to the right of the main clock face, 'pulls on a rope and turns over his hourglass. Then up there,' she pointed again to a narrow doorway above the clock, 'the eleven apostles – plus St Paul – come out in a little procession.'

Ollie squinted upwards.

'Afterwards, a cock crows, and then the hour will chime,' she added, referring to the book to make sure she was getting it right.

'What about the other clock, the one underneath?' Ollie asked.

'That one shows the movement of the sun through the signs of the zodiac,' she told him, retrieving her camera from her bag and pointing it upwards. The lower clock face was predominantly gold, with two circular rings of twelve images going from the outside towards the centre. Each one was painted inside a round frame, with the outer images depicting the months of the year and the inner selection each zodiac sign.

'There's your sign,' she told Ollie, showing him the photo she'd just taken of the gold, M-shaped logo, complete with tiny tail.

'That doesn't look much like a scorpion to me,' Ollie said.

Megan had her nose in the book again. 'The other figure up there, next to Death, that's the Turk, a symbol of lust,' she told him, blushing as she realised what she was saying.

'I like him,' Ollie said. Of course he did.

'And those two, on the other side,' she went on, ignoring him, 'are Vanity and Greed.'

'I can totally sympathise with Greed after those sausages,' he interjected. Megan tried not to laugh.

'You're such a plank,' she smiled.

'Yes. A greedy one,' Ollie quipped, smiling down at her and giving her a nudge. She wasn't used to him touching her this much. Usually they were on opposite sides of a pub table or far ends of her sofa, but here in Prague they seemed to be constantly side by side.

'Be quiet now, please,' she said, giving him a gentle head butt on the arm. 'The clock is about to begin.'

A hush fell over the square as Death shuffled into life and turned his hourglass over. A light creaking sound followed, and the Apostles appeared, their bearded little faces popping up in Megan's viewfinder one at a time. She was amazed at how different they all looked, and how much care had clearly been taken to create and then keep them in a pristine condition. She was noticing that in general about the city, in fact, just how clean and well cared for it was. The inhabitants of London could learn a lot from the people of Prague.

The clock was chiming now and she could hear the delicious click of cameras going off all around her. A few idiots had even switched on their flashes. There was more than enough natural light still lingering around – plus the gold of the clock was so intense it was almost luminous. If only people went a bit further than just setting their cameras to the auto mode and pressing a button. They were missing so much beauty which could easily be captured with just a few adjustments. Ollie, who was busy taking photos with his phone – his bloody phone! – beside her, was definitely not doing much to support her cause.

'I'm glad we saw that,' he told her when the chimes came to an end. 'I've never seen anything quite like it before. I must make sure I tell the kids about it – perhaps a project on the zodiac signs is in order.'

He was talking more to himself now than Megan, but she nodded along encouragingly. She wished she'd had a teacher like Ollie back in primary school. Her form tutor, Mrs Benstead, had been so old that she used to nod off at her desk at around eleven and not wake up until the bell rang at half three. Megan had gone up into secondary school with terrible handwriting and a total lack of respect for anyone in authority. If she was honest, she still struggled with those types of people even now. She hated anyone telling her what to do, even her boss at the gallery, and she was really nice. Just last week there'd been a tense moment when Sally, the owner, asked Megan to take a bunch of torn wrapping down to the recycling bins on the corner of the road and an engrossed Megan, who was halfway through hanging the latest set of watercolours from one of their best artists, unthinkingly snapped at her to do it herself. A cup of tea and a stern chat followed, and Megan had been apologising to Sally ever since.

'Cheer up, chicken,' Ollie prodded her out of her unpleasant train of thought. 'Shall we go and get on the beer?'

Megan thought about the Charles Bridge with its army of statues, Prague Castle and its promise of history, and all the narrow, cobbled alleyways in between, just waiting to be discovered. But they had four more days after this one. The city could wait. And anyway, she couldn't even feel her toes any more.

'I'm bored of being the boss now,' she said, putting her hands in her pockets. 'You lead the way.'

8

Sophie pushed the edge of her spoon through the corner of the apple strudel, relishing the cracking sound of the light, crispy pastry as it gave way beneath the stainless steel.

After walking through the Little Quarter all the way up to the castle gates, she'd sat on a low stone wall watching scores of tourists passing by until she couldn't feel her hands and feet any more. There was a stall selling fold-out maps and hot drinks nearby, and the vendor kept smiling at her from underneath his thick woollen hat. He had kind blue eyes and a thick white beard, and his skin looked tarnished with age. While the people of Prague weren't the chattiest, they were always ready to smile. In ten years she'd never encountered even a smidgeon of rudeness in the city – it was just one of the many reasons why she and Robin loved it so much.

It hadn't taken her long to get from the castle back down the hill to Café Cukr, the very same place that Robin had brought her for that first magical breakfast all those years ago, and she was thrilled to discover that it hadn't changed at all.

The décor inside was basic but attractive, with lots of dark wood, cosy alcoves and a large mural of happy diners painted on the ceiling. Each table was covered in a plain yellow cloth, and in the centre sat the traditional Prague offering of supersized soft pretzels, dangling from their specially made wooden racks. Sophie wasn't much of a fan, but Robin loved them. The last time they'd come here, he'd broken bits off and dunked them in his pint of beer. She smiled fondly at the memory.

She'd almost finished her strudel as her mind wandered, and all that was left on her plate was a puddle of cooked apple and a smear of cream. Nowhere she'd been in the world did strudels as delicious as these, and the taste always made her think back to that breakfast; the day her feelings had caught up with Robin's, and she realised that she'd met the love of her life.

'How did you find this place?' she'd asked him, sipping her coffee and peering at him over the rim of her cup. Robin was wearing a dark blue hoodie, which made his eyes gleam, and his chin-length blond hair had been flattened by his hat.

Café Cukr was located halfway along a tiny cobbled street in the depths of Mala Strana, and from the outside it looked like nothing more than an unremarkable plain wooden door. When he'd opened it to reveal a staircase leading straight down and the smell of slow-cooked beef, apple and coffee had floated up to greet them, she'd been seriously impressed.

'Oh, you know, just stumbled across it.'

Robin had a way of looking at her that was cheeky at the same time as being intense.

'I bet you bring all the strange girls you meet on snowy bridges here,' she joked.

'Well.' He grinned at her and took a big bite of pretzel. 'You are pretty strange, I'll give you that.'

'Hey!'

'I don't mean in a bad way; I just mean that any girl who chooses to spend her leisure time with me must be strange. I mean, you could probably have your pick of all the boys in Prague, yet here you are.'

I would choose you every single time, over every single other person in the world, not just in Prague, she thought, but she kept her mouth closed.

'I wish I could tell what you're thinking,' he said then, reaching his hand across as though to stroke her cheek and then changing his mind at the last moment. Sophie couldn't stop thinking about the way he'd kissed her fingertips the night before. She wanted him to do it again, but this time she didn't want him to stop at just her hands.

'I'm thinking that this is the best breakfast I've ever had,' she said, scooping up some cream and offering him her spoon.

'Mmmm.' He grinned, deliberately letting a large splodge dribble on to his chin. 'What?' he asked, as she started laughing. 'Is there something on my face?'

He ran his tongue around his mouth, missing the splodge of cream on purpose and looking at her in pretend panic.

'Save me!' he implored. 'Save me from the cream!'

Before she had time to think about what she was doing or what his reaction would be, Sophie had launched herself across the table and was kissing him full on the mouth, licking away the cream as she did so.

Momentarily taken aback, Robin soon followed suit, sliding his hands clumsily around her back. It was only when a nearby diner coughed loudly and scraped his chair pointedly across the wooden floor that they came up for air and sat back down in their seats, gazing at each other in awe over the remains of their breakfast.

Robin recovered first.

'Is it gone – the cream?'

And then they laughed, and it was perfect.

Inspired by her memory, Sophie took out her phone and snapped a photo of her empty plate, making sure she got the dangling pretzels in the background. She hoped Robin wouldn't be cross with her for coming back to this place without him. He could be a bit hot-headed at times, always led by his heart rather than his mind, but Sophie could count the number of arguments they'd had on just one hand. As she pondered, the shadow of a dark memory loomed over her, and Sophie shook her head, shoving the thought away before it took root.

From down here in the warmth of the café, it was hard to tell just how dark it had become outside. She knew that the sun would start to go down no later than four at this time of year, but she had no fear about making her way back to the hotel. She always told family and friends that Prague was a city where getting lost was almost an impossibility. There were so many landmarks to follow, and everything was accessible on foot – even the outer boroughs were only a forty-minute stroll away from the city centre. There was barely a corner of Prague that she and Robin had not explored, and they'd discovered some real treasures as a result: lively beer gardens hidden away in remote parks; cocktail bars in basements on distant back streets; restaurants where you could get three courses for less than ten pounds each – and that included copious amounts of beer to wash it all down with.

Sophie loved the fact that she and Robin had their own version of Prague, the side that most people would never see. It made the place all the more special to them.

'Would you like anything else?'

A waitress had appeared at the table to clear away her plate, and Sophie looked up at her and smiled.

'No, thank you – *dekuji*.'

She should really learn more Czech, Sophie thought. She'd almost bought one of those online language courses for Robin's birthday a few years ago, but then changed her mind at the last minute and got him a watch instead. She'd had it engraved with the date they met.

In return, just a few weeks later, he'd bought her a beautiful gold pendant with a photo of himself inside, doing a thumbs up, and had their entwined initials engraved on the back. Sophie hadn't taken it off since. She could feel it now resting against her chest, still slightly cold from her time spent sitting on the wall up by the castle, and it comforted her. Even if Robin couldn't be here with her right now, she still had him next to her heart. If only she could wish away the next few days until it was time for him to arrive.

As she made her way back up the stairs, buttoning up her coat and pulling on Robin's battered old hat as she went, Sophie felt her phone vibrate in her pocket. Removing her gloves despite the freezing air, she tapped on the screen to read her message, the light above the café doorway casting a contorted human shadow across the icy cobbles.

For a few seconds she didn't move, and then, as slowly and softly as the sleet that had just started to fall, she wrapped her arms tightly around her shoulders and made her way back along the street.

9

'Are you sure about this place?'

Hope put her hand on Charlie's arm as they reached the entrance to the restaurant.

'I told you this trip was going to be a treat,' he reminded her. 'And I intend to spoil you.'

They had crossed the Charles Bridge to get here, Charlie hurrying her past all the statues with the promise that they would come back the next day. Hope felt drawn to the bridge as soon as she set foot on it, and was disappointed when they reached the other side and turned right, heading down towards the edge of the water. The pathway up to the restaurant was dotted with lanterns, each one throwing a golden shaft of light across paving stones that were wet with sleet. The rain had started coming down in the late afternoon, leaving them both numb with cold, but it had also washed away a good portion of the frost, and Hope was able to brave the pair of high heels she'd brought along.

'You look beautiful,' Charlie told her now, for at least the tenth time since she'd slipped into her clinging black dress with the lace panels all down the back. She was still becoming accustomed to his constant flattery, and blushed with mild discomfort at the compliment. The hostess at the restaurant had just returned from the cloakroom, and handed Charlie two coat tickets before beckoning for them to follow her.

'Wow,' Hope said, a few minutes later. They had been given a table overlooking the Vltava River. Blue and amber lights from both the Charles Bridge and the surrounding buildings were reflected in the rippling surface of the water, and as the rain continued to hit the windows, the scene beyond was lent a smudged, almost dream-like quality. Hope could barely drag her eyes away for long enough to take her seat.

'Like I said,' Charlie told her, opening the wine menu, 'I wanted to spoil you.'

'Well, you've truly outdone yourself.' She finally looked away from the view and at him. 'First the amazing hotel and now this – I don't deserve any of it.'

'Nonsense.' Charlie waved a hand in the air. 'You deserve all this and so much more. I meant it when I told you I wanted to make you happy. That's all I've ever wanted to do.'

'I just don't understand how this can be my life,' she admitted, looking around the restaurant with its candlelit tables and vases packed with extravagant blooms. 'If you'd shown me a photo of this place a few months ago and told me that I would be sitting here, with you – well, I would've laughed you into the middle of next week.'

'Are you really happy?' Charlie asked her now, lowering the menu. His eyes looked serious and Hope felt the all-too-familiar guilt brush over her again. She thought about Annette, back home in Manchester, crying about the fact that her mum had left her dad. How could she be happy when her poor baby girl was so sad?

'Of course I am.' She reached over and took his hand. 'I honestly couldn't wish for more.'

It was the first proper lie she'd ever told him, and it sat uncomfortably in the back of her throat like a part-digested painkiller, bitter yet so necessary. It wasn't Charlie's fault that Annette had reacted this way. It wouldn't be fair to him if she let herself dwell on it – especially not at this beautiful table with this stunning view.

Charlie was clearly feeling spurred on by the opulent setting, and chose a red wine with an alarming number of zeroes printed next to it on the menu. Hope, who had been surviving on her own meagre savings plus Charlie's generosity for the past few weeks, felt enormously uncomfortable with such an extravagance. But if it made Charlie happy, then she supposed it was okay.

'To us,' he said, raising his glass and clinking it against hers.

They ordered a starter each, then Charlie chose a ludicrously expensive steak while Hope went for the cheaper fish option. It was hard not to just sit and gaze out at the view of the bridge, but Hope dragged her eyes away and focused on Charlie. He was quiet, which was unlike him, and she shifted in her seat. It was strange when they encountered these momentary glitches of awkwardness, but then it was still early days. She'd only known Charlie for five months – hardly enough time to be completely relaxed with someone.

'What do you fancy doing tomorrow?' she piped up, unable to bear the silence any longer.

He shrugged, a smile playing in the corner of his mouth. She wondered if he was feeling the effects of their hectic day. She could easily have nodded off in the bath back at the hotel before dinner.

'Maybe head to the bridge first, then go from there?' he suggested.

The candle in the centre of their table danced as the breath from their shared conversation passed through it, casting patches of light across Charlie's face. He has such nice eyes, Hope thought, and such a good strong jaw. He'd looked after himself well over the years, playing football at the weekends and hitting the gym. Unlike Dave, who'd increasingly begun to let himself go. It wasn't that she even minded a bit of a belly; it was more that her husband seemed to have given up on looking good. Surely if he cared about her even the tiniest bit, then he would want to look nice? It was the one thing that had kept Hope going to her spinning classes and her Zumba, but Dave had never seemed to notice. Charlie was the total opposite – he loved every single inch of her, and she felt ten feet taller when she was with him.

'What are you looking at me like that for?' Charlie asked. He had finished his first glass of wine, and topped up hers before refilling his own.

'I was just thinking how handsome you are.' She beamed. 'You really are. I feel like the luckiest lady in Prague.'

'Who knows?' Charlie lifted an eyebrow. 'You may be about to get even luckier, because I . . .'

'Scallops?'

The waitress slid Hope's starter on to the table and placed Charlie's tuna carpaccio down in front of him with a flourish.

'What were you about to say?' Hope asked when she'd gone, picking up her cutlery and feeling her mouth water with anticipation.

'Oh, nothing important.' Charlie shook out his napkin and spread it across his lap. 'It can wait.'

10

'Why don't they have beer like this at home?' Ollie lifted up his enormous pint and gazed at it in wonder.

'They do, you big ape – it just looks different.'

Ollie pulled a face. 'And tastes different.'

Megan nodded. 'And costs a very different amount.'

'I ordered a pint the other day in this pub near King's Cross and it cost me a fiver!' Ollie exclaimed. 'I asked the guy behind the bar if there was a lump of gold in the bottom of the glass.'

'You didn't!'

'No, but I should have. Five whole pounds – I felt like I'd been robbed.'

Megan took a sip of her own beer and paused to enjoy the rich, almost honey-like flavour as it slid down her throat.

'Don't you think it's weird that we'll happily spend a fiver on a pint of beer, but then grumble over paying more than a quid for an entire loaf of bread?' she pondered.

'Yes.' Ollie nodded until his glasses slid down his nose. 'But then I happily pay over a quid every morning for two slices of toast from the café opposite the school. What is that about?'

'We're being fleeced, every single day of our lives,' Megan stated, her voice deliberately solemn.

'Same again?' Ollie was holding up his already empty pint glass.

This wasn't all that weird, Megan thought, watching as the barman selected two clean glasses and angled them under the beer tap. There was a tattoo on his forearm of what looked like two single quote marks lying top to tail, and she immediately recognised it as the symbol for Cancer, her star sign. Not long after she'd first met Ollie, Megan had – for a joke – looked up the compatibility of her star sign and his. According to the worldwide web, Scorpio and Cancer were a near-perfect match, with soulmate potential. She didn't believe in all that nonsense, of course, but she couldn't argue with the fact that he had become a very good friend.

Ollie nipped off to the toilet and Megan stared pensively at the grooves that his recently departed bottom had left in the cushion of the bar stool. Were her mum and the internet right? Was Ollie perfect for her? She frowned as an image of the last man she'd thought was perfect for her flashed up in her mind – a man who had done his best to chew her up, only for her to spit him out before he got the chance.

'You okay?'

Ollie was back and his glasses had misted up again.

'You're all steamy,' she informed him, blinking away the grubby memory from her mind.

'I may have found a fault in this otherwise perfect pub,' he told her, throwing in an exaggerated sigh for effect. 'The toilets are bloody freezing. I had to run my hands under the hot tap for ages just to get the feeling back into them.'

'Well, I did suggest we keep looking, but you seemed so sure that an Irish-themed pub with a Mexican name was the right way to go,' she said, raising an eyebrow at him while he polished his glasses with the bottom of his shirt.

'I applaud the blatant eccentricity of the place,' he said.

He wasn't wrong, either – Don Pisto's was certainly eccentric. Multi-coloured sombreros battled for space alongside comedy Guinness hats on the wall behind the bar, a shelf groaned under the weight of a truly spectacular selection of tequila, and the speakers were blasting out an eclectic mix of U2 interspersed with what sounded a lot like a mariachi band. It was barmy, but utterly brilliant.

'I agree.' She bashed her beer against his. 'Shall we get on the tequilas after this?'

'One, two, three . . . and slam!'

Megan knocked back her second shot of tequila and banged the empty glass on the table. They'd moved over from the bar to a corner, where they could continue to sing bad renditions of cheesy eighties tunes at the top of their voices without having to face bemused stares from the other customers.

'This ish the besh holday I've ever had,' Ollie told her, bending over and planting a huge, wet kiss on the side of her face. He'd had double the amount of tequila she'd had, and was also a pint of beer ahead.

'Urgh,' Megan grumbled, wiping his saliva off her cheek with her sleeve and pulling a mock-revolted face at him.

It wasn't the first time she'd got drunk with Ollie. In fact, the very first time they met had ended in a similar way to this. The local pub quiz wasn't exactly the most thrilling of settings, but on that particular evening the Nag's Head had been packed. Megan was there with her Polish friend Magda, who worked with her at the gallery on the weekends and was utterly useless at general knowledge, and Magda's boyfriend Neil, who looked so much like a bird with his narrow pointy nose and his spindly little fingers that Megan was always surprised that he didn't take off in flight at the end of the night.

Ollie was on the next table along in a much stronger team of six schoolteacher friends, all of whom were predictably very good at general knowledge. Megan would have cursed them as geeks, but she was being kept constantly amused by the fact that they all seemed to raise a hand whenever they knew an answer, even though all they actually had to do was write it on the sheet. Ollie himself was the most noticeable, simply because he was the tallest, and so when his arm shot up like a frightened cat every three or four minutes, it was hard to miss.

He told her later that he hadn't actually noticed her at all until it happened, but Megan knew that was rubbish. She'd totally seen him checking her out when he thought her attention was on the quiz sheet.

'Right, boys and girls, it's time for my favourite part of the night – the free-drink round!'

Everyone had spun around in their seats to face the Quiz Master. He wasn't hard to miss, either, given the silver-sequinned jacket he was wearing – 'Talk about over the top,' Megan had whispered to Magda, who didn't hear and said 'What?' very loudly in response.

The rules of this round were simple: Sequins would ask a question, and instead of writing down the answer, you had to jump to your feet and yell it. Whoever yelled the quickest, and quite often the loudest, would be rewarded with a drink of their choice from the bar absolutely free. Apparently this didn't stretch to an actual pint of vodka, as Megan had disappointingly discovered the previous Sunday.

'Are we ready? Who's the thirstiest in here? I want to feel your anticipation, ladies and gents – I want to feel it all over me until it tingles!'

'This man is an idiot,' Magda said, doodling a heart next to where Neil had written his name.

Megan took a deep breath.

'Which male British singer has won the most Brit Awa—'

'ROBBIE WILLIAMS!'

They were both right, they were both quick, they were both loud, and they were both on their feet.

'I said it first!' Megan yelled, so loudly that Sequins took an actual step backwards.

'I had my hand up first,' Ollie said, far more calmly and therefore a lot more annoyingly than Megan.

'Whatever happened to chivalry?' Megan tutted, putting her hands on her hips and glaring him down as best she could, which wasn't easy given that he was way over six feet tall.

'I suppose you'd like me to take off my coat and lay it over the puddle outside for you, too?' Ollie replied, but the challenging tone had vanished from his voice. Worse than that, he now appeared to be laughing at her.

'Don't mock me!' she warned, taking a hand off one hip so she could waggle it at him. 'You know I stood up first.

I was on my feet before he'd even finished the question.'

'Okay, okay.' Ollie held up both hands and laughed. 'You can have the free drink, as it clearly means so much to you.'

'Thank you.'

'And because I'm a gentleman in an age where chivalry is all but dead.'

'Careful.'

'And because I know it will taste horrible anyway, given that you're cheating your way into drinking it.'

'That's *it*!'

Just as Megan was about to march over and put him firmly in his place, Sequins had stepped between them and put a hand on each of their chests.

'Now, now,' he said, putting on what sounded dangerously like a baby voice. 'Play nice, you two. I tell you what, as I'm feeling extra-generous and sparkly tonight, I'm going to say that it was a tiebreaker, and award you both with a free drink.'

Megan opened her mouth to retort, then shut it again.

'Thank you,' Ollie said for both of them, stepping around Megan and heading towards the bar, a look of wry amusement on his face. The whole pub was staring over at her, and Megan suddenly felt like the biggest prat in all of London.

'Go and talk to him,' Magda whispered, as Megan sat down and attempted to hide behind her glass of wine.

'Talk to who?'

Magda gave her a look stern enough to turn milk.

'Don't be playing the silly buggers with me. You know who I mean. That man with the long arms.'

Megan felt her cheeks redden and shook her head. 'Him? No!'

'He is handsome.' Magda threw an apologetic glance at Neil. 'When was the last time you had sex – when the *T. rex* was still roaming about on the Earth?'

'Oi!' Megan pulled a wounded expression.

'It is hard to find a nice man in this godforsaken country,' Magda went on. 'I was very lucky to find my Neil.' She squeezed his twig-like fingers. 'But you might not be so lucky. You have to jump on the iron when it is burning, right?'

'Something like that,' Megan agreed.

Ollie had collected his free pint of beer and was laughing at something the girl behind the bar had said.

'He fancies the barmaid, though,' she hissed. 'And anyway, he's a giant. He's probably a secret BFG who steals children in the night and eats them.'

Magda blinked at her. 'What are you talking about, eating the children? Are you crazy?'

Surely she'd read the book. Everyone had, hadn't they? Even Polish people? Perhaps not.

'Go on!' Magda actually jabbed her in the ribs this time and Megan leapt up off her chair, promptly spilling the dregs that were left in her own glass all over the table.

'See,' piped up Neil. 'Now you actually need another drink.'

'I hate you both,' she told them, heading over to Ollie. 'I'd like a free red wine, please.'

'Well, if it isn't Emmeline Pankhurst.' Ollie gave her a lazy smirk.

'My name is Megan.'

'Much better. I'm Ollie.' They shook hands, hers so small in his huge one, and Megan felt herself begin to thaw. Now that she was standing so close to him, she noticed his kind eyes and his plump lips, the way he kept pushing his glasses up his nose every few seconds and running his hand through his hair.

'I'm sorry I chewed your ear off,' she said. 'I have a bit of a competitive streak and sometimes it gets the better of me.'

'No need to be sorry.' Ollie shrugged. 'I'm glad you did – it got me a free drink.'

'In that case,' she said, baulking inwardly at her boldness, 'the next one's on you.'

He laughed at that, and Megan relaxed a notch more. She could see Madga doing an exaggerated thumbs up in her direction and swiftly diverted Ollie's attention to a stuffed owl that was for some reason nailed up behind the bar.

'Bit odd, don't you think?' she said, unable to come up with anything more intelligent in time.

He considered it for a few seconds before turning to face her.

'Oh, I don't know. I kind of like it. I've always thought it would be nice to be an owl.'

'So you could fly?' Megan guessed.

'Nope.' Ollie paused, a gleam appearing in his narrowed eyes. 'So I could swivel my head right around.'

Megan was aware of her face contorting into a bemused expression, and snatched up her glass from the bar.

'Humans are so limited in that way,' Ollie went on, his tone mock-serious. 'I like the idea of being able to see everything. From every single angle.'

Megan almost choked on her wine as she laughed.

'You're unbelievable!' she told him.

'Maybe I am.' He gave her a sideways look. 'But you totally fancy me – I can tell.'

'Is that right?'

In that moment, it was – she knew it, he knew it, everyone in the pub knew it. She didn't even care about missing the final ten questions of the quiz, and it was the popular culture round.

'You tell me.' His eyes were suddenly challenging and she stared at him for a few seconds, feeling the colour flood into her cheeks. The sounds of the pub seemed to quieten around them, as if they'd both dipped their heads in a bucket and were trying to hear through the water. For a few seconds, Megan was only aware of him and of her, and it was delicious.

They were still propping up the bar long after last orders had been called. Megan had no idea who had won the quiz, what time Magda had left or what Ollie's friends must think of her – and she didn't care, either. It had been such a long time since she'd met a man who made her laugh this much. She'd been on plenty of dates during her past three single years, but this was the first time she'd felt able to just be herself. In the end, and after a good few more glasses of wine, it was she who suggested he come back to her flat for coffee.

Ollie hadn't even hesitated, necking the last of his beer and pulling on his coat. Once outside, however, Megan sensed a shift in her mood. Under the bright lights of the cosy pub and the watchful eyes of the staff, she'd felt confident – invincible, even. Ollie was laughing at her jokes and grinning through her various anecdotes, his cheeks growing pink with what she knew was pleasure in their shared connection. Out here, though, with nobody around but the two of them, he all of a sudden became a stranger again, and the easiness she'd felt started to slip away.

When Ollie reached down and tried to take her hand, she actually snatched it up and recoiled from him, stumbling sideways into someone's unruly conifer.

'I don't bite,' Ollie said, more bemused than alarmed by her bizarre behaviour.

'I know. I just . . .' She stopped.

Ollie slowed to a halt and looked at her properly, his smile deflating at the edges like a sad lilo.

'I don't have to come back to yours if you've changed your mind.'

She squirmed.

'It's not that.'

They had reached the corner of her road already, and Megan forced herself to start walking again, beckoning for Ollie to follow her. She could do this, she told herself. He was a schoolteacher, not a crazed killer. They had chemistry and he was interested in her, in her work. He seemed to be a genuinely nice man, so what the hell was wrong with her?

'Home sweet home,' she proclaimed, turning the key in the lock and giving the door a shove. It had been sticking for months, but she never seemed to have the time to do anything about it.

'Are these yours?' Ollie asked, whistling in appreciation as he stopped to admire the mosaic of photographs that were hanging in frames along the wall leading into the kitchen.

'Guilty as charged,' she replied, taking out the cafetière. For some reason, it had become absolutely paramount that she actually make the promised coffee.

'Can I do anything to help?' Ollie had appeared in the doorway.

'No, that's fine. Just, er, just make yourself at home.' The spoon clattered into the sink and Megan swore at it far louder and with more vitriol than was strictly necessary.

Joining Ollie in the living room a few minutes later, she found that he'd taken her at her word and settled himself cross-legged on her sofa, his mismatched socks clashing merrily with her patchwork throw.

'Nice place,' he said, never taking his eyes off her as she put the cups down on the table and perched awkwardly next to him.

'My parents lent me the deposit,' she mumbled, feeling embarrassed. 'It's not much, but at least it's mine.'

Ollie opened his mouth to reply, but then closed it again. She knew what he was thinking: why were they bothering with small talk now that they were here? There was a line that needed to be crossed, and they were both balanced on the very edge of it, each waiting for a sign from the other. In the end, it was Ollie who moved first, untangling his legs and moving towards her, his gaze making her feel excited and fearful all at the same time.

Just let him kiss you, she thought to herself, watching the coffee grounds dance in their glass chamber. *What's the worst that could happen?*

'Megan?'

She turned to find his face an inch from her own, his smile back in place and his lips moist with expectation. For a few seconds the intensity was almost uncomfortable, and then she closed her eyes.

It was a soft kiss, delicate and shy, and Megan could taste the beer on Ollie's tongue. She waited for her body to respond, to feel that need course through her and force her hands up and across his back. It didn't come. Instead, she thought about all the reasons why this kiss was a bad idea. Hadn't she promised herself that a relationship had to wait until she'd achieved what she needed to? Wasn't this the very worst thing that could happen now, right when she was on the verge of taking back the life that had already been stolen from her by the last man she kissed?

She sneaked an eye open and saw Ollie, his own eyes closed and his brow knotted with concentration. No, this was wrong. It wasn't what she wanted.

'Sorry.' She pulled backwards and looked down at her lap.

Ollie took a breath before he answered. Evidently he'd felt a lot more during that kiss than she had.

'Beer breath that bad?' he joked, but the delivery was feeble.

'I'm just not sure I can,' she mumbled. 'It's not you, it's . . .'

'Me?' he finished, shifting away from her a fraction.

'Oh no, it's me. Definitely me,' she assured him.

Ollie watched her for a few seconds in silence. He could have got up and left, politely told her that it was nice to meet her and then scarpered, never to be seen again, but he didn't. Instead, he smiled at her, poured them both a coffee, and asked her to tell him more about her photography.

They could have just become those two strangers who hooked up on a whim, believing that the lust they were feeling meant something more, only to wake up the following day under a heavy blanket of mutual awkwardness and regret. But they didn't. In choosing not to sleep with Ollie, Megan had inadvertently laid the foundations for something much more: a genuine friendship.

Megan snapped out of her momentary trance to find that Ollie had actually fallen asleep with his face on the table, an empty shot glass still clutched in his hand.

'Come on.' She poked him hard on the thigh until he grunted. 'Time to get you back to the hotel, lightweight.'

The earlier sleet had frozen hard on the cobbles, and Megan almost lost her balance as they rounded the corner by the Old Town Square. The streets were alive with packs of stag and hen parties, all of them in an even worse state than herself and Ollie, who was now half-awake but still leaning a large proportion of his weight on her shoulder.

'The closch looks so pree,' he slurred in her ear, swinging up an arm as they made their clumsy way back past the Astronomical Clock. There were lights around it, and Ollie was absolutely right, it did look pretty. There was barely a corner of the square that hadn't been lit perfectly.

'I wuv yew.'

'What?'

Megan's reply echoed loudly into the quiet street that led to the hotel. She'd replied before her brain had really had time to process the words, and now she felt herself freeze with shock.

I love you – that's what he'd said. Okay, so he was as pissed as that man in Camden Market that marched around with a loaf of bread tied to his head and climbed into bins, but he'd still said it.

Either her reply hadn't registered with Ollie, or he'd been shocked into silence by the ferocity with which she'd delivered it, because he didn't say another word to her as they crunched the final few yards along the flat cobbles and up the steps into the warmth and relative normality of the hotel reception. Mumbling something about needing the toilet, Ollie stumbled ahead of her and into the bar, where he made a beeline for the gents.

Ollie loved her? No, he was just drunk. But he'd said it, hadn't he? Did he still fancy her, then?

'Megan?'

She turned to see Hope, the woman she'd met in the bar that morning, nursing what looked like a nightcap. Sitting beside her, clutching what also looked like something with an alcohol percentage in the double figures, was the tiny, short-haired girl they'd both seen that same morning. Megan waved and pulled what she hoped was a friendly smile.

'Join us for a swift one?' Hope asked, making to get out of her seat.

'Oh no.' Megan shook her head. 'I've had far too many swift ones already, trust me. And I need to get this one,' she pointed at Ollie as he crashed sideways through the toilet door, 'up to bed before he falls over.'

'Maybe see you at breakfast, then?' Hope chirped.

'Definitely.'

Ollie staggered off ahead of her again and she waved to the two women, pulling a face at his departing back for effect. She hoped they hadn't been able to see the confusion she was feeling on the inside.

Luckily, any awkwardness Megan might have felt about the prospect of climbing into the same bed as Ollie was eradicated when they got upstairs and he fell unceremoniously on to it face first, immediately passing out. She thought about taking off his shoes, then changed her mind, suddenly uncomfortable at the thought of touching him.

Why had he gone and blurted that out? Now she wasn't sure what he was thinking, or, even worse, quite what she felt towards him. And the most troubling aspect of all, she admitted to herself twenty minutes later as she listened to Ollie's gentle snores in the darkness, was that a tiny little piece of her had enjoyed hearing him say it.

11

Sophie bent her knees and let her head slide under the water, closing her eyes as the warmth flooded over her. She'd run the bath so hot that her heart was hammering, and from under the water it sounded incredibly loud, as if a drummer from a marching band was doing a solo show between her ears. She shifted slightly so that her nose and mouth broke the surface, and drew in some air.

The cold of the late afternoon had worked its way deep into her bones, and by the time she'd returned from her long, meandering walk back to the hotel, her teeth were chattering like a pair of gossipy old women.

St Nicholas Church, which had always been her favourite of the many churches in Prague, had been almost deserted when she got there, but she welcomed the relative silence with pleasure. The sheer scale and grandeur of the place never failed to hush her in both heart and mind, and standing in front of the altar looking up into the far reaches of the vast, ornate dome, Sophie felt tiny and insignificant.

Robin always giggled when she dragged him in there. Being restless and gregarious, he usually found quiet spaces uncomfortable, often giving in to an overgrown teenage need to misbehave.

It was strange being there alone, and Sophie found that her eyes were taking in more than they usually did.

She took a seat on one of the dark wooden pews close to the front and gazed at the golden cherubs up in the pulpit, their intricately sculpted faces shining brightly in the gloom. When you had someone with you, she thought, it made sense that you would try to look for things to point out to them, rather than just allowing your senses to be purely selfish. For as long as she could remember, she'd had Robin with her, and was always thinking what he would like or be interested in looking at. It was a simple enough realisation, but Sophie had never properly considered what a difference being here without him would make.

Before meeting Robin, she'd done everything on her own – often to the despair of her parents, who complained that they never saw her. But rather than losing her independence through her relationship with Robin, he had simply become her partner in crime – an organic extension. Now being here on her own felt alien to Sophie, and she forced herself to take comfort from her surroundings. There was barely a nook in the church that wasn't adorned with decoration, and the light that was streaming in through the stained-glass windows had turned the walls and even the air a dusty pink. It was as if she was floating in the middle of a sunset, the ambient glow tricking her mind into feeling warm.

She sat back on the hard wood and let her head roll backwards until she could see the fresco that covered the ceiling and a good portion of the walls on each side of the church. There was so much colour, and so much beauty – it was mind-boggling to imagine the painters up there on their rickety scaffolding, a brush in hand and sheer force of will enabling them to complete their masterpieces. Had they sat where she was sitting now and admired their own handiwork? Had they wondered if people would still come to admire it centuries later? It must be one of the greatest things about being an artist – the fact that you got to leave something behind in the world, something that people would enjoy and talk about. There was a sort of magic to it.

Unfortunately for Sophie, she wasn't very artistic at all. She could just about manage a stick man, if she had to, but she wouldn't have the first clue how to sit down and paint the view from her bedroom window back home, or the faces of the people she loved. She and Robin had discussed the idea of having their portrait painted a few times over the years, but there never seemed to be time. When he got here she must ask him again – she liked the idea of a painting of the two of them surviving, and of strangers from an unknown future discovering the portrait and wondering who they were. Sophie always did the same pose in photos with Robin: eyes to him rather than the camera and a wide, adoring smile on her face. That was the portrait she wanted.

After the warmth of the café, the church felt draughty, and Sophie could feel her bottom turning slowly into a block of ice on the pew. She shuffled to her feet and took the winding stone staircase up to the gallery level, panting slightly with the effort and almost tripping over a wooden beam that was fixed across the middle of the floor. Prague was full of these anomalies – a random lump of wood here and a slab of stone there – but they all added to the charm of the place. As Sophie righted herself, she noticed a little old man standing guard over the gallery artwork. Seeing her almost take a tumble had clearly amused him, and again she thought how much she loved the people here for their cheeriness.

There was a sign pinned to one of the stone pillars warning visitors not to lean over the edge of the balcony, and Sophie felt her legs wobble just below the knee. She didn't have a particular fear of heights, but every so often her body would betray her, turning her limbs to jelly at the thought of falling. Robin was the opposite. If he were here now he'd be leaning over the side just to wind her up. When they'd reached Australia for the first time all those years ago, he'd insisted that they immediately look up the nearest place to go skydiving, and Sophie could still remember how it had felt now, standing in the middle of a dusty field, peering through her fingers with trepidation at the image of her brand-new boyfriend hurtling through the air. He certainly knew how to keep a girl on her toes, did Robin.

The old man who had laughed at her cleared his throat, and Sophie pulled back several layers of sleeve to look at her watch. It was almost six, time for this place to close its doors and time for her to leave. Smiling at him and tiptoeing carefully back down the steps, Sophie pulled Robin's hat right down over her ears and headed back out into the cold.

Thud, thud, thud.

Her heart was still hammering away under the water. Sophie lifted up one foot and used her toes to turn on the hot tap. She'd been in here for so long now that the skin on her fingers was starting to pucker, but she didn't relish the idea of getting out. Her room was chilly and felt lonely without Robin. Places where they would usually have cuddled up together felt wrong, somehow. The bed too big, the covers too heavy and the silence oppressive. She turned off the tap now and listened to the nothingness, her ears straining to pick up even the tiniest of sounds. She heard a drip, the distant sound of tinny voices, perhaps from a television, a muffled car door being opened and closed, the gentle rumble of a passing tram, and behind it all the disquieting hum of absolute silence.

Feeling goosebumps start to spring up across her chest and arms, Sophie let out a deep sigh and made herself clamber up and out of the bath. The nagging darkness that had been threatening to creep into her subconscious all day was back, hammering away at her like a ghoulish woodpecker. All at once the need to get out of the room was urgent, and she pulled on her jeans so quickly that she stumbled over and collided with the edge of the desk.

That would leave yet another bruise. They seemed to pop up on her body so easily these days, as if she had the skin of a soft fruit. Sophie winced as she pressed a finger against her flesh, swearing under her breath. What she needed was a distraction. Perhaps there would be some other guests down in the bar that she could chat to. Anything was preferable to staying up here on her own.

Mind made up, she gathered up her bag and key, shut the door behind her with a bang and headed towards the stairs.

12

'I'm not sure if that truffle ravioli second course was such a good idea.'

Hope turned to Charlie as they were crossing the bridge and put her hand on his stomach.

'Oh no, did it not agree with you?'

'Something didn't.' Charlie pulled a face and halted in his tracks.

Hope wanted to point out that it was his own silly fault for being such a pig and having two dinners, but she sensed that it wouldn't go down very well. A bit like Charlie's truffle ravioli, in fact.

'Perhaps you've just had too much to drink today?' she suggested instead.

'Maybe.' Charlie didn't look convinced.

'It has been a very long day,' she said, slowing down as he doubled over, his discomfort clear from his grimace.

'You poor duck.' Hope slipped easily into her motherly role, fussing around him and putting her hand across his forehead to check he wasn't burning up. 'You don't seem to have a temperature.'

'This is embarrassing.' Charlie reddened. 'We're supposed to be on a romantic trip.'

'Doesn't the castle look lovely, all lit up like that,' she said to distract him, pointing behind them to where

Prague Castle loomed on top of the hillside, bright gold against the navy sky.

'Very pretty.' Charlie didn't bother turning around. 'Sorry, love – I just need to get back to the hotel.'

'Of course.' Hope laced her arm through his and they continued in silence.

They'd had such a nice evening at the restaurant, enjoying the atmosphere and the delicious wine, and Hope had chatted away to him about her plans. She had decided that she simply must get a job, she told him, even if it was just something part-time in a shop. She didn't want to be a burden.

Charlie had predictably pulled a face at this, reassuring her that she didn't need to worry, that he was more than happy to support the two of them for as long as she wanted. It should have made her happy, but Hope found her hackles rising slightly and had concentrated on her food until the feeling slipped away. Didn't he understand that she needed to work? She wanted to do it for herself, not for him. She'd had years of a man being the one in charge of the money, years of having to pluck up the courage to beg Dave for an extra tenner if the groceries were running low. There was no way that she was ever letting that happen again, even if Charlie did have the very best intentions.

As they skirted the edge of the Old Town Square and made their way along the street towards the hotel, Hope wondered what her ex-husband would have made of Prague. She seriously doubted that its beauty and charm would have got under his skin as it had hers – but he hadn't always been so unresponsive. She tried to remember now when he'd changed into that person, someone who was no longer her friend, but she couldn't quite see past the heavy curtain of time.

Charlie stopped her in the hotel reception, his cheeks red and beads of sweat forming on his top lip.

'Do you mind if I . . . ? I mean, can you wait until . . . ?'

'You want me to wait down here for a bit?' she guessed, feeling herself soften as he nodded with relief. The poor man.

'I'll treat myself to a nightcap in the bar,' she assured him, letting her hand rest on his arm for a second. 'You go on up.'

He nodded again, and Hope watched as he limped slowly away like a soldier back from war. Men and their ailments – they really were ridiculous, she thought, smiling to herself as she pushed open the door to the bar.

'Oh, hello there.'

The small girl with the short hair who she'd seen that morning was sitting alone at a table next to the window, a half-full glass of white wine in front of her and a faraway look on her face.

'Hi,' she replied, her voice subdued.

'Are you okay, sweetheart?' Hope took in the dark shadows underneath the big, startled eyes. 'You look miles away.'

The girl shook her head and smiled. 'I was. It's been a long day.'

The barman appeared next to them and asked Hope what she'd like.

'Do you mind?' Hope pointed to the chair next to the girl and she nodded.

'In that case,' she beamed at the barman, 'I'll have a large gin and tonic, please.'

'Very good.' He trotted off.

'My other half had to go up ahead of me,' Hope said, wriggling out of her coat. 'I think he overindulged at dinner.'

'Where did you go?' the girl asked. She had a slight accent, but Hope wasn't sure where it heralded from. Close up she was stunningly pretty and so elfin in size that Hope half-expected her to have tiny wings sprouting out from between her shoulder blades.

'Oh God, the name escapes me now. All these long Czech words get into a tangle on my tongue, but it was on the other side of the river, down by the water.'

The girl's eyes widened. 'I know the one, Kampa – it's quite posh, isn't it?'

Hope flushed. 'Do you know what, it was a bit! But Charlie, that's who I'm here with, he wanted to spoil me.'

'And so he should.' The girl smiled and took a sip of wine. She was wearing a thick cable-knit jumper, the sleeves rolled up to reveal twig-like wrists. 'Was the food any good?'

'Well.' Hope looked over in the direction of the door. 'I'll have to let you know about that when I find out what's happened upstairs.'

The girl laughed at that and held up her hands. 'I don't need details – honestly!'

'I'm Hope, by the way.'

'Sophie.' The girl smiled back.

'It's lovely to meet you. Are you here alone?' Hope asked, realising a fraction too late that it was probably a bit nosy of her to enquire.

'Just for a few days.' Sophie sipped at her wine. 'My boyfriend – actually, he's my fiancé now, I keep forgetting that – he's coming to join me.'

'Congratulations!' Hope picked up her glass to toast the engagement. 'I'm guessing it's a recent thing?'

'He proposed last month.' Sophie had a faraway look on her face again. 'It was a total surprise, which I suppose is why I'm still getting used to the idea.'

'Was it very romantic?' Hope asked. She loved a good proposal story.

Sophie smiled. 'Not really, to be honest. I was drying my hair and he was still in bed. He actually chucked a pillow at me to get my attention, and then I turned around to tell him off and he just had this really serious look on his face all of a sudden.'

'Oh, but that is romantic,' Hope assured her. 'I had bubbly and flowers and music and everything for mine, and the marriage ended up being a total sham.'

'Oh, I'm so sorry.' Sophie was all concern. 'The man upstairs isn't your husband, then?'

'Charlie? God, no! He's my upgrade.' She laughed and Sophie politely followed suit, but the amusement didn't quite reach her eyes.

'My husband and I . . . we'd been having problems for years. Well, probably forever.' She took a gulp of gin. 'I decided to have driving lessons, because I'd never bothered to learn, and there Charlie was – my knight in a shining white Vauxhall Corsa.'

What Hope failed to mention was that she and Charlie had started up their relationship quite a while before she'd ended her marriage, but it was a tough thing to admit to someone you'd just met. Sophie had only just got engaged, too – Hope didn't want to put a dampener on the mood by reminding her that people cheat on each other.

If Sophie suspected there was more to the story, she didn't say. She simply smiled at Hope and asked, 'Do you love each other?'

Hope nodded.

'Well, that's all that really matters.'

Was it? Hope wasn't sure, but Sophie looked so sincere and non-judgemental. Hope was reminded horribly of Annette, looking at her with such disgust, her hatred and bewilderment clear as she raged at her mother that she was a slut. And she was right, too – Hope agreed that her behaviour had been abhorrent. She never imagined that she would turn her back on the vows that had once meant so much to her, that she would take the coward's way out and choose infidelity over decency.

Getting together with Charlie had felt like the ultimate rebellion, the first purely selfish thing that Hope had ever done in her life. Of course, she should have ended her marriage before starting a new relationship, but she had convinced herself that Dave wouldn't care even if he did find out – there were plenty of couples in open relationships, after all. But it was a lie. While there was no doubt in her mind that Dave didn't love her the way he once had, that didn't give her an excuse to play away. She tried to imagine how she would have felt if it had been him instead of her who had found someone else. Would she have cared? It was impossible to know that now, after so much had happened. What she did know was that she hadn't loved Dave for a very long time – and she hadn't loved herself either. But how could she explain all of that to Annette? She'd made such a mess of everything, and now she was paying the price.

'I hope you're right.' She smiled at Sophie and took another sip of her drink.

'I just think that when you know, you know.' Sophie had finished her own drink and thanked the barman as he scurried over to take her order.

'I guess.' Hope was well aware that she had been spurred into a flurry of probably inappropriate oversharing by all the alcohol she'd had over the past few hours, but she couldn't seem to stop. It felt nice to talk to someone who wasn't a part of her inner circle. Her mum had been appalled when she left Dave, despite knowing full well how unhappy she had been for so long, and her friends didn't understand it either.

'I've only ever loved one boy,' Sophie said now, a dreamy expression clouding her Bambi eyes.

'Have you been together long?' Hope asked, sensing her turn to spill was over.

'Ten years.'

'Wow!' Hope almost choked. 'Did you meet at nursery school?'

Sophie laughed. 'I'm twenty-eight!'

Hope shook her head in disbelief. 'Are you taking the mickey?'

'No.' Sophie was amused. 'I'm definitely twenty-eight, I promise. And we met here, in Prague, Robin and me. We were both backpacking around Europe, as you do, and he just walked up to me.'

'Is that why you're here?' Hope guessed. 'Is it your ten-year anniversary?'

Sophie nodded.

'Well, that is just the loveliest thing.' Hope reached over and gave her an awkward one-armed hug. 'And what a place to meet.'

'It's very special,' Sophie agreed, her fingers playing with the stem of her glass. 'Robin and me, we come back here every year.'

'How soon is he arriving?' Hope asked.

'He should be here in a few days,' she said, her voice small again. 'Probably Sunday.'

'I'm here until Monday.' Hope clapped in delight. 'I should so like to shake his hand and tell him how lucky he is to have you.'

Sophie blushed.

'No, I mean it – you're a beautiful girl with a kind heart and a good soul. You don't get to the age of fifty without learning a few things along the way, I can tell you – and I know a good person when I meet them.'

They both looked up as there was a crashing sound and Megan's face appeared at the door, bright pink from the cold. The guy she was with was in a terribly drunken state, and Hope barely had time to get a look at him before he stumbled through the door leading to the gents. She wasn't all that surprised when Megan turned down her offer of a nightcap – they'd all had such a long day.

'That's Megan,' Hope told Sophie when the two of them had gone. 'I met her this morning. She's very nice.'

'Her friend's very drunk.' Sophie giggled.

'Speaking of which . . .' Hope picked up her empty

glass and lifted it up to her lips, tapping the bottom in an attempt to get every last drop. 'I should get upstairs and check on Charlie – but we should do this again.'

'I'd like that.' Sophie smiled at her. The wine had added some colour to her cheeks and Hope felt herself drawn again to the younger girl. A motherly instinct is a hard habit to shrug off, she told herself as she walked up the stairs. She was just feeling protective towards Sophie because she hadn't seen Annette in so long.

All the same, she thought, letting herself into the bedroom and groaning as she saw light streaking out from under the closed bathroom door, there was something about Sophie that made her want to wrap the girl up in a wad of cotton wool and put her somewhere safe.

13

It was still dark when Megan crept along the deserted hotel corridor and down the stairs. A bad dream had woken her an hour ago and left her feeling so shaken that sleep was an impossibility. Ollie was passed out beside her, totally oblivious, his mouth hanging open and his breath faintly metallic from all the tequila.

Instead of staying put, where she knew she'd only fidget with frustration until she ended up waking him, Megan stole carefully out from under the covers and quietly got dressed, cleaning her teeth by the light of her phone and tiptoeing around to get her clothes in the manner of a sneaky cartoon character. Her plan was simple: head to the Charles Bridge to take some photos as the sun came up. She felt a tiny bit guilty that she would be seeing it for the first time alone, without Ollie, but she needed some space. Plus, the upcoming exhibition was at the front of her mind, wagging its finger and telling her to get a move on. It was so important, and so much of her future hinged on it, that of course this just made it feel like a tyrant. She had been at this point in her career before, her memory helpfully reminded her. It had been hers for the taking, until somebody else took it all away.

Any lingering tiredness she might have felt vanished as soon as she stepped outside into the freezing early-morning air. The sky was dark grey, rather than black, with a hint of dawn at its corners. Knotting up her scarf and pulling her hat further down over her ears, Megan set off determinedly through the crunchy frost.

She wasn't going to think about what Ollie had said to her last night, because it obviously didn't mean anything. Even if he had meant to say that he loved her, it was only in an affectionate, friendly way, because she had been helping carry his drunken arse back to the hotel. If he said anything about it today she would just laugh it off, she decided. Tell him that he'd said no such thing and that his hungover brain must be playing tricks on him. She had a sneaking suspicion that her nightmare had been triggered by Ollie's words, and if that were the case then she needed to discourage him from saying anything else. Megan had never been a particularly open person, and struggled to tell her own mother that she loved her, let alone her friends. She had thought that Ollie was the same, but perhaps not.

The Old Town Square was deserted, piles of rubbish from last night's revellers sitting morosely by overflowing bins. It still looked beautiful, though, the rich gold from the Astronomical Clock gleaming under its spotlights and the proud, Gothic spires of the big church staring down at her from their lofty perch above the cobbles. Again Megan felt that sense of history seeping into her. So much had happened in this place, and now she was making her way across it, creating her own path through the course of history. It made her feel very small, yet at the same time important.

Despite the fact she'd only been in Prague for a single day, Megan already found it familiar and welcoming, even at this time in the morning when she was practically the only person out on the streets. It was so easy to navigate, and she only needed a brief glance at the map in order to find her way through the twisty maze of streets leading to the vast and imposing Old Town Bridge Tower, which served as the ancient gateway to the Charles Bridge. Once she was on the threshold, Megan found herself unable to take another step, the sight before her too awesome and too mesmerising. She didn't even reach for her camera, instead preferring to let her eyes survey the scene first and wait for the inevitable rush of emotions that would follow.

The light was just beginning to creep its fingers up from the water and over the stone edges of the bridge walls, illuminating the thick fog. The dark ridges of the bridge's many statues were just visible through the gloom, their bold silhouettes cutting eerie holes in the gently shifting mist. Megan crouched down on the smooth, curved cobbles and started to record the scene, her fingers expertly caressing the rough casing of the lens as she went in for a closer look, before pulling back again, capturing the bridge in all its glory.

It had been a while since she'd experienced a rush like this, where the images slipped faultlessly into their own narrative and she had the sense that she was merely the tool allowing them to do so. The story was already there, and it was simply up to her to uncover it. It was at moments like this that Megan knew she was at her most whole, as if the entire reason for her existence was to take these photos, to record an event that she could show to others – hopefully to the entire world – so they could feel transported, just as she did.

Was this it? Could her inspiration have been waiting for

her on this bridge for all this time? The more photos she took, the more she started to believe it could be true, and as the fog began to be chased away by the unstoppable power of the dawn, more shapes revealed themselves on the horizon. There was Prague Castle, its outline faint but regal up on the far right, and beside it the dark spires of St Vitus's Cathedral. As she made her way further along the bridge, she could even make out the green domed roof of the Church of St Nicholas, which she'd read about in her guidebook and desperately wanted to see.

Megan's heart was racing, her breath in the cold air rising upwards like a halo. She knew she was capturing something very special here, something unlike anything she ever had before, and the knowledge made her feel giddy with excitement, as if she were light enough to take flight and soar off the edge of the bridge to join the swans on the surface of the Vltava River below. She was exhilarated, and the feeling was better than anything she had encountered before.

She was brought back down to earth by the sound of bells ringing, and took out her phone to check the time. It was eight already – she'd been out here for ninety minutes and she'd barely been aware of the time passing. Her fingers were stinging from the cold, but she could hardly feel them. All she wanted to do was keep going, right into the depths of the city where she now knew that a wealth of visual treasures awaited her, but she hesitated. She couldn't very well go wandering off all day and leave Ollie on his own.

Megan groaned with the unfairness of it all and gazed longingly over at the left bank. This was exactly the reason she'd halted that first kiss with Ollie all those months ago – boyfriends got in the way of her plans. How could she throw herself on the mercy of her inspiration when she was chained down by commitment and responsibility? She'd allowed herself to believe that she could have both once before, and look how that had ended. With tears and jealousy and destruction. Nope, if she was ever going to make a go of it as a professional photographer, then she had to be willing to give it everything. Half measures were not going to be enough. And anyway, if the past few hours had taught Megan anything, it was that this feeling, the one she had experienced as soon as she first set eyes on the Charles Bridge, was what she wanted to experience every day. A relationship just couldn't compete with it, and that was a fact.

The bells had stopped, but in the echoing silence that followed, Megan began to hear signs of life, of car doors slamming shut, shutters being pulled upwards and radios starting up. The city of Prague was beginning to awake, and the magical sense of being alone in a moment melted slowly away as Megan made her way back to face Ollie.

'Why did you let me order tequila? Why?'

Ollie was talking to her through the bathroom door, where he'd been since she returned from her early morning adventure.

'I feel absolutely fine,' she told him cheerily. It wasn't strictly true – she'd actually woken up with a clanging headache, but the cold air had soon cleared it.

'I hate you,' he groaned, and she laughed, ridiculously relieved to have him back being cheeky rather than soppy.

'I think we should go up to the castle today,' she called, peeling off her jumper and swapping it for a thicker one. 'We can go through the park – the walk will do you good.'

'Pah,' came the response.

'Well, that's what I'm doing – it's up to you if you want to come or not.'

There was a pause, and Megan wondered if she'd gone a bit far.

'What happened to me being the boss?' he said at last, his tone not altogether sincere.

'You milked that one yesterday,' she informed him. 'Pints of beer in the airport at seven in the morning, tequilas in the bar . . .'

'Don't say that word!'

'Tequila, tequila, tequilaaaaaaaa,' she sang, her mouth up against the door.

Ollie groaned and kicked the wood.

'I'm going to go downstairs and get breakfast,' she said, slipping her camera into its bag and zipping it up carefully. 'Shall I see you down there?'

'Okay.'

She sighed. 'Don't be grumpy – I promise you'll feel better as soon as we're outside.'

She didn't hear his response, but it sounded like a cross between a swear word and another moan. God, he really was suffering. She'd have to make sure she cheered him up today.

'Morning!'

It was Hope, and this time she had her boyfriend with her. He also looked a bit green round the gills, Megan noticed, as she shook his hand and joined them at their table.

'Sophie's just getting herself some strudel,' Hope told her, pointing over to the buffet, where the small girl Megan recognised from the bar last night was hovering.

'I might join her,' Megan said, sniffing the air appreciatively. 'I'm absolutely starving.'

Charlie let out a low moan and clutched his stomach.

'Poor Charlie had a touch of food poisoning last night,' Hope explained, giving Megan a quick look that said, 'you know what men are like'. Megan did know, and she told them all about Ollie and his tequila misadventure.

'I wish I'd had tequila instead,' Charlie grimaced. 'Booze I can handle, rich food, not so much.'

Sophie was back with her strudel and said a shy hello to Megan before taking her seat. The cutlery looked enormous in her tiny hands, and Megan wondered if she'd even manage to hold it up long enough to transfer the warm apple and crisp pastry from her plate to her mouth.

'It's good,' Sophie said after the first forkful had gone in. The icing sugar from the strudel was all over her top lip, and Megan saw Hope pick up a napkin and instinctively go to wipe it off, before stopping herself at the last second.

'You've got sugar on your face,' Megan said instead, laughing as Sophie looked horrified and hurriedly licked it off.

'Has it gone? Oh my God – I'm so disgusting. You can't take me anywhere. That's what Robin always says – he thinks I eat like a dog.'

'Robin?' Megan enquired politely, thanking the waitress who had just come over with coffee for the table.

'He's her fiancé,' Hope said, sounding like a proud mother.

'Oh.' Megan suppressed a yawn. 'Congrats on the engagement. Sorry – I didn't sleep very well.'

'Me neither,' Charlie grumbled, and Hope met Megan's eye again across the table. Megan considered telling them all about her walk to the Charles Bridge that morning, then hesitated. She wanted to keep that moment private for now.

'Is Robin here with you?' she asked Sophie instead, immediately noticing the girl's smile drop from her lips.

'He's been held up at home,' she replied, nudging her knife through the puddle of leftover cream on her plate. 'He'll be here in a few days.'

As she said it, the phone on the table in front of her lit up, and Megan saw a picture flash up of a man with messy blond hair and a big grin.

Sophie jumped on it and leapt to her feet. 'I should take this,' she told them, and slipped out of the glass doors into the courtyard.

Megan busied herself by going to fill up a plate from the buffet, which offered just about every breakfast food you could ever want, including some other delicacies that she couldn't imagine ever craving at this time in the morning. Radishes? Really? And piles of pickled gherkins and coleslaw? There were also spicy frankfurter-style sausages sliced into chunks, and some rather dubious-looking pasta salad. Clearly the Czechs liked to have every single taste catered for, even those that belonged firmly in the later part of the eating day. Thankfully, there was also eggs, toast and a copious amount of strudel.

'I think I'm dying.'

She turned to find Ollie, staring down at a platter of dressed boiled eggs and gripping the edge of the wooden counter.

'Eat something,' she chided. 'It will make you feel better.'

Ollie pulled a face and reached limply for some bread.

'How come you're so chirpy?' he demanded. 'You had pretty much the same amount to drink as me and you look fine.'

'I've got youth on my side,' she said. 'You're an old man, don't forget.'

'Thirty-five is not old,' he muttered, adding bacon to his scrambled eggs.

They joined the others and Megan introduced Ollie to Hope and Charlie. The two men seemed to hit it off immediately, linked as they were by their individual ailments and shared self-pity. Sophie was still outside in the courtyard, her phone clamped to her ear and her arms wrapped around herself.

'She must be freezing out there,' Hope said, her face full of concern.

'I'm sure she'll come back in if she is,' Megan replied, smiling to reassure her.

Ollie was telling Charlie about his job, and Hope turned her attention to the two men as Megan got stuck in to her breakfast.

'I don't know how you do it,' Charlie was saying. 'I only have to teach one person at a time and that's hard enough. How the hell do you cope with a whole classroom full?'

'You get used to it.' Ollie shrugged. He had a bit of colour back in his cheeks now that he'd eaten something, and Megan watched as he told the other two a story about his early days as a trainee teacher, when he'd been left to cover a class of year tens at a secondary school and they'd locked him in the stationery cupboard.

'I was in there until the caretaker found me at six,' he said, as Charlie laughed his head off. 'I even offered to pay them if they let me out, but they were having none of it. I was quite impressed in a way, but I was also busting for a pee, which wasn't quite so good. After that I decided that primary school kids were the way forward.'

'I'm amazed you ever went back at all,' Hope said, wiping her eyes with her napkin.

'Well, I love teaching,' he said simply. 'I see children as the future, and being part of that, and being able to help those kids find their way through those tricky few years . . . Well, that's what keeps me motivated, I suppose. Even when they're swearing at me.'

'I wish my Annette had been taught by someone like you,' Hope told him. 'She had terrible teachers all the way through. She never really gelled with school; she always preferred talking to people than reading books, you know? It's no wonder she became a hairdresser. But she's happy, and that's all I care about.'

Megan was reminded of her own parents saying the same thing about her when she'd informed them that she wanted to go to art college, and felt punched with emotion. Thankfully, a shivering Sophie chose that moment to come back to the table and the conversation was forgotten as Hope stood up to put a tentative arm around her.

'Oh, darling, you're absolutely cold right through – do you want my cardi?'

Sophie shook her head. Her teeth were chattering and her fingers looked almost blue.

'Here.' Ollie handed her a cup of hot chocolate that he'd managed to conjure up from somewhere.

'Thanks.' She smiled at him, and Megan quickly introduced them.

'Was that your fella on the phone?' Charlie asked.

Sophie nodded, smiling as she sipped her drink.

'Did he say when he'd be here?' Hope asked excitedly.

'In a few days,' Sophie said, her shoulders dropping as she started to thaw a bit. 'I told him about you all – he can't wait to meet you.'

'And we can't wait to meet him,' Hope exclaimed. Megan was still playing catch-up, but she smiled encouragingly at Sophie, wondering then what the rest of the group thought about her being here with Ollie, who was neither boyfriend nor fiancé. Megan had never been away with a male friend before, but then she'd never really had a man in her life that she was this close to before. It shouldn't be any more awkward than if she were here with a girl, but for some reason it felt different. When she'd told Magda that she was coming over to Prague with Ollie, her Polish friend had raised a suggestive eyebrow immediately. Did Sophie, Hope and Charlie feel the same way? Did they assume there was more to her and Ollie's relationship than friendship?

'We should get going,' she said to Ollie, who downed his coffee and nodded. 'Maybe we'll see you all later, in the bar?'

'For a soft drink,' Ollie quickly added, pulling a face and making Charlie chuckle again.

Megan caught Hope's eye once more before they left and could almost see the loaded questions behind her lashes. Thinking back to Ollie's affectionate words last night made Megan's stomach lurch – the poor thing must have been seriously drunk to blurt them out like that. Although perhaps it was time to tell him the truth about her past and put a stop to the uneasiness she was beginning to feel once again.

The only problem was, she had no idea where to even start.

14

Charlie insisted on a lie-down after breakfast to make sure his stomach was fully recovered, so Hope used the time to paint her nails and check her phone – not looking for messages from Annette, of course. She'd sent her a text when she'd come up to bed last night, and every minute that passed without so much as a few words of abuse in return broke Hope's heart a little bit more. It was hopeless, and she felt too sad to even appreciate the irony.

She glanced over at Charlie, who was fully clothed on top of the covers, his eyes closed and his breathing slow and steady. She knew he wasn't asleep, because he always made these sweet little snuffling noises when he was really out for the count. She'd never known him to be so silent, and it was disquieting. Should she say something? Attempt to cheer him up? When Dave had been feeling ill he'd wanted her to fuss around him, fetching him tea and bringing him a cold flannel for his head, but poorly Charlie was a new one on her. It only reminded her of how little she really knew him.

It had been easier in a way when their relationship was all a big secret. She'd kept waiting for the day that her guilt would charge to the surface and force her to confess what she was up to, but it never arrived, and now her single biggest regret in life was how the affair had come out in the open. It had happened in the worst possible way imaginable, and she supposed that was her punishment. Cheating on your husband wasn't a very nice thing to do, even if your marriage was as lifeless as road kill, but being caught in the act by your own daughter? Well, that was a karma kick in the teeth too far. She didn't know how to say sorry to Annette.

Charlie had been just as mortified as her, especially given that they were sitting in the back seat of his car at the time, kissing each other with abandon. It had been reckless to do such a thing only a few streets from her front door, but Hope had fallen for Charlie like a stone into a pond, her feelings when she was with him stamping all over the qualms she was having. Annette, who was on her way over following an argument with her boyfriend Patrick and ironically had been looking for comfort and reassurance from her mum, had glanced through the car window purely by chance as she passed.

Hope actually winced whenever she thought about it, and she understood why her daughter was finding it difficult to move past her anger. Annette hadn't even stopped to think after her eyes had met Hope's through that window; she'd sprinted straight off in the direction of home to tell her dad exactly what she'd just seen. Hope, who'd been rendered temporarily immovable by horrified shock, caught up with her daughter just as the words were spilling out of her mouth. Dave had simply glared at her, shaking his head from side to side while he attempted to console a now-hysterical Annette. It had been so awful.

'Ready to go in a bit, love?'

Charlie was sitting up and smiling at her now, a lopsided look of adoration on his face.

'Yes, of course.' Hope rubbed her eyes. 'Sorry, sweetheart, I was miles away.'

'Luckily not literally.' Charlie swung his legs round and made his way across the room. 'I like having you right here, right where I can kiss you whenever I want.'

'Feeling better, then?' she guessed.

'A bit.' He looked down at her. 'But feel free to keep fussing over me – I love it.'

They headed straight to the Charles Bridge, Hope almost bouncing up and down inside her boots with excitement. She could feel Prague easing its way into her, its beauty and inherent sense of magic lifting her spirits. Wherever she looked, there was an ornate building to make her gasp, a street entertainer to make her giggle, or a young couple snuggling under a blanket together watching the world go by. It was such a happy place, and she was content to let herself fall under its spell.

'Here we are,' Charlie announced, as they crossed the road and walked under the huge arch of the Old Town Bridge Tower. 'Welcome to my bridge!'

It was a terrible joke, but Hope felt so cheered by the walk that she indulged him in a laugh.

Wide as a road and dappled with cobbles, the bridge stretched out ahead of them enticingly, both sides lined with entertainers, stall-owners and artists, each offering to paint portraits on the spot or sketch a caricature. Small tables were covered in trinkets, ornaments and photos, and statues stood grandly at irregular intervals upon the outer walls, surveying the bubbling brook of tourists making their way past.

Hope was rummaging in her handbag for the guidebook, but Charlie put a hand on her arm. 'Don't bother with that,' he hissed under his breath. 'Let's just tag along to one of these tours.'

'Isn't that a bit naughty?'

'It is a bit.' He winked at her. 'But I'm game if you are?'

They strolled as nonchalantly as possible to the opposite side of the bridge, where a walking tour had come to a halt beside a large statue of a woman holding a baby in her arms, surrounded by worshipping men.

'This is the statue of the Madonna, St Dominic and St Thomas,' droned the guide. 'It was placed here in 1708 and shows the Dominicans, the Madonna and, if you look here, there is also their emblem, a dog.'

'They all look pretty stoned to me,' Charlie whispered, earning himself a yelp of amusement from Hope. The guide turned towards them and frowned at the interruption, and Hope quickly scuttled away.

'Where are you going?' Charlie plodded after her. 'You've blown our cover – now we'll have to find another tour to crash.'

'You are a bad man,' she chided, taking his hand.

They continued along the bridge, stopping every few metres to gaze out at the view or admire a brazen pigeon washing itself on the wall. A lot of the statues had birds sitting up on their shoulders and heads, and Hope found herself amused by their audacity.

'Wouldn't it be great to be able to fly?' she said now, looking up to where two seagulls were fighting over the remains of a hotdog bun in mid-air.

'I'd rather be on the ground with you.'

He pulled her to him, and for a while they just stood

leaning against the wall at the edge of the bridge. Hope thought she could spend all day here, her eyes drawn upwards by a never-ending mosaic of red rooftops, clock faces and the spires of centuries-old churches. It felt like they'd opened the pages of a fairy-tale book and stepped inside, and with every minute that passed, she was aware of her senses unfurling like a creature coming out of hibernation. The air that passed held an intriguing mixture of scents, and her ears picked out the distant clicking sound of passing trams and the throbbing swell of the Vltava River below them.

After a time, Hope found her eyes drawn to a statue up ahead with a large crowd around its base. Taking Charlie's hand, she made her way over and found them a spot not too far from the tour guide, who was clearly enjoying having such a rapt audience.

'This is the statue of St John Nepomuk,' the woman announced, waiting while everyone raised their cameras and snapped away at the figure above them. St John was clad in robes and a hat, a small replica of Christ on the cross in one of his hands and a large golden feather in the other. Behind his head there was a halo punctuated by five gold stars. He looked sad, but also wise, and Hope felt a shiver run through her that was nothing to do with the cold.

'This was the first statue to be placed on the Charles Bridge in 1683,' the tour guide continued. 'St John is very famous here in Prague, and his tomb can be found in St Vitus's Cathedral.' Everyone craned their heads around to where Gothic spires were clearly visible on the hill.

'St John was arrested by King Wenceslas in 1393 and

tortured,' she went on, causing many members of the crowd to widen their eyes.

'It was later claimed that the Queen had confessed to St John, but that he would not tell the King what she had said. After he was tortured, St John was brought down to the bridge, his arms were chained and wood tied in his mouth, and he was thrown over the side.'

'Bloody hell,' whispered Charlie. 'That's a bit barbaric.'

'The legend says that after St John went under the water, five stars rose up, and later his followers recovered his body. People now like to come and touch this statue for luck,' she added, moving aside to reveal the base of the plinth. On one side there was a plaque depicting the moment St John was thrown, the figure of his tiny body polished gold by the many hands that had touched him. On the other side, another plaque showed a soldier petting a bright golden dog.

The tour guide smiled to herself as the crowd surged forward, taking it in turns to touch the plaques. Hope couldn't stop looking up at the face of St John above them.

'Do you not want a turn?' the guide asked. She had taken a step back from the rest of the group and was making sure that only Hope and Charlie could hear what she was saying.

'It is said that touching the falling Saint will bring you luck and ensure you come back to Prague one day, but there is a better way to make your luck on this bridge.'

'Oh?' She had Hope's full attention.

'If you go back along the bridge on this side, you will find another small structure, not like a statue, but an ornament, which is also showing St John in the water,' she whispered conspiratorially. 'In front of this is a golden cross, embedded in the stone. If you touch this cross and make a wish, it will come true one year and one day later.'

'A year and a day?' Hope repeated.

The guide nodded, looking very pleased with herself.

'Not everyone is knowing this secret,' she said, turning away so that the rest of the crowd didn't hear her. 'I like to tell only a few people.'

'We'll definitely go and find it.' Hope could feel her excitement bubbling again. She knew there was something special about this bridge, something that had made it sneak its way under her skin as soon as she stepped on to it.

'Come on.' She grabbed Charlie's arm. 'Thanks again,' she said over her shoulder, before hurrying back the way they'd just come.

It didn't take Hope long to find what she was looking for. The rectangular structure was far smaller than any of the statues, its decorative lattice made from twisted curls of bronze. In the centre was a separate, smoother section depicting the Charles Bridge and St John Nepomuk in the water below, his eyes closed and the five stars in a halo around his head. In front of this, set into the stone of the bridge, was a gold cross with an extra branch through its centre, and on the end of each branch was a star.

'This must be it!' Hope clapped her hands in delight. 'It feels magical; don't you think?'

Charlie pulled a face. 'I'm not really into all this hocus-pocus stuff.'

Hope felt herself deflate. For the first time since they'd

met, he had just reminded her exactly of Dave, and it wasn't a pleasant realisation. She had thought that Charlie was Dave's opposite in pretty much every way, but perhaps she had been mistaken.

'But what if it is true?' she persisted. 'It's got to be worth a try.'

Charlie shrugged again. 'I already have everything I could ever wish for; I don't need anything else.'

'You're very sweet,' she said, reaching up a hand to stroke his cheek.

As he leaned down to kiss her, his warm body so solid against her own, Hope slid her other hand behind her and made a silent wish in her head.

15

Prague felt smaller today.

Perhaps it was because there was barely a corner of it that she and Robin had not explored, or maybe it was just that overwhelming sense of familiarity. Sophie felt the same way when she stood at her bedroom window back at the farm and looked out towards the distant hills. She knew exactly how many miles there were between herself and the horizon, how many acres of green and brown patchwork land lay stretched from the edge of the farmland to the bottom of those faraway clouds, but she still felt as though she could gather it all up into her arms.

Hope and Charlie had asked her if she wanted to head to the Charles Bridge with them, which was very sweet, but Sophie had politely declined. She'd already made up her mind that she wanted to come up here, to Letna Park, where she could enjoy a view of the whole city without having to jostle for space beside the tourists.

Letna Park was situated in the north of Prague, just above where the Vltava River curved its way around the city's Jewish Quarter, and it was largely uncluttered by foreign visitors – especially at this time of year, when last week's leftover snow still lay in thick drifts on the grass. Holidaymakers were also put off by the number of steps you were required to climb to reach the top, and even now

Sophie could feel the muscles in her legs tingling with fatigue.

She'd crossed the road at the base of the hill and taken the steps leading up to the right of the park, which would bring her out not far from the large red and black metronome sculpture where all the paths converged. Sophie didn't care much for the structure itself, thinking it too industrial in style, but she did have a special reason for coming up here. The last time she and Robin had visited Prague during the summer, over two years ago now, they'd headed up to Letna Park on a Sunday afternoon to take advantage of the large beer garden over on the eastern side. They had taken the same route as Sophie had today, and upon reaching the summit they'd come across a group of young Czechs tossing their trainers high up in the air, where they snagged and hung on a thin strip of rope that had been strung from the metronome to a nearby tree.

Robin had laughed his head off as they watched pair after pair being flung into the air, only to come crashing back down to the ground, narrowly missing the heads of their exuberant owners. Someone had brought a radio up with them and the atmosphere was one of such frivolity that it was impossible not to get caught up in it. In true Czech style, it wasn't long before one of the teenagers approached Sophie and Robin and beckoned them to join the party.

'I think we should add our shoes,' Robin said, grabbing her hands. 'Come on! It'll be fun.'

'You're mad,' Sophie told him, pointing down at her trainers. 'I only brought one pair with me. I can't really spend the next four days wandering around in my socks.'

'You can buy some more.'

'We're on a budget as it is, you wally. And anyway, these are brand-new Converse – there's no way I'm tossing them up on that rope for anyone. Not even for you,' she added, as she saw him start to make that ridiculous face that he always pulled when he wanted to get his own way.

'Spoilsport,' he laughed, leaning over to kiss her before leaping to his feet. 'You can be boring if you like, but I'm going for it.'

And he did, too. He undid his battered old trainers and tied the laces together, frowning with concentration as he made sure the knot was secure, and then positioned himself right underneath the rope.

'You reckon I can get them up there first time?' he asked.

Sophie nodded. 'I have no doubt in my mind.'

The Czech teenagers began to clap and whoop as Robin got into position, his legs stretched apart and his now-bare feet planted firmly on the stone floor.

'After three!' he yelled, and they all began to chant.

'Three . . . Two . . . One . . . TOSS!' screamed Sophie, totally caught up in the moment, her eyes never leaving her boyfriend's face as he frowned, squinted, bent his knees, raised his arms and threw the shoes high into the air. For a few seconds everyone held their breath, and then there was a thunder of rapturous applause. He had done it: Robin had thrown his only pair of shoes up on to a rope – and got them to snag and catch on his first try.

He flopped back down next to Sophie to accept his victory kiss, laughing into her mouth as one teenager after another ran over to pat him on the back.

'My boyfriend, the hero,' she said, one eyebrow firmly raised.

'Never let it be said that I'm not adept at tossing,' he quipped. 'If the tossers of the world were to adopt a king, I think I could fulfil that role with aplomb.'

'Idiot.' Sophie poked him in the ribs, but Robin hadn't finished.

'If I don't answer my phone, just assume that I'm off somewhere perfecting the art of tossing,' he told her. 'Some people are just natural-born tossers, and I am proud to call myself a tosser!'

'Shut up!' Sophie clambered on top of him and tried to stop him talking by putting her hand over his mouth, but Robin simply bit her.

'Ow!' She laughed. 'Just promise me you'll stop saying the word "tosser" and I'll get off.'

'But getting off is one of the aims of tossing.' He grinned at her mischievously.

'Robin Palmer, you are a very naughty boy!' she scolded, but didn't move from his lap. She liked having him here, clamped between her thighs, his lips at the perfect height for her to kiss them. Robin seemed to sense the slight change in mood and ran his hands around her waist, gripping the small of her back.

'All this talk of tossing is making me thirsty,' he murmured.

'Me too,' she agreed. 'I suppose we should go to the beer garden.'

'We should.' He looked down at his shorts and then

back up into her eyes. 'If I don't take you off my lap soon, I'm going to lose whatever I have left of my self-control, which isn't much – and there are children present.'

She giggled at this and shuffled backwards off his knees, averting her eyes while he rearranged his shorts and stood up.

They waved to the group of locals still attempting to throw their shoes up on to the rope and strolled off into the depths of the park. Sliding his arm around Sophie's shoulder, Robin leaned across and said, 'Do you think there's a shoe shop anywhere in this park?'

It had been such a fun day, and after they'd collected their beers they'd spent hours sitting side by side in the grass, chatting about everything and nothing, about their future plans and their past adventures. Sophie made a daisy chain and put it carefully on the top of Robin's blond head, and he in turn made her squeal by threatening to stick his muddy big toe in her mouth. It had just been the two of them, the park and the sunshine, but it had been perfect.

Letna Park looked very different today, the trees stripped of their leaves by the unstoppable cold fingers of winter and the grassy banks transformed by the snow. But Robin's shoes were still there, blackened by age and exposure but unmistakably his. After all, Sophie thought with a smile as she stood staring up at them, who else would wear floral trainers and get away with it?

She left the metronome and hanging shoes behind and took the path along to the pavilion. There was a café at the front with a terrace that overlooked the city, but there were no signs of life coming from inside as she approached.

Sophie didn't mind – in fact, she was grateful to have the view all to herself.

The weather wasn't the greatest today, with thick grey and white clouds blocking out the sun and a persistent drizzle making everything smell damp and musty. Very little could distract from the beauty of this view, however, and Sophie stood for a time just letting her eyes devour every little detail. There was the Charles Bridge, so distinct from the five others she could see, with its statues silhouetted like chess pieces against the grey sky. She could see the castle from here, as well as the Observation Tower on the top of Petrin Hill. To the east she could make out the futuristic outline of the Zizkov TV Tower, so unusual yet somehow so at home, and on the opposite side of the Vltava River, right in front of her, the various towers looming out of the Old Town Square. Again she had that feeling, that impression of the city shrinking in around her.

It didn't make sense to feel suffocated up here on the hill, with so much space around, but as she looked out at the familiar landmarks, Sophie felt a heaviness on her chest. It was as if someone had reached inside her and was gripping her heart, and she closed her eyes, gulping in mouthfuls of air until she heard her heart begin to slow down. Not caring about the wet ground, Sophie allowed her knees to buckle and sat on the concrete floor, her head resting against the metal bars of the terrace and black spots dancing in her eyes. Her brain was suddenly a lava lamp, her heart a shattered stone. It should have been frightening, but Sophie felt oddly calm. She concentrated on her breathing, counting to four with each breath and watching drips of melted snow fall from the branches of the trees on to the ground.

'Just a few more days,' she whispered. 'Not long now.'

She could feel the snow seeping through her jeans and forced herself to stand, her legs shaking as she walked slowly away from the view and back down the steps into the park.

16

'Remind me again why we didn't take the funicular?'

Megan sighed. 'Because, unlike the name suggests, they aren't very fun.'

Ollie rolled his eyes. 'How do you know? You've never been on one.'

'Well, I've been on the Docklands Light Railway, and that's no fun at all,' she told him. 'And anyway, I thought your hangover could use a walk.'

'And?' Ollie had stopped walking and she turned to face him.

'And what?'

'There's always another "and" with you, Ms Spencer. Out with it.'

'Okay, okay – and I want to take photos for my exhibition. Happy now?'

'Yes. But my feet are still cold. And I think one of my shoes must have a hole in it.'

Megan looked down at Ollie's waterlogged trainers and laughed. 'Why didn't you bring some proper boots, you idiot? I told you it had been snowing over here.'

'But there isn't any snow down in the city bit,' Ollie grumbled, looking around them at the snow-covered grass of Petrin Hill. 'I didn't know you were going to make me wade through it.'

Megan, who was feeling very smug with her feet cosily

laced up in a pair of fur-lined boots, jumped from the path on to the grass and kicked a big lump of snow in Ollie's direction.'

'Very mature,' he said drily, wiping the end of his nose on his glove and removing his glasses. 'You do know what you've done now, though, don't you?'

Megan laughed and skipped through the snow some more, bringing her leg back as if to kick another clump at him, but then stopping at the last minute, just as Ollie flinched and raised his hands up to shield his face.

'What's the matter?' she taunted. 'Afraid of a bit of snow, Mr Morris?'

Ollie didn't move for a second or two, just stood there giving her a look that she was pretty sure he usually reserved for the naughtiest children in his classroom, and then suddenly lurched forward and grabbed two huge handfuls of snow. Before she could really register what was happening, he'd pulled down the back of her coat and her scarf and rammed the whole lot down her back.

'AARGH!' she screamed, dancing around in circles. 'It's in my knickers!' She raised her fist but missed him completely. Ollie was resting both his hands on his knees and roaring with laughter, his cheeks pink with mirth.

'I'm going to kill you!' she raged, grabbing up her own snowball and tearing after him down the path. Unfortunately, she didn't see the big patch of black ice, and the next second she was lying on her back, the wind knocked out of her lungs and the snowball she'd been carrying to hurl at Ollie plastered all over her own face.

'Shit!' Ollie came running back and knelt down beside her. 'Are you okay, Megs?'

'No,' she snapped, but she couldn't help but laugh, which wasn't easy without any air left to laugh with.

'You went down like a sack of sh—'

'Don't say it,' she growled at him. 'Pick me up.'

He did as he was told and hauled her to her feet, letting go of her hand a fraction later than was strictly necessary.

'Here.' He scooped up a handful of snow. 'I'll let you get me back with this. Go on, right down the pants – I won't even fight you.'

'What's the fun in that?' she muttered, but took the snow anyway and dumped the lot on his head.

'And to think I was worried about one cold, wet foot,' Ollie said, blinking as part-melted snow dripped down his face and over his glasses.

'I think you're right,' Megan groaned, rubbing her back and sending up a silent prayer of thanks that Ollie had offered to carry her camera bag up the hill. If she'd come down on her back and destroyed that . . . It didn't bear thinking about. 'I think we should have taken the bloody funicular.'

Ollie pulled a face. 'Don't be like that,' he said, unzipping her bag. 'Here, take some photos – it always cheers you up.'

As usual, he was absolutely right, and he even leapt around in the snow making various stupid faces to make her laugh.

'These are all NFF, by the way,' he warned, poking his head out from behind a tree and grimacing at her like a gargoyle.

'NF what?' Megan asked, zooming right in for an extreme close-up.

'NFF: Not for Facebook. It's what all the cool kids are saying.'

'I'm pretty sure cool kids don't use Facebook,' she informed him. She knew this to be true because she used it all the time, and she was probably the least trendy person on the planet.

'That Eiffel Tower place still looks miles away,' Ollie said, changing the subject and peering up through the twisted mesh of branches to where the Observation Tower loomed over the crest of the hill.

'It is pretty steep,' Megan agreed. Her legs were on fire and her back still ached from where she'd taken a tumble, but she wasn't about to admit that to Ollie, who had barely broken a sweat since they set out that morning.

They carried on along a gently sloping path for a while, and occasionally Megan would hang back to take photos. It was such a treat to be in real snow. It hadn't snowed in London for what felt like years, and she loved the way it gave everything such a fresh canvas. Bland, brown forests were instantly transformed into magical fairylands, leaking roof gutters dripped into sparkling icicles and the sky was washed white and clean, as if someone had thrown a dust sheet over the sun.

Not all the photos she took were of her surroundings, though – she was also taking lots of photos of Ollie that he wasn't posing for. He looked far better when he was bent over examining an abandoned water fountain, or a submerged patch of flowers, than he did when he was doing his best Golem impression. In some of her photos, he looked really handsome, not that she would ever tell him that.

After a time, they reached a very long and very steep set of stone steps, all covered in a frozen layer of snow that looked dangerously slippery. Megan and Ollie exchanged a look.

'Do you think this is the only way up?' he asked, peering at the little brown sign which clearly indicated that the Observation Tower was indeed at the top of this death trap.

'Well . . .' Megan considered the question. 'We could go back down and pick up the funicular after all, but it might take ages.'

'Nah.' Ollie shook his head. 'This will be fine. There's a handrail. You go up first, then if you fall again I can catch you.'

'My hero,' she drawled, blowing a kiss at him.

They set off determinedly up the hill, their concentration disintegrating quickly into shared giggles as they skated around on the ice like a couple of drunks. Halfway up, the steps gave way and became a smooth, steep slope, and Ollie and Megan had to stop just to laugh as a young Italian couple slid past them on their bottoms, both hysterically cackling as they held hands and tried to stop each other from careering right off the path.

'It's even harder to balance when you're laughing,' Ollie called, turning to see Megan flail helplessly into a tree. 'I see now why this is more fun than the funicular.'

'Don't make me laugh!' she yelled back, creasing up as Ollie's right leg zoomed out from under him so he was forced to do a mini-jig on the ice to stay upright. Megan's legs and arms had turned wobbly from laughing and she was on the verge of going down on to her hands and knees and crawling up the hill that way when they reached another set of steps.

'Not more bloody steps,' Ollie groaned humorously, patting her on the back as she finally caught up with him. She was panting with the effort, but she felt good. She loved being outside, sucking clean air into her lungs and taking in all the natural beauty around them.

'Look at this.' Ollie was beckoning to her, and as she reached him he pointed to the bottom of the thin metal handrail that was attached to the stairway wall.

The red padlock was so small that they could easily have missed it, and Megan bent down for a closer look.

'It's got something written on it,' she said. 'Hang on.'

'Do you think it's like the ones on that bridge in Paris?' Ollie asked. 'People in love write their names on them and attach them there for luck.'

'It says R & S,' she told him. 'And there's a heart drawn around the letters.'

'R & S?' Ollie thought for a moment. 'Hang on – didn't that Sophie girl say that her boyfriend's name was Robin?'

'I think she did.' Megan stood up again. 'Do you think it could be theirs? I'm sure she said that they'd been coming here for years.'

'Doubt it.' Ollie bent over to take a look for himself. 'There must be loads of couples in the world whose names start with R and S.'

'It would be nice if it was them, though, wouldn't it?' she said, crouching down once again so she could snap a few frames.

'It would,' he allowed, and Megan thought for a moment that he sounded almost wistful. Was he just pretending not to be the big soppy romantic that she suspected he was? He never made any complaints when she insisted they watch *PS I Love You* for the third hungover Sunday in a row. Hell, she'd even caught him having a little cry over it the first time, even though he'd claimed there was something in his eye. No, she was pretty convinced that Ollie was exactly the type of person to leave a love padlock in a remote location and believe that it meant something. Had her initial rejection all those months ago made him feel like he couldn't be his true self? Megan really hoped it hadn't.

'Come on,' Ollie said as she stood up. 'At this rate all the snow will have melted by the time we reach the tower.'

He turned and put one wet trainer on the first step, only to have it promptly slide right back off again.

'Here's hoping,' she quipped, following him unsteadily upwards.

From a distance, the Observation Tower looked much larger than it actually was when you were standing right underneath it, although, as Megan pointed out to Ollie, that was probably just because it looked exactly like the top part of the Eiffel Tower, and that thing was absolutely monstrous in comparison to this.

They paid their ninety Czech korunas each, which was about three British pounds, and made their slow – and in Megan's case, weary – way up the endless winding metal stairs to the top. Ollie must have thought the view had left her lost for words, but in reality she couldn't speak at first because she was so knackered.

'See! Totally worth all those stairs,' Ollie said triumphantly, pointing excitedly to all the landmarks he recognised in the city below them. 'That's the Charles Bridge, look. You can just make out all the statues. And there's that weird TV tower again, the one with all the babies, and look at that church.'

'Jesus, boy – I thought the climb up here was exhausting, but it's got nothing on you.'

Ollie pouted. 'I'm just excited.'

Megan took her camera out of its bag and started fiddling, selecting the right lens from the three in her pouch. While Ollie was nattering away to an old couple that had just emerged from the stairwell looking far less exhausted than Megan had been a few minutes ago, she slyly took a few more photos of his profile. With this lens in, she could see the pores of his skin and the pink indent that his glasses left on his nose. He was smiling at something the old man had just said, and she watched through the viewfinder as laughter lines popped up around his eyes and in the creases of his mouth. She didn't even realise that she was still taking photos until her lens abruptly stuck mid-rotation, causing her to swear under her breath.

'Now, now.' Ollie had popped up behind her. 'The air up here is blue enough from the cold without you adding to it.'

'Got it,' she said, breathing a sigh of relief as her camera sprang obediently back to life.

'So, after this, how do you fancy going to a hall of mirrors?'

Megan hated mirrors possibly more than she hated selfie sticks, which was a lot.

'I don't fancy that at all.'

'Oh, come on, Little Miss Misery. The old couple over

there have just been and they told me it was a hoot. They actually used the word "hoot", too, so it must be pretty special.'

He looked like a child on Christmas morning.

'It's going to cost you.'

'What? Anything!'

'Dinner tonight,' she told him, giving in to a wry grin as he started nodding wildly like a mad pigeon. 'And I mean a proper dinner, not a couple of those sausages from the market.'

He saluted. 'Whatever you want – although those sausages are really good. You'll be missing out.'

'I'll have to take your word for it,' she said, lifting her camera up to her face and turning her back on him.

Time spent in Ollie's company was so easy, she reflected, watching with fondness as he went back to join the elderly couple again, leaning down so he could point something out to them in their guidebook. The woman had taken off her gloves in order to flick through the pages, and the skin on her hands was translucent against her knuckles. Through the lens of her camera, Megan could make out the spidery purple lines of veins as they chased around liver spots and knotted ligaments worn with age. Megan knew that a lot of her friends were paranoid about getting old. Hell, some of them had even started having Botox, although none would admit it, which was ridiculous. Ageing was just a part of life, Megan would tell them, and to her eye, there was just as much beauty in decay as there was in youth.

She thought about this as she continued to press the shutter and capture a visual narrative of her train of thought. Prague was the perfect example of something that was definitely old, but all the more beautiful for it. If only humans were able to embrace the fascinating tale behind the lines on someone's face as much as they could stare up in awe at a centuries-old monument. The world would be so much happier if they could all just stop and think a bit more, and a bit harder – appreciate the visage and think about the life that had gone before, rather than the road ahead.

She had talked about this idea with her ex, once. Andre had sniffed in that infuriating way that he always did, dismissing her observations as if she was a stray cat begging for a morsel. He was a photographer, too, but he didn't see beauty in the same way as Megan always had. To Andre, true beauty could only be achieved through perfection, and his work was a continuing example of this. He wasn't interested in the story behind each face at all, just the way it looked on his canvas.

Megan gave an audible sigh and let her camera rest against her chest. The wind was playing a game of chase around the top of the tower, nipping its icy fingers through the open gaps every now and then to pinch her exposed cheeks. She could hear it if she concentrated, a low whistle that carried with it a multitude of other sounds – the clattering of a tram against its tracks, the cry of a lone bird, a distant strain of music and, of course, Ollie's voice. The wind was carrying that back around the tower to her, too, and she felt her insides warm in response.

His friendship had become so important to her, but more than that, she craved his company. She'd grown accustomed to the smell, sight and sound of him, and the way she felt about herself when he was around, so different to the way she'd felt with Andre. With her ex, she had always been wary of saying the wrong thing, of upsetting the fragile shelf upon which their strange little relationship was precariously balanced. But with Ollie she could say anything, be completely herself, and he would like her all the same. And he did care about her, didn't he? He'd said as much.

Even now the thought of those silly drunken words made Megan itch with unease. It was totally okay for him to love her as a friend, she knew that, but for some reason the weight of those words felt to Megan like a metaphorical rucksack packed with stones. Friendship carried less expectation than love, it was more flexible, and it wouldn't betray you as love had so cruelly betrayed her once before. Despite all this, though, Megan found her legs moving her around the top of the tower until she was standing beside Ollie. He was apparently lost in thought, his eyes on the horizon and a contented smile just lifting one corner of his mouth. Very slowly, Megan took a small step forward and rested her head gently against his shoulder.

17

Of all the toilets in Prague, of course she had chosen the one with no loo roll. Hope supposed she ought to be thankful that she'd only come in here for a cry, but that didn't really help her runny nose situation.

Annette had replied to her text at last. Hope glanced down at the phone in her hand, even though she knew it would only unleash another torrent.

> I don't want to speak to you
> ever again. Leave me alone.

It was so cold, so unlike anything that her bubbly, loving daughter would ever say, and every time she read it, Hope felt another part of her heart break off and turn to mush inside her chest. She knew she should reply, but for the first time since giving birth to her daughter over twenty-five years ago, she had no idea what to say. The misery was clogging her up, making it hard to think straight. She'd never known a pain like this, not ever.

And then there was Charlie, who was being so sweet to her, and who had brought her out here to this magical place. She felt wretched at the idea of ruining their trip with her tears, but what ate away at her even more was not being honest with him. She should be able to let him comfort her, but for some reason, she couldn't.

When she finally emerged, Charlie was just as

attentive as she had come to expect over the past few weeks.

'You've been in there for ages. I was getting worried.'

'Oh, you know.' She waved a vague arm around. 'There was a queue, and then I had to do my make-up.'

'We're the only people in here,' he pointed out gently. It was true. Aside from one girl behind the bar who seemed to be the hostess, waitress, barmaid and chef, they really were the only people.

'Is it Annette?' he guessed, pulling her towards him as her face crumpled.

'I'm sorry,' she said through her tears. 'I just got a message from her and it—'

'There, there.' Charlie patted her head until she could speak again.

'It said that she doesn't ever want to see me again. She told me to leave her alone – but how can I? I'm her mum.'

'Of course you are,' he soothed, nodding reassuringly at the waitress as she hovered uncertainly by their table. They'd stumbled across this place quite by accident as they explored the narrow street that wrapped around the church in the Old Town Square. Drawn to the doorway by the faint sounds of jazz music and the aroma of hot wine, they'd discovered a quaint little café full of mismatched cushions, neat little tables made from old wooden doors, and an array of different-sized mirrors fixed to the walls and parts of the ceiling. When Hope had found that she could order a cup of English breakfast tea in a proper teacup and have it arrive with a matching saucer, she'd been enchanted.

'What am I going to do?' she mumbled, catching sight

of her blotchy face in one of the mirrors and recoiling in horror.

'She'll come around eventually,' Charlie said, sounding less confident than his words suggested. 'You two are so close.'

'That's why this hurts so much,' she wailed.

The waitress stepped forward and slid a plate across the table towards them.

'This is honey cake,' she told Hope. 'You will feel better, I think.'

This act of kindness only set Hope off again, but Charlie was full of thanks.

'The people here are so nice,' he marvelled, breaking off a corner of the cake and holding it up to her mouth. 'Try it. It might make you feel better.'

Hope did as she was told, smiling as the warm, sticky cake sent her taste buds into a frenzy.

'It's really nice,' she said when she'd swallowed. 'Have some.'

'Mmmm.' Charlie gave the waitress a thumbs up.

'I'm sorry to be so wet,' Hope said, sitting up properly and breaking off another piece of the cake. 'I don't know what's wrong with me.'

'It's fine,' Charlie soothed. 'You never have to be sorry for being sad, but please tell me if you're upset. Don't go into the toilet to cry all by yourself. You don't need to face these things on your own any more; you have me now and I want to look after you.'

'I didn't want to ruin the trip,' she mumbled.

'You could never ruin anything,' he told her, breaking off another sticky morsel. 'Honestly. Hope, look at me.'

She looked at him.

'I could be in the worst place in the world, with no money, no shirt on my back and no way of escape, but as long as I had you by my side, then I'd be able to face it. I would have hope.'

'Do you mean me, Hope, or just hope?' she asked, reaching for his hand.

'One equals the other,' he told her. 'The only thing that scares me is being hopeless – in both senses. I don't ever want to lose you.'

In answer, Hope wrapped her arms around him and gripped tight.

As Hope had chosen the Charles Bridge for their morning excursion, it was Charlie's turn to pick a destination for the afternoon. Rather unimaginatively, Hope privately thought, he decided they should head to the shops in Wenceslas Square, where he wanted to treat her to a new outfit.

'It will cheer you up,' he said when she shook her head. And usually he'd be right, but Hope was starting to feel uncomfortable about the amount he was splurging on her. Still, she had promised herself that she'd make an effort, so she let herself be led away from the café and underneath the arch of the vast Powder Gate.

She wasn't sure what she was expecting to find, but she was surprised to discover that Wenceslas Square was not actually a square at all. It was, in fact, a wide boulevard dotted with shops, bars, casinos and restaurants. Of all the places they'd visited in the city so far, this seemed the most modern, but Hope still found herself entranced by some of the architecture.

‘Look at that place,’ she said to Charlie, pointing to a tall yellow building that was coming up on their left.

Charlie squinted at the sign. ‘Grand Hotel Europa,’ he told her.

‘It’s stunning,’ she exclaimed as they drew closer.

‘What’s that style of design?’ he asked, peering up at the curved stone arches.

Hope didn’t answer him for a few minutes because she was flicking through the guidebook.

‘Art Nouveau,’ she said. ‘First opened in 1889, but now closed. Oh, that’s a shame.’

They were right in front of the striking building now, both craning their necks back to get a good look, and they could see that the entrance and lower windows had been boarded up.

‘If I ever won the lottery, I’d buy this place and restore it to its former glory,’ Hope said, picturing herself standing up on the threshold, welcoming guests with a tray full of complimentary hot grog. She had tried for years to persuade Dave to buy and open a B&B. She would do all the cleaning and cooking, she told him. All he’d have to take care of was the paperwork. It was a job that Hope knew she’d love and that she’d be great at, but Dave had refused to consider it.

‘I don’t want some stranger sitting with their feet up in my living room,’ he’d grumbled.

‘But we’d have our own part of the house,’ she’d pleaded. ‘We could even move out of the city a bit, go to Wales or the Lake District. It would be so nice for Annette to be out in the open more.’

He’d glared at her then for trying to use Annette as a

bargaining tool, and argued that his daughter would be bored in the countryside and so would he. 'Why would you want to upset your own daughter by taking her away from her school and her friends?' he'd asked, deliberately picking the one subject he knew she'd cave in on.

So that had been the end of it.

Hope had never told Charlie about her secret ambition, but she suspected that he'd love the idea. Like Hope, he was sociable and outgoing, and a driving instructor could really base themselves anywhere in the country. But something had always held her back so far. Was it the fear that he wouldn't like the idea, or the fear that he would?

They carried on along the wide pavement, stopping every now and then to venture into clothes shops but coming away empty-handed each time. Hope seemed to have lost her shopping mojo – no amount of dresses and shoes could heal her today. Charlie pretended to be fine about it, but Hope could tell he was worried, and after they'd been into five shops with no joy, he stopped pointing them out as they passed.

'Oh, look at that,' she murmured.

A small crowd had gathered around a wooden bench outside an Italian restaurant, as people took it in turns to have their photo taken next to the model of a man that was sitting on it. He was a dirty gold colour, with one leg crossed at a jaunty angle and an arm stretched invitingly along the back of the seat.

'Go on – sit down and I'll take a photo,' Charlie urged, but Hope shook her head.

'Not in front of all these people.'

'Oh, go on.' Charlie gave her a little nudge. 'You danced

across the square yesterday, and there were far more people watching then.'

He made a good point.

She stepped forward and sat down, shuffling her bottom along until she was sitting almost on the lap of the golden man. Up close his eyes were cold and staring, as if he'd been frozen solid at just the split second he'd realised something was going to happen. It reminded her of the creatures that the White Witch had turned to stone in *The Lion, the Witch and the Wardrobe*. She had read the whole collection of C. S. Lewis books to Annette when her daughter was growing up, and that scene had frightened her. Hope had always had to reassure Annette that the animals didn't stay trapped in stone forever, and that Aslan the lion would be along soon to save them.

Now it was almost as if Annette had turned to stone, trapped under the weight of her anger, and there was nothing Hope could do to save her.

'Smile!' Charlie called out, snapping Hope out of Narnia and back into the present.

She was holding up the queue, she realised, pulling herself together and making a silly face for the camera.

'Enough!' she said, getting to her feet and letting an older Swedish woman take her place.

Charlie showed her the photos and she groaned. They were absolutely frightful.

'Delete those right away, you naughty man,' she said, trying and failing to snatch his phone out of his hands. As she did so, it started ringing loudly and he pulled it away out of reach.

'Ow.' She rubbed her fingers.

'Sorry, love.' He reached for her absently, still holding his phone at arm's-length. 'I have to take this.'

She watched as he darted off and vanished into the crowd. Being secretive wasn't like Charlie at all, and Hope felt herself shrinking inwards on the spot. Who could be calling to make him scarper off like this? He wouldn't have answered if it was just a customer – she'd watched him ignore a few work-related calls since they'd arrived. The idea of it being another woman was so absurd that Hope almost laughed, but then she remembered the circumstances that had led to them being here together in the first place. Although she'd been cheating on Dave, neither she nor Charlie had ever brought up what would happen if they got caught, or if she would leave her husband. It had happened out of the blue, and now Charlie was stuck with her – he was doing the honourable thing because she'd been kicked out. There was so much that she still didn't know about him.

As she stood mulling this over and gazing up at one of the city's many clocks, Charlie reappeared, a wide smile on his face and two takeaway cups in his hands.

'I'm so sorry.' He balanced the cups on top of a blue postbox and scooped her into his arms.

'You're shivering,' he said, hugging her tighter.

'Who was that on the phone?' she said against his chest, feeling him tense up a fraction.

'Oh, that? It was just some business to do with the flat, nothing you need to worry about.'

'The flat?' She wanted to believe him, he'd given her no real reason not to.

'I wanted to get it valued,' he told her. 'I figured we'd be needing a bit more room, and—'

He didn't get to say anything else, because Hope had grabbed his face and was kissing him harder and with more passion than she ever had before, and when she eventually let him go he looked bewildered.

'Sorry,' she murmured. 'I just . . .'

'Don't apologise.' Charlie picked up the cups and handed one to her before taking her spare hand. 'I thought we could drink these hot chocolates while we walked, but now I'm thinking they'd taste much better back at the hotel.'

Hope nodded, feeling a tug of longing. She needed to connect with him again and chase these dark thoughts from her mind.

'Let's go and find out.'

18

The gargoyle glared down from its perch on the cathedral roof, its body and face contorted with discomfort. The water that usually poured down from the spires and out through its open mouth had frozen, adorning the gaping monster with a jagged flat tongue of ice which sparkled pleasantly in the faint afternoon sunshine.

Sophie knew that the gargoyles were designed to protect the cathedral from evil spirits, which was why they had to look so terrifying, but she found the various creatures more amusing than alarming. In fact, over the years she'd grown quite fond of them.

'Just like looking in a mirror, Bug,' Robin would have quipped if he were here. His absence was starting to feel like an ache, and Sophie glanced up to the cathedral clock, willing the hands to move around faster. Why was it that when you wanted time to pass by in a blur, it always seemed to slow to a crawl? And the reverse was also true – standing here now looking up into the vacant eyes of the scowling stone creatures above her, Sophie felt as if every other moment before had rushed away from her. She wished that she could reach back into the past and grab her memories with both hands, lay them out flat and safe somewhere, like dried flowers in a press, so she could return to them whenever she chose.

As if on cue, the city clocks started to strike, almost as

if they were mocking her silly fantasy. There was no escaping the fact that time was beating on, they seemed to chime. It was one thing you could never get away from in this city – the sense of time passing. From pretty much every part of Prague, you could see a clock. They were everywhere – not just on the churches, monasteries and more official buildings, but also on the front of shops, at the top of poles and on the walls of every household that had its curtains pulled aside. Sophie was sure that if she closed her eyes and concentrated hard enough, she would be able to hear the ticking.

There was a large crowd of tourists waiting to enter the cathedral, so Sophie stood back and waited while they filed in one behind the other. A small boy in a bright-green hat was dragging his feet, imploring his mother in a language that Sophie couldn't understand. If she'd had to hazard a guess, though, it would be that he was bored, that he'd seen the inside of enough churches and cathedrals to last his whole life and could they go somewhere a bit more fun, please? She watched the mother bend down and whisper something in her son's ear, only for him to gaze up at the roof in awe. The gargoyles had won a new fan.

Sophie's parents had often told her that she was a horror as a child. Not so much badly behaved as inquisitive and fiercely independent, which meant she thought nothing of running off to take a closer look at something or begin a game, without telling her mum and dad where she was going. She used to find their exasperation bewildering, until she met Robin. Now she understood completely how frustrating it could be when the person you cared about more than any other thought nothing of vanishing for hours at a time. But just as her parents had discovered time and again, trying to tell someone off for simply doing what they want is never an easy task.

'I'm going to kill him!' Sophie had raged to her mum the last time Robin had disappeared off on one of his 'walk-abouts', as he liked to call them. What was endearing in a film about an Australian man who wrestles crocodiles did not translate into real life, when your boyfriend hadn't been seen or heard from for eight hours and had switched off his phone.

'He'll turn up soon,' Sophie's mum soothed. 'He always does.'

'I just don't understand why he does this,' she moaned, accepting the mug of tea her dad had just made for her and kicking the leg of the kitchen table in irritation.

'It's not the table's fault,' her mum pointed out, which wasn't helpful.

'He makes me feel like a nag, and I'm not!' Sophie went on. 'I don't care if he wants to go off and do his own thing – I just like to know that he's okay.'

'I understand, darling,' her mum said, pulling her best sympathetic face as she knelt down on the floor to empty the washing machine. 'But unfortunately you can't change people. If you try to, you'll only end up pushing them away.'

'I don't want him to change, I just want him to send me a bloody text.' Sophie was aware that she was repeating herself. It wasn't the first time that Robin had done this, and every time it happened they ended up having the same silly debate, and her poor parents ended up hearing the same complaints from her. She didn't know why she let it wind her up so much, because she also knew that as soon as he came back, his camera loaded with photos that he'd taken on his solitary adventure and a look of exhilarated contentment on his face, she would forgive him instantly.

'Why don't you go out on your own walkabout?' her dad suggested. 'You used to do it all the time when you were little. It drove me and your mother half-mad.'

'I've grown up,' she pointed out sulkily. 'And I wish Robin would, too.'

The truth was, Sophie had never been able to bear being away from Robin for long – not since that very first day on the snowy bridge. It wasn't that she hated his independent streak, more that she cherished every second that she spent with him.

'Are you in the queue?'

Sophie was distracted from her thoughts by the question, turning to find an elderly couple peering at her, their gnarled hands clasped together and a dash of colour in their cheeks. She hadn't realised that she'd come to an abrupt standstill outside the cathedral entrance, and shook her head to clear it.

'You go ahead,' she told them, smiling as she stepped to one side. She loved seeing old couples together, so in tune with one another that they were almost more like a single person than two separate entities. Growing old together was an expression she'd never really appreciated when she was younger, but now she understood it completely. She wanted to be by Robin's side when the first grey hairs stole through on his temples, and when the skin on his eyelids sagged with the weight of time passing. She wanted to run her fingers across the lines that appeared on his face, watch his skin begin to droop under his chin and his veins stand up to attention on the back of his hands. She wanted to be the one who could look into his eyes even when they were misted with age, and still see the sparkle beneath the milky surface. It was all she wanted, just to always be with him.

When she finally shuffled forward through the slush and made her way into the cavernous cathedral, the large crowd of tourists had long since vanished, and she stood for a time in the entrance chamber, waiting for her eyes to adjust to the muted darkness. On either side, stained-glass windows stretched high above her towards the Gothic vaulted ceiling, each one a riot of colour, resplendent against the surrounding stone walls.

Sophie had a sudden recollection of when she'd made her own stained-glass window from coloured strips of plastic at primary school. She tried to walk right back into the memory now and feel the scissors in her hands, smell the glue and remember how the slippery plastic had felt between her fingers, but of course she couldn't. The passing of time had placed layer after layer of new memories on top of that one, and it was now nothing more than a smudge of colour in her mind. Sophie wondered why it was that the mind dug these snippets out from time to time only to snatch them away again. She'd talked about it to Robin often, but he'd just patted her head and told her she was crazy.

'I think there's only so much room in there,' he said,

tapping the side of his head. 'I think you need to accept that some memories aren't really worth saving.'

'But what if you forget the ones you want to save?' she pressed.

'Silly Bug.' He kissed the end of her nose. 'I don't think it works like that. The ones you like the most – the really good memories, like your wedding day, or, say, the day you first saw me.' He gave her a cheeky look. 'Those are the ones you can always call up. But what you had for dinner on a random Thursday night in October ten years ago isn't all that important, so you don't need to remember it anyway.'

Sophie stared at the stained-glass windows in the cathedral until her eyes started to sting, wondering if by standing here now she was pushing out an old, treasured memory to make room for this new one. It scared her to think that one day in the future, she might not be able to remember every little detail of the things that had mattered the most to her. She wished there was a way to store them, emotions and all, in a jar, and then she could screw the lid on tight and peer at them through the glass.

She watched as the little old couple she'd spoken to outside made their slow way up towards the centre of the cathedral. She had been in here many times now, but today she had a goal in mind. There was something in here that she wanted to see. More than that, she needed to see it.

Sophie padded quietly past the pulpit and carried on around the corner until she could see what she was looking for – her whole reason for making the journey up here. The silver looked almost golden in this light, gleaming with unapologetic pride in its dingy setting. There was a rope around the base – a gentle reminder to visitors that this was not something they were permitted to touch – but Sophie almost gave in to the urge she had to cross that threshold. She settled instead for kneeling on the cold, hard floor in front of it, so close to the thick velvet rope that she could smell the mustiness of age clinging to its fibres. She closed her eyes and concentrated on what she was feeling, for once content to sweep away a space in her mind to make way for this new moment.

It was cold in the cathedral, but as she knelt there, her gloved hands resting in her lap and Robin's tatty old hat pulled down so far that it almost covered her still-closed eyes, Sophie felt a brilliant warmth steal its way through her.

19

'Ah, to have legs this long and thin.'

Megan turned to Ollie and they both looked back at her reflection in the warped glass, pausing to pull faces at one another before collapsing into laughter. Ollie took a step to the left, and immediately one half of his face grew huge and stretched in the mirrored wall, his mouth an enormous, bloated strawberry and his nose a giant aubergine. Megan giggled and fell into him, only for her reflected chin to be sucked suddenly downwards until it reached her toes.

'This was a great idea of yours,' she told him when she had regained the power of speech. She much preferred this final room of the Mirror Maze, with its funny, distorting glass, to the labyrinth of regular mirrored passageways that they'd had to navigate to get here. It was just wrong that a girl should be able to see her face and her bottom at the same time – and from at least five different angles at once. Especially when it was a bottom as unwieldy as hers.

'Don't thank me – this was all that old couple's idea,' Ollie told her, stepping backward and forward so he could watch his face bend and twist.

'Still,' she grinned at him with hugely enlarged teeth, 'I'm glad you nagged me into it. Now I get to laugh at you in here *and* have you buy me dinner later – sweet deal.'

'I would have bought you dinner anyway,' he said, nudging her forward until her legs vanished completely in the glass and her shrunken little body floated just above her boots.

There was a group of young children in the long, rectangular-shaped room with them, all squealing with delight at their reflections. Megan watched Ollie as he turned to look at them, affection and amusement written on his face as he listened to their happy shouts. Her camera was resting on her chest, the wide canvas strap around her neck, and she surreptitiously removed the lens cap.

'Do you think you'll ever have any kids?' Ollie asked, not looking at her but at the giggling children. They were now doing some sort of strange dance in front of one of the mirrors, and a few of the younger ones were literally doubled over laughing at their classmates.

Megan took her finger off the shutter release button and sighed. It wasn't the first time Ollie had asked her this question, and he already knew the answer.

'I don't know,' she told him truthfully, just as she had the other times he'd asked. It wasn't that she didn't want to have any children, it was just that she hadn't ever really given the idea that much consideration. The thing she had always wanted was to take photos, that was all she had really cared about for as long as she could remember. And anyway, she had plenty of time yet before she had to worry about kids.

'I know you want them,' she added, leaning against a pillar as the group of children were called away by their teacher and began filing out of the room in neat pairs. 'I bet you want a whole football team.'

'Nah.' Ollie shook his head slowly as he turned back to face her. 'I reckon two would be enough – a girl and a boy, ideally.'

'You'd have to name the girl Megan, obviously,' she told him. Ollie didn't respond, but Megan was sure she heard him mutter something under his breath.

'What was that?' she asked, twisting around so she could talk to him in the mirror. The one they were both facing made their middles stretch outwards, as if someone had trodden downwards on their heads and squashed them.

Ollie waited until their eyes met before he replied, taking a deep breath and rubbing his hair away from his face.

'What would you say if I told you I'd met someone?'

Megan's stomach lurched lower than it had in the warped glass.

'Have you?'

Ollie screwed up his face a fraction. 'No, but that's not the point.'

'What is the point, then?' she asked, genuinely mystified.

'I just mean, would you mind? We spend a lot of time together, and if I had a girlfriend then I imagine that would have to change.'

Megan considered this for a moment. The idea of Ollie with a girlfriend was unsettling, and she didn't want to dwell on the reasons why.

'I'd be fine with it,' she told him, stepping forward until she was only a few inches from the glass wall and could no longer see his expression. 'You're my friend, Ollie – I want you to be happy.'

'Did you ever . . . ?' he began, and she turned again to look at him.

'Ever what?'

'Ever think about what would have happened if we had, you know?'

She did know. She'd allowed herself to imagine it many times over the past six months, but she also knew why it couldn't happen. Why they couldn't happen.

She hadn't meant to sigh, and flinched when she saw the immediate hurt reflected in Ollie's eyes. As he went to turn away from her, she reached across and caught his arm.

'I haven't ever told you about my ex, have I?' she said. They were alone in the mirrored chamber now, and Megan led Ollie into the centre of the room where their reflections wouldn't be distorted. She couldn't really have a serious conversation with him when his feet were the size of boats and his head looked like a huge lump of tofu.

'I hate him already,' Ollie joked, but his brow was furrowed with interest.

'His name is Andre, and he's quite a famous photographer. I applied for an internship at his London studio about five years ago and he invited me in for a chat.'

She stopped, suddenly aware of how sleazy the next part of her story was going to sound. Ollie already had his nose curled up in distaste.

'You can probably guess what happened next,' she said. 'But it wasn't as bad as you're imagining it to be. I was a grown woman, not a teenager, and he's only six years older than me. It's not as if he was some perverted old man leering over a young, impressionable girl. Although,' she added, giving a small shrug, 'I was impressed by him. In the beginning, at least.'

'What happened?' Ollie prompted. He'd folded his arms as she started talking and looked almost defensive. She hoped it was because he was feeling protective on her behalf rather than wary of her words.

'I wanted to enter this competition. You won't have heard of it, probably, but it's only open to upcoming talent – people like me, who have never won an award for their photography.'

He nodded.

'I'd been working on the project for months, and at first Andre was encouraging. He was always critical of my work, but that was part of his job as a mentor . . .'

'And an arsehole,' Ollie put in.

'Yes, that too – but you have to understand that I was in awe of him at this point. I thought that everything he said was gospel. It was only when I started to question his ideas that things turned sour.'

'So, he's an egomaniac?' Ollie guessed.

'Oh, very much so.' Megan gritted her teeth as she pictured her ex-boyfriend: his velvet jackets and his wavy, unkempt hair, that permanent smug snarl plastered across his narrow face. Thinking about him now made her flesh creep off into a corner to hide, and she shuddered involuntarily before continuing.

'On the day I had to submit my work for the competition, I couldn't find it.'

'What do you mean?' Ollie looked puzzled. 'I thought everything was digital these days?'

'It is.' Megan shook her head now as the memory of

her past anguish assaulted her once again. 'I had the files saved on my laptop and on a memory stick, as well as on Andre's private computer. He wiped the lot.'

'What a bastard!'

'He was.' She nodded. 'He is.'

'But why?' Ollie's expression was so wounded that Megan felt an overwhelming urge to kiss him. She had known he'd be angry at such an injustice, and it was immediately and undeniably attractive. But no – she mustn't let herself get carried away. Look what had happened the last time she kissed Ollie. Closing her eyes for a split second, Megan shoved the feelings to one side and went back to her story.

'He told me that he did it to protect me – can you believe that?' Megan grimaced as she conjured up the conversation in her head. 'He said I'd have embarrassed myself and him if I'd entered, but in reality he was just jealous. He was threatened by me – and I know that sounds really arrogant, but it's absolutely the truth.'

'It doesn't.' Ollie held up a hand. 'You're incredibly talented, Megs – even I can see that, and I don't have a single artistic bone in my body.'

Megan smiled at this before continuing. 'When I realised what he'd done, it was as if the drapes fell from my eyes,' she recalled. 'I could suddenly see him for what he really is – a nasty little man with a spiteful nature, minimal talent and the personality of a paving slab.'

'Wow!' Ollie's eyes widened. 'Remind me never to get on the wrong side of you.'

'I told him he could stick his internship and the relationship,' she went on, smiling grimly as she remembered the look on Andre's face when she'd yelled at him. 'He didn't like that very much.'

'Well done you.' Ollie put his hand up for a high-five, but she didn't move. 'There's a "but", isn't there?'

'Andre didn't appreciate being put in his place,' Megan told him. 'The photography world is very small, and he's bad-mouthed me to just about everyone in London.'

'Prick.' Ollie was looking mutinous.

'This exhibition, the one I have booked in for May . . .' Megan said, and Ollie nodded. 'It's the first time I'll have shown my work since the whole Andre thing ended. It's been three years since we broke up, but it's taken me until now to feel ready to face that world again, and those people who were so ready to write me off.'

'Oh Megs . . .' Ollie unfolded his arms and pulled her into a hug. 'I had no idea.'

'I just want a chance to prove to everyone that he was wrong,' she said into his coat. 'I want to get some recognition on my own terms, without needing Andre . . .' She hesitated. 'Or anyone else.'

She felt his body stiffen at her words and knew he must finally understand why she was so reluctant to have another relationship. The last man she had trusted had betrayed her in the worst possible way, and she needed to know that she could make it on her own. She didn't want to need someone or feel vulnerable – what she wanted was to concentrate on achieving her dream.

For a time, they just stood in companionable silence, and Megan gradually relaxed her weight against Ollie's chest, listening to the methodical rhythm of his heart and enjoying the sensation of closeness that for so long had been missing from her life. There was so much else she wished she could put into words for him, but she couldn't articulate what she was feeling even to herself, let alone share it. For now, it was enough to simply feel understood.

'I think we should get going,' she said eventually, lifting her head and smiling at him. 'That monastery further along the hill is supposed to be amazing.'

'Right.' Ollie blinked as he gathered up his backpack from the floor. 'Whatever you say.'

They had to make their way back down the slippery, snow-covered slopes and steps to reach the path, but there was far less merriment between them now than there had been on the journey up. Ollie seemed to be lost in thought, and had been unusually quiet ever since she finished telling him about Andre. Megan hoped he understood why she'd kept it a secret until now. It wasn't something she really liked talking about, and only her family and very closest friends were aware of exactly how much the whole experience had affected her. It wasn't that she had any lingering feelings for her ex – on the contrary, she was actually repulsed by him now – but she did remember with acute clarity just how bad it had felt in the immediate aftermath of their break-up. Despite his actions, she and Andre had been together for a long time and she had loved him. No matter how angry she'd been, switching off her feelings had proved to be trickier than she'd imagined, and she was still fearful of getting hurt. Perhaps if she'd met Ollie before Andre, then she would have taken a chance on him, but she hadn't.

She tried to force her mind away from the subject as

they continued walking, staring upwards to where the stripped branches of the many trees sagged under their piggyback of snow, and flocks of small birds flew in hurried circles high above the hill, their beating wings warming their fragile feathered bodies. Everything else around her was serene and magical, but despite such beauty, Megan didn't find herself moved enough to bother lifting up her camera. This was the problem with discussing feelings and digging up the relics of her past – they killed her creative mojo. To make this exhibition a success, what she needed to be was focused, but at the moment all Megan felt was confused.

'I'm just going to nip to the gents,' Ollie said, veering away to the right as they reached the entrance to the Strahov Monastery.

She nodded and returned his smile, then stepped off the cobbles and spent the next few minutes kicking a disgruntled figure-of-eight pathway through the snow covering the lawn. Ollie's question back in the Mirror Maze had left her guts churning with a mixture of dread and of something else, which Megan couldn't quite find a label for. Clearly he had been thinking about that first shared kiss and, if Megan was completely honest with herself, she often did, too. At the time she had convinced herself that it was the wrong thing to do, but all of Ollie's actions since that day had been so lovely and warm. She didn't want to lose him, that much she was sure about, but what if this friendship she so cherished wasn't enough for him?

In many ways it was a blessing that the Strahov Monastery was much like a museum, both in the fact that it was filled with interesting historical artefacts, and also that it had that uniquely silent atmosphere. After just ten minutes spent examining books dating back to the thirteenth and fourteenth century, collections of stuffed animals, armour and trinkets, plus some truly beautiful jewellery, Megan was already feeling much calmer. Ollie had wandered off in the opposite direction to her after they'd paid their entrance fee, and she was enjoying taking her time at each display.

There was so much history here, she thought, her eyes coming to rest on a book which had been adorned with gold and silver decorations and large precious gems. 'Strahov Gospel Book' she read on the label, her mouth forming a perfect 'O' as she saw that it dated from the ninth century.

When Megan thought about the world existing at that time, and indeed all of the centuries before and since, right up until this exact point in the calendar, it did make her recent freak-out seem rather silly. Wars had been fought, cities burned to the ground, empires built and destroyed. Hell, this monastery in which she was standing right now was over 800 years old – the things it must have been witness to in that time . . . Scholars had come here to study, visiting dignitaries to pray, local people to pay their respects over many hundreds of years. But today, this grand, striking, monumental and truly awe-inspiring place was being forced to bear witness to her silly internal turmoil. Megan all at once felt small, insignificant and, most acutely of all, really bloody foolish. What she needed was to lighten up, and for that she needed Ollie. Making her way quietly across the wooden floor, she came to a halt just behind him.

'Are you okay?'

It was barely a whisper, and at first Megan thought Ollie hadn't heard her; then she saw him smile.

'There's a cabinet full of dried out, very dead fish up that end,' he told her under his breath. 'Even funnier than the Mirror Maze, if you can believe that.'

Feeling overwhelmingly relieved to have her friend back on his usual cheeky form, Megan let Ollie take her hand and lead her down to the other end of the room by the gift shop, where there was, as promised, a truly hideous and downright hilarious menagerie of toothy, crusty sea creatures.

'I'm pretty sure I went on a blind date with her once,' Ollie said, pointing to a particularly snarly-faced specimen.

Megan burst out laughing. She still had her gloved hand in Ollie's, and she could feel her skin becoming clammy beneath the material.

'Go on many of those, do you?' she enquired. She'd meant it to come out nonchalantly, so was appalled to hear an edge of genuine trepidation in her voice. If Ollie realised this, he didn't rise to it.

'A few.' He lifted his shoulders. 'But not for a while now. Fish lady put me right off.'

'That one looks like Andre,' she told him, keen to join in on his joke. Pulling the glove off her free hand with her teeth, she pressed a finger up against the glass, only for one of the staff members to immediately hurry forward and point at the 'do not touch' sign.

'Yeah, Megan – stop touching stuff,' taunted Ollie, dropping her hand for a moment and skipping away as she raised a playful fist to hit him.

They were both hushed back into silence when they

reached the doorway facing into the Philosophical Hall, and Megan felt Ollie's fingers grip hers a fraction tighter as he gazed up at the stunning fresco on the vaulted ceiling above them. The entrance was open, but roped off, and when Megan lifted her camera to capture the array of colours from the intricate artwork and the oak shelves packed with books, another member of staff appeared out of nowhere to inform her that she had to pay extra for taking photos.

Ollie curled his nose up a fraction at this news, but Megan didn't hesitate to hand over some coins – there was no way she could leave this magnificent place without capturing a memory of it for herself, and for others. It was breathtaking.

'Feeling inspired?' whispered Ollie, after she'd fired through at least fifty frames.

Megan could only nod. She knew she must look mad, with her cheeks flushed and her boots up in the air as she crawled around on the wooden floor on her tummy, trying out different angles. She wanted to see the arcs of light from every possible position, find a corner of the hall that nobody had discovered before, not even in all the centuries it had been standing. She wanted to bring something new to this place, something magical. This was what she did, what she was passionate about, and for the few minutes that she was in this bubble, nothing else really mattered.

It was only after she had clambered back up on to her feet, finally satisfied that she'd captured an image she could be proud of, that she realised Ollie hadn't moved. He'd stayed right where he was, watching her in action, and she blushed right to the roots of her blonde hair.

'What are you staring at?' she said, brushing what felt like eight centuries' worth of dust off the front of her coat.

'Just you.' Ollie narrowed his eyes a fraction. 'Doing your thing.'

'You must think I'm a right weirdo,' she said, a half-laugh escaping her mouth as she spoke.

'I thought that already.' He grinned at her. 'But actually, I don't think you're weird at all. I was, in all honesty, thinking how nice it was to see the real you. I don't think you've ever shown her to me before.'

'It was an accident,' Megan admitted, astounded at her own honesty. 'I just saw that room and I . . .' She stopped, searching for the right word, but Ollie silenced her with a raised hand.

'There's no need to explain,' he assured her. 'But I do think I understand you better now – and I mean that in a good way.'

Megan thought back to the night they'd met, to Ollie's confused yet sympathetic expression when she'd pulled back and put a stopper in the bubbling pot of their shared chemistry before it spilled over into their lives, and wondered if maybe, just maybe, he might finally be beginning to appreciate exactly why she'd done it.

20

Hope waited until Charlie was snoring before slipping out from beneath the sheets and tiptoeing into the bathroom for some much-needed time alone. Dropping her towel, she stood naked in front of the full-length mirror, frowning as her eyes ran over the drooping skin around her breasts. She did what she could to stay in good shape, but fifty wasn't thirty, and there was only so much of a battle you could really put up against gravity. She still had decent legs, she thought, turning to the side to admire her defined calf muscles. Despite what some people may think, being a housewife didn't mean that you sat around on your bottom all day watching daytime telly; it meant you were always on the go.

She pulled the skin across her stomach taut and sucked in her breath until her ribs were visible. Would she look better like this, with no excess flesh? Charlie seemed to fancy her just the way she was, but Hope had to admit that she wasn't completely happy with her appearance. It should be enough that Charlie found her desirable – and for a while, in the beginning, it had been the hook on which she had hung her self-worth – but now she had to admit that she'd been left wanting. It wasn't simply about what Charlie – or any man, for that matter – thought of her, it was really all about how she saw herself. And what a silly thing to be concerned about anyway: looks. There was so much more to being a person, so much more that Hope knew she wanted to enable her to feel good about herself: things like her own money, her own home and – God forbid – perhaps even her very own career one day.

She let go of her stomach and watched as it sagged back to its original position, the redness where her fingers had dug into the flesh turning slowly pink. The scar was still there, the skin on either side of it puckered inwards where the doctor had run his blade across. She had so wanted to give birth naturally, but after almost fourteen hours she had no choice but to admit defeat and let the medical professionals take over. It was the only time she could remember seeing Dave cry. Hope, by contrast, had been oddly calm – a fact she later attributed to all the drugs that had been pumped into her – and it was she who ended up comforting her husband as he wept tears of fright all over the blue scrubs that the nurses had hurriedly thrust in his direction. When Annette had at last been lifted out and placed in her arms, Hope could remember thinking that everything was going to be perfect. Dave had been entranced from the first second, his eyes widening as his tiny, perfect daughter squirmed against Hope's chest, never crying, just cooing like a newborn baby bird.

While she and Charlie had been making good use of their king-sized bed, the light outside had faded and she could now see the moon through the open bathroom window. It was a three-quarter one tonight, and so bright that she squinted as she gazed at it. Steam from the bath she was running rushed out of the gap, and she leaned across to breathe in the cold air on the other side of the glass. It smelled clean and fresh, and Hope felt her brain start to wake up. It would have been easy just to snuggle down next to Charlie until the morning, but she was restless. There was so much more of the city to explore, and she didn't want to waste another second trapped up here away from the sights. Slipping her body below the bubbles, she lay for a few seconds with her eyes closed, feeling the fatigue of the day ease away.

'That looks like fun.'

Charlie was standing in the doorway, one side of his face crushed by sleep.

'I was just about to get out, actually,' she said, wondering as she did so why she was lying.

'Shall I help you to wash your hair first?' Charlie asked, sounding less sure of himself than he had a few seconds ago.

Without waiting for an answer, he sat on the downturned toilet seat and ran his fingers into her damp hair, massaging her scalp in strong, circular motions. It felt absolutely heavenly, and Hope told him so as he reached for her shampoo.

'Why are you being so nice to me?' she asked, her toes curling as his fingers rotated.

'Does there have to be a reason?'

'I suppose not.' She smiled and arched her back so he could rinse out the suds.

'I'd say you could return the favour.' He paused, waiting for her to re-emerge from under the water. 'But there wouldn't be much point.'

Hope had always felt sorry for men who lost their hair.

Dave still had a fairly decent thatch, but Charlie had barely a strand. Then again, she'd never known him to be anything other than bald, so she didn't have any basis for comparison.

She closed her eyes again as Charlie combed the conditioner through her hair with his fingers, and thought back to the first time they'd kissed.

It was her sixteenth lesson with him, and he'd instructed her to drive out of town to a large industrial estate. There had once been a supermarket out there but it had closed down the previous winter, and Charlie explained that the vacant car park was a perfect place to practise manoeuvres without getting in anyone's way.

What had started off being simply friendly chat between the two of them had blossomed over the weeks into a teasing flirtation. Hope had started to look forward to her twice-weekly lessons perhaps more than she strictly should have. Charlie was so easy to talk to, and he made her laugh more than she had in years. When she attempted to discuss anything topical with Dave, he'd barely move an eyelash in response, but Charlie seemed enthralled by her opinions. They talked about everything from politics to reality TV shows to relationships, and over time Hope began to bring up the subject of her own marriage. Charlie was always sympathetic, but very careful never to criticise Dave – even though Hope realised later that he must have wanted to air his views on the matter.

Fifteen lessons equated to thirty hours spent in each other's company, and they had spent at least the last five of those growing increasingly bold. Hope knew that she liked Charlie a lot and had an inkling that he felt the same way, but neither of them had crossed that forbidden but invisible line. On this particular day, Hope had been wearing a new pair of over-the-knee boots, which Annette had urged her to order from a catalogue, and they kept catching on the edge of her seat.

'Are you going somewhere nice after this?' Charlie asked, as she stalled for the third time during a three-point turn.

'No.' She shook her head and tried in vain to roll the boot down out of the way.

'You look . . .' Charlie paused as he filtered through his mind for the appropriate word. 'Really nice. Sorry, I know it's not my place to say.'

'Don't apologise,' she told him, glancing around. 'It's your place just as much as anyone else's.'

Charlie seemed to consider this as she attempted the manoeuvre again, this time managing to stop her foot from slipping off the pedal.

'Bravo!' He clapped as she triumphantly yanked up the handbrake. 'If you can drive in those things, you can drive in anything.'

'They probably weren't the best idea.' She grinned, taking her hands off the wheel and clasping them shyly in her lap.

'Don't apologise,' he said, imitating her earlier retort. His voice was soft and Hope sensed a shift in the atmosphere, as if someone had dimmed the lights for them.

'Hope, I . . .' Charlie's cheeks were brushed pink as he looked at her, and her heartbeat quickened.

'I really want to kiss you,' he finished at last. He looked almost sorry, as if he'd said something unforgivable. 'I know, I know!' He shook his head. 'It's completely ridiculous – and I shouldn't have said anything. I'm sorry, I'm really sorry, I will ne—'

She'd silenced him with a kiss, her body moving across the space between them before she realised what was happening. It was timid at first, each of them afraid that they were heading in a direction that a few moments ago had been nothing but a shared fantasy. In the end it was Hope, not Charlie, who took things further, sliding her hand across and along his thigh.

She forced herself not to think about Dave, but she could never shut out Annette. Her daughter was always there in the wings when she kissed Charlie, but even that wasn't enough of a reason to stop. Time with Charlie was like a drug that Hope couldn't get enough of, the thing that got her out of bed in the morning. For the first time since Annette was born, she felt loved, understood, cherished and desirable – but she was still ashamed even now to admit just how much she'd relished those feelings.

Hope kept her eyes closed as Charlie's hands continued to massage her head.

That strong connection was still there between them now, as much as it had ever been, but since that night, since she'd seen that look of disgust on her daughter's face, it was tinged with guilt, too. Hope couldn't let herself go in the way that she felt she should. The betrayal she'd been responsible for was making her relationship with Charlie seem seedy and cheap; at times it felt purely physical rather than an act founded on real love. She had been trying to switch her mind off from the incessant niggles since they arrived in Prague, but she wasn't having any luck, and now, as Charlie's fingers crept lower and she heard his towel slither to the floor, Hope felt herself completely tense up.

'What's the matter?' Charlie said, rocking backwards on to his heels as she sat bolt upright, spilling a good portion of water over the side of the tub.

'My head was spinning,' she lied, gripping his arm as if to illustrate the point.

'It is very hot in here,' he agreed, but he sounded puzzled.

'And I'm hungry,' she added, moving away from him and yanking out the plug. 'Shall we go out for dinner?'

'Okay.' Charlie's whole body seemed to droop at her words, and Hope kissed the top of his shiny head as she gathered up her towel.

'We could go back to the place we found earlier, with the honey cake?'

'Whatever you say.'

He seemed worried that he'd done something wrong now, but Hope wasn't sure how to put his mind at rest. The uncomfortable truth was that she was starting to question how she really felt about this relationship. Charlie was a decent man and deserved better than what she was currently able to offer. The problem was, she'd spent so much of her life putting a man's needs in front of her own that to do it again with Charlie now seemed like a mistake.

He was so willing to support her and look after her, but Hope was beginning to realise that both those jobs belonged not to Charlie – or to any man, for that matter. They belonged solely to her.

21

A small, crescent-shaped crowd had gathered in the Old Town Square to watch a group of musicians, and Sophie stood on the very edge, a cup of hot wine clutched in her hands.

The band was made up of four men, all over the age of fifty, each with their own instrument. One held a clarinet, one a huge double bass, the third a banjo and the lead singer, whose voice was providing Sophie with even more goosebumps than the plummeting temperatures, had a ribbed wooden board hanging around his neck, two small cymbals fixed to its base. He played it simply by scraping or tapping with his fingers, most of which were adorned with thick silver rings.

Gershwin's 'Summertime' was the song of choice, and Sophie let the slow jazz melody creep its way through her senses. Everyone seemed entranced by the haunting lyrics and the gravelly voice of the singer, and Sophie watched as couples leaned into one another. Taking a sip of wine, she swayed gently from side to side, closing her eyes momentarily as the music continued to cast its slow spell.

The snow that had fallen in the days before she arrived had been swept into large piles around the edges of the square, and the mounds looked almost purple in the fading light. The band had set themselves up far enough away from the Christmas Market so as not to be competing with the shrieks of laughter coming from the beer hut or the music churning out of the merry-go-round. Each musician was wrapped up against the cold of the evening in a woolly hat and thick coat, but Sophie could see how pink their fingers were as they teased out note after delicious note from their instruments.

Robin had started to learn the guitar, but he was a terrible singer. The first time she'd heard him warbling away in the shower, Sophie had actually felt relieved. Finally, she had found a chink in his perfect armour, a reason to believe that he was a human being, just like her, and not some godlike creature sent down from the heavens, or more likely, she would tell him, an alien being from another planet. In the first few weeks after they met, Sophie had been in awe of Robin, of just how gorgeous, passionate, smart and funny he was. She'd put him up on a pedestal so high that she feared he was vanishing from sight, so hearing him sing that Elvis song completely wrong and totally out of tune had made her feel a lot better.

Robin had predictably found the entire situation baffling, telling her that she was completely mental to think all those lovely things about him, and that if anyone was punching above their weight in their relationship, then it was him. She was perfect, he told her, like a lone star in a dark night sky. She was extraordinary and remarkable and he was . . . Well, he was just Robin Palmer, scruffy surfer from Cornwall with only seven GCSEs to his name. Sophie hadn't told him so at the time, but what she'd been thinking was that he was far more than just himself – he was the half of her that she'd been searching for all her life without even realising it. He was her missing piece, her soulmate, her everything.

'Sophie?'

She swung around in surprise at the sound of a male voice, expecting to miraculously find Robin standing behind her, then immediately felt like a fool. Ollie grinned down at her, the lenses of his glasses half-covered with condensation. Megan was beside him, and she smiled at Sophie, too, nodding her head towards where the four men were still playing.

'They're amazing,' she said in a low voice, and Sophie could see the lights from the market reflected in her eyes. 'We've been standing here for ages watching them, then Ollie spotted you so we thought we'd come and say hi. Have you had a good day?'

Sophie nodded. She waited until the song came to an end before turning to address the two of them properly. 'I have, thanks – how about you two?'

'We discovered the Mirror Maze,' Ollie told her. 'Although we had to wade through a ton of snow to get there.'

'Hardly a ton!' Megan chided, rolling her eyes for Sophie's benefit. 'This one decided not to bring any boots to Prague, in the depths of winter,' she added, looking down at Ollie's big wet trainers.

Sophie grinned and pulled a sympathetic face at Megan's tall companion, who was now stamping his feet on the spot and complaining that he hadn't been able to feel his toes since lunchtime.

'We went to the Strahov Monastery, too,' Megan was

now telling her. 'It's amazing up there – you can see the whole city spread out below you.'

Sophie nodded. 'It's great, isn't it?'

'I'd love to come back in the summer,' Megan went on. 'I'd like to see how it contrasts to this time of year.'

'It's stunning at every time of year,' Sophie assured her. 'But the snow does give it that something special.'

'Freezing feet is what it gives you,' put in Ollie, making both girls laugh.

'Are you heading back to the hotel?' Megan asked Sophie now. The band were taking a well-earned break and Ollie had just nipped off to throw some coins into their box.

'I guess so.' Sophie shrugged. 'I didn't really have any plans set in stone.'

'Us neither,' Megan admitted.

She was very pretty, Sophie thought, with those golden curls snaking out from under her hat to frame her face. Megan's nose was small and upturned slightly at the end, and her lashes were long enough not to need any mascara to enhance them. Ollie must have a huge crush on her. In fact now that she considered it, Sophie realised that she could almost hear the air crackling between them, and wondered why she hadn't noticed it sooner.

'Did you take many photos today?' she asked, motioning to the camera that was hanging around Megan's neck.

'So many.' Megan grinned broadly at her. 'I haven't felt this inspired in a long time, to be honest. Coming to Prague feels like someone's flicked a switch on in my head. And the light when the sun's out . . . I mean, just wow.'

'Talking about me again?' quipped Ollie. He'd come

back laden with three of the CDs that the band were selling, and he presented one to each of them.

'Oh, you shouldn't have,' Sophie said, immediately blushing.

'Oh, I should.' He shrugged. 'I think we all felt something special listening to them, so why not take a bit of that feeling home with us?'

Sophie thought privately that it was impossible to ever leave Prague without taking some new feelings away with you – it was just that kind of place – but instead she merely smiled and slipped the CD into her bag.

'Ollie's offered to buy me dinner tonight,' Megan told her as they moved away from the square and headed in the direction of the hotel. 'I don't suppose you know where the most expensive restaurant in Prague is, do you?'

'Great friend, isn't she?' Ollie deadpanned, winking at Sophie as she looked at each of them in turn. His easy banter reminded her of Robin.

'I know a few,' she replied, happy to play along. 'But to be honest, the best places are the ones more tucked away. The further out of the centre you go, the better the food becomes.'

'I haven't even tried any goulash yet,' Ollie said, sniffing the air appreciatively as they passed a traditional Czech restaurant.

'You know, most Czech people don't actually eat that much goulash or onion soup,' Sophie told them. 'They go mad for Italian food, believe it or not. You're much more likely to find a Prague family at a pizza parlour than you are in one of these taverns.'

'I think they're crazy,' Megan said, kicking a lump of

slushy snow in Ollie's direction as they crossed the cobbled street. 'I love all that meat and dumplings and potatoes.'

'Nothing better than a girl who loves her me—' began Ollie, only to have his hat pulled down right over his face by an indignant Megan.

'You two are hilarious,' Sophie told them, laughing as Ollie staggered about pretending to be blind. 'You're like an old married couple.'

'Oi!' Ollie reappeared and pushed his glasses back up on to his nose. 'Less of the old. I turned thirty-five not long ago and I'm feeling very sensitive about my impending old age.'

'Thirty-five isn't old,' Sophie told him, deciding as she did so that she liked Ollie very much. 'My mother would tell you that you're in your prime.'

'Is she single?' He laughed at his own joke and Sophie joined in, shaking her head from side to side in an apology.

'Sorry, no – she's very much spoken for.'

'Another one bites the dust,' Ollie sighed, sneaking a glance at Megan.

There was definitely something going on between these two, Sophie decided, watching smudges of colour emerge on Ollie's cheeks as Megan returned his smile.

'Is that Hope and Charlie?' Megan suddenly said, pointing across the street to where a couple were picking their way carefully through the puddles, her arm firmly linked through his. Sophie and Ollie watched as she bounded over to greet them, following suit as soon as they heard Hope's delighted cry of recognition.

'We're off to dinner at this lovely little place behind the

church,' Hope told them after everyone had shaken hands or hugged. 'Why don't we all go together?'

'Fine by me,' Megan was quick to reply, and Ollie nodded, presumably happy to go along with whatever she wanted.

Sophie hesitated. Her phone was almost out of battery and her charger was back at the hotel. Then again, dinner did sound like a nice idea, and far more fun than sitting in her room on her own. A day spent completely alone had left her feeling uneasy, and her sensible side was urging her to go ahead. Company would be a good thing, a distraction. It would make the evening pass by more quickly, and the date of Robin's arrival draw closer.

That decided it.

22

As soon as they'd made their way into the little café-cum-restaurant behind the church in the Old Town Square, Megan excused herself and nipped off to the ladies. She'd been wearing a woolly hat pulled right down over her ears all day and she just knew that her long blonde hair would have tangled into a solid lump beneath it. If it was just herself and Ollie, she'd have brushed it out at the table, but she thought she'd better not be quite so casual now that they had company.

'Owwwww,' she cried, grimacing at her reflection in the mirror as her fold-up brush became caught in a particularly matted chunk of hair and stuck fast to the strands.

'Do you need some help?'

It was Sophie. She'd just pushed the door open and was grimacing almost as much as Megan as she took in the scene of carnage.

'I used to have this problem all the time,' she told her, stepping forward and slipping her tiny fingers around the plastic brush. 'My hair was long enough to sit on, once upon a time.'

'Wow.' Megan's eyes widened in the mirror. 'It's so short now – it must have been a big deal when you cut it all off.'

Sophie had taken her own enormous striped beanie hat off already, and her pixie crop was sticking up in all directions. Rather than look messy, however, the haphazard style lent her a sort of vulnerability, and Megan felt herself soften as she watched her new friend gently ease the bristles from her hair.

Sophie looked nonplussed as she handed Megan the brush back. 'It's only hair, right? It'll grow back eventually.'

'What did your boyfriend – sorry, fiancé – say when you did it?' Megan asked, pulling her hair back into a ponytail and aggressively brushing the ends.

Sophie paused for a moment, not quite meeting Megan's eyes in the mirror as she replied.

'He cried,' she said, then immediately started laughing.

They both jumped as a phone started ringing, and Sophie snatched hers out of her coat pocket.

'I'd better take this,' she said, and Megan saw the photo of the good-looking, smiley blond guy that had flashed up earlier at the hotel.

She nodded, watching as Sophie scurried back out of the toilet, letting the wooden door bang shut behind her. The girl was clearly besotted, and Megan sighed as she continued to detangle her hair. Why was it that other people found it so easy to be in a relationship? Why had she been unfortunate enough to end up with a shit like Andre when there were nice men like Sophie's Robin in the world? And why couldn't she move past what had happened?

The sink was filling up with broken strands of hair now, and Megan scooped them all up and tossed them into the bin. The truth was, she knew the answer to all of those questions. She was who she was, after all, and being Megan Spencer came with certain limitations. She would have time for all that love nonsense one day, she told herself. It just wasn't the right time for her at the moment.

'What have you done with Sophie?' Ollie asked as she joined them at the table a few minutes later. He'd taken the liberty of ordering her a hot wine, and she sipped it gratefully.

'She's on the phone – her fiancé,' she told him, pointing vaguely in the direction of outside.

'Aww.' Hope grinned. 'Young love, eh?'

'Not so different from old love, really,' said Charlie, putting his hand over hers. Megan stared resolutely at the menu.

The café was small and cosy, with a curved ceiling that made the place feel almost like a cave. There were mirrors on nearly every wall, and a number of ancient-looking musical instruments had been hung up in the corners. The tables were all wooden, and there were cushions of all shapes and sizes scattered across the chairs and bench seats. Megan picked one up now and hugged it against herself, her fingers playing absent-mindedly with a loose thread that was dangling out from the zip.

In the far corner, tucked away almost out of sight, she could see a piano, and beyond that more tables, each with a candle in the centre.

It was warm in the café, and felt immediately comforting and homely – not least because the waitress, who was now standing at their table to take their food order, was so utterly enchanting. She loved that about this city, how friendly and welcoming the people were. It made you feel more like a treasured guest than a tourist, and Megan was reminded guiltily of all the times she'd barged past bewildered travellers in London, tutting at them when they stopped dead in the middle of the pavement and refusing to stop and help when they needed directions. She really must try harder to be a better person when she got home.

Ollie's glasses had steamed up as usual, and he was now cleaning them with a napkin while he and Hope discussed what they were going to order.

'I'm becoming obsessed with apple strudel,' he told her, finding it on the menu and giving the air a small fist-pump. 'I might just order three of those and not bother with dinner.'

'I wish I could do the same,' Hope said. 'But if I put away puddings like that then none of my clothes would fit any more. You're very lucky, being so tall and slim like you are. I bet you can eat whatever you want.'

'He does,' Megan interrupted. 'You should see what he puts away. It's so annoying; I can't even sniff a plate of chips without gaining half a stone.'

'I think you ladies are crazy,' Ollie told them. 'You both look perfect to me. And what's the point in life if you don't allow yourself a little indulgence now and again?'

'That's what I'm always telling her,' put in Charlie. 'But you know what women are like.'

'Oh, careful.' Ollie glanced sideways at Megan, his expression mock-fearful. 'This one will put her feminist hat on and give you a telling-off soon.'

Megan glared at him and forced out a bitter laugh. 'He's right,' she told Charlie, taking another sip of her wine. 'I will.'

Charlie held up his hands in surrender.

'I'm all for equal rights,' he assured her. 'But I do like to treat a lady, you know? Hold open the door, pick up the bill – that sort of thing. I don't think being a gentleman should be discouraged. It's a nice gesture, that's all, not a threat to womankind.'

Megan could hear Ollie giggling as she gritted her teeth.

'Of course those sort of things are nice gestures,' she agreed. 'And believe me, I'm all for being spoilt every now and again – just as long as the man in question doesn't treat me like a helpless little fawn that needs looking after at all times. That I couldn't bear.'

'We've been friends for over six months now and she doesn't let me do anything to help,' Ollie told them, laughing at the expression of fury on Megan's face. 'Oh, come on – it's true! You wouldn't let me help you put those shelves up in your kitchen, because you were too proud, and now they're so wonky that you lose at least three mugs a week.'

'It's my flat, not my DIY skills,' she cried. 'The whole building is wonky. I swear it's going to vanish into a sinkhole one day, and then I'll lose more than a few mugs.'

'I actually believe there are just certain things that men are better at than women, and vice versa,' Hope said, smiling an apology at the waitress for the third time. They were still waiting for Sophie to come back inside so they could order food.

'Like what?' Ollie asked, earning himself another stern glare from Megan. He knew this line of conversation was going to wind her up, and he was encouraging Hope on purpose.

'Well, you know, stuff like mending the washing machine, or changing the tyre on a car.'

Megan rolled her eyes.

'But you could do both those things perfectly well if you wanted to,' she argued, being careful to keep her tone light. 'I don't think we should roll over and accept we can't do things, just because a man is more willing to try.'

Hope opened her mouth to reply, then shut it again. She looked downcast all of a sudden, and Megan felt horrible.

'I'm sorry,' she said, her voice small. 'I didn't mean to insult you, I just—'

'You're right,' Hope interrupted, glancing at Charlie before continuing. 'I was married to a man who did everything for me. Well, when I say everything, I mean the more traditional male jobs, you know, such as dealing with the household bills, taxing the car and mowing the lawn. I took care of all the cleaning and cooking and washing. I guess I never really thought anything of it. My mother had done the same thing with my father and us kids, and I never had any real reason to question it.'

'That makes sense.' Megan smiled at her.

'And there's nothing wrong with it either,' Ollie added defiantly. 'I think people should do what makes them happy, and screw what society thinks.'

'What about ironing?' Charlie asked. 'No one should be made to do that, male or female.'

'Very true,' Ollie laughed.

Megan was about to agree, when they were all assailed by an icy draught and Sophie rejoined them at the table.

'Sorry,' she said, picking up a menu as she sat down on the bench seat next to Hope.

'Was that Mr Wonderful?' Hope guessed, smiling at her with a genuine warmth.

Sophie nodded, glancing again at the menu before putting it down.

'You shouldn't have waited to order,' she told them.

'Nonsense,' Charlie assured her. 'We're not in any hurry, are we? Now, who wants to share some wine?'

As soon as their glasses were full, Hope asked Ollie about his job as a teacher.

'I found it noisy just having one child in the house,' she admitted, her face wistful as she described her now-twenty-five-year-old daughter as a toddler. Apparently, Annette had been a big fan of putting things in her mouth that she really shouldn't. Ollie laughed as Hope told them about a particular occasion when she'd taken off her engagement and wedding rings to do the washing up, only to find that Annette had swallowed them when her back was turned.

'I was too relieved that she hadn't choked to be cross at the time,' she told them. 'But those rings never were quite the same after I got them back.'

'There's a little boy called Bertie in my class who loves eating mud,' Ollie said. 'I call him Dirty Bertie – but not out loud, of course. The rest of the children play nice games together or kick a ball around, but Bertie just sits cross-legged in the flower bed scooping up handfuls of soil and posting them into his mouth like biscuit crumbs.'

'I ate a snail once,' piped up Sophie, taking a sip of her wine as they all turned to look at her. Her eyes were so huge, Megan thought, feeling her hands tingle with the idea of taking her photo. Usually she would just ask her to sit for a few portraits, but for some reason she had an inkling that Sophie wouldn't be keen. She fidgeted almost constantly, and kept glancing to her right as if someone were standing next to her, even though they weren't.

'In my first year as a teacher, there was a little girl in my class called Molly who had an imaginary pet alligator,' Ollie was now telling them. 'She would crawl under the table and bite the ankles of the other kids, then blame it on Snappy.'

'I like the sound of her.' Megan grinned, reaching for the open bottle of wine and topping up each of their glasses in turn. Hope was making quick work of hers, she noticed, but Sophie had barely drunk a thing.

'She even did it to me once,' Ollie continued. 'It bloody hurt, I can tell you. I was hopping around the room saying every non-swearword under the sun.'

Hope's face had turned pink as she laughed, and Megan watched Charlie gazing at her. Sophie clearly wasn't the only besotted person sitting at the table. She sneaked a look at Ollie as he reeled off another story. The candle on the table was reflected in his glasses and his dark brown hair was sticking out just above each of his ears. The temptation to reach over and tuck it away into a tidier position was a tough one to quell, and Megan only just managed to resist. As she looked back down at her bread, she caught Hope staring at her.

'Do you get all the mums at the school flirting with you?' Hope asked Ollie now, glancing briefly at him and then back at Megan.

He shook his head. 'No. I keep waiting for that to happen, but it never does. I think it's just a myth they tell people to make them agree to be teachers.'

'I used to have the biggest crush on Annette's history

teacher,' Hope went on, earning herself a look of surprise from Charlie.

'He was called Mr Johnson and he had a big ginger beard, but there was just something about him.'

'Maybe that's where I'm going wrong,' mused Ollie, stroking his clean-shaven jaw with a frown. 'Clearly the caveman look is the way forward.'

'Surely you're not really allowed to date the mothers of your pupils, though?' Megan asked, her tone more accusatory than she'd meant it to be.

Ollie paused with a chunk of buttered bread halfway to his mouth.

'I've never been told it's against the rules.'

'It would be too weird for the kid in question,' she went on. 'Imagine your mum having a fling with your teacher – you'd never live it down.'

Hope had gone a rather unflattering shade of maroon, and Megan got the sense she'd hit on something inadvertently. Her and her huge gob.

Ollie's mouth was too full for him to reply, but he looked as if he wanted to laugh.

'Have you two never . . . ?' Charlie suddenly asked.

Now it was Megan's turn to resemble a tomato.

Sophie emitted a small cough of embarrassed pity, but Charlie was still looking at Megan and Ollie in turn, waiting for an answer to what he must assume was a totally innocent question.

Ollie got there first.

'Megan's a beard fan, too,' he shrugged. 'I'm not her type.'

'You seem to get on well,' Charlie went on, looking to

Hope for confirmation. There was a beat of silence as Hope shook her head just a fraction, and Megan wondered seriously about slipping under the table and setting her own version of Snappy loose on the lot of them.

'We do,' said Ollie eventually, after it became clear that Megan wasn't going to reply. 'But we don't see each other as anything other than friends.'

For some inexplicable reason, Megan felt tears prickling in her eyes. She was used to being the one who scrutinised people, not the other way around. Ollie was doing his best to laugh the whole thing off now, but she couldn't help but feel hurt by the casual way he'd just dismissed her – dismissed them. What the hell was wrong with her?

The next time she braved a glance across the table, she caught Hope's eye and saw the older woman mouth the word 'sorry'. It was only a matter of time before the subject of her and Ollie came up again, she realised. Hope would have questions for her the next time the men were out of earshot, of that much she was pretty certain, but Megan didn't have any answers for her. She wondered what Sophie was thinking, and whether she had an opinion on the matter, but when she tried to get her attention with a silent gaze, she found that the other girl was staring off in the opposite direction, her eyes wide and her small mouth open, as if marooned halfway through a memory.

She felt rather than saw Ollie shift in his seat, the wood creaking beneath his weight, and knew that he was looking at her. This time, however, she managed to fight the urge to lift her eyes up to where she knew his would be waiting.

23

There was an uneasy atmosphere at the table, and Hope was relieved when the food arrived and they all had an excuse to stop talking.

She couldn't stop thinking about what Megan had said, about women being able to do whatever they wanted, regardless of whether or not it was a 'man's job'. She knew it was true, of course. The reason she'd signed up for driving lessons in the first place was to gain a bit more independence. In the past, she'd always had to rely on Dave driving her over to the supermarket to do the big shop at the weekend, and increasingly he'd been reluctant to move from his chair in front of the TV. Rather than turn into a nag, as so often occurred, she decided to take matters into her own hands. And then, of course, she'd met Charlie.

Hope had always been content to take care of the house. After all, Dave was the one going out to work, and she enjoyed being there when Annette came home from school. She could have gone out and got herself a job at any time, really, but she was afraid. Hope knew how to be a mother and a wife, but when it came to working out in the real world, she didn't have the first clue.

She watched Megan now across the table; the younger woman seemed so strong and self-assured, with her highlighted hair and her eyeliner drawn on in those trendy little flicks. She and Ollie were obviously close. He was watching her now out of the corner of his eye, Hope noticed. In fact, thinking about it, he barely seemed to take his eyes off her.

The goulash she'd ordered was delicious, with tender chunks of beef that melted in her mouth, sweet red onion and a rich, warming gravy, which she was busy soaking up with her beautifully moist bacon dumplings. Megan had ordered the same as her, but the boys had opted for the pork shoulder, which came with a generous helping of sauerkraut and mashed salted potatoes. Sophie, by comparison, had chosen a beef broth, which was rather adorably served inside a bread bowl. It smelled heavenly, but Hope could tell that she was only pretending to eat it.

'Are you okay, love?' she whispered, as Sophie brought a full spoon up to her mouth, then lowered it back down again.

'I'm fine.' Sophie gave her a half-smile.

She clearly didn't want to elaborate, so Hope merely gave her arm a light squeeze before turning her attention back to the rest of the group.

'We went to the Charles Bridge today,' she announced.

'Me, too,' Megan replied, nodding her head with enthusiasm. 'I went there first thing this morning to take photos.'

'Is photography what you do, then?' Charlie enquired.

'It's what I'm trying to do,' Megan admitted, pushing her fork into a lump of meat and scooping it into her mouth with some onion.

'What she isn't telling you is that she's brilliant,' Ollie added. 'Honestly – if I was rich enough then I'd pay her to quit her job and just take photos all day long.'

'That's so sweet.' Hope clasped her hands together.

'I would never let him,' Megan was quick to put in. 'And anyway, my job isn't all that bad. I work in a gallery,' she added.

'That must be fun?'

Megan merely nodded. 'It's okay. Some of the customers are awful, but we don't get that many of them, so it could be worse.'

'I get some right sorts booking driving lessons with me,' Charlie told them. 'This one lady was really superstitious, and every time I picked her up she had to open and close all the car doors three times before she'd even get in. Apparently if she didn't, we'd be certain to crash.'

'Sounds exhausting,' said Megan.

'It was,' Charlie agreed. 'But she was very nice. Never made it through the test, though. I think she gave up after the thirteenth attempt, which must be some sort of record.'

'I haven't got a licence,' Sophie admitted, causing them all to turn to her. 'I mean, I can drive – my dad taught me on the farm when I was about twelve, but I've never bothered making it official.'

'Same here,' Megan said. 'My parents offered to pay for lessons when I was seventeen, but I wanted a camera instead. And anyway, I live in London now – you don't really need a car in London.'

Hope thought fleetingly of the day she'd taken her driving test. She'd passed first time, which had both surprised and delighted her, and afterwards Charlie had driven them out to a country pub for a celebratory lunch. She could remember how proud she'd felt, and how she'd refused his offer of champagne because she'd wanted to drive the car back into Manchester. It was only a week later that Annette caught them.

'Did you see the gold cross on the bridge?' Hope asked Megan now, steering the conversation back to the city, and away from her memories.

'I saw *a lot* of crosses.'

'This one isn't on a statue,' Hope explained. 'It's on the wall of the bridge itself, at the spot where a saint was thrown off into the river.'

Megan was looking at her, nonplussed, so Hope told them all the story that she and Charlie had learned earlier that day.

'I think it's a load of gobbledegook,' Charlie admitted sheepishly, putting his knife and fork together. 'Just a story they tell tourists to keep them interested.'

'You're such an old cynic,' Hope scolded. 'I think it's a beautiful idea.'

'I'm going down there tomorrow to wish for a pay rise,' Ollie said, causing Charlie to chuckle. The girls, however, were both looking thoughtful.

'There is something magical about this city,' Hope went on defiantly, picking up her wine. 'You can feel it. There's something in the air here, like a whispered secret drifting around on the wind. I sound mad, I know.'

'You don't.' Megan was nodding in agreement now. 'I know exactly what you mean. I felt it this morning on the Charles Bridge and at the monastery up on the hill. It's as if the city is haunted, but not in a bad or a spooky way.'

'I think you girls have had too much wine,' Charlie joked.

Hope turned to Sophie. 'You agree with us, don't you, love?'

Sophie put her spoon down and nudged her plate forward a fraction. 'I just love this place,' she told them simply. 'I've been all over the world, but this is the one place I keep coming back to – and it's where I met Robin.'

'There must be a reason why so many people keep coming back here year after year,' Hope said.

'The cheap beer?' Ollie suggested.

Hope smiled, but she was glad she wasn't the only one who had sensed something special about Prague. When she had made her silent wish on the Charles Bridge that morning, she'd truly believed in what she was asking. In that moment, with the cold wind biting at her cheeks and the distant sound of church bells ringing, she'd let herself believe in real magic. A year and a day was a long time to wait for her particular wish to come true, however. Perhaps what she should really be focusing on was how to create a little magic of her own.

When the last of the apple strudel and cream had been scraped off their plates and a generous tip had been heaped on to the table next to several empty wine bottles, Hope suggested that they all take a wander around the square before heading back to the hotel. She watched Sophie pull her oversized hat back on and button up her coat against the freezing night air. She was so tiny that Hope couldn't help but feel a maternal pull towards her. She wanted to wrap her up in her arms and protect her from the world, which was of course ridiculous. Here was a girl who was not only here in the city on her own, but had also travelled around the whole world. She was probably far more capable of looking after herself than Hope ever could be, yet that overwhelming urge to mother was still there, refusing to dip below an urgent bubbling simmer. It must be because she was missing Annette.

While her daughter was outgoing and outspoken, she still came running to Hope whenever she was in trouble. Well, she had until recently. Hope found it impossible to look at Annette and see a mature twenty-five-year-old woman with her own career, relationship and home – all she saw was her baby. She didn't think that would ever change, either. The fact that her own daughter now wanted nothing to do with her cut into Hope like a scalpel through the skin of a peach.

'Will you look at this cheeky fellow,' Charlie said, coming to a stop beside a makeshift set of stables. The floor of each stall was covered with straw, and there were three goats, one miniature pony and a donkey, all with their noses poking over the bolted doors. At the far end of the stables, a coin-operated sweet dispenser had been fixed to the wall, its plastic tub filled with pony nuts. The donkey, whose stall was at the end nearest this contraption, waited until he had their full attention before reaching his head around and curling his hairy grey upper lip over the dial in an attempt to make some nuts drop down.

'How adorable!' Hope cried, putting a timid hand between the donkey's lopsided ears and rubbing his knotted fur.

Ollie was rooting in his pocket for change, and Megan already had her camera poised. Hope could hear her clicking away furiously as Ollie collected a generous serving of nuts and poured a heap into Hope's hands, and then

Sophie's. The donkey barged forward immediately, lifting up his top lip and showing them his teeth.

'He is very happy,' the man looking after the stall told them, slapping his hands on his thighs as the donkey turned and gave his pony stablemate a warning nip.

Holding her palm flat under the donkey's muzzle and watching him gobble up her offering, Hope guessed this floppy-eared creature's little routine was keeping him very well fed, to judge from the size of his tummy. As she took a step back and wiped the dust from the nuts off her hands, she noticed that Charlie wasn't anywhere to be seen.

'Did you see where he went?' she asked Megan, who was still holding her camera in her gloved hands.

Megan shook her head. 'Sorry.'

'He's over there.' Sophie pointed through the enormous ears of the donkey at another stall a few yards away. Charlie had his back to them, but his height and his bright red hat gave him away. Hope felt her stomach churn with unease as she noticed the mobile phone clamped against his ear. It couldn't possibly be an estate agent at this time of night.

Ollie must have noticed the stricken look on her face, because he quickly inserted another coin into the pony-nut dispenser and beckoned for her to join him.

'Come on,' he said, excitement taking his voice up an octave. 'Let's see if we can get the donkey and the pony to have a punch-up.'

Hope held her hand out gratefully and crouched down to where the determined chestnut mare had forced her tiny nose through the slots in the fence. She could still see the top of Charlie's head, and she heard rather than saw Megan begin to take photos again.

How had she ended up here? she wondered. A few days ago she had felt as if she'd found someone she could trust, someone who loved her, but now, here in Prague with her knees on the cold, damp cobbles and her fingers pink from the icy air, she realised with a creeping dread that she didn't really know Charlie that well after all.

24

The sky the next morning was white and heavy with snow. Sophie could almost feel the weight of it as she slipped out of the hotel and crunched through the piles of grubby slush on the pavements. Stopping only to buy herself a cup of fresh ginger tea from a small vendor on the far side of the river, she headed down past the Kafka Museum until she was on the banks of the Vltava.

Ahead of her was a large, weathered tree, its roots poking up sporadically through the muddy ground and its lowest branches trailing down into the surface of the water. The only colours down here were whites, browns and greys, the Vltava River itself bleached into a murky beige by the reflection of the pale sky above. Sophie sniffed the somewhat stagnant air and wrinkled her nose, bringing her cup up to mask the aroma of duck dung with the sweet scent of ginger.

She had filled her coat pockets with bread from the breakfast buffet that morning, and now she settled herself down on a large tree root and began breaking it up into chunks. It didn't take long for the local contingent of swans, ducks and seagulls to pick up the fresh, doughy scent on the air, and soon the puddles around Sophie's feet were obscured by a multitude of feathered scavengers.

She took her time choosing which ones to feed,

throwing chunks right over the heads of the expectant swans that had barged aggressively to the front of the pack. Her reluctance to reward their bullying behaviour enraged them, and she cowered as one particularly affronted beast stretched out its wings and made a lunge for her ankles.

'Sod off!' she yelped, making shooing motions and almost losing her arm to the swan's equally bolshie friend in the process. The way that the birds were all bashing against each other as they jostled for space reminded her of the Underground in London. So many people down there behaved just as these swans were, as if they were the most important people on the planet, and so should be treated as such. Sophie found them ridiculous, and she smiled as she thought fondly of the relative quiet of home. There was no need for anyone to push each other around in the village. When Sophie had been a child, she'd often lamented this fact to her parents, moaning that the village was 'boring' and that she was going to move to London as soon as she was old enough. What an idiot she'd been.

There was a sudden flurry of movement in front of her and several ducks set off squawking towards the water. At first Sophie thought one of the swans had kicked off again, but then she saw a flash of brown fur amid the melee of feathers.

'What the hell?' she gasped, drenching one of her gloves in lukewarm ginger tea as she recoiled in shock.

She had definitely seen fur. And some sort of tail. And teeth. But it couldn't be a rat. She'd seen some big rats in her time – it was one of the many joys of living on a farm

– but this thing was something else. It was bigger than the ducks that were now waddling away from it.

The urge to clamber up and run away was overwhelming, but Sophie found she couldn't move. She could feel her skin tingling with discomfort, and for some reason her mind was conjuring up images of the wet, slimy creature scuttling up her legs. If ever she needed Robin to be here, it was now. He would know what to do – he wouldn't be afraid.

She let out a huge shudder as the rodent re-emerged from behind a cluster of angry drakes and started sniffing at the rubbish that had washed up on shore a few metres down from her spot beneath the tree. From this safe distance, she realised that it wasn't actually all that bad. In fact, it was quite sweet. Its face was flatter than a rat's and its paws seemed to Sophie to look more like flippers than claws. As it turned its back on her and slithered down into the water, she caught sight of its tail again and actually laughed out loud at herself. It was a beaver, not a rat.

She and Robin had seen dolphins in Mexico, crocodiles in Australia, an eagle catching fish from a lagoon in Sri Lanka and countless thousands of pigeons as they'd made their way around the world, but they had never seen a beaver before. As her relief that it hadn't been a giant rat slipped away, Sophie was hit by a new emotion: regret. She couldn't believe that Robin hadn't been here to see this.

Taking out her phone, Sophie padded through the mud to the edge of the water, looking in vain for the animal that she'd been desperate to run screaming from just a few minutes ago. She could at least take a photo. It wouldn't be the same, though.

She and Robin had been through so much together. They'd barely spent a day apart since they'd met – and certainly not since he'd left his home in Cornwall and taken up residence in her attic bedroom at the farm. It felt intrinsically wrong that she was here alone now, having a new experience that he would never be a part of.

Her mind flickered involuntarily back to a memory she'd tried hard to bury – of an argument that had marked a shift in their relationship. He had arrived home later than planned, his breath laced with the yeasty stench of beer and his demeanour edgy and excited. When Robin was in this sort of mood he found it impossible to sit still, and would pace around the room fidgeting with things. When Sophie pointed this out and asked why he seemed so exhilarated, he'd suddenly turned coy and unusually mute.

'What aren't you telling me?' she demanded, watching as he picked up a CD case and pretended to read the back.

'Nothing.'

'Why are you so late?'

A shrug. 'I just went for a drink after work, that's all.'

'Who with?'

Sophie saw his shoulders tense up a fraction.

'Just the lads, and . . .' He put the CD down and tucked his hair behind his ears, his eyes on the carpet rather than her.

'And who?' She tried to stop her anguish from seeping into her words, but it was impossible. It wasn't like Robin to be cagey like this.

He gave a deep sigh and looked at her finally.

'Nobody,' he said.

Sophie took a deep breath. He obviously wasn't going to tell her the truth.

'I see.'

Robin groaned and tapped his fingers impatiently on the dressing table. 'This is exactly why I never tell you when I go out with the boys. I knew you'd overreact.'

'I'm not overreacting. You're the one who's acting all guilty.'

'Come on, Bug.'

'That's right,' she snapped, turning her back on him as he tried to put his arms around her. 'I'm an insignificant bug – no wonder you'd rather be out with your friends.'

'Now you're being really stupid.' He was looking at her with a mixture of dismay and amusement, but it was the hint of laughter in his voice that really rankled. How dare he laugh at her?

Her face must have portrayed her feelings, because Robin took one look at her and backed down.

'I'm sorry,' he said, his bravado vanishing like water down a drain. 'I should have invited you, too. The lads aren't a threat to you, Bug – you should know that. You know you're more important to me than any of them.'

'I'm just scared of losing you,' she said, her voice small, and he pulled her against his chest.

'That's never going to happen,' he promised, and she felt him smile. 'I'm afraid you're stuck with me for life.'

The sob erupted from the very depths of her chest so suddenly that it startled the few ducks and seagulls that were still hovering around hoping for bread. She was being ridiculous now – there wasn't any need for all these tears. That argument had happened months ago, and she and Robin had long since made up again.

Sophie wasn't sure how long she sat there, lost in the past, but after a time the beaver popped its smooth head back through the surface of the water right in front of her and sniffed the air with interest. Sophie didn't move a muscle as it made its way past her, so close that she could have reached out a hand and stroked a finger along the slick fur on its back.

The birds had quietened down now and on the opposite shore the city was coming to life. Sophie strained her ears and heard the tell-tale clicking sound coming from the crossing by the Charles Bridge, where the trams squealed up and down the banks of the Vltava. There was a faint trace of music drifting down from somewhere behind her, and the wind was busy chasing fallen leaves along the cobbles.

The temperature was slowly dropping, and Sophie sighed as she looked down at her sodden gloves. She was glad of her long coat, which would hide the wet patch on the back of her jeans. At least she would have a tale to tell the others that evening, she thought, cursing herself again for not getting a photo of the beaver. Perhaps if Megan came down here, then she would be able to take some, and she'd do a far better job of it.

They had all agreed to head out for dinner again as a group that evening, and she was grateful that they were all being so welcoming. She pictured Robin again, with his kind, smiling eyes and his untidy blond hair. How she missed him – his smell, his touch, the pure essence of him. After this trip, she was never going to let him get away from her again.

25

'Have you ever had a go on a Segway?'

Megan pulled a face. 'No.' She stepped to one side as yet another group of tourists rumbled past them on the strange two-wheeled contraptions. 'If anyone rode one to work in London, they'd definitely get lynched,' she added, eyeing the Segways as they vanished around a cobbled corner up ahead. 'Can you imagine?'

'Yeah, they would,' Ollie agreed. 'And robbed. Remind me again why we live in that city.'

'Because it's where everything happens,' she informed him. 'If you want to be a somebody, then you can't hide away in a little village.'

'Is that why you're there?' He peered at her in interest. The cold wind had turned his nose the same colour as a ripe apple.

Megan shrugged uncomfortably. 'I guess so. But it's not that I want to be famous or anything like that, it's just that there are more exhibitions and opportunities for photographers in London. If I'd stayed in the Kent countryside with my parents, I'd never have got anywhere.'

Ollie looked an awful lot like he didn't believe her, and Megan felt herself bristle with mild irritation.

'I mean it,' she said. 'I want people to look at my work, not at me.'

'No, you hate people looking at you,' he agreed.

She wasn't sure from his neutral tone whether he meant exactly that, or if he was making a small dig about the night they'd met, when she'd squirmed uneasily under his gaze as they'd sat side by side on her sofa. She hadn't been comfortable with the intensity of Ollie's feelings towards her in that moment, that much was true – but it wasn't because she hated the idea of being wanted by him. Or was it? Megan was feeling increasingly confused about the whole situation with every hour she spent here in Prague with Ollie. Just that morning, she'd woken up to find that he'd sneaked his hand into hers while they slept. She didn't actually know if he'd done it intentionally – it could have been an unconscious movement – but the thing that had worried her most was how much she'd liked it. She'd genuinely felt sad when he'd started to stir and had rolled away from her.

Megan had always thought of herself as an independent spirit, someone who was easily strong enough to cope just fine without a man in her life. This new neediness she was feeling towards Ollie was unsettling, and it made her feel weak. One thing Megan did not want in her life was weakness – not after what had happened with Andre, when her terrible judgement had led her to such misery. She knew that the only way she could confidently take back the life she wanted, and show the world exactly what she was made of, was to create the best launch exhibition that London had ever seen – and she wanted to do it alone.

However, the more time she spent with Ollie, the more she found herself drawn to him. Her feelings kept creeping up behind her and tapping her on the shoulder, demanding attention.

'Look at him,' they seemed to nag. 'He's lovely and tall and funny, with all his own hair. Go over there and kiss him!'

But Megan would shake her head and shoo them away. Ollie was just one complication too far at the moment, and it wouldn't be fair to act on what she was feeling. She cast her mind back to the previous evening, when events had taken a rather strange turn.

After they had all left the quirky café behind the Old Town Square and stumbled across that brilliant, mischievous donkey – Megan grinned to herself now as she remembered all the photos she'd taken – Charlie had wandered off to make a phone call and the atmosphere between him and Hope had immediately turned even colder than the weather, which was really saying something, given that it had been below freezing. Hope had asked him who he'd been talking to, only for Charlie to bizarrely accuse her of imagining things. They'd all seen Charlie with his phone clamped to his ear, so it was odd to hear him deny it outright, and Megan had turned to Hope to find her muttering under her breath. The awkwardness level soon cranked up to a solid, skin-itching ten, and Sophie's huge eyes had met Megan's and widened.

Ollie, ever the pragmatist, had stepped in and rescued the situation by suggesting that he and Charlie head off for a 'man's pint' in one of the horrible-looking English-themed pubs on the other side of the square, leaving Hope to silently seethe with the two remaining girls.

'Another wine?' Megan had suggested, for want of anything better to say.

Hope had arranged her features into something resembling a smile, and shaken her head.

'I think I'll go back to the hotel, but you girls go ahead.'

Megan looked to Sophie for help, but she merely brought her shoulders up to her ears and shivered.

'Come on,' Megan pleaded. 'There are so many nice bars. Why don't we go to that one over there, with the heated lamps outside? I fancy a hot wine under a blanket, don't you two? It's been, oh, at least ten minutes since the last one, and I'm already freezing again.'

Hope looked from her, to Sophie and back again, and finally managed a proper smile.

'Oh, go on then – you've twisted my arm.'

There was barely a cloud in the sky, but the artificial lights illuminating the impressive architecture of the Old Town Square cast a glow that obscured the stars. Thankfully the wind had dropped, so they were all relatively cosy as they sipped their hot drinks under three thick red blankets. The waiter, Megan noticed, who was impressively tall with a rather large nose, took his time tucking hers in around her waist and thighs.

'You've got yourself an admirer there,' Hope chuckled, winking at her as the man weaved his way back through the tables. He was dressed in a smart shirt and tie with absolutely no jacket, and Megan shivered in sympathy.

'The cold has clearly addled his brain,' she said.

'Good thing Ollie didn't see,' Hope went on, nudging Megan's arm conspiratorially.

Megan ignored her, picking up her glass instead and then swearing as the hot, spicy liquid burned the back of her throat.

'I'm afraid it's obvious that he fancies you,' Hope continued. 'He can't take his eyes off you.'

'You heard what he said at dinner,' Megan reminded her. 'He only sees me as a friend. There was a time when . . .' She stopped, unsure of how to continue.

'You don't have to talk about it,' Sophie piped up from across the table.

For one so quiet, she was clearly very astute, thought Megan. But actually, perhaps it would do her good to talk about it.

'I broke it off with Ollie before it really even started,' she told them, explaining between tentative sips of wine how the two of them had met and kissed on that first night after the pub quiz. 'I had a bad break-up a few years ago,' she added, deciding not to go into detail. 'It's not that I think Ollie's a bad person, quite the opposite, in fact. I love being his friend.'

'How did you end up here together?' Hope asked, putting her pretty head on one side. With her blonde hair set in curls, she reminded Megan of one of the many carved stone angels and cherubs dotted around the city.

'Ollie wanted to come and check the place out before he taught the kids in his class about it, and he thought I could help by taking photos for him.' She paused, realising as she said it that all she'd really done since they arrived was focus on taking her own photos. Had Ollie noticed and simply not said anything? That would be just like him.

'How's it been?' Hope went on, looking towards Sophie, who smiled.

'It's been really fun,' Megan admitted, then grimaced as she remembered Ollie's drunken confession on the first night out. 'But there have been a few awkward moments.

I sometimes get the impression that he's annoyed with me.'

'Why would he be?' asked Hope, pulling her blanket up a fraction higher and clasping her gloved hands around her glass.

Megan shook her head. 'Maybe because I never let that kiss go any further? I don't know. Or maybe I'm just annoying?' She laughed, but the other two didn't join in.

'Why didn't you let it go any further?' Hope asked gently.

'You must have had your reasons,' Sophie interrupted. 'There's always a reason.'

She was shivering, Megan realised.

'Do you want another blanket?' she asked. 'Or we can ask for a table inside?'

'Oh no, I'm fine.' Sophie hunched up her shoulders.

There was a loud sound of metal scraping against stone as Hope dragged her chair closer to Sophie's and put a protective arm around her shoulders, rubbing her hand vigorously up and down to warm her up.

'Ollie needs a proper girlfriend,' Megan told them. 'Someone who is free to spend all their time with him. He deserves that. But I'm not that person – I'm too selfish.'

'I'm sure you're not,' argued Hope, but Megan shook her head.

'I am, believe me. At least, when it comes to my career. The thing is with photography, it's not a nine-to-five job. I can't just clock off at the end of the day and put it out of my mind until the morning. Sometimes I'm up for hours just editing one frame, only to dump it in the trash at three in the morning. Other times I get up before dawn to work.

It really depends on my mood, but the fact is that I have the freedom to do what I like. If I had a boyfriend, I'd have to sacrifice some of that free time, and I'm not prepared to do that.'

'Do you love him?'

This had come from Sophie, while Hope stared at Megan in bewilderment.

'You mean Ollie?' Megan coloured and laughed a little too loudly. 'No! I mean, yes, as a friend. Oh, I don't know.'

'Love isn't always straightforward,' Hope said gravely. 'Sometimes you can feel like you are in love with someone, only to realise years later that you never really were at all. In love with the idea of love, rather than the person.'

'You have to be sure,' Sophie said quietly. 'I always have been with Robin. There has never been a day since I met him that I wasn't absolutely sure I loved him. I think if you know, then you just know.'

'It's rare, love like that,' Hope told them, her eyes misty as she gazed up at the lights of the square. 'Some folk never know for sure if what they're feeling is the real thing.'

'How do you know?' Megan asked them. 'I mean, is there a moment, like a firework going off in your brain?'

There was a pause while they all considered the question, then Sophie spoke first.

'When I met Robin – and I mean literally the moment he first spoke to me – I just felt something change in me. It was like the hands of a clock going round and clicking into place as they reached the hour. He told me that he felt the same thing. It was like the universe brought us together.'

'I did have fireworks in my pants when I first met Ollie,' Megan admitted. The mood had turned far too serious for her liking, and she was keen to lighten it.

Hope giggled and signalled to the lanky waiter for more wine.

'Don't you ever worry, though?' Sophie asked Megan.

'Worry about what?'

'That Ollie could be the one? What if you've been brought together for a reason and you're doing the wrong thing by keeping him at arm's-length?'

'I know it's not the wrong thing,' Megan said automatically. 'I can just feel it, you know, in my gut. It's not right.'

'What do you think Ollie's gut is telling him?' Sophie asked. She didn't appear to mean it as a dig, but Megan narrowed her eyes a fraction. This scrutiny was starting to get to her, and she felt a bit as if she was being ganged up on. It was always the same when the subject of Ollie came up – her family and friends all adored him, all thought she was crazy for not taking the friendship to the next level, and now these two had closed ranks against her too.

'I think Ollie knows we're just friends,' she said simply. 'Even if he doesn't understand my reasons for not being with him, I think he tries to.'

Hope took her hand off her glass of wine and squeezed Megan's arm through the blanket. 'You have to do what's best for you,' she said. 'Don't put anyone else first. I did that with my Dave for so many years, and now I'd do anything to turn back the clock.'

'Sometimes I wish I could stop all the clocks,' Sophie said dreamily. 'I'd give anything to have hundreds of extra years with Robin.'

'I cannot wait to meet this fella of yours.' Hope grinned. 'He sounds so perfect.'

Sophie smiled at that. 'He is. Well, he's perfect for me.'

She'd gone on to tell them more about her fiancé, the plans they had for their wedding and all the places in the world they still wanted to visit together. Megan had been glad for the change of subject, but she'd also found herself feeling jealous of Sophie's happy relationship. Why had it all come so easily to her, yet seemed such an impossibility for Megan?

Megan glanced up at Ollie now, at his red nose with the glasses perched on the tip, at his pink cheeks and the ugly fur-lined hat that he'd picked up from a stall on the way over the Charles Bridge, and tried to concentrate on what she was feeling. Whatever it was, it was warm. She could feel it oozing through her insides like melted caramel. Her limbs felt lighter and her heart quicker, the cold barely distinguishable. Was this love? And if it was, what kind of love was it? How could she be sure that she didn't simply love Ollie as a friend? Sophie had said she'd just known she loved Robin as soon as she met him, so why was she, Megan, finding it so difficult?

'I think the John Lennon Wall is this way,' Ollie announced, cutting abruptly through her meandering train of thought. He was in charge of the map, holding it folded open in his gloved hands.

They'd left the Charles Bridge now and headed left, entering into a series of twisty streets flanked by high-walled yellow buildings. Smooth cobbles decorated the ground beneath their feet, each one adorned with a glittering spider's web of frost, and swept snow sat in sad, forgotten heaps by the kerb. The sound of chattering tourists faded the further they went.

It would be the perfect place for a kiss, Megan was horrified to find herself thinking. Nobody around to interrupt them. It had been so long now since she'd first kissed Ollie, but she could still recall the tentative way he'd slid his tongue against her own, not awkward or clumsy, just measured and tender. Her knees throbbed and she instinctively reached down to rub them.

'Are your joints still aching from that climb we did yesterday, old lady?' Ollie asked in amusement.

If only he knew . . .

'Who are you calling old, Mister Closer-to-forty-than-thirty?'

Ollie stuck his tongue out.

The next corner they took brought them out on a small bridge, which had a low wall on one side and wrought-iron bars on the other. Attached to these bars were literally hundreds of padlocks in a multitude of colours, sizes and styles, each bearing the names or initials of the couples who had placed them there. Megan thought of the lone padlock she and Ollie had found halfway up Petrin Hill the previous day, and smiled. If she was ever going to leave a love padlock anywhere in Prague – not that she ever would, of course – then she would definitely follow the lead of that couple and hide it away somewhere discreet.

'There are a lot of people in love in this city,' Ollie remarked, flicking over a few of the padlocks closest to him.

Megan didn't reply, because she was too busy taking photos from every angle imaginable. It was nice not to feel inhibited in front of Ollie any more. After yesterday's moment of mad abandon in the monastery, she'd come to the conclusion that it didn't matter what he saw her do. If they were going to be friends, then he had to know the real her – and this was the real her.

'Are you actually going to lie down on the . . . ? Oh.' Ollie hopped aside as Megan wriggled along the ground by his feet. 'You are.'

All Megan could see was colour and love and joy – and as she framed her shots, she tried to feel what the owners of these locks must have felt when they brought them here. Those feelings of mutual affection, a longing to be sure that what they were feeling for one another would last for always. A solid guarantee, one that they could see and hold in their hands, perhaps revisit when the going got tough. Which it almost always did, as far as Megan was aware.

'You're making a face like a baby filling its nappy,' Ollie pointed out, unhelpfully.

'It must be like looking in a mirror,' she quipped back sweetly, finally struggling to her feet as yet another Segway tour came hurtling around the corner behind them.

Ollie took her hand to help steady her, crushing her fingers gently between his own, as if trying to communicate something he wasn't prepared to say out loud. Megan thought again about the kiss, and forced herself to step away.

'It's freezing,' she stated, looking down at her now-damp clothes and shivering violently to illustrate the point. 'Let's go and find this wall you won't stop going on about.'

Ollie looked down at her through the smeary glass of his spectacles and brought his hand up to brush away a single strand of blonde hair that had adhered itself to her lip balm.

There it was again, that warmth.

'You're very beautiful,' he told her. 'I think it every time I look at you, and most of the time I can stop myself from telling you. But not this time.'

Megan said nothing, but she felt herself tremble. For once she didn't turn away from his gaze either; she simply stood as still as one of the statues up on the bridge and stared back at him.

'Come on, then,' he said eventually, visibly shaking himself out of the trance he'd lulled them into and reaching for her hand. 'Let the teacher lead the way.'

26

When the soft morning light had snaked through the curtains just after dawn that morning, tiptoeing its pale fingers down on to the carpet, across the ornate rug and up across the tangled sheets of the bed, it found that Hope was already awake. She had been awake for hours. Ever since the screaming woke her.

Charlie lay beside her, his head facing the opposite direction, a few sparse hairs just visible on the back of his shoulders. Hope could hear his gentle snores, but she took no comfort from the sound. They had gone to sleep on a row – the first proper one they'd ever had – and Hope could still feel the sting of their angry words.

'You're imagining things, love,' he had argued, when she'd accused him of taking a secret call on his phone in the market while she was distracted by the donkey. 'Why are you having a go at me?'

But Hope hadn't been imagining anything – she had seen him. When she told him so, Charlie had looked at her with scorn, as though the mere sight of her was an irritation. It was so unlike the gentle, loving Charlie that she'd grown accustomed to, that Hope had been momentarily stunned into silence. She'd tried a different tack.

'Whatever it is, you can tell me,' she'd said, forcing a conciliatory tone into her voice. 'I won't be cross, I promise.'

'There's nothing to tell,' came his reply. He wouldn't even meet her eyes.

It was so strange to feel disconnected from him like this. Their relationship had always been passionate, but, as Hope now acknowledged, it had always been very physical, too. Had the two of them simply got carried away with the lust that had consumed them and failed to notice the gap opening up like a chasm between them? Had they been too impatient to fall in love? Hope had been so sure of her feelings – even a few days ago she had felt certain that Charlie was the answer to her puzzle – but had she been wrong? Had her desire to change her life propelled her into something that wasn't real?

The sticking point Hope kept coming back to was that she did care about Charlie, but she wasn't ready to let him look after her in the way that he wanted – and she was going to have to face up to it.

The light shifted as she peeled back the covers and walked quietly across to the bathroom. She groaned out loud when she saw herself in the mirror, the complicated map of lines on her face testament to how little sleep she'd managed to get. She thought again about those screams she'd heard from one of the other rooms – so miserable and so wretched that she'd been compelled to dash out into the corridor and call out, 'Hello? Is everything okay?'

Nobody had replied. The only sound had come from the slight hum of the automatic light which had flickered on above her head and a gentle ticking from a nearby radiator. The scream apparently hadn't woken up anyone else, and Hope had started to think that she must have imagined it. She was tired, both mentally and emotionally, and it wasn't hard to believe that her mind could be playing tricks on her. Defeated, she'd returned to bed, gazing in wide-eyed agitation at the dark ceiling.

Charlie woke late and rubbed his eyes, reaching instinctively for his watch and then for Hope. She watched him from her position in the chair by the window, where she'd been for the past half-hour, fully dressed and tight-lipped.

He shook his head as he looked at her.

'I'm sorry,' he mumbled.

There was a silence. Hope wasn't sure what she was supposed to say. She knew he was waiting for her to say that she was sorry too, but she didn't. She wasn't sorry – she hadn't done anything wrong. Too many times she'd apologised to Dave during their marriage, too many times she'd let him get away with making her feel like she was the one to blame, when she was anything but. She wasn't going to be that person any more.

'Let's just draw a line through last night, shall we?' she said instead. 'Let's try to have a good day today, explore more of the city.'

He nodded. 'Chuck us that towel, would you?'

He was being overly self-conscious, Hope thought, as she watched him carefully cover himself from the waist down before leaving the bed. Despite her earlier resolve, she felt guilty.

'I'll meet you downstairs,' she said through the closed bathroom door, unable to bear the atmosphere in the room a second longer, and quietly slipped out into the hallway.

'I thought we could go on a boat trip today,' Charlie said. After they'd left the hotel, he'd resolutely put both his hands deep into his coat pockets instead of taking one of hers, but at least he had stopped speaking to her in monosyllables.

'That's a lovely idea,' she trilled, expressing far more enthusiasm than she actually felt. Her earlier irritation had been softened by a hearty breakfast and several cups of strong black coffee, and all she wanted now was for things between them to go back to normal.

The sky was pure white today and looked almost heavy, as if someone had knocked over a tin of gloss paint and obliterated all the scuffs and stains. Hope said as much to Charlie, and he looked up, squinting slightly.

'I think it might snow,' he said. 'It has that feeling today, doesn't it?'

Hope smiled her agreement, thinking privately that the foreboding in the air probably had more to do with the deterioration of their relationship than the threatening weather.

They meandered through the streets of the Old Town in the vague direction of the Vltava River, stopping briefly to admire a man sitting on the edge of a disused water fountain dressed from head to toe in plastic foliage. He'd clamped a small pipe between his teeth that was emitting a steady stream of water into a bucket on his lap, and as they stood and stared he raised a leafy hand in greeting. It was a far cry from some of the naff living statues Hope had seen in Manchester, and she rummaged in her purse for some korunas to drop in his bucket.

'He must be freezing!' she exclaimed, hugging herself as a gust of wind whipped around them.

'Rather him than me,' Charlie agreed, although his

usual playful humour was notably absent, and Hope winced inwardly as she took in the deep worry lines etched between his eyes.

'Are you okay?' she asked, braving a gentle touch on his arm.

Charlie took a deep breath. 'Of course I am,' he said.

After strolling up and down along the bank of the Vltava River, they settled on the Prague Historical River Cruise, which included a free drink and cake as part of the ticket price. The boat, which was wide and finished in beautiful polished wood, sat low in the water, and their two tour guides were dressed in traditional sailor costumes. Hope was enchanted, and only just managed to stop herself blurting out how much Annette would have loved this trip as a child. She must remember that her daughter was an adult now – a woman with her own mind, who no longer needed Hope fussing around her. But being Annette's mum was all Hope knew how to do, and having that role torn away from her so abruptly had left her floating, rudderless, in an ocean of uncertainty.

As the engine began to rumble beneath them and the boat edged its way out into the river, Hope let her head rest tentatively on Charlie's shoulder, and was hugely gratified when he slid his hand across her knee in response. It was nice to be wrapped up under a blanket, a cup of hot wine in her hand as the tour guide chatted away about the history of the city. Hope noticed that this guide didn't mention the special wish you could make on the bridge, instead sticking to the more traditional story about touching the statue for luck. She was fascinated to hear more about St John of Nepomuk, though, whose tomb up in St Vitus's Cathedral was apparently topped by a huge silver monument. In a hushed voice, the guide told them about the saint's supernatural powers, and how his tongue had been discovered still intact inside his skull three whole centuries after his death. Hope thought again of the wish she'd made, and crossed her fingers beneath the blanket.

'And now we have arrived at the Devil's Channel,' announced the guide, with an over-the-top dramatic tone, 'thought to have been created in the twelfth century. Here in Prague, we call it Certovka.'

They were now on the opposite side of the river in the Mala Strana area of the city, and their guide happily informed them that this part was largely unspoilt.

'Hardly any building has taken place here since the late eighteenth century,' he explained, pausing as his audience emitted the 'oohs' and 'ahhhs' which he'd clearly grown accustomed to. 'And we have two medieval mills in this channel; the wheel of one of them still turns to this day.'

There was a series of clicks as the passengers pressed their cameras up against the glass to capture the passing architecture. Hope could only stare, transfixed, trying to picture the city as it had been then, so many centuries before. Had people taken the time to sit on the banks of the Vltava and let their minds stray into an unknown future? Would they have been able to imagine a boatload of tourists staring at their homes?

'Look!' Charlie said suddenly, standing up in his seat so the blanket fell to the floor. 'Isn't that Ollie and Megan?'

Hope got to her feet so she could see out through the glass front of the boat. Ahead of them was a large mill wheel, half its wooden body obscured by water, and beyond that a narrow bridge decorated with . . .

'What are those?' she asked Charlie.

'Padlocks,' the tour guide interrupted. 'People put them there for luck, or to preserve their love for each other.'

'That is definitely Ollie,' Charlie went on, pointing. 'Megan was there a second ago, but she's vanished.'

Hope could see Ollie now, his glasses catching the light as he peered through the gaps between the padlocks. She had developed a real soft spot for him over the past few days, and Megan, too. The two of them seemed to be such a good match, and her romantic side couldn't help but will them to become more than just good friends.

'Oh, there's Megan!' she cried, as a blonde head popped up from somewhere below Ollie's knees. 'I wonder what she was doing on the ground.'

'Well . . .' Charlie gave her a sideways look.

'Don't you dare!' she shrieked, giving him a playful slap as they sat back down again.

Charlie laughed and at last slid his arm around her shoulder and pulled her against him. It felt so good to be forgiven, to be back in the cosy nook of his affection, that Hope could have wept. Thank goodness for Ollie and Megan.

The guide was now chatting away to them about the history of Kampa Island, which was up ahead on the right.

'I love how this place has so many little stories and myths,' Hope told Charlie, lacing her fingers through his. 'It makes me feel as if we're in a fairy tale. I keep expecting to look up and see Rapunzel letting down her hair from one of the windows, or an army of dwarves marching to work over one of these bridges.'

'You are a funny one,' Charlie told her.

'And so are you,' she replied, snuggling up against him.

Whatever that phone call had been, he clearly had his reasons for keeping it a secret from her, and she should accept it. The idea of losing Charlie as well as Annette was just too much for her to face at the moment. They had a chance, the two of them – this was just a tricky fork in the river. She had to believe it.

After all, Hope realised as the boat headed back out towards the Old Town, Charlie was all she had left now.

27

Sophie stared down at the puddle of bile, her arms on each side of the toilet, her chin resting on the seat.

She had skipped breakfast that morning, so there was nothing in her stomach to throw up, but still her body lurched violently forward, desperate in its attempts to rid itself of whatever poison it decreed was inside. The revolting sight below her began to spin, and her eyes filled with tears of frustration.

What was happening to her?

After spotting the beaver down by the river, she had headed out of the city and into the suburbs, her plan being to find the little bakery she and Robin had come across the previous winter. It had been years since she'd needed a map to navigate Prague, but today she seemed unable to find her way around. After walking for over half an hour only to realise that she'd ended up in almost exactly the same place as she'd started, Sophie had begun to feel faint. Her skin was hot to the touch and black spots clouded her vision. Gripping a wall for support, she'd been approached by a young Polish couple, who'd helped her to the nearest café and told her very sternly to sip some sweet, black tea. Her body, however, clearly had other ideas.

She must have been in here for some time, she realised, because her feet had turned numb from the lack of blood flow. There was hardly any room in the cubicle, and her knees were bent awkwardly underneath her body, her jeans still damp from where she'd knelt on the wet ground by the river. The Polish girl had followed her into the bathroom when she ran in here, but Sophie had assured her between bouts of sickness that she would be okay. Whether or not her words had been understood, Sophie didn't know, but the girl had now left her alone.

She could feel the familiar weight of her phone in her coat pocket, and wished she had the strength to take it out and make a call.

She lunged forward as another spasm juddered through her. The room wobbled again, and she let out a weary sob of self-pity. She'd always hated being sick.

Robin would rub her back if he was here and soothe her with nonsense words and silly jokes. He'd hold her hair back off her face, perhaps plait it between nervous fingers, pretending that he wasn't worried about her when he clearly was. He'd had to look after her once before, when they were in Sri Lanka. She'd picked up something nasty during their day out exploring, and had woken in the night in their crowded hostel dormitory with the worst stomach cramps of her life.

'Robin,' she'd whispered, keeping her voice low so as not to wake all the other travellers in the room. 'I'm going to the bathroom. I don't feel well.'

'I'll come with you.' He was already clambering down from his top bunk, ignoring the shaking of her head.

It was a good thing he did, in the end, because her legs gave out long before she reached the end of the corridor.

'Whoa there!' he said, grabbing her underneath her

arms and propping her up. Robin wasn't very tall, but he was strong. And, as he pointed out to her later, she weighed almost nothing.

They made it to the toilet just in time for her to heave up the remnants of their dinner, all the time crying out because the pain in her stomach was so bad. As the vomiting increased and her temperature soared, Sophie slipped rapidly into a fever of which she had absolutely no memory afterwards. Robin had described it to her days later – how she'd flailed and wept and begged him to make it stop. How she'd coughed and spluttered and sobbed in agony. It was the worst six hours of his life, he told her, but he'd never once left her side.

When she'd stopped being sick but was still horribly feverish, Robin had tried to gently persuade her to return to the dormitory so she could rest, but Sophie had refused. The thought of the covers touching her burning hot skin was unbearable. She wanted to sleep right there, on the dirty cold tiles, and no amount of begging by Robin would change her mind. In the end, rather than battle with her, he'd simply fetched two pillows and lain down on the floor next to her, running his fingers gently through her hair and stroking a single finger along her spine. The incessant shaking soon dissolved into shivers, and then, finally, blissfully, into slumber, and still Robin stayed beside her.

'You looked so at peace on that grotty floor,' he told her later. 'I didn't have it in me to move you. I was so scared that you'd feel that pain again – I wanted more than anything to take it away from you, to have it myself instead.'

That was Robin, always stepping forward to ease her suffering; always far more willing to feel pain himself than watch her go through it. And it was a turning point for Sophie, too, because she realised afterwards that Robin was the only person she'd really wanted in her time of need. Not her mum or her dad or any of her friends – just Robin. Nobody else would do.

But she'd never been sick in Prague before – not even after those misguided evenings spent sampling the city's wide variety of absinthe. And certainly not like this. It felt as if her body was trying to cleanse itself from the inside out, and she had no control over what was happening.

There was a crash as the door to the toilets opened and the sound of voices as two girls – Italian, she guessed from their accents – went into the stalls on either side of her. Sophie realised that her feet must be visible under the partition wall, and forced herself to shuffle on to her knees, using the toilet bowl to steady herself as the feeling slowly seeped back into her lower legs. By the time the girls were flushing and then washing their hands, Sophie was back up in a sitting position, wiping her face with tissue paper and taking deep breaths to quell the nausea.

She tried not to think of the germs she had probably picked up, and as soon as she heard the Italians leave, she stumbled across to the basin and turned on the hot tap to wash her hands. The water turned her skin pink and she winced with discomfort, but at least she felt able to stand again. Her heart had slowed its relentless crashing and there was a bit of colour in her cheeks. She would be fine, she reassured herself. She'd get something to eat, and then she'd be fine.

It was late afternoon now, and the sky had turned from white to a putty shade of grey. Sophie had thought it would snow, but now it seemed more likely that rain was on its way. She felt disoriented after spending such a long time bent over the toilet, and stepping out into the cold air felt like she had been slammed against a brick wall. She stopped to put her gloves on and pulled Robin's hat down so far over her ears that she could barely see where she was going. No matter how many layers she piled on in the morning, the cold always seemed to work its way through each and every one, until her very bones felt like icicles. She knew it must be below freezing, but how far below? She had never known Prague to feel this cold before.

There was a cart selling pretzels up ahead, and Sophie bought a large plain one and nibbled at it as she made her slow way back into the hub of the city. The pavements in this part of Prague were wide and pebbled, and the road beside her was a piebald pattern of black concrete and frozen puddles. Halfway up the hill, overlooked by the towering spires of St Vitus's Cathedral, there was a wide rectangular viewing platform. Tourists stood in clusters around the edges, taking it in turns to pose for a photo with the city spread out behind them. Pigeons picked their way through the morsels of discarded food around the rubbish bins, paying no attention to the constant footfall around them.

Sophie broke off a small piece of pretzel and tossed it

in their direction, watching as a wily seagull swooped down as if from nowhere, scattering its moonwalking companions with an indignant squawk. Unlike their cousins over in London, the pigeons here looked sleek and clean, their claws perfectly formed and their eyes bright. Sophie wondered why some of them stayed through the winter rather than migrating. She would give anything for some sunshine right now; something to reheat her limbs and offer her some comfort.

By the time she reached the turnstiles marking the entrance to Golden Lane, the pretzel was doing the trick and she was starting to feel a bit more human again. It now seemed absurd that she had ever been sick in the first place.

This narrow little lane was one of her favourite places in the city, and she happily handed over her entrance fee to the smiling man in the booth. He was wrapped up against the cold, too, in what looked like at least three scarves and two coats, and he shivered for effect when he caught her looking.

Sophie knew from earlier trips to Prague that the Golden Lane was named after the goldsmiths who lived here back in the seventeenth century, and that the collection of tiny two-storey houses had been built right into the arches of the castle walls.

Each little abode was painted a different colour, and the palette varied from yellow to blue to red and even pink. Most of the houses were now gift shops or galleries, but some still remained closed to the prying eyes of the public. Sophie peered through the latticed window of one shop selling Bohemian glass, taking in the riot of colour on the shelves. The light inside was arranged to show the ornaments at their most alluring, and she could see the plan working its magic on the tourists. She and Robin had bought their first piece of Prague glassware the previous year. It was just a simple blue bowl, but she loved how it looked in the centre of the chest of drawers in their bedroom. When she opened the curtains in the morning, the light would stream in and the bowl would glow, as if lit up from within.

A gust of wind scurried down the lane, and Sophie felt it pass right through her like an errant ghost. She often thought that Prague must be haunted, given its age and bloody history, but this didn't bother her in the slightest. On the contrary, she found it hard to imagine anyone in Prague being vengeful, whether they were spirit or still living. The city was a place of hope and of happiness; of magic and wishes and beauty. It was this that drew her and Robin back, time and time again. In all the places they'd visited around the world, none compelled them as much as Prague – and their belief in this place and its magic was one of the things they'd held on to over the years. Sophie could feel the spirit of the city creeping into her as it always did, the sense of history a comfort and the promise of dreams coming true a tonic to her melancholy.

She stayed on Golden Lane until dusk crept up behind daylight and threw its grey shroud over the sky. By now her limbs were stiff with cold and her breath was pooling into the air like smoke. Another day almost over, another cycle of the clock complete. The golden hands of the clock on St Vitus's Cathedral informed her that she had just a few hours until she had to meet the others as arranged.

The rain finally started as she made her way back past the viewing platform, the fat droplets chasing a group of tourists down the hill. She looked up just in time to see a flash of untidy blond hair tucked into the collar of a coat.

'Robin!' she said, loud enough to cause several people to stop and stare. Pushing her way through them, Sophie searched desperately for the man she'd just seen, but he seemed to have vanished completely. There were woolly hats of all colours, a blond head here and a hastily opened umbrella there, but no Robin. Feeling stupid, Sophie put her chin down and hunched her shoulders, slipping off the edge of the pavement and almost losing her footing entirely as her boot landed in an icy puddle. The sudden lurch seemed to unsettle her guts, and an immediate coldness started to creep through her now-shaking legs.

She was going to be sick again.

Staggering into people and almost blinded by a combination of nausea and falling rain, Sophie made it to the bottom of the hill and straight through the door of the first restaurant in her path. She barely acknowledged the waitress who stepped forward to greet her, lunging instead for the sign indicating the toilet and clamping a gloved hand over her mouth.

As she made her way unsteadily through the tables and pushed open the heavy wooden door that led to the ladies, she was vaguely aware of someone saying her name, and then she was on her knees on the cold, tiled floor again, and all she was aware of was pain.

28

'"Drink the life!"'

'What does that even mean?' asked Megan, a laugh punctuating her question like a jolly exclamation mark.

'What about this one?' Ollie went on, pointing above her head. '"Smile when you read this".' The message was written in blue pen, and a smiley face had been added for good measure.

'I am smiling,' Megan said, searching the surface of the wall for more amusing graffiti. 'Oh look – here's one: "Wolf pack 2002. Don't stop believing". Believing in what, do you reckon?'

'In the wolf pack, of course,' Ollie said with a grin, glancing up to the top of the wall before turning to her and taking her hands in his.

'Megan Spencer,' he began, 'how can I express that you are awesome?'

For a few beats, she flushed at the close contact and the intensity in his eyes, but then she recognised the gleam of humour that was also there. Glancing up to where he had been looking, she saw the same question written above their heads in thick black letters, the yellow paint behind them making the words stand out against the brick.

'I like this one,' she told him, coughing to mask the slight wobble in her voice. Taking back her hands, she walked along the wall and pointed upwards.

'"May the best of your past be the worst of your future".'

'Poetic.' Ollie grinned at her.

'I like it,' she repeated. 'It's a nice notion, isn't it? The idea that the future will be better than the past. What could be more inspirational than that?'

Ollie nodded. 'I still prefer the wolf pack,' he told her. 'You know, just for the sheer entertainment value.'

Megan thought about the gloomier moments of her own past, and how every single second since she'd made the decision to walk away from Andre had been a better one. There had been times with him, especially in the early days of their relationship, when she'd genuinely believed that she was happier than she ever had been – or ever could be. How ludicrous that seemed now. If she'd stayed with Andre, she realised, she might never have found her way to Prague. Or to Ollie, for that matter. The idea of a life with no Ollie in it was a horrible one, and Megan felt her cheeks heat up as the realisation took hold of her.

They'd reached the centre of the long, high wall now, where a black and white painting of John Lennon's face peered out at them from among the surrounding graffiti. He had no hair, chin or visible cheeks, but it was still undeniably the Beatles star. Megan knew she would recognise those kind, wise eyes behind the tell-tale round-rimmed glasses anywhere, and she immediately lifted her camera.

'Over here,' Ollie called a few minutes later. He'd found another poetic quote scrawled on the concrete in permanent marker, and he read it out to her as she crouched down beside him to get a better angle.

'"Don't tell me the sky's the limit, when there are footprints on the moon". Now that is deep.'

'I thought you'd love all this stuff,' Megan said, genuinely surprised at the irony in his tone. 'You're all about the positivity usually.'

'I still am.' Ollie was indignant. 'Maybe I've just seen too many inspirational quotes on Instagram.'

'Oh God, I know exactly what you mean,' she agreed. 'But I prefer reading them here on this wall to off an app on my phone. They seem less cheesy somehow. Less try-hard and in your face.'

'If there's anyone I know who would leave footprints on the moon, it's you,' Ollie told her, turning from the wall and fixing her with one of his serious-teacher expressions.

'Don't be daft.' She batted away the compliment with a flick of her wrist.

'I mean it,' he said, taking a step towards her and reaching out a gloved hand to touch her cheek. 'You're the most determined woman I've ever met, Megs. This whole exhibition you have planned is just incredible – even more so now that I know how much you've had to overcome to get to this point. Honestly, you're an inspiration.'

'Oh shush!' Megan was blushing so much now that she no longer even felt cold.

'Seriously.' There was that look again. Ollie hadn't taken his hand away from the side of her face, but Megan found she enjoyed the feel of it there, so firm but still gentle. 'I'd be tempted to ask you into the school to speak to the kids about all your achievements, but I'm not sure if I can trust you not to swear.'

'Bloody cheek!' She laughed.

Ollie removed his hand at last. 'I rest my case.'

Any awkwardness that might have been churning in the air between them was interrupted by a gust of wind so cold that it actually caused Megan to shiver from head to toe like a jelly on a bulldozer. Rubbing her hands over the tops of her arms and stamping her feet, she turned her attention back to the wall.

'Oh, this is cute,' she said a minute later, lowering the camera so Ollie could read it over her head. '"Bob loves Bug – now and forever".'

'Very sweet,' he agreed. 'Bob and Bug sound like they could be cartoon characters. I'm pretty sure there's a children's storybook with a character called Bug, who oddly isn't an insect. In fact, I think he's a dog. Honestly, kids' books are weird.'

He took a few steps back and watched Megan as she continued to snap away, the mechanical clicking of her camera holding a metaphorical hand up to the silence. There was a lot of wall to cover, and she didn't want to miss any of it. Each of these drawings and scribbles had their own story, their own individual meaning, and she wanted to capture as many as she possibly could for her exhibition.

The people who had come here and made their mark on the John Lennon Wall had done so with a wish in their heart, a sense of hope that their words would make a difference. Megan could feel the emotions radiating out from the cold stone, the colours intermingling in an untidy mess of love, desire, anger and pain. There was a rawness to the place that she loved, but there was also a sense of constraint. This was a place where it was permitted and even encouraged to make a statement, and as such there was an unbroken promise that whatever you put here would remain. Layer upon layer of words and images and feelings – it was almost overwhelming.

She couldn't be sure how long she'd been taking photos, but when she finally took a step back and looked again for Ollie, he was holding two steaming cups in his hands.

'I went to get tea,' he told her. 'It's bloody freezing standing here, watching you be all Rankin.'

She opened her mouth to retort, but he cut across her.

'Not that I'm complaining. You know I love watching you work. It's mesmerising, fascinating and, well, it's pretty awesome.'

'Oh, stop that,' she told him, but her smile was making her face ache.

Something was different between the two of them today. At times when she was with Ollie, Megan felt unsure of how to be – the reminder of that first night when she'd put a halt to the romantic progression of their relationship always lingering in the background, like a nervous toddler behind the legs of its mother. But today, and actually on every day since they'd arrived in Prague, she didn't feel that same sense of pressure or confusion. What she did feel was content, but it was more than that. She was starting to feel drawn to Ollie in a way that felt like more than the gentle pull of friendship, and increasingly she found herself aware of exactly where he was – of how close he might be to her, how easy it would be for her to reach out and touch him. Their relationship had always been seasoned with mutual banter and teasing, but today they were both being far more mellow with each other – almost tender at times – and far from feeling unnatural or uncomfortable, Megan sensed a part of herself thawing. It may be below freezing in this city, but her insides were bubbling away like a milk frother.

'Did Charlie say anything to you last night?' she asked him now, accepting her cup of tea with a grateful smile. It was lemon and honey, and smelled delicious.

'About what?' he asked, casually rearranging the strap of her camera which had twisted on her neck.

'Thanks,' she said, wriggling to free her trapped strands of hair. 'I mean about that phone call, which he seemed so keen to keep a secret.'

'He didn't mention it, and I didn't like to ask,' Ollie told her, nudging her in the ribs as a particularly overenthusiastic Segway driver almost came a cropper in front of John Lennon's face.

'Hope didn't really say anything to us, either,' Megan said, blowing on her tea to cool it down. 'She seemed upset, though.'

'Charlie too,' Ollie said, pausing to take a sip. 'He did tell me how much he loved Hope, though, and how much he wanted to take care of her. It's obvious that he's besotted.'

'I know what you mean,' Megan said, but she frowned as she remembered the look on the older woman's face the night before when she'd been urging Megan to follow her heart, and telling her that she must put herself first. Was Hope starting to have doubts about Charlie?

'Why do relationships always end up being so complicated?' Ollie asked now. 'Charlie and Hope clearly love each other, so why can't that just be enough? Why are they falling out over nothing?'

'Maybe it's not nothing to her,' Megan pointed out, remembering the stricken look on Hope's face when she realised Charlie had slipped away to make that phone call. 'And I think it's all well and good to hold love up as some sort of medal, but that's just the beginning of making something work, surely? Love is at its best when it's uncomplicated.'

'What do you mean?' Ollie pressed. He'd brought his cup of tea up to his mouth, and the steam coming off the top had turned the lenses of his glasses white in the cold.

She sighed, suddenly reluctant to be in this territory with him. 'I just mean that you can love someone all you want, but sometimes that isn't enough.'

'It should be,' Ollie said simply.

'Perhaps.' She shrugged again and looked up at him. His lips were beginning to chap in the cold, and she reached into her bag for the tin of salve she carried everywhere and offered it to him. 'But look at Romeo and Juliet, Rose and Jack on the *Titantic*, Ross and Rachel from *Friends* – they all loved each other, but there were other factors to consider.'

'You do realise those are all fictional characters?' Ollie was looking at her with ill-disguised bemusement as he dug a finger into her proffered tin.

'Durr.' She swiped an arm at him. 'Of course I do. But I'm just using those as examples. You only have to look at poetry and literature from across the ages to understand that the concept of love has been puzzling people since the dawn of time.'

'That's true.' Ollie took her empty cup from her hands and looked around them for a bin. 'But it's not much of a comfort.'

'Look at Sophie and her fiancé. What's his name again?'

Ollie thought for a moment. 'Robert? No, Robin!'

'Yes, that's it. Look at those two. They fell in love pretty much at first sight and haven't looked back since. The way she talks about him, you'd think they were a single entity rather than two people living their own lives.'

'It's adorable,' Ollie said, a smile playing on his lips as they left the wall behind and strolled back towards the river.

'Perhaps.' Megan waited a few beats before continuing. 'But that level of devotion makes me feel uneasy. I mean, what if he cheats on her or does something unforgivable like Andre did to me? What would she do without him? She's put so much of herself into him that I'd worry there would be nothing left for her.'

'I guess she just trusts him,' Ollie replied, but he didn't sound as sure as he had before.

'I suppose she must,' Megan said, stepping sideways to avoid a puddle and bashing against him. Ollie's response was to lean his body back against hers, and she felt that tingle again. She wished he would hold her hand as he had earlier, or put his arm around her to keep her warm, as Hope had done with Sophie. Shaking her head and taking a determined step away from him again, she forced her mind back to the subject they were discussing.

'I just hope he feels the same way, this Robin bloke,' she

said. 'I hardly know the girl, but for some reason the thought of Sophie being upset just kills me.'

'I know what you mean.' Ollie was nodding. 'She reminds me of this baby bird we found in the playground last spring. The kids were adamant that we nurse the poor little thing back to health, but of course it never made it through the first night. I sat up with it and tried to feed it bread soaked in warm milk, but its tiny body was just so fragile and—' He stopped abruptly, and Megan looked up to find his eyes shining beneath his glasses.

'Are you okay?' she asked, finally giving in to the nagging urge in her limbs and sneaking a hand into his.

Ollie looked down at their entwined fingers in surprise, then sniffed.

'I'm fine,' he assured her. 'Now I don't know about you, but I could eat a small building. Shall we wander up towards the castle and stop for a very late lunch?'

In that moment, and as suddenly as the sharp-edged gusts of wind that kept assaulting them, Megan desperately wanted Ollie to kiss her, but instead she nodded, braving a light squeeze through the layers of gloves.

'Sounds good to me.'

By the time they'd meandered slowly through the slush-splattered streets of Mala Strana and up past the impressive facade of St Nicholas Church, Megan's hand had grown hot with longing. Ollie hadn't let go of her for a second, and she was finding it increasingly difficult to ignore the need that had begun to pulse through her. She could blame the strong tea on top of a small breakfast, but in truth she knew what was happening. After all, she hadn't put a stop to that kiss with Ollie all those months ago because she wasn't attracted to him – it had been more complicated than that. The truth was that she was extremely attracted to him, and she wasn't sure how much longer she would be able to keep that information to herself.

'This place looks nice,' Ollie said, his words yanking apart the thick curtains of lust that had closed up around her.

The inside of the restaurant was pleasingly traditional, with heavy wooden furniture, giant pretzels hanging from their specially made stands in the centre of each table and a delicious smell of goulash and hot wine in the air.

They were shown to a small table at the back, and Ollie let go of her hand as they took off their coats, hats and scarves, only to snatch it up again as soon as they sat down. Megan knew she should pull away and break the undeniable spell that had somehow been conjured up between them, but she didn't. It felt too nice to have him touch her; she wanted to feel him, skin against skin. For once in her life, she was happy to be losing control of the situation, and a thrill trickled through her as she pictured where it could potentially end.

'What are you going to get?' Ollie asked. He was peering at her curiously, and she wondered if her expression was giving her away. She was surprised there wasn't a line of drool connecting her bottom lip to the table.

'Oh, probably goulash.' She narrowed her eyes at his amusement. 'What? I'm an addict, okay? What's wrong with a girl liking a bit of meat every once in a while?'

'Oh.' Ollie licked his lips as he looked at her, his eyes

wide with the cheeky sense of humour she'd loved so much when they first met. 'There's definitely nothing wrong with that. In fact— Hang on – is that Sophie? Sophie!'

Megan was aware of a blur of colour as Sophie and her multi-coloured hat clattered past them at speed. She hesitated for just a split second in front of the toilet door, her hand over her mouth, and then she was gone.

Ollie let go of Megan's hand.

'She didn't look well, did she?'

Megan looked over her shoulder at the door.

'No, she didn't.'

They paused for a moment, Megan allowing herself to look right into his eyes. Where there had been playfulness and desire just a few seconds ago, there was now nothing but concern, and she pushed back her chair.

'I'm going to go and see if she's okay. Order for me, will you?'

He nodded, worry etched on his face, and Megan forced herself not to feel dismayed. Poor Sophie couldn't help the fact that she'd interrupted a nice moment between the two of them. And anyway, she told herself sternly, it was probably best that she not venture down this path with Ollie – it would only confuse things.

But as she pushed her way through the door towards the toilets, Megan could still feel the warmth of his hand in her own.

29

'Is that pressure okay?'

'It's perfect.'

Hope stretched out her toes and looped her fingers together under the blanket. It had been Charlie's suggestion that she pop in for a hand, head and foot massage at one of Prague's many drop-in parlours. After the bad night's sleep she'd had, it would do her good to relax a bit. She couldn't argue with that. Plus, she wanted to please him after the rocky start to their day, so for once she let him treat her without complaint.

It was so warm in here, and Hope felt her eyelids grow heavy as the young Thai girl slid expert fingers through her hair, down the back of her neck and across her bare shoulders. She'd taken off her jumper and rolled down the straps of her bra as instructed, the blanket providing a barrier from the prying eyes of the passing public. This wasn't a massage parlour like any Hope had ever been in before, but they seemed to be dotted around everywhere in the touristy areas of the city. Each one had a ridiculously over-the-top statue of a dragon by the entrance, painted a lurid shade of bright green.

Charlie had recovered some of his good humour since the boat trip, and as they wandered down the bank of the Vltava to the Jewish Quarter to visit the old cemetery and synagogue, he'd taken her hand in his again. Hope had been moved to tears by the thousands of headstones, stacked so close together in the small courtyard that they were almost on top of each other, and she was genuinely horrified to discover that due to a lack of burial space, some graves ran twelve deep.

Charlie did his best to distract her, pointing out how the hands on the synagogue clock looked like the seats of a bicycle, how the winter flowers were pushing their way through the snow in the banks around the edge of the cemetery, and the tiny birds that were playing a game of hide-and-seek among the monuments. It was too late, though, because a tangle of confusion had already taken root in Hope's mind.

There was nothing quite like a graveyard to make you evaluate your own life and where it was heading, and Hope realised now that her own had come to a standstill.

If she really had lost Annette, as she feared she had, then what was next for her? Was she destined to become Charlie's wife and swap one household's washing and cooking for another? Surely there had to be more than that. Maybe now was the time to do something for herself. She thought back to what Megan had said over drinks in the square, about how she wanted to achieve her ambitions without a man by her side. Hope had assumed up to now that she was afraid to be on her own, that she wouldn't know who to be, but being here in Prague had made her consider that perhaps she would be okay. Or better than that, she might even be happier than she was with Charlie.

Wondering which path was best was becoming exhausting, though, and it didn't help that wherever she seemed to look in Prague there was a clock. What had felt charming when she first arrived now felt like a constant taunt. Time was ticking past – time away from Annette, time that she could be using to sort her life out. She almost felt as if she could hear the seconds all ticking away inside her head.

Assuming that her melancholy was down to their surroundings, Charlie had hurried Hope out of the cemetery and back into the Old Town, where the Christmas Market provided a welcome change in atmosphere. Once there, he bought her a cup of hot grog and a traditional sugary Czech Danish called a *trdelnik*, and Hope, who hadn't even realised that she was hungry, gobbled it down in a few bites. It was then that Charlie had suggested the massage.

'What are you going to do while I'm in there?' she asked when they reached the doorway guarded by its dragon.

'Oh, you know, just grab a coffee – nothing special.'

She nodded, watching him weave his way slowly through the groups of tourists as he headed back in the direction of the square. How simple life would be if happiness were as attainable as Charlie seemed to think it was. She could vaguely remember a time when she'd been overwhelmed with how happy she felt, years ago, in the months leading up to her wedding. Dave had been so attentive in the early days of their relationship – she had felt as if she was walking on air, buoyed as she was by the strength of his love for her. It had all seemed so simple: he loved her, she loved him, and they would live happily together until the end of their lives. But then Annette had arrived.

Even Hope had been surprised by just how hard she

fell for her baby daughter. It was an immediate, urgent and all-consuming love, one that left little room for anyone else, and one that Dave found difficult to understand. He loved Annette, of course he did, but it wasn't the same fearful, borderline neurotic love that Hope was experiencing. She began to find excuses not to let him hold her precious bundle, inexplicably concerned that he wouldn't do it right. It was her job, she would tell him. She was Annette's mother, she had carried her, she had given birth to her – it was her right.

Dave was sympathetic at first, muttering things about 'bloody hormones' under his breath, but when Annette reached her first birthday and Hope was still a clinging, panicking mess, he'd put his foot down and insisted she go and talk to someone. Hope tried a few sessions, but found the therapist patronising and hated being separated from her daughter, so refused to go back. It was the start of the arguments between them that had continued for the best part of two decades, until eventually they both retreated into themselves, weary of battling but too stubborn to admit defeat.

Hope clung fiercely to her role as mother and wife, never imagining that she wanted to do anything else – especially since Dave had refused unequivocally to try for a second child. Hope could still remember the day he'd gone to have a vasectomy with painful clarity. She had begged him to reconsider, but his mind had been made up, and any lingering strands of love that remained at that time were swiftly washed away. Annette had only been ten at the time, on the verge of going to secondary school and only just coming out from her favourite hiding place behind Hope's legs. It was inconceivable to shatter her world at such a pivotal moment, and Hope forced herself to bury the smouldering resentment she felt towards Dave. After a time, the two of them settled into a stilted routine of pretend normality, and it wasn't until Annette moved out that the harsh reality set in. Both of them were guilty of ignoring what was going on, and Hope accepted now that she should have left Dave then. She had been a coward, but then so had he. Her affair with Charlie had been her way of lashing out, her misguided payback for what Dave had done all those years before, but now it had spiralled out of control and ended up in a situation that Hope wasn't sure she really wanted.

'We are finished.'

Hope snapped her eyes open and pushed the past from her mind.

'Thank you. That was lovely – just what I needed.'

Charlie was waiting for her in the doorway, a faraway look on his face. Hope wondered if he, too, had been giving their relationship some thought. Did he wake up every day and wonder how this had happened, just as she did?

'I think we need to talk,' she said as soon as she reached him, not realising what words were going to spill out until she uttered them.

Charlie gave her a grim smile. 'I know we do, but how about we save it until tomorrow? Let's just have a nice time tonight, try to forget all the other stuff for a few hours.'

He looked so handsome and sincere, Hope felt her resolve weakening.

'Okay.' She smiled back.

'There's a jazz band playing in the square,' he told her, looking over his shoulder. 'How about we start there?'

As they slipped and slid together across the cobbles, the late-afternoon air scratching its icy spindles across their exposed cheeks, Hope looked up and saw the gold hands of a clock illuminated by a trickle of sunlight.

30

'Are you okay in there?'

There was a gentle tapping on the door of the toilet cubicle and Sophie groaned. The remains of her soft pretzel bobbed on the surface of the water below her, half-digested and stringy. She closed her eyes.

'It's Megan. Are you sick?'

'I'm okay,' Sophie managed, yanking the flush and pulling herself up off the floor for the second time that day. Whatever germ it was that had worked its way into her system, it meant business.

When Sophie emerged, Megan was leaning against the wall by the basin, her blonde hair a tangled mess and an expression of genuine concern on her face.

'You don't sound very okay,' she said.

'It's just something I ate,' muttered Sophie, sucking in her breath as the hot water from the tap made contact with the cold skin of her hands. Her mouth was dry and her throat itched unpleasantly, but she still forced herself to smile at Megan.

'Listen.' Megan took a step towards her and their eyes met in the mirror. 'It's none of my business, but are you . . . You know?'

Sophie coughed out a bark of laughter. 'No!'

'Sorry. I shouldn't have asked. My brain always has been a good few steps behind my gob.'

'Don't be sorry.' Sophie smiled at her properly this time. 'I would probably have thought the same thing – but it's not that. I feel fine now, anyway,' she lied. 'Probably too much wine last night.'

'We did drink a fair amount,' Megan agreed.

They left the bathroom together and headed back up the stairs. As soon as he saw them, Ollie leapt up from his chair and offered it to Sophie.

'There's no need.' She held up a hand. 'I'm fine, honestly.'

Ollie looked across at Megan for confirmation.

'Well, at least join us then?' he offered, pulling out a third chair from a nearby table that was unoccupied. 'I've ordered us lunch – plus some strudel, obviously,' he told Megan.

'I'm not really hungry,' Sophie tried again.

'Just some water then, or a tea?' Megan insisted, steering her gently into the seat. 'It's raining outside, and you look so pale. Once we're done here, we'll walk you back to the hotel so you can rest properly, won't we, Ollie?'

He nodded, reaching over to pat Sophie's arm. The two of them seemed different today, she realised. Closer somehow, not bickering in their usual way. Megan had a softness to her that Sophie hadn't seen yet, and it was nice. She forced herself to ignore the creeping feelings of sickness that were threatening to overwhelm her again, and stared instead at the menu.

The waitress appeared with beer for Ollie and Megan, so Sophie ordered herself a tea as instructed. It would undoubtedly make her sick again, but she supposed that she should at least try. Her broken night's sleep and the constant nausea had left her feeling woozy, and she was worried that she might faint. She watched through hazy eyes as Ollie slid his hand across the table and picked up a few of Megan's outstretched fingers, rubbing them lightly between his own. While Megan didn't reciprocate, Sophie noticed that she didn't pull her hand away either. She merely tensed her shoulders a fraction and sipped her drink. So, her earlier assumption about Ollie's feelings had been right, but she couldn't quite work out whether or not Megan felt the same way. Sophie hoped she did.

Witnessing the casual way that Ollie touched her, almost as if it was a need rather than a choice, something he did without thinking, like scratching his nose or yawning, made Sophie yearn for Robin. The two of them were always touching one another when they were together, a trail of fingertips across a cheek, the brush of a hand across a thigh or the rub of a foot against another. It was impossible for the two of them to be in the same room together and not come into contact.

Ollie didn't let go of Megan's fingers until their food arrived, and then Sophie could sense that he only relinquished them with reluctance. She watched as Megan paused, curled her fingers inwards, then brought her hand up to her face, stroking herself almost absent-mindedly.

'I really should leave you two alone,' Sophie said, pushing her empty cup and saucer to one side. 'I don't want to intrude.'

'You're not intruding,' Megan was quick to reply. 'Honestly – I'm sick of Ollie's company anyway. He's a right bore, you know?'

She was obviously teasing, and Ollie balled up a nugget of bread and threw it at her across the table.

'Tell us more about your travels,' Megan pushed, bringing her soup spoon up to her mouth. 'Didn't you say you'd been around the world?'

Sophie nodded. 'That's right. I went with Robin.'

'Tell us all about it,' Megan said again. 'I want to know where to go on my next holiday.'

And so Sophie started talking. She told them about the giant statue of Buddha she and Robin had visited in Sri Lanka, about how it was common over there to see stray cows wandering around in the cities, and pass trucks with an elephant tethered in a trailer on the back. She told them about how the sun in Los Angeles sits low in the sky, casting an eerie light over the beaches and skyscrapers, making you squint almost constantly, as if you've just woken up.

Megan, in particular, was fascinated by this, the photographer in her itching to experience it for herself. Ollie was more interested in what the people were like in other countries, asking her endless questions about poverty and culture. Megan was far more concerned with which places were the most beautiful, the most picturesque, and Sophie saw her eyes widen as she described places like Phuket, New Zealand and Buenos Aires.

'I must travel more,' Megan said, her voice dreamy. 'No wonder I never feel inspired, living in London.'

'London has its moments,' said Ollie. 'Richmond Park is stunning – and what about the Thames at sunset?'

'London just has a noise to it,' Megan said, flapping her arms in agitation. 'There never seems to be a respite from all the people and traffic and smog. I can hear it in all the photos I take, and it makes me hate them.'

'Really?' Ollie looked genuinely surprised to hear her

say this, and Sophie wondered how often they had talked about her work. She'd only known Megan a few days, but she could tell that her new acquaintance was passionate about what she did. And she thought she could understand what Megan said about a photograph feeling noisy. You found it in paintings all the time, after all, and London was one of the busiest and loudest cities in the world.

'You know I hate most of the photos I take,' Megan was saying now, her tone one of resignation rather than irritation. 'I can't always get the emotions to translate.'

'I think your work is amazing,' Ollie told her, and Sophie smiled. He was such a nice man, and his devotion to Megan really didn't have a ceiling. If only she could see that and just accept it. Sophie had always accepted the fact that Robin loved her, and she him, even if she had experienced the odd wobble over the years. It had never felt like a struggle, their relationship. She heard friends talk about the difficulties they went through, their constant internal battle with themselves over whether or not they were truly happy, or if there was something or someone better out there for them. There was nobody and nothing better out there for Sophie – Robin was all she needed, and she'd never doubted that fact for even a second.

Ollie had now pulled up Megan's website on his phone and was showing Sophie some of the photos. He was right, they were spectacular, but clearly Megan didn't agree.

'I want people to have an emotional reaction to my work,' she was telling Sophie now. 'I know people are impressed with my angles and perspective, and with how I use light – but that's all so dry and technical. I want people to be moved by what I do, just like I am when I'm taking the photo in the first place.'

'Have you been moved by Prague?' Sophie asked, already knowing the answer.

'Oh, yes!' Megan cried, mopping up the last of her soup with a chunk of bread. 'It's so beautiful here, I feel like I've barely put my camera down. Everywhere you go, there's a moment to capture. I just hope I can do the place justice.'

'I'm sure you will,' Ollie said. His hand was back on the table top, Sophie noticed, poised and ready to reach over and touch Megan again. This was what he must love about her the most – her passion. It was quite a rare quality, passion, and Sophie could understand why people who didn't have it themselves were drawn to those that did. A person with passion, such as Megan and Robin, always burned so much brighter than the rest, so it was no wonder that they always found themselves surrounded by others, all keen for some of that fiery sheen to rub off on them.

Megan signalled for the bill, waving away Sophie's offer of payment – 'You only had a tea!' – and the three of them left the restaurant and headed in the direction of the hotel.

The Charles Bridge was throbbing with tourists, each one of them wearing a hat and gloves to keep out the chilly air. The earlier clouds had shifted apart a fraction, and the dusky sky was now a murky mixture of greys. The water of the River Vltava below them was a deep, impenetrable slate, its surface broken only by the white flashes of seagulls. Every so often the birds would let out a shrill squawk and fly up above the bridge, ducking and swirling to catch morsels of food that had either been dropped or were being tossed into the air on purpose.

Pigeons lined the low walls on either side of the vast stone structure, playing a game of copycat with the many statues dotted along beside them. Megan had her camera up to her face and was grinning behind the lens as she snapped away. Ollie walked just behind Sophie, his eyes on her rather than the scenery, almost as if he feared she might keel over at any moment.

'I'm feeling much better now,' she told him, trying to scatter a sprinkle of truth in amongst her words. The tea had mercifully stayed down, and the three sugars she'd heaped into it were beginning to take effect. Her hands had stopped shaking now, but she still felt unsteady. It was as if the ground below her feet were nothing more than the closed mouth of a terrifying monster, content to go hungry for now, but always ready to open its jaws and swallow her whole.

She stepped out of the way just in time to avoid being clouted by yet another selfie stick and crashed into Ollie, who had come to a standstill right behind her. Megan, it seemed, had found something exciting on the wall of the bridge and was beckoning for them both to join her.

'Is this what Hope was telling us about?' she asked them, as soon as they were in range. Sophie looked down to where Megan's gloved hand was resting, the brushed gold of the two-armed cross dulled by the pale early evening light.

'I think it must be.' Ollie had answered before Sophie had a chance, so instead she stood nodding her agreement, watching as Megan whipped off her glove and ran her fingers over each of the five golden stars in turn.

'What are you going to wish for?' asked Ollie. He sounded almost hopeful.

Megan paused, then closed her eyes, her lips moving soundlessly, her bare fingers still touching the cross.

'There.' She smiled as she opened her eyes. 'All done.'

'Come on, then!' Ollie urged. 'Don't keep us in suspense.'

'I can't tell you what I wished for.' Megan was aghast. 'If you tell people your wishes, then they don't ever come true – everyone knows that.'

They both turned to Sophie, but she couldn't reply. Her legs had suddenly turned to tissue paper beneath her, and she crumpled on to the cobbles like a dry autumn leaf.

'Jesus!' Ollie caught her just before she went right over, and Megan rushed across and knelt beside them.

'I think we need to find you a doctor,' she said, her face creased with worry. 'Someone at the hotel will know how to get hold of one.'

Sophie shook her head weakly from side to side.

'No. I'm fine.'

'Come on.' Ollie ignored her protestations and hoisted her up. Handing his rucksack to Megan, he crouched down and instructed Sophie to clamber on to his back.

'I'll piggyback you to the hotel,' he told her. 'It's the most sensible idea. You can have a nap, then if you still feel ill this evening, we'll help you find a doctor. Deal?'

Sophie could see that she had very little choice in the matter, so she climbed on, her stomach groaning in protest as Ollie shuffled her up into a more comfortable position.

'I might stay here and take a few more photos,' Megan said, patting Sophie gently in the small of her back. 'Shall I meet you in that bar, Don Pisto's, in half an hour or so?'

Ollie agreed, and Sophie watched from her perch up on his back as he picked up Megan's hand and gave it another squeeze. She knew people were turning to look at her, but she didn't care. It felt nice to be up here, shielded from the world by the bulk of Ollie's six-foot frame. She wanted to thank him, tell him how grateful she was, how she felt protected and secure, but her nausea was so acute that she didn't dare even open her mouth.

As Ollie bounded off along the Charles Bridge, his fingers laced together across his front to stop her legs from slipping, Sophie thought how nice it would be if she could simply close her eyes right now and sleep, just like a child. Then she could wake and it would be the next day – the day that Robin would come back to her.

31

Megan watched until Ollie and Sophie vanished from view before turning her attention back to the swooping gaggle of seagulls above her head. Adjusting the shutter speed on her camera, she tried a series of shots in auto mode, before switching over to manual. She wanted to capture the kinetic frenzy of the birds' beating wings as they jostled for position in mid-air, and for once she wanted the sound to translate into the image, too – all the squawks and cries and shouts from those throwing seed and bread up into the air.

As she worked, Megan thought about Sophie. There was something going on with her that left a nagging trail of worry in her wake. She was so fragile, like a tiny origami bird, and Megan was proud of Ollie for stepping in and playing the hero, even if she had felt a smear of jealousy stain her mood as she'd watched the small girl wrap her arms and legs around him.

She remembered Ollie's comment in the Mirror Maze about meeting someone. It had felt like odd timing, because her mum had asked her just a few days ago how she'd feel if she saw Ollie with another woman. Ever since Megan had introduced the two of them that summer, her mum had been waging a not-so-subtle campaign to get them together. When her gentle hints had no effect, she started resorting to actual begging. Then, when even that failed to dent the resolve Megan had put up like scaffolding, she had turned to sly little remarks like this one, presumably under the impression that her daughter had somehow reached the age of thirty without recognising a blatant attempt at reverse psychology when she heard it.

The idea of Ollie taking up with someone else had felt unimaginable to her then, but the image had stayed with her and now it was becoming impossible to ignore. Could she really be that girl? Someone who didn't want a man, but didn't want anyone else to have him either?

Megan curled her nose up in self-disgust. It wasn't a nice trait, jealousy, and selfishness was an even worse one, but there it was. She didn't want anyone else to have Ollie, but she knew that eventually someone would. He was far too good a man to be passed up by anyone with even the slightest bit of sense.

Megan couldn't ignore the way she had been feeling today, the tingles when he played with her fingers across the table, and that constant, almost burning need she had to kiss him. She knew she was veering into very dangerous and very selfish territory indeed, but her loins were beginning to win the battle with her common sense – and it would only take a few helpings of Dutch courage for lust to be crowned overall champion.

She reached the end of the Charles Bridge and strolled out under the soaring Gothic arch of the Old Town Bridge Tower. The slush covering the cobbles had frozen throughout the afternoon, and Megan relished the crunching sound it made as she stamped over it in her boots. Arriving at the road, she pressed the button and watched as the illuminated sign opposite counted down from thirteen to zero, a cacophony of clicks sounding to let her know it was safe to cross. She loved how the roads here were laced together with tram tracks, the light catching the polished silver as it peeked out from between buildings and statues.

She had been told once by a walking tour guide in London that you always saw the best of a city by looking upwards as you explored. Even somewhere as outwardly dull and modern as Oxford Street could be transformed if you lifted your eyes above the shop fronts to the often stunning buildings above. Megan loved looking at old photos of London from the years before chain stores took over, vomiting their trashy modern lights and signs up and down the high streets. Her favourites were always the photos of small businesses, such as the local grocery shop or fishmonger's, with the shopkeeper, his staff and their families lined up outside. Children with grubby cheeks and bright eyes, harassed-looking mothers with a baby balanced on one hip, an old-fashioned wicker basket in their hand, and the men with their trousers hoisted up by vast leather braces, a hat balanced at a jaunty angle on their head and a pipe hanging out from their smiling mouth. Each of those characters had their own story, and Megan could spend hours gazing into their faces, trying to work out what those tales might be.

She'd been walking without really paying attention to the direction she was heading, and now realised that she'd missed the turning that took her back to the Old Town, and was instead heading east to Wenceslas Square. Shrugging, she carried on, thinking that it would be just as easy to loop around in a circle as it would be to turn back. And anyway, she was enjoying having the city all to herself for a while. She was free to stop and gaze at how the yellow leaves of a distant tree stood out against the slate-grey of the building behind it. A burst of colour, like one of nature's very own fireworks, so beautiful that it made her heart beat faster inside her chest. She lifted her camera again and again, pausing to check on her progress and shaking her head when she found it lacking.

How could anyone ever find this endearing? she thought. She annoyed even herself when she stumbled around over a shot like this, so it must be borderline infuriating for anyone else in the vicinity. It was one of the reasons she knew it was better for her to be single – then she could do whatever she wanted without feeling guilty.

Megan heard the sound of excited yelps carrying on the breeze and followed her ears to a small open square. A man was standing amid a large group of young children, all of whom were abuzz with excitement as they watched him dip his long rope into a bucket at his feet. He paused for effect, laughing as some of the children began jumping up and down on the spot with anticipation, then he swung up his arm with a flourish and spun around, the giant bubble trailing out behind him from the loop of twine.

Megan lifted up her camera, feeling the freezing air hit her gums as she smiled behind it. The children had charged forward to try and burst the bubble, and the man was already following it with another, and then a cluster of smaller bubbles. She edged closer, taking a photo of one stray orb just before it burst over the front of her lens, and giggling as the manic kids ran around her legs. They were only marginally less frantic than the birds back on the bridge, and far noisier, but their joy was infectious. Megan wished Ollie had been here to see them, realising as she thought of him that she was probably going to be late to meet him. It was hard to tear herself away, though, and she could still hear the children's shrieks and cackles long after she turned and headed in the opposite direction.

Ollie was sitting up at the bar when she arrived, his long legs wrapped untidily around the wooden limbs of a stool and two pints of dark Czech beer in front of him. He hadn't heard her come in, and she took advantage of the fact to stand and watch him for a time. His floppy brown hair had been turned slightly static by the combination of his ridiculous hat and the tropical central heating in Don Pisto's, and a few strands were swaying drunkenly up in the air away from the rest. His trainers were stained and looked soggy from the wet ground outside, and one of the sleeves of his coat had turned inside out when he took it off.

For some reason, that final small detail suddenly and inexplicably made up Megan's mind, and she walked straight over to the bar, pulled Ollie's arm until he swung around to face her, and kissed him full and hard on the mouth.

There was a beat as Ollie registered what was happening, then he kissed her back with a keen urgency that made her grip the bar to stay upright. Pulling off her hat, he ran his hands into her tangle of hair, his fingers massaging her scalp as his tongue tasted first the inside of her top lip, then the fleshy part of her bottom lip. One of her hands was still on his arm, but she lifted the other one off the bar and used it to pull his body against hers, slipping between his legs and feeling the rigid edge of the stool against her stomach.

Around them, music played and people continued to chat, their own world totally unaffected by the two people kissing at the bar beside them. Megan heard herself gasp with pleasure, letting her head droop backwards and feeling Ollie's lips on her throat, behind her ear, on her flushed cheeks. She kissed the lobe of his ear, keeping her eyes closed and feeling her way across his face until she found his glasses, slipping them off so she could push her face even closer to his. Their breath was becoming ragged, and as he pulled her further forward against him, Megan could immediately feel how much he wanted her. She, too, was aware of an intense throbbing between her legs, that sensation of wanting him, of needing him.

'Shall we go back to the hotel?' Ollie's breath was hot against her neck.

'Yes!' her body screamed, but she slowly shook her head.

'Not yet.'

Ollie nodded, resting his forehead against hers and waiting while his heart rate returned to normal. Megan leaned in and kissed him again, lightly this time, her smile tickling his cheek. She could already feel the light burn on her face where his faint stubble had made contact, and she shivered with happiness. Ollie pulled back a fraction and kissed the top of her head, her eyelids, and her brows, before stopping to stare at her.

'Megan, I don't . . .' he began, but hesitated when he saw the look on her face.

'Can we not talk about it?' she begged, her voice small. 'Please.'

He frowned momentarily but didn't say anything else; instead picking up his pint and taking a long, deep, gulp.

The temptation to pull him back towards her was palpable, but Megan forced herself to stare at the floor until her heart stopped its incessant clattering. This was new territory for both of them, and she had no idea what to say to him.

'How was Sophie when you left her?' she asked at last, steering the conversation firmly on to neutral ground. She'd shrugged her own coat off now and was busy unravelling her scarf from where Ollie had yanked it down out of the way. Their kiss had left her flushed and sweaty with exertion, and she gratefully reached for her beer as she clambered up on to the stool next to him.

'She was very quiet.' Ollie hesitated for a moment and then put his free hand on her thigh. 'I bought her a bottle of Prague's finest cola from the bar. I thought she should have some sugar.'

'Good thinking.' Megan smiled at him over the top of her glass, slipping her foot across so it rested on the wooden rung between his feet. She could still feel the imprint of his kisses on her throat, and put up an instinctive hand to touch herself. Had it really just happened? Had she really just walked in here and kissed Ollie?

'I hope she's okay,' Megan went on, pressing her knee against his leg. 'It was crazy the way she just keeled over like that on the bridge.'

'Do you think she might have an eating disorder or something?' Ollie asked. He hadn't put his glasses back on yet, and Megan studied his eyes as he spoke. She must have looked into them hundreds of times, but today they looked more vibrant than ever. In the dim light of the bar, their hazel colour had been turned so dark that it could almost be mistaken for black, and the lashes framing them were short and thick.

'I'm not sure.' Megan frowned. 'I thought she might be pregnant, but she laughed at me when I suggested it.'

'Do you think it's weird that she's here on her own?' Ollie asked, reaching up and tucking a strand of her hair behind her ear. She knew she should really go to the bathroom and brush it, but she was worried that leaving Ollie, even for a few minutes, would pop the nice bubble they were floating in.

'I don't think she planned it that way,' Megan replied, turning her head so that her lips brushed against his fingers. 'From what I gather, they were supposed to come here together, her and her bloke, but he then got held up at home.'

'I'm not convinced he'll even show up.' Ollie looked concerned as he said it, as if the idea had only just occurred to him. 'Why would he wait so long?'

Megan resisted the temptation to pull him off his stool and back into her arms. 'This isn't like you, Mr Morris,' she said quietly. 'What happened to love conquering all? Isn't that what you usually say?'

She couldn't stop staring at his lips, wishing that he would kiss her again.

'That was the old me,' he said, one eyebrow arching upwards, mocking her. 'I'm not sure I'm brave enough to believe that any more.'

'Well,' she told him, 'we'll find out soon, won't we? Sophie told Hope and me that Robin's flight gets in tomorrow afternoon.'

'I hope he comes,' Ollie said, stepping down from his stool and finally pulling her gently forward into his arms. 'She's such a sweet girl – she deserves to be happy.'

Megan closed her eyes and enjoyed the sensation of his chest against her cheek. She could hear his heart beating through his thick jumper – a slow, steady, comforting rhythm – and wrapped her hands around so she could slip them into the back pockets of his jeans. For a tall man, Ollie had a pleasingly round bottom, and she squeezed it appreciatively.

'Now, now,' Ollie whispered. 'Any more of that and I'll be piggybacking you to the hotel, too.'

'It's your fault for being so damn sexy,' she murmured, digging her nails in a fraction harder.

In all the time that they'd been friends, Megan had never paid Ollie a compliment – certainly not one like this. He was forever telling her how talented she was, how much he admired her work, how much she made him laugh. Then today he'd told her that she was beautiful, and she'd actually believed him. Andre had never commented on her looks, and the more time she spent with him, the more she hid herself away under baggy clothes. When she looked at herself in the mirror now and saw her ribbons of golden hair, her mother's bright eyes and the neat way her lips were tucked under her small nose, she wasn't appalled, but she wasn't totally satisfied either. To Ollie, however, it seemed that she was everything. Megan had never needed a man's approval – she hated the idea that her self-worth could be reliant on someone's opinion – but she had to admit it felt nice to be cherished in this way.

She listened to Ollie's heartbeat quicken as she moved her fingers across the small of his back. They had spent so much time alone together over the past few months, sitting in the pub on a Sunday afternoon, playing beer pong on a rooftop bar in Brixton, walking up Parliament Hill and eating ice cream with the capital city spread out below them – but nothing had ever happened. He'd never reached for her hand or touched her face, as he had here in Prague, and she'd never really wanted him to. The fact that they seemed to have slipped so seamlessly and suddenly into this shared cubicle of intimacy surprised Megan as much as it delighted her. There wasn't any awkwardness at all this time, and his kiss had felt right. Better than that, it had felt almost inevitable.

Despite the delicious, trembling warmth that was tiptoeing through her bit by bit, Megan was aware of a tiny nagging voice coming from a very remote part of her mind, asking her what the hell she was doing. She ignored it, instead removing her hands from Ollie's pockets and sliding them over either side of his face. As he bent his head to kiss her again, Megan was sure she saw a flash of something like sadness pass across his eyes.

32

'I don't think anyone's coming.'

Hope and Charlie were sitting in the bar of the hotel, two full cocktail glasses on the table in front of them. They'd spent the rest of the afternoon after Hope's massage wandering around Mala Strana, picking up trinkets and giggling at the faces on the wooden puppets that were leering out at them through the glass-fronted windows of gift shops. As the hours had slipped away, so had the uneasy atmosphere that had snuck its way between them.

Ignoring the throb of their chilly fingers and toes, Hope and Charlie strolled hand in hand up the steep, winding hill to Prague Castle, where they marvelled at the dedication – and apparent immunity to the icy temperatures – of the guards outside the entrance. Looking utterly cool, calm and unflinching in their furry grey hats and matching lapels, they glared steadfastly ahead through their sunglasses, a rifle clutched tightly in one white-gloved hand. Charlie stood next to one of their blue and white striped sentry boxes, laughing as he saluted into Hope's camera.

To escape the determinedly freezing weather, which seemed to be growing colder with every rotation of the long hand around each of the city's clocks, they explored the inside of St George's Basilica. Hope gasped with awe as she squinted up at the paintings covering the vaulted ceiling, the reds and golds so regal in the dim light of the chapel. The open space was peppered with shifting dust, and she could smell age and history in the air. Crossing the threshold into these places felt to Hope as if she was stepping into the past, and the magnitude of that feeling blissfully eradicated the mess of other emotions that were coursing through her. For those few precious hours, Hope had let herself off the hook and allowed herself to simply absorb what she was seeing. The longer she spent in Prague, the more she believed that the magic in the city was real – she could feel it.

'Perhaps Ollie finally wore Megan down?' suggested Charlie, a mischievous look on his face.

Hope tutted. 'I doubt it. Not after what she was saying last night.'

'Oh?' Charlie leaned across the table.

'I can't tell you,' Hope said. 'Girls' honour and all that.'

'I see.' He took a sip of his drink. 'In that case, I'd better not tell you what he was saying about her, either.'

That got her attention.

'What? You have to tell me!'

Charlie shook his head. 'Can't. Boys' code and all that.'

'Oh, all right.' Hope gave in, throwing up her hands in defeat. 'I'll tell you, but only if you tell me *and* swear not to say anything the next time we see them.'

Charlie brought two fingers up to his forehead in a mock salute. 'Scout's promise.'

So Hope told him, watching him frown as she explained what Megan had said about not having enough room in her life for a boyfriend, and how she wanted to put her career first.

'Sounds barmy to me,' he said, sucking on his straw.

'But she also said that she doesn't feel as if it's right, you know, in her gut. And you should never ignore a gut feeling.' As she said it, Hope was reminded of the gut feeling she'd experienced earlier that day, in the massage parlour, and felt her cheeks begin to redden with discomfort.

'But what if that gut feeling is just fear?' Charlie said. 'Sometimes your instincts can be right, I agree – but there's an awful lot of fear involved a lot of the time. Ollie didn't say all that much to me, to be honest. I think he's too much of a decent bloke to talk about Megan behind her back, but he did say that he'd like them to be more than just friends. If you ask me, those two seem made for each other, and *my* gut feeling is that they belong together.'

She wondered what Charlie would say to her when she voiced her concerns about *their* relationship, that they may have cut off a bigger slice of the pie than they could manage. Would he understand, or would he just accuse her, too, of being crippled by a fear that would turn out to be unfounded?

Just then they were interrupted by the sound of laughter coming from the hotel lobby. The door into the bar was propped open just enough for the two of them to catch a glimpse of Ollie and Megan scurrying past towards the stairs, their arms wrapped around each other.

Hope let out a small squeak of delight, and Charlie grinned, smug in the knowledge that his prediction had been correct. There was no doubt where Megan and Ollie were heading, and it definitely wasn't out to dinner with them.

'I wonder where Sophie has got to?' she said after

they'd gone, downing the last of her drink and putting the empty glass on the table. 'I haven't seen her all day.'

'Perhaps her boyfriend turned up at last?' Charlie suggested, glancing at his watch.

'I wish I knew her surname, so I could check on her at reception,' she told him. 'I worry about her wandering the streets all by herself.'

'That's because you're lovely.' Charlie smiled at her. 'But don't forget, this is a girl who's been all over the world – she probably knows this place better than we know Manchester.'

He was right, of course, but Hope couldn't shake off the feeling that something was going on with their new friend. When they'd all agreed to meet in the hotel bar the previous evening, Sophie had nodded along with enthusiasm, but it hadn't quite reached her eyes. Perhaps Robin had turned up early, or maybe Sophie just wanted to spend some time on her own, rather than with two middle-aged bores like herself and Charlie. She wasn't the girl's mother, after all.

The clock on the wall behind the bar was nearing seven-thirty. 'Come on, then,' she said to Charlie, unable to stop herself giggling at the speed with which he ejected from his chair. 'Let's go and get some food in you before you pass out.'

Outside, the cold bit into them like a rabid dog, senseless and unyielding in its grip. Hope felt the skin on her cheeks tighten, and stuffed her gloved hands as deep as they would go into her pockets. The clouds that had hung over the sky like a wet blanket all day had finally shifted, and looking up she could see a multitude of stars scattered across the blackness.

It was cold enough to silence their conversation, so Hope listened instead to the crunching of the frost beneath her boots and the various strains of music leaking out from the windows and doorways of the bars they passed. It was never silent in Prague, but it wasn't a noisy city either. Where Manchester would assault her ears with a cacophony of rumbling traffic, passing planes and grinding roadworks, Prague filled them pleasantly with song.

It was Saturday night, and the beautiful cobbled streets of Wenceslas Square were packed with a shouting array of stag and hen dos, all doing their home country no favours at all with their atrocious behaviour. Hope grimaced as a passing hen, decked from head to toe in the traditional get-up of feather boa, bright pink tutu, fishnet tights and giant inflatable penis, staggered sideways into an overflowing bin and promptly kicked a pile of rubbish into the air.

'Disgusting,' she muttered to Charlie, but he was distracted by a queue of lads waiting to order giant *klobasa* sausages from a stall. The groom, who was being held up by two guffawing friends, was wearing a bright green dress and a blonde wig.

'What would you like?' the Czech woman on the stall asked, polite even in the face of such a ridiculous drunken display.

'Ham, egg and tits, please, love,' he bellowed, earning himself a rapturous round of applause from his mates.

The woman rolled her eyes but didn't retort, and Hope

was appalled to feel Charlie's body shaking with silent mirth.

They arrived at the restaurant without getting lost once, which was a good thing, Hope remarked to Charlie, because any longer outside in the cold and Prague would have two new statues to add to its already huge collection. It was wonderfully cosy in the basement dining hall, with a fire crackling merrily at one end and candlelight dancing up the walls towards the domed ceiling. The wooden bench seats were decorated with cushions, and old framed photographs of Prague were dotted around on the brick walls.

They ordered a bottle of red wine, which arrived in its very own wicker basket, and dawdled deliberately over the menu, waiting for their fingers and toes to return to normal temperature. The ambience in here was so different to the chaos of tourists up in Wenceslas Square, and Hope could feel herself relaxing more with every delicious sip.

Charlie took out his phone and placed it on the table, frowning slightly.

'Something wrong?' she asked.

'There's no signal down here,' he grunted.

'Are you expecting a call?' She tried to keep the suspicious edge out of her voice.

He sighed. 'No. Well, maybe. I don't know.'

'Is everything okay?' she asked. He suddenly looked so tired, and so much older than his forty-eight years, that Hope was genuinely concerned.

'Of course.' He feigned indifference. 'It's totally fine, love. Don't worry.'

'I do worry,' she said gently. 'I worry because I care.'

'I care, too.' He gazed at her until her eyes began to burn, and she dropped them down to her menu. She watched from beneath her lashes as he fiddled with the edge of the tablecloth, his wine glass, the plastic sheaths of the menu, his phone – he was agitated, and she had no idea what to do or say to help him.

It was a relief when the bread appeared, still warm from the oven, and Charlie's hands at last had a use. They hadn't discussed what they would order, and Hope was surprised to discover they'd both picked the same dish – Czech fried cheese with a baked potato and tartar sauce. Charlie almost always had meat, and there was an abundance of it on offer. When she questioned him, he shrugged.

'I fancied a change.'

Something about the way he said it, so flippant and throwaway, made the foreboding she'd experienced that afternoon creep back through Hope. The persistent doubt that had been rising like hot milk in a pan over the past few days had reached such a height now that she could no longer ignore it. At this moment, sitting here in this beautiful restaurant, Hope could put her hand across her heart and say that she wanted to be with Charlie. But when she looked further forward into the future, towards their shared life in Manchester, her confidence in what they had together began to unravel. If she didn't know with her whole heart that she and Charlie were going to make it, then was it fair of her to stay with him at all? She had already broken one set of vows and it had nearly destroyed her – she wasn't about to do that again.

She thought of Sophie, so resolute about her feelings,

so secure in the love she and Robin felt for one another. How lucky she was, thought Hope, to have found something so strong and so real. Even in her very best moments with Dave, Hope had never known in her gut that he was the right man for her. That was why she understood where Megan was coming from – if neither of them could have what Sophie and Robin had, was it really worth the effort? Perhaps not. Perhaps it was better to be alone. While she hated the idea of losing Charlie, she had to admit that the idea of being completely independent appealed to her, too. Something had changed inside Hope since she'd come to Prague, and it was becoming increasingly difficult to keep a lid on it.

Charlie excused himself, but instead of heading towards the toilets, he jogged up the stairs towards the exit. Hope turned her eyes back to the table and took a deep breath – his phone was gone, too.

33

Sophie was dreaming. She knew it was a dream, because her hair was long and she could feel the warmth of the sun on her shoulders. Robin was running down the beach ahead of her, his bare feet leaving prints in the wet sand.

She often had these dreams, the kind where she was consciously aware that what she was seeing wasn't real, but unconscious enough to enjoy it. She was at the helm of her own imagination, steering her way through her favourite memories, and it felt fantastic.

Sophie watched as Dream Robin launched himself into an untidy cartwheel, laughing as his hands and feet sprayed goblets of soggy sand into the air.

'Monkey!' she yelled, running after him and leaping up on to his back. Robin's legs buckled in surprise, but he managed not to drop her, instead grasping her feet in both hands and tickling her until she shrieked and squirmed against him.

'Who are you calling Monkey?' he laughed, as she wrapped her legs tighter around him, knotting her ankles together and burying her face in his neck.

'You!' she cried, wriggling against his back. She was only wearing a bikini, tatty denim shorts and her locket, and her hair was wet from a recent swim. As she looked to the left, away from the ocean, Sophie could see palm trees, and above them a sky as tropically blue as a peacock's feather.

Where were they? she wondered vaguely. Sri Lanka? Bali? Mexico? Malaysia? Thailand? Did it even matter?

Robin came to a halt and sat down, twisting Sophie around so she was facing him, her legs still on either side of his body. She was missing the view of the horizon, that mesmerising line where ocean and sky merged to a shimmering point, the promise of adventure whispering out from beyond where the eye could ever take you, but Sophie didn't care. The view of Robin was far superior – his eyes, so full of joy, the pupils widening to take her in; his mouth, so generous and welcoming, the bottom lip full and darkened by the sun; and his tangle of golden hair, stuck to the sides of his face and beginning to crisp as the salt water dried. She gazed at him as she always did, with wonder and with love, and he moved his head forward to rub his nose against her cheek.

'Let's never go home,' he said, his lips sending a whisper of pleasure down her spine. 'Let's stay here forever.'

She smiled. 'What about our families? What would we tell them?'

'They would understand,' he said, a seriousness in his eyes. 'I don't need anyone but you, anyway.'

Sophie opened her mouth to agree with him, but the dream had rendered her suddenly mute. Her jaw gaped ajar, but her words weren't even whispers. She screamed the thoughts at him over and over, but he couldn't hear her. He simply stared past her towards the ocean, a serene smile lifting the corners of his mouth.

'Me too!' she thought, trying to fight the limitations of her dream. She could feel the edges of her picture beginning to crumble, as the image and feeling of him slipped away like sand through a sieve, and she wrapped her arms around Robin, clinging on to him with alarm. When she braved a look at his face once again, the beach around them had grown darker. A sudden wind blew in and stirred the palm trees into a shuffling, cracking frenzy. Sophie's contentment began to break off into jigsaw pieces of fear and uncertainty, all hard edges and jagged holes. Now Robin was starting to darken, too, his smile lost in the fog. Sophie was no longer on the beach, but on the very edge of a precipice, the wind pushing at her and threatening to topple her right over. She blinked with desperation, trying with all her might to claw back the sunny part of her dream, but it was gone. In place of her beach was the gloomy, unfamiliar shape of her hotel room, the only light coming from a pinch between the heavy drawn curtains.

The bed beside her was empty, and a howl of frustration rose up from her chest. She closed her eyes again and forced herself to breathe deeply, willing her dream to come back and steal her away. She wanted to be back on that beach with Robin, the smell of salt in the air and the warm breeze caressing them as they caressed one another. Silent tears rolled down her cheeks.

Alas, sleep was not forthcoming, and after a time Sophie gave up and peeled her eyes back open, staring into the shadowy corners of the room as she tried to decide what to do. She had a vague inkling that she was supposed to meet Hope, Charlie and the others downstairs in the bar, but she couldn't remember what time they'd agreed. And anyway, she reminded herself as her bleariness cleared, Ollie and Megan wouldn't be expecting her to make an appearance after her earlier collapse on the Charles Bridge. She blushed as she recalled the way she'd clung to Ollie's back like a limpet. Maybe that was why she'd been piggybacking with Robin in her dream? How would she ever face him and Megan again? God knows what they thought of her after all the puking and the fainting. Sophie felt her heart begin to speed up and forced herself to take a deep breath.

She reached for her phone to find six missed calls, all from the same number, and quickly shuffled herself up into a sitting position. There were text messages, too, and she skim-read them in turn, her fingers nimble on the screen as she tapped out a reply.

This time tomorrow, Robin should be with her. The thought was enough to propel her out from beneath the covers into the bathroom, where she ran the hot tap until it was scorching and splashed water across her cheeks. Her earlier sickness had left her with a greyish pallor, and her eyes were bloodshot, but at least the nausea seemed to have gone. She noticed that her hands were trembling slightly as she dried them, and tried to remember the last time she'd eaten anything. There had been that pretzel, but most of that had come back up. And then Ollie had told her to try and nibble at the hotel room's complimentary biscuits when he dropped her off at her door. Had she done as instructed? Sophie couldn't remember.

She must have had a slight fever as she slept, because her clothes were clinging to her back and sides with stale sweat. Peeling them off and dumping them in a heap on the bathroom floor, Sophie clambered over the edge of the bathtub and switched on the shower, opening her mouth as the warm water rushed over her face and down her chest.

Ollie had told her his room number, too, she remembered, raising her hands to rub shampoo through her short spiky hair. He'd told her to call or knock if she felt ill, whatever time it was, and he and Megan would make sure she saw a doctor.

She washed briskly, not wanting to dwell too long on her body now that it was no longer hidden under layers of clothing. Her ribs protruded through her skin like a morbid xylophone, her hip bones jutting out unpleasantly below them, high enough to cast shadows on the concave nest of her stomach. Sophie knew that her arms were beginning to lose their tone, and that her collarbones resembled the holds on a climbing wall, but it was as if she was staring down at a figure belonging to someone else. She'd always been small, but athletically so – not this scrawny bag of bones that she had become over the past few weeks.

She wondered if Robin would notice the difference in her body. They hadn't been apart that long, but he had always been so attentive. Sometimes she thought he knew her body better than she did, knew the location of every hidden freckle and dimple. He'd become a bona fide Sophie expert, he'd tell her proudly, his head popping up from below the covers, where he'd been on one of his 'expeditions', as he liked to call them. He always told her that he could spend all day every day just looking at her and that he'd never get bored, that there would always be something new and delicious to discover.

What if he was disgusted by her now? Sophie froze

mid-rinse. He loved her the way she was, but she had changed. Would he take off her clothes and be appalled by what he found? Would he shake his head in dismay and turn away? Sophie didn't think she would be able to bear that.

The water suddenly began to run cold, and Sophie jumped out of the way with a yelp. How long had she been standing there? Reaching for a towel, she was relieved to see that the full-length mirror had steamed up, allowing her ample time to dry and dress without her reflection distracting her. Every now and then a wave of dizziness would take hold, and she'd be forced to put out a hand to stop herself tumbling over sideways. She really must eat.

Having made the decision to venture downstairs and see if she could find the others, Sophie was now painstakingly applying a thick layer of foundation in an attempt to conceal the greenish tinge on her cheeks. Surely Megan and Ollie would have filled Hope and Charlie in on what had happened that afternoon, and she knew that Hope, especially, would be worried. She kept catching the older woman watching her when she thought Sophie wasn't looking, her expression always one of concern. None of them had any need to worry about her, though. As soon as Robin arrived, they would see for themselves that she was absolutely fine.

Closing her bedroom door carefully behind her, Sophie made her way along the landing towards the stairs, her boots making barely a sound on the thick carpet. Mounted to the wall at the top of each flight of steps was a vast, ornate mirror, and she paused in front of the first one.

The make-up definitely helped, as did the extra jumper she'd pulled on over the first, but her hair still looked terrible. She had grown so accustomed to hiding behind her long hair over the years that she was still having a tough time readjusting – and tonight she needed that reassuring veil even more than usual.

When she reached the second landing down, Sophie heard the sound of laughter heading her way. Overcome with absurd shyness, she darted towards a nearby window and pulled the heavy floor-length curtain across until she was concealed from view. Peering through a small hole in the fabric, she watched as Megan and Ollie came into view, her hand clasped firmly in his and a look of flushed excitement on her face. At the bottom of the stairs heading up towards the bedrooms, Megan hesitated, pulling on Ollie's hand to stop him.

'What's the matter?' he asked, his tone gentle but urgent.

Sophie watched as Megan looked down at her feet, and then back up at him.

'Are you sure you want to do this?'

It was almost a whisper, and Sophie held her breath, appalled to have intruded accidentally into such a private moment between the two of them.

'Of course I'm sure.' Ollie stepped down from the bottom stair and took her other hand. 'I want this to happen more than anything.'

This seemed to work, and Megan moved closer to him.

'It would be a shame to waste that bed,' she said finally, her meaning clear. Sophie's eyes widened behind the curtain.

Ollie chuckled and pulled her against him, bending

forward and kissing her with such ferocity and passion that Sophie felt herself blush. She looked away, feeling embarrassed, but she could still hear their short breaths and gasps as they feasted on one another with a hunger that Sophie recognised all too well.

She turned to face the window instead, her skin prickling as the cold night air stole through the gaps, its icy fingers stroking the tendrils of hair that half-covered her ears. She could see the stars in the sky above the buildings, each one burning with a brightness that made her eyes swim, and she blinked away the moisture.

When she turned back to her shameful peephole to check if the coast was clear, Megan and Ollie had gone.

34

The vibration from Megan's phone woke her, and she groped to pick it up from where it had buzzed across the wooden top of the bedside cabinet. It was a notification from one of the apps she used to edit photos on her phone, informing her that three new filters had been added. Great. Nice of them to tell her that, in the middle of the bloody night.

Putting her phone back down with a mild grumble, Megan caught sight of something else on the polished wood, and felt all the blood drain out of her. The condom wrapper winked back at her, its foil edges a merry silver in the blue light of her phone, so innocuous, yet so damning.

She and Ollie had done it. They'd had sex.

Megan peered over the edge of the bed and surveyed the carpeted floor.

They'd had sex at least three times!

It was very hard not to groan out loud, and only the fear of waking Ollie stopped her. He was stretched out beside her, a casual arm flung across his head, hiding his eyes from view, and he was absolutely, unashamedly and quite startlingly naked.

Wincing as the bed springs creaked below her, Megan hooked the cover over her foot and dragged it slowly back up from where the two of them must have kicked it out of the way. When it was safely up at waist height, she let it drop, her heart racing as Ollie shifted and turned, his face now just inches from her own. In the darkness he reached out, searching for her, but she remained rigid and unyielding as his warm hand came to rest on her bare shoulder.

The room all at once felt suffocating, the unmistakable scent of sex in the air making her feel as if she was choking. She tried closing her eyes, but all she could see was Ollie – his mouth on her breasts, his torso above her, his hands clutching her waist, her bottom, and his eyes, always looking into hers with such intensity. Megan began to trace their steps backwards, to the bar where she – yes, it had been she – had walked over and kissed him with no warning. She hadn't planned it, she knew that, but she also knew that she had wanted it to happen.

After that there had been drinks, then more kissing. When had they come back to the hotel? She couldn't be sure. Had anyone seen them? Oh God, they had been all over each other in that bar, she realised. It was so unlike her to be even the slightest bit affectionate in public, but she could clearly picture herself lost in the moment with Ollie, her eyes closed and her hands everywhere. They hadn't even moved from the bar, but stayed in full view of the staff and all the customers, kissing each other like a pair of randy teenagers.

The shame was so acute that for a moment Megan thought she was going to throw up. Ollie, apparently unfazed by this extraordinary turn of events, continued to snooze contentedly beside her. She envied him, but felt cross with him at the same time. This was all her fault, she knew that, but she wished he had done the right thing and told her where to go, turned his head away and refused to kiss her back. He would think that this changed everything, and he would be right – but rather than feel happy, she was already beginning to experience the chokehold of regret.

She closed her eyes again, but this time she could see herself, her head thrown backwards and her back arched in pleasure, her hands raking through Ollie's hair as he kissed his way down her body, pausing only to carefully but persistently lick her into a near-frenzy of ecstatic release.

It had been heavenly, but it had been a mistake.

Megan waited until she was sure that Ollie was completely sound asleep, then lifted one side of the cover and slithered silently to the floor, crawling on her hands and knees to her open case and extracting her clothes without making a sound. She needed a shower desperately, but her need for escape was far greater, so she wriggled into jeans and a jumper, found her shoes and bag, and managed to get out into the hallway without waking him.

The breakfast room downstairs was deserted save for one lone girl who was setting up the buffet. She smiled shyly at Megan when she saw her hovering in the doorway, pointing at the clock on the wall and telling her they would be ready soon. Megan, who was overwhelmed by the need to put a safe distance between herself and Ollie, merely smiled back and scuttled past, pulling on her gloves as she reached the exit.

The cold morning air lashed at her exposed skin like a whip, but being outside sharpened her senses immediately. By the time she'd made it to the far end of the road and could no longer see the hotel, she had begun to calm down. The pavements were almost completely bare, with only a few weary-looking souls passing by as she made her way towards the Charles Bridge. She had no plan in mind, but for some reason the bridge seemed to be the place she always ended up.

It was a beautiful morning, the clear sky a freshly laundered blue and the promise of later sunshine glowing faintly in the deepest corner of the horizon. Megan lifted up her camera ready to capture the moment, but found herself incapable. She couldn't see the beauty through the lens, and tried again, tears of frustration building as the emotions she so longed for failed to materialise.

The camera sat forlornly against her chest, as redundant a tool to her now as a chocolate teapot. Without that feeling, that connection, she couldn't even call herself a photographer – she may as well hurl her bloody camera off the bridge and into the Vltava.

What had she been thinking, sleeping with Ollie like that? After days of self-control, she'd given in, and now there was no going back. He would never accept her excuses now, never understand why she couldn't be with him – but this right now, these horrible, confused feelings of guilt and regret, this was exactly why. Ollie had wormed his way under her skin, and her ability to take photos had vanished overnight. She could not have both things in her life – that much was now achingly clear – and she wanted to follow her dreams more than her heart.

It was all so unfair. So many of her friends had rolled their eyes at her when she explained why she couldn't be with Ollie. Her own mother had been scathing of the decision, warning Megan against making a mistake that she might regret for a long time – but what none of them realised was that she was heartbroken, too. She knew that it was her neuroses and her fear that had kept them apart, even if she hadn't been able to admit as much to herself until now. She cared deeply for Ollie, she always had, and she didn't want to hurt him, but wasn't that exactly what she was about to do?

Megan had been walking without really paying attention to where she was going, and looking up she realised that she had no idea where she was. The houses here were several storeys taller than those back in the Old Town, and many of the large rectangular windows were encased by wrought-iron balconies, each one cluttered with the debris of different lives. Using her camera lens as a makeshift telescope, Megan could see plant pots choked with winter flowers, children's bicycles and overflowing ashtrays. As she watched, one of the glass doors opened and a woman emerged. She was wrapped in a dark-grey dressing gown and her black hair had been pulled into an untidy bun on the top of her head. Megan squinted through the viewfinder and saw a pair of what looked like red slippers poking out from below the robe.

The woman hadn't seen her yet, and Megan let her finger rest on the shutter release button. She loved it when this happened, when she stumbled accidentally into another person's private world and got the chance to observe, unnoticed. The lady had clearly just woken up, and Megan smiled to herself as she watched her yawn and stretch out her arms above her head. She was looking towards the horizon, to where the sun was continuing to rise slowly into the day like a baked muffin, throwing out ropes of light so that the frost on the rooftops of the city twinkled like an endless string of fairy lights.

What was she thinking? Megan wondered. What would her day ahead entail?

As Megan stood there, the woman turned and looked directly at her, as though she'd been able to feel the heat of Megan's gaze from all the way up there. For a second, it looked as though she was going to smile, but instead she just shook her head, her lips moving soundlessly, and went back inside.

Instead of heading back in what she thought was the right direction, Megan continued to weave her way through the wide cobbled streets and deeper into what she assumed must be the residential area of Prague's west bank. She was enjoying being away from the busier, more touristy areas of the city, where it was easy to be distracted by all the grand architecture and miss all those little details that she so cherished. To truly understand a place, she'd learned that you needed to peel up the corner of perception and stick a big spoon of curiosity into whatever you discovered underneath.

A bakery was just opening its doors as she passed, and Megan hesitated for a moment before pushing open the glass door and stepping inside. Almost immediately, she smiled – partly because the merry-looking man behind the counter actually stretched out his arms in welcome, but mostly because the smell wafting out from an array of pastries, loaves and buns was absolutely amazing. She wished she could capture it all on camera, but she didn't want to be rude. Megan had struggled to even learn the Czech words for 'please' and 'thank you' since she'd arrived, let alone figure out how to ask this man if photography was permitted. She settled instead for just using her eyes, and eventually chose herself a pastry that looked like a giant jam tart.

'This, please,' she stammered, feeling like a fool as she pointed at the glass front of the counter.

The man clapped his hands.

'Ah, *kolache*! Very good.' He busied himself with a paper bag and some metal tongs. 'This one is jam,' he went on, pausing just as he was about to pick it up. 'I have also cheese and meat.'

'Cheese?' she asked. Now he was talking.

The man's grey beard wobbled a fraction as he nodded his head, moving his hand to the left, where another row of pastries sat waiting, their circular centres filled with oozing, yellow goodness.

'Yes, please! *Prosim*,' she said, matching the man's grin as he acknowledged her attempt at the Czech language.

As he was handing back her change, the bell above the door tinkled and an old lady shuffled in. She was wearing a big felt hat over rollers, a pink overcoat and bright green wellington boots, and she immediately launched into an animated babble of Czech that Megan had absolutely no chance of understanding. The man followed suit, and soon the two of them were talking happily over each other, paying no attention at all to Megan, who was leaning against the window eating her delicious cheese pastry and taking it all in. Daily life in Prague seemed friendly and simple, she thought. The city still had that almost village feel to it, split as it was into separate boroughs where everybody seemed to know each other. There was a sense of community here, she realised, giving the baker a shy wave as she headed back out into the cold street. It was the one thing that London was really lacking, and it wasn't until she witnessed an exchange such as this one that Megan appreciated how much she craved it. Perhaps she had been wrong about needing to live in London. Yes, there were more opportunities, but wasn't there a chance to make something of yourself wherever you ended up in the world? She wished Ollie was here to ask, but of course he wasn't – she had made sure he couldn't be.

She meandered through the suburbs until her legs began to ache with cold, then turned reluctantly north and quickly found her way back to the base of Petrin Hill. The park stretched up above her, still coated by a generous helping of snow, and Megan paused to catch her breath, her eyes stinging in the freezing air. As she stood by the entrance, a man passed by with a dog at his heel. It was small and scrubby, its brown and black hair standing upright in wiry clumps, but its expression of pure joy made Megan smile. The owner had no ball, but instead was reaching down for piles of snow, which he flung into the undergrowth for the dog to chase. Every time the bewildered pooch returned with nothing, its muzzle frosted white from all its determined excavations, the man roared with delighted laughter. It was such a simple tableau, but so beautiful, and Megan watched until the two of them were out of sight.

For once, she didn't feel the need to capture the scene, and was simply content to have something to save for herself – a memory of Prague not coloured by history or magic or even by Ollie, just a moment of companionship between a man and his best friend.

She took out her phone to check the time. It was nearing

nine now, and there had been no word from Ollie. She wondered if he'd woken up to find her gone again, and how he would feel about it. He'd been so understanding of her odd behaviour up till now, but she wasn't sure he'd be so forgiving of her this time. If only she could make sense of what she was feeling, take it out and pin it up on a wall so she could study it, as she did with photographs, looking for hidden meaning amongst the colours and shapes.

She continued uphill through the snow, pausing only when she was high enough to see the bed of the city spread out beneath her. Even the vast, six-storey buildings along the banks of the Vltava looked tiny from up here, and Megan was reminded of the time she and Ollie had played Monopoly one Saturday night. They'd shared a bottle of bubbly as she systematically took him to the cleaners, buying up everything of value and refusing to budge an inch when he landed on one of her properties. Unlike Megan, Ollie wasn't in the slightest bit competitive – a trait that she found both endearing and frustrating in equal measure. Beating someone who didn't care about winning was no fun, she'd pointed out to him, and his response had been to blow her a playful kiss across the board.

By the time she reached Prague Castle, the city's many clocks were striking the hour, and Megan knew she must head back to the hotel. It wasn't fair to ruin what was left of this trip by freaking out. And freaking out was exactly what she was doing. Instead, she'd try to act as if nothing was wrong, then talk to Ollie properly when they were back in London.

Sex with Ollie had been a one-off; something that they should and would be able to put behind them – a bit of holiday fun. Their friendship was the most important thing at stake here – at least it was for Megan. It would be tricky at first, sure – the hairy mammoth in the room with them until some time had passed – but she believed in the power of their united will to be in each other's lives. She knew she would hate to lose Ollie, and felt pretty confident that he wouldn't want to cut her out of his life either. Then again, if Ollie's feelings for her had moved past friendship, he might not be so keen to pretend that nothing had happened. There was only one way to really know for certain how Ollie was feeling about the whole mess, and that was to face up to him.

He'd always been so lovely to her, and such a supportive friend. Megan couldn't imagine him turning on her now. But then why, she asked herself, as she came to a nervous halt on the corner of the street leading down to the hotel, was she feeling so utterly terrified that he might?

35

Hope woke with the light, as she so often did, letting her eyes adjust at their own pace as she squinted into the half-darkness. She was lying on her side, facing away from Charlie's side of the bed. It was the same position she'd adopted before falling asleep, the troubling nature of the evening's events sitting like a boulder on the sheets between them.

After dinner, Hope had suggested they get an early night. She was exhausted, but she also wanted to check if Sophie was in the bar waiting for them. When Charlie had returned to the table after his pretend trip to the gents, his phone clutched in his hand, Hope had decided not to mention it. She felt like she'd learned a lot about her boyfriend over the past few days, the main thing being that he didn't like it when she accused him of keeping secrets. He had never been married, unlike her, and hadn't had a serious relationship for years, so being entirely open with another person must seem like a strange concept. She understood that, sympathised with it even, but his secretiveness still rankled.

They got as far as the street leading down towards the hotel before Charlie stopped and turned to her, his eyes black under the gleam of a nearby street light and his breath visible in the freezing air.

'I want you to know that I love you,' he said, catching

her by surprise. 'It's important to me that you know how I feel.'

'Oh, Charlie.' She reached for him. 'I never thought you didn't. I . . .' She stopped, unsure of how to continue.

'It's okay.' He cupped her face with a gloved hand. 'I don't need you to say anything to me, I just wanted to tell you.'

Trepidation crept through Hope's stomach like a prowling cat.

'Charlie, are you okay?' she asked, hearing the fear in her own voice. 'You're not, you know, ill or something?'

He shook his head. 'No.'

'Do you promise?'

The thought of this big, strong, loving man being poorly, of suffering in any way at all, was unbearable.

'I promise. Now, please will you let me take you back to the hotel?'

She nodded. 'Of course.'

They'd made the rest of the journey in silence, and Hope was ashamed to find herself relieved when a glimpse into the bar revealed no sign of Sophie. Much as she wanted to check on her, she sensed that Charlie needed her more.

Once upstairs, they made love, but there was a sense of finality to it all that unnerved Hope, and she lay awake long after Charlie dropped to sleep beside her, worry working its way around her mind.

Now it was morning, and they had another full day to get through. Another whole morning where she said anything but the things she needed to, another afternoon where he hid secrets from her and vanished to take mysterious calls. And what then? On Monday they would fly home, and she would still be living in his tiny flat. Annette would still be lost to her and she would still be lost in her own life, trapped in a maze of confusion, fear and discontent.

Hope made herself sit up as these thoughts whirred around in her mind, realising as she did so that the bed beside her was empty.

'Charlie?'

No answer.

She sat up and rubbed her eyes.

'Charlie?' She said it louder this time, thinking that perhaps the bathroom door had muffled her call.

Nothing.

Hope got up and padded over to the en suite, opening the door and blinking rapidly as the light stung her eyes. There was no sign of him, and his washbag was gone from the edge of the basin. Perhaps he'd just popped downstairs to get them some coffee, she thought. Or even buy her some flowers. She knew how fond he was of a gesture, and last night had been . . . Well, she wasn't sure what it had been.

She was further alarmed to find Charlie's coat and hat missing and his case neatly packed, so she quickly showered and dressed, keeping half an eye on the time, then carefully applied her make-up and dried her hair. There was still no sign of Charlie, and she was beginning to feel sick with the sense of foreboding.

Hope pottered around the room, folding up her worn clothes and hanging up last night's discarded dress. She made the bed and opened the curtains, pausing to take in the view. The Prague skyline never failed to stop her in her tracks, and she let herself gaze at it for a few moments.

How much longer should she wait up here? The breakfast room would be closed in half an hour. Perhaps Charlie was already down there, nursing his tenth cup of tea and wondering what the hell she was playing at. It didn't seem very likely, but it was all she had. Decision made, Hope sat down on the bed and started pulling on her shoes, just as there was a tentative knock on the door.

'Hello?'

There was a silence, and then she heard Charlie's voice.

'Go on in,' he was saying. 'She'll be so glad to see you.'

Abandoning her other shoe and walking briskly over to the door, Hope flung it open and almost collapsed in shock.

There in the hallway, looking tired, scared and more than a little like she was about to burst into tears, was Annette.

36

'More coffee?'

Megan held up Ollie's empty cup in front of him, her eyebrow raised.

'Sure.'

She pushed her chair back and headed over to the machine, letting two women go ahead of her. The atmosphere at the breakfast table was becoming unbearable, and she had no desire to rush back.

'Here you go,' she said, putting the full cup back down on his saucer with more of an enthusiastic flourish than was strictly necessary. Ollie didn't smile.

When she'd finally made it back to the hotel after her early-morning jaunt, Megan had found Ollie very much awake and dressed. He'd tidied away the remnants of their previous evening and opened a window, so the bedroom no longer had the tell-tale musky scent that had so freaked her out when she woke up – and he'd even gone out and got her a bunch of flowers. She'd spent the entire walk back going over what she was going to say to him, about how she could make it clear that last night was a one-off, a slip-up, something that would never happen again – but none of it had been necessary. As soon as she'd gaped in ill-disguised horror at his proffered bouquet, Ollie had simply shaken his head.

'It's okay,' he'd told her, putting the flowers down on

the table and going back to his packing. 'You don't need to say anything. I understand.'

She was relieved, of course, but the defeated look on his face as he'd said those words had almost brought her to her knees with distress. She didn't think anyone could hate themselves as much as she did right at that moment. She remembered the look on his face the night before in the bar, when he'd kissed her with such a sadness. Had he known all along that she would change her mind? She hated the idea of being that predictable. But what was the alternative – that he didn't want more than a one-night thing with her anyway, and was glad? That was even worse.

'I went to check on Sophie,' Ollie added then, changing the subject.

Megan somehow found her voice. 'Oh?'

Ollie frowned. 'She wasn't in her room. Well, if she was, she wasn't answering. I couldn't find her downstairs, either.'

Megan took her phone out of her pocket. 'Well, it is getting on a bit,' she said. 'She's probably just headed out for the day.'

'Perhaps.' Ollie didn't look convinced.

He'd waited in the bedroom while she showered and dressed again in the bathroom, feeling a fresh stab of guilt as she discovered the tiny bruises on her neck and chest where Ollie had nibbled and sucked at her. In just a few hours, that closeness between them had evaporated, and now they were trapped in a more uncomfortable place than they had been before coming to Prague – she full of guilt and he muted by resentment. It wasn't a great combination.

Megan sipped her own coffee and toyed with the remains of her breakfast. The guidebook was open on the table between them, and she picked it up and flicked to the section covering Nove Mesto – the New Town.

'Shall we go and see this Dancing House?' she asked, pointing down at the building on the page.

Ollie's glasses slid down his nose a fraction as he bent his head to look.

'Sure. Whatever you want.'

It was as she had feared: he was angry with her. And who could blame him? What she had allowed to happen was so selfish, so stupid, so misguided . . .

'Megan?'

She glanced up at him, hopeful. 'Yes?'

He scrutinised her for a few seconds. 'You've got egg on your chin.'

She laughed and reached for a napkin, smiling at him as relief walloped through her. 'Thank you for telling me,' she said, dipping the edge of the material into her water glass and dabbing it over her face. 'You didn't have to.'

'No.' Ollie pulled his lips into a thin line. 'I didn't. And I was tempted not to.'

'I wouldn't blame you.' She sighed, aware that she was straying dangerously close to the subject she didn't want to discuss. 'It's what I deserve, after all.'

Ollie didn't say anything to that, just picked up his coffee and continued to stare at her until she looked away.

Why? She cursed herself. Why had she let this happen? She knew why, though, of course – it was because she had wanted it to happen. She had yearned for it a bit more with every passing hour they'd spent in Prague.

But now she'd gone and ruined everything – it was all such a mess.

They lingered in the breakfast room until the staff began to clear up around them, Megan half-hoping that they'd see Charlie and Hope so she could apologise for failing to meet them the night before. She suspected that Ollie was waiting there in case Sophie showed her face, but there was no sign of anyone else.

Outside the sun had risen to a middle point in the sky, and the two of them automatically brought their hands up to shield their eyes.

'Wow,' Ollie remarked, pulling his hat on. 'Look at that sun. You'll get some amazing photos today.'

Little did he realise how much those words stung. If she wasn't so obsessed with her work, with this exhibition that she'd foolishly gone and booked, then perhaps she wouldn't be so emotionally crippled. She knew what had happened with Andre had made her wary, but she also knew Ollie was a better man than him. She trusted him not to hurt or betray her, so what the hell was her problem?

'I'll try my best,' she muttered, digging around in her bag for her sunglasses.

They walked in silence for a while, gazing upwards to where the city's multi-coloured rooftops and dark church spires sat framed against the blue. The sunshine had brought out the tourists, but the temperature prevented anyone from lingering too long in one place. Megan took a few token photos – a tiny dog picking its way over the frozen cobbles with dainty paws, an elderly couple strolling hand in hand through a hidden square among the back streets, their noses bright pink as they took it in turns to point things out to one another – but her heart failed to flutter with inspiration. Beside her, Ollie was quiet, thoughtful and calm – his playful mood of the past few days clearly packed away with the worn socks and pants he'd stowed in his suitcase that morning.

They made it to the banks of the Vltava, the sunshine casting impressive shadows as it streamed through the neat gaps in the stone wall that ran along the edge of the river. Megan lifted her camera and captured the gulls perched on the wooden struts of the dam, and the ducks bobbing merrily on the surface of the water below. To the right she could see the impressive arches of the Charles Bridge, its statues merely silhouettes in the bright light of the day, and above the bridge, clustered against the side of the hill, Mala Strana stretched upwards to Hradcany and Prague Castle. Black and green spires jostled for space among the textured red rooftops, the riot of colour broken in places by the yellow wash of a building or the curling dance of chimney smoke. Everything was bathed in the strange, slanting sunlight, and right at the top of the hill, St Vitus's Cathedral loomed, dark and bold and reeking of history. It was a few minutes before Megan realised that she was looking at the scene through the lens of her camera, and she felt a tear of silent jubilation slide down her cheek.

'Hello there.'

Megan turned at the sound of Ollie's voice, but he wasn't talking to her. A pigeon had landed on the wall in front of them, shuffling from side to side on its scrawny pink claws and staring at them through bright beady eyes. Very slowly, Ollie reached out a hand towards it. The pigeon didn't move, just cocked its smooth head a fraction and considered him. Then, just as Ollie's hand was about to make contact, it lifted its wings and flew up on to his shoulder.

'Oh my God!' Megan squealed, her camera slipping in her haste to capture the moment.

She waited for Ollie to say something cheeky about being irresistible to birds, but he didn't. He seemed mesmerised by his feathery new friend, and Megan was able to snap away for ages. There was a similar photo of a young Megan framed in her parents' hallway back home. She was standing in the middle of Trafalgar Square in London with her arms outstretched, covered from hand to hand with pigeons. There was even one on the top of her head. She remembered being dismayed when she'd heard that they were getting rid of those pigeons – what harm could a load of birds really do? Well, now she knew where to bring her children for their own pigeon encounter. If she ever had any children . . .

'You're clearly a bird magnet,' she said, when it became apparent that Ollie wasn't going to bother making the joke himself.

'Clearly.'

He wasn't going to bite. Megan took a deep breath and forced herself to smile. They just had to get through today. Just a few more hours until they'd be on their way home, and could put this trip behind them.

The pigeon took one last look at Ollie, then launched itself untidily off his shoulder back down to the wall, before taking off to join its friends by the water below. Megan followed it with her camera, feeling exhilarated as she saw the wind rustle its outstretched feathers. Even pigeons could look majestic when they were mid-flight.

'It left me a little gift,' muttered Ollie, peering at a white stain that had appeared on the shoulder of his coat.

Megan burst out laughing, letting her camera drop back on its strap and rummaging in her bag for a tissue.

'It's supposed to be lucky,' she told him, standing on tiptoes and gingerly attempting to wipe away the poo.

'The only people that say that are people who haven't been shat on,' Ollie replied. He wasn't laughing, but Megan thought she could see the hint of a smile beginning in the corners of his mouth.

'Oh, come on.' She nudged him as hard as she dared. 'You have to admit, it's pretty funny.'

'Birds shitting on me is the story of my life,' he muttered, then almost immediately threw her an apologetic glance. 'Sorry.'

Megan finished wiping and dropped her grubby tissues into a nearby bin, taking a deep breath before she answered.

'It's okay,' she told him, a smile cracking her set jaw. 'It's no more than I deserve.'

Ollie opened his mouth to argue, but then shut it again. After all, he knew just as well as she did that what she'd said was right – she did deserve his resentment. She'd rejected him once, and now she was doing it all over again. No wonder he could hardly bear to look at her.

'Come on,' he said instead, starting to walk away from the view. 'Let's go and find this weird dancing house you're so keen to see.'

37

'Mum?'

Hope stood frozen on the threshold of the room, gazing at her daughter. Could she really be here? Was she still dreaming?

'How?' she finally managed, gripping the wooden door frame for support.

Annette fought down her tears, taking a large gulp before she spoke.

'Charlie,' she said. 'He's been calling me for days. When I eventually answered, he told me how upset you were.' She had to pause again as the sobs threatened, and Hope braved a look at Charlie. He looked close to tears, too.

'He told me you'd been crying, and that you kept talking about me and . . .' Annette couldn't hold her tears in any longer, and her face screwed up in agony. She looked just as she had as a small child, all red and blotchy and vulnerable. Hope finally regained her power of movement and gathered her daughter into her arms, stroking her hair and making soothing noises into her ear. It wasn't long before both women were crying, clinging on to one another with a desperate mixture of love and relief.

Hope heard Charlie cough under his breath. Looking up, she saw that his cheeks were wet with tears, but he was smiling.

'I'm going to head downstairs and get a coffee,' he told her. 'Leave you two girls to catch up.'

'Thank you,' she mouthed, still holding Annette as tightly as she could. Charlie nodded, turning away and heading for the stairs.

Hope ushered Annette into the bedroom, sending up a silent prayer of thanks that she'd taken the time to tidy the place and make the bed. Annette didn't seem to notice the lavish décor or the beautiful details – she only had eyes for Hope.

'I've missed you, Mum,' she admitted, finally letting go of Hope and allowing herself to be gently manoeuvred into a chair.

'Oh, darling – I've missed you so much.' Hope clasped her hand. 'I've felt like my heart is breaking every day.'

'I was so angry,' Annette confessed. 'I just didn't understand why you would do that to Dad.'

'I'm so sorry you found out the way you did,' Hope said, twisting her body in discomfort as she remembered Annette's face peering at her and Charlie through the car window. 'I'd never in a million years have wanted that to happen.'

To her surprise, Annette suddenly started chuckling.

'What's so funny?'

'Just you – snogging a man in a parked car. My mum! Honestly, when I think about it now, I'm actually quite impressed.'

'Oh, don't!' Hope slapped playfully at the air. 'You'll make me blush.'

'Charlie's a nice man,' Annette said now, surprising her again. 'I thought I hated him, but I don't. I just hate the situation.'

'He is a nice man.' Hope nodded. Annette looked so drawn and pale. She must have had a very early flight from Manchester to be here by this time. Hope wanted to get up and make her some tea, urge her to eat some biscuits to get the colour back in her cheeks, but she resisted. This was the first time they'd properly talked to one another in weeks, and she was reluctant to upset the calm that had settled between them.

'When he called me,' Annette went on, staring down at Hope's hand holding her own, 'he told me – begged me – that he would do anything to reunite us. He paid for my flight over here and arranged a car from the airport and everything. He wouldn't take no for an answer. Patrick was sick of me moping around the house anyway.' She looked up and smiled. 'I think he was as relieved as I was that someone else was taking charge of things.'

Hope thought of all those calls Charlie had made, at how he'd hidden the truth from her, presumably so as not to raise her hopes. How horrible she'd been to distrust him. All that time he was trying to do something nice for her, something vital, and she'd assumed that he was up to no good. And now there was an uncomfortable rift between them that she wasn't sure how to mend.

'I can't believe he managed it,' she told Annette. 'I honestly thought you might never speak to me again.'

'I thought so, too,' Annette admitted, and Hope flinched. 'But then I went to see Dad, and he told me I was being unfair.'

'Did he?' Hope's eyeballs bulged in surprise.

'He told me that your . . . well, that you and he hadn't been a real couple for a long time. I don't think he was surprised when I ran in there and shouted my head off about you and Charlie – in the end, I think he was relieved.'

Hope felt a huge metaphorical weight lift off her shoulders.

'Really?'

'You should see him, Mum – he's been like a new man these past few weeks. He's started jogging!'

'No!' Hope actually laughed.

'I said to him, I said, "Mum's gone out there and found herself someone who makes her happy – and you should do the same." I think he took it to heart, because the next time I went over, I found him in the kitchen with one of your Jamie Oliver books open, trying to cook himself a decent meal.'

'I can't imagine it.' Hope clapped her hands together.

'The place was a bomb site, obviously,' Annette added. 'But at least he was trying. I was so proud of him.'

'I am, too.' Hope smiled. 'I never wanted to hurt your dad, but what he told you is right. We hadn't really been a proper husband and wife for years. Neither of us ever had the guts to say anything about it, so for ages we just sort of existed. Meeting Charlie made me realise that I was still a woman as well as a wife, but more than that, he gave me the excuse I needed to escape.'

She trailed off, not wanting to sound too damning of Dave and their relationship, but Annette was looking at her eagerly.

'Go on.'

Hope took a deep breath. 'The thing is, love, I've been thinking about this since I've been here, actually. For such a long time, I've been Dave's wife and your mum. And you know there's nothing I love more than being your mum, but somewhere along the way I lost who I really was. Can you understand that?'

Annette nodded, tears making her eyes shine.

'I felt like I was invisible half the time,' Hope admitted. 'You and your dad, you had jobs and lives outside of the house, but I felt as if I didn't, not really. Not in the way I wanted. Now I've realised that what I want is a life all of my own. Oh love, don't cry.'

'I just wish you'd talked to me about it.' Annette sniffed and wiped her face with the back of her hand. 'If I'd known how unhappy you were I could have done something.'

'I've never been unhappy being your mum,' Hope assured her. 'Don't ever think that. Promise me?'

Annette nodded, taking a deep breath to control her sobs.

'Being a mum to you is the best thing I've ever done or ever could do, and it was only when you moved in with Patrick that I started to feel as if I was in the wrong place. Charlie just came along at the right time, I suppose. He saw me as a woman and as a person – I was Hope to him. Am I making any sense?'

'So much sense.' Annette sniffed. 'I behaved like such a brat. I'm so ashamed of myself.'

Hope shook her head. 'Don't be. I would have done exactly the same thing. And anyway, you're here now and that's all that matters. I'm so glad you are, too, because you're going to love Prague.'

Annette got up from the chair and wandered over to the window, peering out at the brilliant blue sky.

'It's so cold!' she said. 'I didn't even bring a scarf.'

'Well, we'll just have to get you one,' Hope told her, thinking of a beautiful stall down in the market.

Annette took a breath. 'I'm sorry, Mum,' she said. 'I'm sorry for everything.'

'Enough of that,' Hope chided, swallowing her own tears yet again. 'You must be starving, are you? Let's go down and see if we can't find some late breakfast.'

'Can Charlie come with us?' Annette was suddenly urgent. 'If it wasn't for him, I wouldn't even be here. I'd like to thank him properly.'

'Of course.' Hope took her hand.

As they shut the bedroom door behind them and made their way hand in hand down the carpeted staircase, Hope thought about the wish she'd made on the Charles Bridge. A year and a day to get her daughter back had felt like such a desirable prospect at that moment, but now that she had her here, Hope knew a wait that long would have been unendurable. It turned out that she hadn't needed Prague's hidden magic to have her wish granted – she had just needed Charlie.

38

'Do you remember that advert, the one with Mr Soft?'

Megan frowned. 'The Softmints one?'

Ollie looked at her, then again at the building in front of them. 'Yeah, he had a little song and everything. It was a bit creepy, but I used to love it.'

'I remember,' she said.

'Well, this place looks like something that would be in that advert. It's all squashed.'

He wasn't wrong, thought Megan. The Dancing House did look a lot like a mistake from a potter's wheel, with its irregular edges and bizarre curves, but she liked it all the same. It had so many windows dotted up its height in random places that it reminded her of something you'd see in a cartoon, or in a fairy tale.

'Apparently, it's known as the Fred and Ginger building,' Ollie told her, reading from the guidebook. 'There's a swanky restaurant on the top floor, too.'

Megan didn't reply, because she'd crouched down at his feet to get a good angle. The Dancing House was situated on the corner of a very busy crossroads, with cars and trams hurtling past them from every direction.

'I'm just going to cross the road,' she told Ollie, pressing the big red button and waiting for the ticking noise that would indicate she could go. 'I can't get the right frame from here.'

Ollie went to follow her, but then thought better of it. 'I'll just have a wander down there,' he said, pointing to a road heading off to the right. 'Find myself a tea or something.'

She watched him lope off, his hands deep in his pockets and his head down, and resisted a strong urge to run after him. Was her mother right? Was she making a mistake by refusing to be with Ollie? Last night had felt so amazing, but more than that, it had felt right. Any niggles she had about the way she felt towards him were eradicated by the strength of their connection. But now, with the alcohol out of her system and reality holding up huge placards in her mind, that creeping feeling had worked its way back into her gut, and she couldn't ignore it. If she truly loved Ollie, then why wasn't she doing everything she could to be with him, rather than running away?

When she had taken as many photos from as many different positions as she could of the Dancing House, all the while growing more and more impressed with the sheer ambition of the architect who had created it, Megan made her way back across the road in search of Ollie.

Aside from a cat café, the street seemed to be purely residential. But Ollie wouldn't have gone into a cat café, would he? Shrugging, she made her way along the wide pavement, which was inlaid with flat grey pebbles, until she reached the black-and-white sign featuring a little cat and a steaming cup of coffee. Peering through the glass, she emitted a small murmur of delight.

Ollie was sitting cross-legged on the floor, a large red cushion underneath him and at least four cats crawling all over him. A petite Czech girl was sitting on a chair nearby, and she watched as Ollie said something that made her laugh. Very slowly, she lifted up her camera.

One of the cats had curled up in the space between Ollie's gangly legs, and another, which looked much younger, was crawling up his arm to reach its tortoiseshell friend. That one, having scaled Ollie's other arm, had settled down on his shoulder and was now calmly washing its own bottom. Ollie waited until the young cat had reached the summit of his head before picking up his mug of coffee, laughing as the Czech girl clapped her hands and pointed.

From behind two layers of glass – the window and the lens of her camera – Megan experienced a stirring of jealousy. She would never get to be that girl again, the one who Ollie would flirt with, or laugh with. It felt like too much had happened between them now for her ever to be that girl again. There was too much resentment and distrust on his side, too many memories of how great things had been between them before she'd ruined it all. On her side it was more complicated, because she felt guilty. Not only about hurting Ollie's feelings, but also for allowing herself to feel miserable, too. What a stupid mess she'd made of everything.

Ollie suddenly looked up and saw her through the glass. He hesitated for a split second, then beckoned to her, gesturing to the cats and giving her a half-hearted thumbs up. Inside, the smell of cat litter was almost overwhelming – even the aroma of freshly ground coffee came a poor second.

'You're a regular Doctor Doolittle today,' she told him, shaking her head at the young Czech girl to indicate that she didn't want to order anything.

'Did you get some good photos of Mr Soft's house?' he asked.

She nodded, looking anywhere but at him. There were more cats sitting on chairs and along a wide wooden rail above the windows at the back of the café. Some appeared to be sleeping peacefully, while others stared across at her, in that quietly judgemental way cats always do, their tails twitching with displeasure at this strange, foreign newcomer.

Ollie must have sensed her impatience to leave, because the next time he picked up his cup of coffee, he drained it in one gulp.

'Shall we?' he said, indicating the door.

Megan was relieved. The combination of cat litter and curious stares from the girl – who, she'd decided in the past five minutes, had clearly developed a major crush on Ollie – was making her feel extremely uncomfortable. Once outside, she sucked in the cold, clean air gratefully.

'How could you stand the smell in there?' she asked, when they were a safe distance away from the café.

'Smell?' Ollie seemed genuinely at a loss.

'The cat litter. I thought I was going to heave.'

Ollie shrugged. 'My parents have got loads of cats. I'm probably immune to the smell of them by now. Plus, we have loads of animals in the classroom. They come round on rotation for the children to care for. At the moment, I'm looking after three guinea pigs and a degu.'

'What the hell is a degu?' Megan asked as they crossed the road. They had made their way back to the main road that ran alongside the Vltava River, and the sun was still dancing merrily off the surface of the water below them.

Ollie pulled a face while he searched for the words. 'Like a big gerbil,' he told her. 'Sounds awful, but he's actually quite a character. He seems to love the children, too.'

'I don't know how you do your job,' she told him honestly.

That shrug again. 'I don't know how you do yours,' he said.

'Don't you ever have days where the kids annoy you?' she persisted, steering them towards a wide bridge that would take them across the river.

Ollie shook his head. 'Not really. The thing is with young children, even when they're naughty, it's rarely coming from a bad place. They don't understand what it is to be spiteful. It's almost always to do with attention. And if there is some persistent bad behaviour, it usually indicates a bigger problem.

'I had a boy in my class a few years ago who turned from behaving impeccably to literally tearing the place apart, and when I finally sat down with him, one-to-one, it turned out that his mum was sick with cancer.'

'Oh.' Megan put a gloved hand up to her mouth. 'That's awful.'

'There was no dad in the picture, so little Ryan and his older brother, who was only about thirteen, they were doing the lion's share of the housework and the food shopping. The mother's sister was helping out, but they were all struggling, and poor Ryan was just falling apart.'

'What happened?' Megan asked. They had crossed the river now and turned right to walk down the other side, back towards the centre of the city. She was becoming accustomed to the click-clicking sounds of the passing trams and the crunching of the frozen slush beneath her feet. It felt oddly comforting – even relaxing – and she stopped in her tracks for a few seconds to take in the view. The glittering ribbon of the Vltava lay flat and calm to their right, the wind only just causing the trees beside them to creak and rustle. She thought again about the golden cross on the Charles Bridge, the promise of a wish coming true. It was easy to believe such a thing was possible on a day like today.

Ollie had slipped into his typically modest mode now, as he explained how he'd contacted a local support group on Ryan's mother's behalf. His self-effacing nature was one of the things she liked most about him, but equally it frustrated her at times. Ollie was incapable of patting himself on the back, even when he really deserved it, and accepted compliments in much the same way that a cat accepted a worming tablet – he found them a very sour pill to swallow.

'You should feel proud of yourself,' she told him, groaning inwardly as he shook his head with predictable disagreement.

'I was just doing my job,' he said, glancing at her. 'Ryan's mum died about a year ago now. He's not in my class any more, but I've been keeping an eye on him, you know, just making sure he's coping okay.'

Megan paused while she tried to imagine what it must be like for poor little Ryan, losing his mum and not having a dad. She was so close to her own parents that the thought seemed absurd – impossible even.

'Is he okay?' she asked, noticing the moisture in Ollie's eyes.

He took a few moments to reply, instead looking out across the water until the twinkling flickers of sunlight calmed him. 'Kids are resilient,' he said, turning to her. 'I'm supposed to be the teacher, but in the end it was him who ended up teaching me a lesson.'

Megan made a small noise of enquiry, silently worried where the conversation was heading.

'I wasn't in a good place when . . . Well, after my last break-up. I've never told you about my ex, have I?'

Megan shook her head, thinking privately that whoever this girl was, she already hated her.

'I thought it was going somewhere, she had other ideas,' he stated, being careful to keep his tone neutral. Even now, Megan thought, he's doing whatever he can to avoid offending me.

'I won't bore you with the details,' he went on. 'It was nothing like what you went through with that Andre moron – but just after it happened I was having a hard time sleeping and was beating myself up about it all, wondering what was wrong with me, what I could have done differently.'

The tears pricked at Megan's eyes behind her sunglasses.

'I was feeling sorry for myself, basically.' He gave her a sheepish half-smile. 'But then I went into school every day and saw this boy. This boy who had lost everything, but who still made it into lessons every day and put his hand up to answer questions, and played football with his mates during break time. He told me once that his mum had made him promise to keep smiling after she went. He'd promised her that he would be brave and that he'd make her proud – and he was doing it, too. He was doing his best.'

A small sob erupted from Megan, and Ollie immediately stopped. For a second she thought he was going to pull her into his arms and comfort her, but he didn't.

'Sorry.' He looked down at the icy pavement. 'I didn't mean to upset you; I was just . . . Well, I just wanted to say that Ryan made me feel like a prize idiot. I had no right to be even a smidgeon as upset as he was, and I was wallowing in it. He made me see that I had to man up a bit.'

'I'm sorry, too,' she muttered, her voice small.

He didn't ask what she was sorry for. He didn't need to.

They stood for a while, side by side, watching as a tour boat chugged past below them, its red and gold awning as bright as a log fire against the dark grey of the river. Megan lifted her camera to catch the moment, relishing the interruption it provided, and she sensed Ollie begin to move away. She didn't need to turn her head to see if he was waiting for her. She knew he would be – he always was.

39

Hope and Annette found Charlie nursing a black coffee in the bar, his coat, scarf and hat laid across the table. When he saw them approaching, he smiled.

'All okay?'

In answer, Hope lifted up her hand so he could see Annette's wrapped around it. 'I don't know how I'll ever thank you,' she told him. 'You've made me the happiest woman in the world.'

He smiled again. 'That's all I wanted.'

There was a silence, and Hope felt Annette shift beside her.

'Mum, I've gone and left my phone up in the room,' she said, finally dropping Hope's hand. 'Can I have the key?'

Charlie's face flickered a fraction, and Hope knew then that Annette hadn't forgotten a thing – her daughter was just perceptive enough to realise that she and Charlie needed a few minutes alone.

'Are you okay?' she asked him, sitting down as soon as Annette was gone.

'I'm more than okay,' he assured her. 'Seeing the look on your face when you opened that door . . . it was amazing. Made all my sneaking around worthwhile.'

'I'm sorry I didn't trust you.' She patted his hand awkwardly. 'You gave me no reason to think badly of you, but I did. It was wrong of me.'

Charlie nodded. 'Yes, it was a bit. But I can understand why.'

Relief coursed through her.

'Where shall we take Annette today?' she asked. 'I must show her the bridge, and perhaps the castle.'

She continued chatting for a few minutes before she realised he was shaking his head.

'What's the matter?'

'I'm not coming with you.'

'What do you mean? You must come!'

Charlie shook his head and started fiddling with the tassels on his scarf.

'I don't think so, love.'

'But I want you and Annette to spend some time together, get to know each other. She was just telling me how much she likes you.'

Charlie stopped her. 'What was it you wanted to talk to me about yesterday, after you had that massage?' he asked, not taking his eyes off her as she shifted uncomfortably in her seat.

'Nothing important.' She shook her head and forced a smile. 'It can wait.'

He frowned at her. 'I don't think it can.'

Hope glanced up towards the door, already missing the sight of her daughter, the smell of her, the feel of her.

'Do we have to go into it now?' she begged. She couldn't bear for Charlie to pull out the stopper of her happiness just yet.

'I've booked a flight,' he told her, tapping at the table, not meeting her eyes. 'I'm leaving in half an hour.'

'But why?'

'I had a little chat with Annette before I brought her up,' he explained. 'She told me she's more than happy for you to go and stay with her and Patrick for a while.'

Hope snorted. 'You're kicking me out?'

His eyes were pure sorrow. 'No, Hope. I'm letting you go.'

'But I don't want to go!'

Even as she said it, she knew it wasn't the whole truth. He knew it just as well as she did.

Charlie didn't bother to argue, instead turning to face her and putting a big hand on her cheek.

'It's okay,' he soothed. 'This wasn't what either of us planned, I know that. I was so excited to have you all to myself, I didn't really stop to think about how it must feel for you, to have to leave behind your home and your life. I was selfish, but only because . . .'

He paused.

'Because you love me?'

'Yes. Because I love you. And I can't believe I'm doing this, but I have to, because I know that you don't love me.'

'I do!' Hope was quick to correct him. 'I just . . . it's complicated.'

He shook his head. 'You don't have to explain.'

'I do. I mean, I don't want to lose you.'

'Would you marry me?'

Hope hadn't been expecting that, and she heard herself gasp.

'Do you know,' Charlie said, staring hard at her as the colour filled her cheeks. 'I almost proposed to you on our first night here, in the restaurant by the river. I had the ring in my pocket and everything.'

Hope's eyes widened.

'I was this close.' He held up his thumb and forefinger. 'But then something stopped me.'

'What?' It was barely a whisper.

He shrugged and sat back in his chair, at last releasing her from that intense stare. 'I just saw something in your face, a flicker of something. And I knew you'd turn me down.'

Hope tried in vain to think back to what she'd been feeling when they were in that restaurant. She could remember being upset about Annette, and trying in vain to pretend she was all right for his sake. Perhaps that was where she'd been going wrong all this time. Pretending to be fine when she was anything but.

'I'm a mess.' She held up her hands in emotional defeat. 'I'm sorry.'

Charlie sighed. 'You're allowed to be a mess,' he said. 'You've just broken up with your husband. If you weren't a bit of a mess, I'd be worried, frankly.'

'But I don't love Dave.' At last Hope had something that she knew was true to tell him.

'I know.' His voice was gentle again. 'And it's okay to admit that – even to Annette.'

'I feel like I've failed her,' Hope admitted.

'Come on, love.' Charlie's expression was all concern. 'That's just not true. You tried your best – sometimes things just don't work out. And you certainly haven't failed as a mother. Do you think Annette would be here now if you had?'

'I suppose not.'

'When I called her the first time, sure she was angry.

But she also wanted to know how you were, what you'd said about her, if you were missing her.'

'Really?'

'Really. As soon as I heard that, I knew I had to bring the two of you together, and I didn't want to wait. I offered her a flight and told her to think about it, and I've been calling to nag her ever since.'

He picked up his phone from the table to check the time. 'My taxi will be here soon and I need to go upstairs and get my stuff,' he said, managing not to betray how Hope knew he must be feeling. She was suddenly hit by a panic, and grasped his arm with both hands.

'What happens next?'

Charlie looked down before he answered. Her knuckles were white with the effort of holding on to him. 'That's not really up to me,' he said. 'I think you know what I want, now you need to work out what you want.'

Hope couldn't remember the last time anyone had put her in this position, asked her what she wanted to do. Dave had always been the chief decision-maker in their family, and after the break-up she had run straight to Charlie, who'd told her, 'Live with me.' So she had. But now, with the offer of a room at Annette's, she had options for the first time.

She shook her head. 'I honestly don't know,' she told him.

Charlie pushed back his chair. 'I have to go.'

'I'm scared I'll never see you again,' she whispered, more to herself than to him, but it was enough to stop Charlie in his tracks. She knew she should leap up and run across the room into his arms, but she didn't. She stayed where she was in the chair, never taking her eyes off him as he opened the door. For a second she thought he wasn't going to look back at her, but then, at the very last moment, he did.

'Goodbye, Hope,' he said. And then he was gone.

40

As the morning rolled up its sleeves and got ready to welcome its friend afternoon, the sunshine held fast in the clear sky. Megan and Ollie made slow progress as they picked their way along the bank of the Vltava towards Kampa Island in the Little Quarter. The baroque-style buildings they passed were tall and square, and many were lavishly decorated. Megan stopped endlessly to take photos, but she never even heard so much as a murmur of complaint from Ollie. He seemed to be lost in his own melancholy thoughts, and was content to stare out across the water while she worked.

The city was even more beautiful when dappled in this strange, muted sunlight, and it wasn't just the surrounding architecture that caused Megan to lift up her camera. The pavements, too, were ornately patterned in red and white square tiles, and someone had taken the time to come out early and sweep the stubborn remnants of melted snow to one side.

Despite the sun standing proudly above the city, it was still bitterly cold, and Ollie was removing his glasses every few minutes to wipe away the condensation. Megan's bare fingers were pink and sore, but she refused to put on her gloves. If she couldn't feel the solid curves of her camera and the satisfying snap of the lens as she rotated it, then she found it harder to connect with what she was doing.

Instead, she paused every few metres to breathe on to her hands or rub them together. Usually Ollie would make fun of her, but not today.

They reached Kampa Island a little before lunchtime, ducking to avoid the droplets of melted snow that were dripping from the stripped branches of the trees. Following the path from the main road into a wide grassy square populated by shrieking groups of children, tiny dogs wearing minuscule waterproof jackets and clusters of tourists, they stopped to consult the guidebook.

'That's the Sova Mill,' Ollie told her, pointing to the right, where an imposing white building loomed over them, half-blocking the light. Glancing upwards, Megan noticed that the roof tiles were black – a rare sight amongst its predominantly red-roofed neighbours.

'The Kampa Museum of modern art is based here,' Ollie went on, flicking over the page. 'Shall we take a look?'

Megan had never been much of a fan of modern art, but she nodded and followed him towards an open gate. The courtyard beyond was paved in crunchy gravel and littered with sculptures, each one more bizarre than the next. Megan stopped next to a large red horse, its male red rider naked and bald, with strange elongated arms that reached all the way down to the ground.

'He must be a bit chilly,' she quipped, but Ollie had already wandered off to look at a cubist-style creation of a woman lying awkwardly on her stomach, her face twisted upwards and her body horribly contorted. The small square paving slabs around the base of her plinth were decorated by tufts of rogue grass and patches of snow, which Megan found far more beautiful than the artwork itself. She didn't share her thoughts with Ollie, however. She sensed a brittleness that hadn't been there earlier in the day. Ever since he'd admitted to her how upset he'd been about his past break-up, it was as if he'd found a fresh reason to be annoyed with her. Megan knew him well enough to know when he was brooding, and that was exactly what he was doing now.

On the far side of the courtyard they discovered another sculpture of a woman, this time standing upright with a long, thin body rolled almost as flat as a sheet of paper. With her head bowed forward and her splayed-out fan of blue hair, she exuded sorrow and defeat, and for the first time since they'd ventured inside, Megan felt moved enough to lift up her camera.

Ollie had made his way back to the red man astride his horse and was crouching down to decipher the label. Megan was so used to feeling his eyes on her at all times that this new deliberate avoidance felt unnatural. She was accustomed to basking in the warm glow of his affection, and now that it was gone she felt as if someone had opened a door and let the cold air in. She and Ollie may never have been a proper couple, but she'd always suspected that he cared about her. She hadn't wanted to admit what had been so blindingly obvious to all their friends – that Ollie fancied her just as much as he had on that first night when they'd kissed – but the tiny part of her that wasn't in denial had known they were right. She knew it was wrong to crave Ollie's love the way she did; she knew she was being selfish – but she also knew that the thought of losing him for good terrified her. He was such a big part of her life, and she was afraid that the void he would leave if he ever went away for good would be so big that it would consume her entirely.

Battling a sudden surge of regret and fear, Megan did what she always did and brought up her camera, shielding her face from the world and venturing into another, one where she was in control. She found Ollie through the lens, saw his breath pooling into the cold air and the colour on his cheeks; saw his eyes shift behind his glasses as he searched for her, and saw the flicker of regret pass across them. His nose was just beginning to run, a glisten of moisture in the groove of his Cupid's bow, and his lips were plump and full.

She watched as he got up and strolled across the gravel to examine another structure, this one made of metal poles and intricate little wheels. He took out his phone to take his own photo, and Megan zoomed closer to see how he framed it. He'd removed one of his gloves, and she could see the torn shards of skin around his nails, the sporadic black hairs on the top of his exposed wrist, the pronounced veins criss-crossing the pale flesh, his ligaments busily working beneath the skin. She felt her heart soar and her pulse quicken, that treasured rush of inspiration so acute as she moved her finger around to compress the shutter. If only he knew how lost she was in him. If only she knew the words to explain it.

After a time, Ollie turned towards her, his expression hard as granite as he made his way back to the open gateway, beckoning her with a hand when she didn't immediately follow. She wondered when he would bring up the events of the previous night. Although he had batted the conversation away that morning, she knew Ollie – he would want to discuss it. If he was feeling anything like she was, then he would be experiencing constant flashbacks – colourful images of twisted bare limbs and open mouths – and it was becoming difficult to ignore the crackling energy in the air between them. She hoped more than anything that he wouldn't make her reiterate why she didn't want to be in a relationship, not least because she was beginning to doubt her own resolve.

'Bloody hell!'

They'd left the courtyard of the museum and made their way back into Kampa Park, taking the path that ran past the rear of the Sova Mill. As they reached the edge of the building, however, Ollie, who was a few metres ahead, actually recoiled in surprise.

'What is it?'

Megan hurried forward through the slush to join him and gasped. There in front of them, frozen on all fours and looking about as ghoulish as anything Megan had ever encountered, were three huge bronze babies.

'Good God!'

She wasn't sure if it was the sheer size of these creations, their random positioning in the park or the fact that instead of facial features each one had a strip of what looked like a window blind stretching from forehead to chin – the bronze skin puckered unpleasantly around the edges – but she was immediately and enormously creeped out.

'Why don't they have faces?' she said, aghast.

Ollie stepped forward and read from a plaque on the

side of the Mill. "'David Cerny, 1967. Mimina/Babies."' Hang on, aren't these the same babies as the ones on that TV Tower we saw in the distance?'

'Yes!' Megan snatched up her camera and starting clicking through the archive. 'Here! There are loads of them.' She paused to count, scrolling up and down her photos and shivering as a gust of wind blew a herd of fallen leaves through the park. 'There are ten of them crawling up the tower.'

'They're quite something,' Ollie said now. He walked over to the nearest sculpture and took off his glove to run his hand over the smooth bronze of its bare shoulder. Ollie was tall, but even he couldn't look one of these things in the eye. Not that they had any eyes . . .

'I hate their latticed faces!' Megan was still rooted to the spot in horror.

Ollie laughed at that, strolling around the back of the same baby and vaulting up on to its back.

'What are you doing?' she shrieked. 'You can't ride the babies!'

'I think you'll find that I can,' he informed her, swinging his leg over so he was sitting astride the vast metal monster. Megan lifted her camera and chuckled against it as he pulled stupid faces and peered at her from over the top of the baby's head. A nearby family of tourists had been watching them and, spurred on by Ollie's antics, the youngest children were demanding to be lifted up on to the backs of the other two babies.

'Now look what you've done,' Megan scolded him playfully. 'As if it isn't bleak enough for these babies, out here in the snow, now they're no better than donkeys.'

Ollie shrugged. 'If I were them, I'd appreciate a bit of human warmth.'

Megan blushed as another flashback of Ollie's own considerable warmth swam into view. She blinked it away, turning to hide her red cheeks.

'"The babies are a symbol of the Communist era,"' Ollie read aloud. He was still sitting up on his bronze baby perch, but now had the guidebook open in his hands. Megan looked up and saw that his glasses had slid so far down his nose that they were in danger of falling right off.

'"They are unable to reach adulthood, their growth stifled by totalitarianism."'

'You can take the teacher out of his classroom . . .' Megan mocked, pleased when Ollie responded by sticking out his tongue at her. 'I couldn't care less what they mean,' she told him, finally feeling brave enough to step forward and touch one. 'I just want to know why they don't have any faces.'

'Perhaps they're shy?' Ollie swung a long leg over and slid down to the ground, his foot slipping on a patch of ice that sent him careering sideways into Megan.

'Sorry!'

For the briefest second, Megan felt herself enjoy the sensation of his weight against her, felt his warmth flow through her. The urge she'd had yesterday, to kiss and touch him, seemed to be making a return. But she mustn't. She wouldn't.

'I don't think they're shy.' She indicated the huge bare bottom by his face. 'I think they're evil.'

'Just because you don't want any babies, don't go slating all the others.'

He'd meant it as a joke, of course, but Ollie's casual assumption made Megan's face pucker up just like the statue next to them.

'I never said I didn't want a baby, I said I wasn't sure.'

Ollie held up his hands. 'Okay, okay – don't bite my head off.'

'I wasn't!'

The last thing she wanted was to argue with him, but he clearly wasn't going to give her even a centimetre today, let alone an inch. She watched as he kicked at a patch of uneven ground, his head down as he bit furiously on his lip. The worst thing was, she didn't even blame him for being fed up with her. She tried to imagine how she would feel in his position, how humiliated she would be if she'd put herself out there twice and he had freaked out, if he had run off and she'd woken up alone in bed, a rapidly cooling groove in the mattress beside her. It would have been horrendous.

Turning from the babies back towards the park, Megan watched the breeze bothering the topmost leaves in the trees. They were a heady autumnal mix of greens, oranges and yellows, and the relentless sunshine lent a startling clarity to the scene. She felt as if she could see every individual strand of grass, every spidery vein on the fallen leaves by her feet. Why, she wondered, when the beauty of the world was so blindingly obvious to her, could she not let herself see it in what she had with Ollie? It wasn't that she didn't trust him not to treat her well, or even to be understanding when she needed time alone to work, it was more that she didn't trust herself not to hurt him.

What Megan really needed was to be able to see into

the future. If only she could reach out a finger and push the hands around on just one of the many clocks in this city. If she could leap forward in time and see herself and Ollie there, together and happy, then she would be able to give in to what she was feeling. She would be free to enjoy all these emotions, rather than feel strangled by them – they would be her wings, rather than her bars.

But nobody could see into the future, and wishes rarely came true – they were empty pockets of hope, a fleeting rush of desire or of need. If Megan thought that there was any truth in the myth surrounding that golden cross up on the Charles Bridge, she would run there right now and wish with all her heart for some certainty. But without an absolute assurance that she wouldn't be responsible for breaking Ollie's heart, she just wasn't willing to take the risk.

41

Annette ran her fingers over the arms of the golden cross and gazed in wonder at her mother. Hope had just relayed the story about St John being tossed over the side of the Charles Bridge.

'Did you really wish for me?' Annette asked for the second time.

Hope nodded. 'I did. I know it's silly, but at that moment it felt possible.'

'A year and a day is a long time,' Annette mused. 'I don't think I would ever have been able to stay away from you for that long.'

'I'm very glad to hear it.' Hope put her arm around her daughter's shoulders and squeezed. How bizarre, she thought. Just a few days ago she'd been standing in this exact place with Charlie, trying not to cry over Annette, and now she was here again with her daughter, trying not to cry over Charlie.

'Are you okay, Mum?'

Hope swallowed. 'Of course. I just wish that . . .' She stopped, realising how ironic it was that she was wishing for things in this particular spot.

'Wish that what?' Annette asked.

'Nothing.' Hope shook her head and smiled. 'Now, come on, let's go and waste some money on one of those people who draw caricatures. I've always wanted to get one done, but Charlie wasn't keen. He was worried they'd draw him to look like a boiled egg.'

'Well,' Annette grinned, 'he does look a bit Humpty Dumpty-ish. Not in a bad way, of course.'

Hope pictured Charlie, his lovely smooth head and his jolly grin. She missed him terribly, but there was also a sense of relief. The past few days had been tough for both of them, and she imagined he was feeling the same way as her.

'Has he texted you since he left?' Annette asked gently, as they made their way slowly along the cobbles. She was all wrapped up now in the hat, scarf and gloves that Hope had insisted they buy, her long brown hair glowing like polished wood against her shoulders.

'Not yet.' Hope looped an arm through her daughter's. 'I'm not sure if he will, to tell you the truth. I think he'll leave it up to me.'

'And will you?'

Hope paused to watch a collection of pigeons that had gathered in a patch of sunlight, each doing that strange head-bobbing dance as they picked at the ground for crumbs.

'I don't know,' she said honestly. 'I care about him, but I don't want to mess him around. My head's been all over the place since me and your dad . . . Well, since it all happened.'

Annette's face fell, and Hope knew she must be picturing the night she'd caught them in the car.

'I don't know why I did that,' Annette said, staring at a gaggle of girls with their selfie sticks held aloft. 'I shouldn't have run off to Dad like that.'

'Please.' Hope squeezed her arm. 'Don't be sorry. I'm the one who cheated.' She had decided not to tell Annette about Dave's vasectomy. The only thing that mattered now was the future, and while it was frightening to know that she now had the freedom to go and seek her own adventure, it also filled her with excitement. Prague, with all its magic, colourful history and inescapable clocks, had reminded her how important it was to live life to the absolute fullest. She wanted to set out and make her mark in her own little corner of the world.

After they'd had their caricatures drawn, Hope took Annette up the hill to visit Prague Castle, the two of them giggling at the stoic guards in their fur hats and grimacing at the gargoyles hanging off the roof of St Vitus's Cathedral. They came across the Golden Lane purely by accident, and spent hours exploring the tiny shops and galleries, luxuriating in the pleasure of each other's company and the warm welcome of the Czech shopkeepers.

As the wind picked up, Hope and Annette scuttled from one pool of sunlight to the next in search of warmth. They bought cups of wine laced with rum, each growing happily merry as the hours passed. For a late lunch, Hope took Annette back to the little café behind the church, ordering them both huge plates of steaming goulash followed by deliciously gooey honey cake. The waitress greeted them like old friends, adding what Hope suspected was a lot of extra cream to their desserts.

As she had anticipated, Annette was absolutely enchanted by Prague, and was now lamenting the fact that the two of them were flying home the following day.

'You will stay with us over Christmas, won't you?' Annette asked now, licking cream off her spoon.

'What about your dad?' Hope asked. She knew Annette was willing to offer her a bed for now, but she didn't want to come between her daughter and Dave, not when she felt responsible for the fact that he might be facing Christmas alone.

'He's going to Granny's.' Annette shrugged. 'Apparently she can't wait to spoil him.'

Hope rolled her eyes in good humour. 'That sounds about right.'

'I meant what I said,' Annette went on. 'You'll have a bed at mine for as long as you need it.'

Hope felt tears in her eyes yet again – she really was a wreck today.

'I'm sorry if I let you down,' she said, her voice small.

'I just wish you'd talked to me,' Annette whispered, playing with the edge of the tablecloth.

'I thought you'd hate me.' Hope shook her head as she realised just how foolish she'd been. 'He's your dad and you love him. I didn't know how to tell you.'

'It's over now,' Annette said, drawing a line under the conversation. 'And now you can do whatever you want.'

'Pah!' Hope laughed. 'I'm too old now. Old and past it.'

'Oi!' Annette scolded. 'I hear that fifty is the new thirty these days.'

'Only if you can afford Botox.'

They laughed for a few seconds, and then Annette looked at her thoughtfully.

'You know Patrick's parents are retiring next month?' she asked.

'Are they?' It was the first Hope had heard about it.

'Well, they're looking for someone to take over the B&B – someone they can trust. Patrick thought you might be up for it.'

Colour flooded into Hope's cheeks. 'Me?'

'No, the Queen's pack of Corgis. Of course you!'

'But I don't have any experience.'

Annette glared at her, mock stern. 'You ran our house for years. And Patrick's dad can teach you anything you need to know. Honestly, Mum, it's not exactly quantum physics we're talking about – you could do the job blindfolded with one arm tied behind your back.'

'I don't think I could,' Hope protested again, but there was a slow excitement building inside her. Wasn't this exactly what she'd been hoping for? Her own income and a chance to do a job she knew she'd love . . .

'Do you really think I could?' she asked, unable to stop herself from grinning when her daughter bobbed her head up and down so rapidly it was in danger of falling right off.

'Of course you could. I'm going to call Patrick right now and let him know.'

'I can't believe this.' Hope's hands were shaking as she counted out some money for the bill and attempted to pull on her gloves. 'I just can't believe it.'

Annette pulled her new hat down over her mess of brown hair and stood up.

'What was it you were saying about Prague being a place where all your wishes come true?'

Yes, thought Hope, as she linked arms with her daughter and led the way back out into the bright afternoon – this was a place where magic happened.

42

'I think it might snow.'

Ollie squinted into the distance, following the direction of Megan's outstretched finger to where an ominous throb of dark clouds sat gloomily in the east.

'I think you might be right.'

'I hope it comes before it gets dark,' she mused. 'I'd love to take some photos of it falling. I bet the Charles Bridge looks amazing in the snow.'

'I bet it does.'

He'd been providing her with these non-committal replies all afternoon, and Megan was beginning to feel irritated. She knew he had every right to be short with her, though, so she swallowed each sarcastic remark as it occurred to her, choking every now and then on the sheer bitterness.

She'd convinced him to walk off their lunch of pork shoulder, bacon dumplings, mashed potatoes and piles of sauerkraut by strolling up to Letna Park, but she hadn't been prepared for just how many steps they would have to climb. The trek up here had been worse than the one up the Observation Tower. However, when they'd reached the summit of the hill, the view over the city had made the arduous ascent more than worth it. Megan had also been delighted to find a rope strung up from the metronome to a nearby tree which had been decorated with loads of discarded trainers – a perfect addition to her album of the past few days. Just when she thought she'd seen all the beauty that Prague could offer, she'd turn a cobbled corner, open a creaky old door or climb a slippery, snow-covered hill and be confronted with gem after gem. It was such a special place.

She should be feeling excited about getting back to London and shutting herself away with her photos, going through the many thousands she'd taken since they arrived and selecting the ones she wanted for the exhibition. But she didn't feel excited at all. Instead, she was filled with an uneasy sort of dread.

'What do you fancy doing now?' she asked Ollie, unable to bear the silence any longer.

He barely turned in her direction before replying.

'I don't mind.'

'Come on,' she forced a note of enthusiasm into her tone. 'I chose this place, so now it's your turn.'

Ollie took a deep breath. 'You mean you'd actually consider doing something that I wanted to do?' he asked.

Megan could detect a tinge of spite in his words, but she wasn't quite sure where he was going with this line of conversation yet, so she decided to play dumb.

'Of course I would.' She smiled stiffly. 'Why wouldn't I?'

'I just didn't think my opinion counted for much in your eyes,' he said, giving her a hard look.

Megan opened her mouth to argue, then shut it again.

'You can't keep doing this to me,' he went on, picking a leaf off a nearby bush and shredding it into tiny pieces. 'Not any more, Megs. Things have changed.'

'Don't let's do this,' she begged. 'I don't want to argue with you.'

‘What about what I want?’ he cut across her, his voice rising an octave as the bits of desecrated leaf fluttered to the ground. ‘Does what I want ever even occur to you?’

‘I thought you wanted to be friends,’ she stammered, following him as he crunched across the frozen grass towards the path.

‘I thought so too.’ He stopped and stared at her. ‘But now I’m not so sure I can be.’

He’d never looked at her like this before, with such dismay, and Megan felt as if she’d been slapped.

‘I’m sorry for what happened,’ she began, although it was a lie. She had wanted it to happen just as much as he had.

Ollie opened his eyes a fraction wider. ‘If you regret it so much,’ he muttered, ‘then why did you do it at all?’

‘It’s not that I regret it!’ she implored. ‘You know I don’t. I just . . .’ She stopped as her thoughts slipped away from her into the quicksand of fear. This was the moment she needed to be honest with him about her own shortcomings and tell him that it was herself she couldn’t trust, not him, but for some reason she couldn’t find the words.

Ollie was blinking rapidly behind his glasses, his cheeks filling with colour as he waited for her to continue.

‘I don’t want to lose you,’ she said eventually, and so quietly that Ollie had to take a step closer in order to hear her.

‘What was that?’

‘I said, I don’t want to lose you,’ she repeated, this time failing to keep the pleading tone from her voice. She wasn’t sure what she was feeling for Ollie any more, but she did know that she wanted him in her life – she knew that for certain. It was one of the only things she really was sure about.

Ollie sighed and folded his arms.

'Have the last few days meant nothing to you at all?' he said then, and she knew what he was asking. All those looks exchanged between the two of them, all the crackling chemistry in the air, the way it had felt to finally touch one another, to taste one another, to be with one another.

'You ask me that question as if you think they didn't,' she mumbled. 'I'm not dead inside, Ollie – I feel things just as much as you do.'

'So then why?' He wrung his hands with exasperation.

Megan didn't have an answer for this, so she just shook her head.

'I've liked you since the first moment we met,' Ollie told her, his voice steady despite the turmoil she could see all over his face. 'When you backed off at the beginning, I thought all you needed was time. I guessed you must have been through something awful in the past, but I didn't want to push you. And being your friend has been amazing, Megs – it really has. But over the past few days, I've started to like you a whole lot more than a friend really should.'

Megan looked up and let her eyes find his. He was saying all the things she couldn't, and alongside the glow she felt at hearing him admit all this, there was also shame.

'I don't want to be your best friend, Megan,' he said, taking another step forward until he was only inches away. 'I want to be your boyfriend. The thing is, I—'

'Don't.' Megan put up a hand, unable to bear hearing him confess his true feelings. Saying it after a night on the tequila was one thing, but for him to admit that he loved her when he was sober? That was a different thing entirely.

Ollie recoiled, his mouth opening in shock.

'I'm sorry,' she said, looking at the ground now instead of him. The snow was thick up here under the trees and she couldn't even see the grass beneath it. 'You deserve better than someone like me.'

'What are you so scared of?' Ollie asked her then, his voice gentle as he noticed her tears beginning to fall. 'Whatever it is, Megs, we can work through it. Just don't give up on us because you're scared.'

Megan closed her eyes and tried to picture what it would be like to be Ollie's girlfriend, to wake up with him by her side every day, as she had done here in Prague. To kiss him whenever she wanted to and bask in the warm glow of his love for her. Then she switched places and pictured herself as Ollie, trying to navigate a path towards happiness with her. She who was so consumed by ambition, screwed up by distrust and crippled by the fear of letting him down. It wasn't Ollie who she didn't love enough, it was herself.

'I can't,' she told him, folding her arms to signal that the subject was closed. 'I'm really sorry.'

It was agonising to stand there and watch the disintegration of his features as he realised what she was saying, that there was no hope for them and that everything they'd felt for each other over the past few exquisite days had all amounted to nothing. Megan knew she would never be able to forgive herself.

This time when Ollie started to walk away, she didn't

follow him, and when he reached the path leading back down the hill he paused, eventually turning again to face her.

'I'm going back to the hotel to check on Sophie,' he said. 'I just need some time on my own, away from you. I need to get my head straight.'

She nodded, biting hard on her lip to stop herself from sobbing in front of him. Ollie looked for a moment like he was going to say something else, but instead he just gazed at her for what felt like an age, before shaking his head and disappearing from view. Megan waited until she could no longer hear the sound of his shoes on the frozen gravel before she let the rest of her tears fall, then angrily wiped them off her cheeks as soon as they appeared. This was all her own fault – she had no right to be feeling sorry for herself.

She didn't want to take the same path down the hill as Ollie, so she wandered around the deserted park looking for an alternative route, her feet turning to ice inside her boots as the snow soaked through the gaps between the stitches and glue. She wished there was someone she could call who would tell her what to do and make her feel better – but she couldn't think of a single soul. Her friends were all exasperated by the subject of herself and Ollie, and she couldn't imagine her mum having much sympathy either.

She thought fleetingly of Hope, who had been so sweet to her when they'd spoken about Ollie the other night. She wondered where in the city she and Charlie were, and what they were getting up to. Then she pictured Sophie, so small and unobtrusive, yet so sure of her love for her fiancé, Robin. Ollie had said he was going to check on her, and Megan realised guiltily that she hadn't even thought about the younger girl since the morning. She had been so ill, collapsing in front of them and everything, and Megan had been too self-absorbed to even care. What a total bitch she had become.

When had it happened? she wondered, kicking a part-collapsed snowman so that his head flew up into the cold air. When had she become more important than everyone else? Why did Ollie even like her, let alone love her? How could he love someone like her? She'd taken advantage of how he felt, that's what she'd done. She'd wanted him and she'd known he would oblige, but she hadn't thought about what it would mean to him. She hadn't just let him down, she'd let herself down.

Slowly realising that she was never going to get very far by trundling around in circles in the snow, Megan returned to the path they'd taken earlier and made her way out of the park, finding the steps down a lot less work than they had been coming up. More clouds had crept along the Vltava River and the sun was beginning to hang heavily in the sky. The city was bathed in a strange yellow glow, as if someone had turned a giant dimmer switch down, and the green-topped towers of the Church of St Nicholas had been turned the colour of sludge in the approaching dusk.

Stopping to take in the view halfway down the steps, Megan took a deep breath, trying to absorb everything that she was seeing. She wanted her eyes to find every individual red roof tile, every curl of chimney smoke, every dark spire and flicker of light against water. Sometimes the enormity of the world exhausted her – there was so much to see and not enough time in which to see it. She knew she must accept that some corners of the world would always remain nothing more than a blur to her, but if she had her way then she'd halt time altogether. Perhaps it was being here in Prague, with all these clocks at every turn, that made her so aware of time passing.

Instead of lifting her camera and capturing the view in front of her, Megan held it out at arm's-length and made herself stare into the dark mirror of the lens, pressing the shutter release and holding it down. When she'd made her way back down to street level, she ventured straight into the nearest bar and ordered herself a cup of hot grog with honey, which she clasped with both hands until the feeling started to come back into her fingers.

The taste of it was sharp, the smell fragrant, but it hit her belly with the required amount of fire to bolster her mood and close the lid on all the conflicting emotions that were busy tying her guts into knots. The alcohol slowed the race of her heart and soothed the corners of her mind, and Megan found that she was again able to breathe without it hurting.

She chose a seat next to a window and picked up her camera to examine the photograph she'd just taken, searching her own face for signs. Of what, she wasn't quite sure, but all she found in her eyes was sorrow. Her skin was blotchy from where she'd rubbed away her tears with the scratchy wool of her gloves, and her lips were beginning to crack from exposure to the cold air. Days of indulging in dehydrating alcohol had deepened the lines around and in between her eyes, and across the part of her forehead not obscured by her hat. Her hair was tatty-looking, the ends frayed, and her mouth was downturned at its edges. There was no joy on her face, no love. What there seemed to be an abundance of was regret, sadness and a real weariness that Megan hadn't realised she was feeling. She was worn out, both physically and emotionally. It was, quite literally, written all over her face.

She sipped her grog and grimaced as the medicinal liquid hit the back of her throat and burnt a path down towards her stomach. She should get up and go back to the hotel, find Ollie and beg him to forgive her, tell him she was sorry. But she didn't move, she couldn't move, and the minutes drifted past in a blur. When her phone suddenly buzzed into life on the table in front of her, she almost jumped out of her seat.

It was Ollie. He'd forgiven her. He must be calling to make amends. Snatching up her phone, she began babbling apologies before he could get a word in, and only stopped when she realised he was actually shouting at her.

'What? What is it?' she gasped.

'We need your help,' Ollie said, the fear horribly apparent in his voice. 'It's Sophie. Something's happened. At the hotel. Where are you?'

Megan felt her heart begin to clatter once more against her ribcage.

'I'm on my way.'

43

The light was beginning to draw in by the time Hope led Annette back to the hotel. They'd spent the afternoon exploring as much of Prague as they could reach, but eventually, the lure of a hot bath became too much to resist – especially as Hope was convinced it was going to snow. She had told Annette all about Megan, Ollie and Sophie, and how the latter's fiancé should have arrived by now. If they camped out in the hotel bar for long enough, she told her daughter, they'd be bound to bump into everyone.

'What will you tell them about Charlie?' Annette asked, as they took off their coats, hats and scarves and settled themselves at a table close to the door.

Hope shuffled in her seat. 'The truth. If the past few months have taught me anything, it's that the truth is always the best option.'

Annette smiled. 'Well, if that's the case, then the truth is I really fancy a cocktail. How about you?'

Hope grinned and picked up a menu. 'I don't see why not.'

They were on their second round of multi-coloured rum concoctions when Ollie appeared in the doorway. Hope took one look at his face and leapt to her feet.

'What's the matter, love?'

Ollie had been staring straight at them, but it seemed to take him a few moments to register that it was her.

'Sorry, I . . .' He stopped, running a hand through his hair. 'Have you seen Sophie?'

'Not since the day before yesterday.' Hope paused. 'Why? What's happened?'

'She was ill.' He faltered for a second as he caught sight of Annette, frowning in confusion.

'This is my daughter, Annette,' Hope explained. 'She . . . Charlie . . . It's a long story.'

'Oh. Hi.' Ollie raised a hand and Annette waved shyly back.

'You were saying about Sophie?' Hope prompted. Ollie looked upset then, and she felt bubbles of panic begin to inflate in her chest.

'She fainted on the Charles Bridge yesterday.' He sighed and looked over his shoulder into the reception area. 'I brought her back here and told her to get some rest, but I haven't seen her since. I just went to check on her and she's not in her room.'

'Fainted?' Hope was shocked. 'We waited for you all in here last night, Charlie and I, but nobody showed up. I assumed she'd made other plans.'

'I should have checked on her myself,' Ollie admitted, suddenly looking sheepish. 'But me and Megan, we . . .' He stopped, obviously realising from the look on Hope's face that he didn't need to explain further.

'What if she fell in the shower or something?' he said, fear grasping him. 'I knew she wasn't quite right. I should have done more. I was so preoccupied.' He paused again and looked down at Hope's hand, which was clasped around his arm.

'Don't go blaming yourself,' she soothed. 'I'm sure she's fine. Her fiancé was due to arrive today, so maybe she's just off somewhere with him.'

Ollie pulled a face. 'I don't know. Something just doesn't feel right. It's been niggling at me all day. I came back to check on her because I just had this sense, this feeling that something was wrong – and now she's not here.'

'Where's Megan?' Hope asked now, and Ollie visibly blanched.

'Out taking photos somewhere,' he muttered, not meeting her eyes.

'Did you two have a row?' she guessed.

'Not really a row.' He sighed again. 'It doesn't matter.'

'Come and sit down for a bit,' she suggested, steering him towards a chair. 'We can keep an eye on the door in case Sophie comes back.'

Ollie collapsed into his seat. He looked utterly defeated, and Hope raised her eyebrows at Annette. The sky beyond the windows was a dark denim blue, and Hope shivered as if she could feel the cold evening air on her skin. It wasn't nice to think of Sophie out there, her frail body no match for the freezing temperature, and she was unnerved by how worried and agitated Ollie seemed to be.

A dark Czech beer arrived and he drank half of it in one long gulp as Annette explained how she had come to be in Prague.

'So, Charlie's already left?' he asked, wiping beer froth off his upper lip.

Hope nodded.

'I really hope the two of you work things out,' he said. 'It's obvious how much he cares about you.'

'It's complicated,' Hope told him, glancing at Annette. 'There's a lot to consider.'

Ollie looked up. 'Is there? It all seems pretty simple to me. If two people care about each other, they should be together. It should be easy.'

'If only it was,' she agreed, knowing that what he was really talking about was his own situation.

'You know, you should do what makes you happy,' she told him, feeling horribly disloyal to Megan. 'If Megan can't make you happy, then you need to move on for your own sake.'

He shook his head, his sadness palpable. 'I know, but the thought of not seeing Meg or talking to her . . .' He took a deep breath and pushed his glass forward a fraction. 'I don't know if I can cut her out of my life.'

Hope wished she could reassure him that Megan would come round, but how could she?

'You deserve to be with a person who is one hundred per cent sure about you,' Annette said now, smiling as Ollie looked at her in surprise. 'They need to know beyond a shadow of a doubt that you're the one they want to be with. There's no room for any uncertainty, not when your heart is on the line.'

'When did you get so wise?' Hope asked, looking from her daughter to Ollie and back again.

'I had a good upbringing,' Annette replied. 'It's what you told me when I was dithering over whether or not to move in with Patrick. In the end I realised that I was just scared. It wasn't that I didn't love him, it was just the fear that I might not. That sounds like nonsense, I know.'

Ollie put his empty glass down. 'It doesn't,' he told her. 'It sounds spot on. I'm so sure of Megan, but I can't be sure for the both of us.'

'And you shouldn't have to be,' Annette said, and Hope nodded in agreement. She remembered what Sophie had told them about how she knew Robin was the one almost as soon as she met him, and how the love they felt for each other had grown stronger with every passing year, until they became how they were now – totally unbreakable.

Glancing out through the open door into the reception area, Hope gave a start. There at the front desk, his blond hair tucked into the collar of his jacket and his cheeks pink from the cold, was a man that could only be Robin.

'Look!' She grabbed Ollie's hand and pointed.

Ollie had to get out of his chair to see, and as soon as he did, he stumbled straight out of the bar, Hope at his heels.

As they neared the blond man, Hope heard him asking the receptionist if Sophie Roberts was a guest. It must be him.

'Robin?' she said, so hesitantly that at first she thought the man hadn't heard her.

'Sorry?' He turned to face them. He had a slight accent and looked at her with seriousness, but his blue eyes were friendly enough.

'Are you Robin?' she repeated. 'Sophie's Robin?'

'Is she here?' the man asked, all at once alert. 'Do you know her?'

'We don't really know her that well,' Ollie explained.

'We just met her a few days ago, but she talked about you. She told us you were coming over.'

Annette had appeared behind them now, too, and the blond man looked at each of them in turn, a mask of utter confusion on his face.

'Are you okay?' Hope asked at last, taking a step towards him. The hotel receptionist was holding out a photocopy of something, and the man turned to look.

'Yes, that's her,' he said, his voice breaking with a mixture of relief and concern. 'That's Sophie.'

Ollie joined the man and glanced at the paper in his hands, nodding across at Hope.

'I'm sure she'll be along soon,' Hope said. 'All she's talked about these past few days is how much she's looking forward to seeing you.'

Ollie was shaking his head. 'He didn't even know she was staying here,' he pointed out, and Hope heard Annette emit a nervous cough.

'You are Robin, aren't you?' Hope turned again to face the other man. He was still holding the photocopy of Sophie's passport, and his hand was trembling. The only sound came from the ticking of the clock on the wall, and Hope held her breath as she waited for what she could sense was bad news. Ollie looked positively terrified, and Annette was clutching the door frame. All their eyes moved slowly to the man as he raised his head.

'I'm his brother,' he said, the words coming out slowly, as if punctured by pain. 'Robin died ten days ago.'

44

It felt like a joke when the doctor told them. A horrible joke, but a joke all the same. Sophie had even laughed out loud, shaking her head and telling the man not to be so silly. Robin wasn't even thirty yet, he wasn't going to die. He couldn't.

But, as it turned out, he could.

Cancer didn't negotiate once it had its hostage. No amount of love or hope or despair could be used as a bargaining tool to win a person back from its clutches. All you could do was stand back and watch as the man you loved so entirely disintegrated in front of your eyes. Watch as the desperate attempts at treatment robbed him of his strength, of his energy and of his beautiful hair, the skin on his sore-covered scalp cold and tinged with grey. Sophie used to run her hands across its fuzzy surface, stroking him as she would a wounded baby bird, all the time telling him how handsome he was, and joking that she could finally see how big his ears were after all these years.

After his initial disbelief that what the doctors were telling him was true, Robin's fiery passion manifested itself in a destructive torrent of rage. Sophie could only sit sobbing on the carpet of their bedroom floor as he shouted at the unfairness of it all. His eyes were wild with fear and anger as he begged for someone, anyone, to take this disease away from him. As she stood up to try and comfort him, Robin swung an angry arm around and sent the blue glass bowl they'd bought together in Prague hurtling across the room, where it smashed into thousands of pieces against the wall.

While this anger had frightened Sophie, she understood it. The thing she feared most of all was that this illness would take away Robin's passion. It never did, though. The one thing the cancer failed to take was his spirit – that had remained intact until the very end, when she'd felt his hand weaken slowly in her own. She hadn't let go of his hand even when it was as cold as porcelain, even when she was asked to, then begged, then ordered, then dragged.

Sophie closed her eyes as the wind blew straight into them, taking with it the tears that now seemed to have taken up residence there. She had walked out of the city in the opposite direction to the one she would usually take, and she hadn't stopped until she reached the huge, futuristic structure of the Zizkov TV Tower, with its bronze babies crawling menacingly up its sides.

She and Robin should have had a baby. They had even talked about it a few months before he was diagnosed. She wanted to get married first, to have their dream wedding at her parents' house and write her new name in the sand. Of course, when it later became clear that cancer had flipped over the hourglass of their happiness, Robin had begged her to marry him before it was too late. Sophie had refused, telling him they would do it when he was better. Someone would find a cure, and he would get well – well enough to take her in his arms and swing her around and around as he used to. She didn't want tears of sadness at her wedding, she wanted tears of joy. She hadn't been ready to give up.

It had grown dark some time ago now, Sophie wasn't sure exactly when, and a glance at the illuminated face of a nearby clock told her it was close to eight p.m. Just four hours left.

It was Robin who had first told her about the golden cross on the Charles Bridge, about the legend of St John Nepomuk and the wishes he could grant. They had visited Prague together so many times over the years, but not once had either of them taken advantage of this myth. They both agreed that they had everything they could ever wish for, that to ask for more would be greedy and needless, so they admired the cross from afar instead. Always in awe, but never tempted. Well, not until the last time they'd visited.

Sophie had begged Robin to come away with her as soon as the doctor delivered that awful news. It was only a few weeks before Christmas, and Robin wanted to wait until the festivities were over to tell his family. That was Robin all over, putting everyone else ahead of himself, not wanting to ruin Christmas. So he and Sophie flew over to Prague as they habitually did, only this time was different. This time she insisted they go straight to the Charles Bridge to make their wish. They couldn't afford to lose even a second, she'd told him, dragging him over the cobbles in her haste to reach the magical spot. Robin's limbs had already begun to weaken, but he never once made even a murmur of complaint. He watched in silence as Sophie got to her knees on the cold ground, her hand firmly on the gold cross, ignoring the stares from passers-by as she whispered her wish again and again into the air.

When it was Robin's turn, he closed his eyes, and she'd stared at his silently moving lips through eyes saturated with tears. It had felt special, and magical, and she knew the city's ghosts were listening to them. She could feel it in the air and smell it in the bricks. So much history, so many spirits. Before Robin, she hadn't been sure if she believed in true love, and before Prague, she had never believed in magic. Now she was convinced that the strength of her belief in both those things was going to bring him back to her.

A year and a day it had been. A year and a day since she had stood on that bridge and wished with every fibre of her soul that Robin would always be with her. It had become the hook on which she hung her hope, and even when it seemed that all was lost, she still believed. She must believe. She could not and would not accept that she had lost him, and that there was nothing ahead of her but emptiness, a missing space where Robin should always be.

She hated this. Being alone here in this city that she loved so very much. But there was nobody she could have brought. Her family and Robin's family were dealing with their own grief, but she knew they were worried about her. Her phone had barely stopped ringing since she arrived, and she knew her parents were growing frantic. None of them understood. None of their words could make a dent in her absolute certainty that Robin would be returned to her – and that it would happen here, in the place where they had met.

Blackness had crept across the city as she walked, and from her position on the road behind Prague's central train station, Sophie could see a mosaic of coloured lights. The Charles Bridge was where she needed to be. That was where he'd be waiting. She could hear the sound of her own heart as it crashed wildly against the inside of her chest, and her legs felt unsteady beneath her. The sickness had not returned, but her breathing had become erratic, and Sophie found that she had to stop often to rest. There was something else, too – a feeling she couldn't find a label for, a complicated mess of trepidation and exhilaration. One second she felt free, as if she could kick off from the ground and take flight over the cobbles, but then, just as quickly, it felt as if those same stones were shifting like quicksand under her feet, threatening to suck her down into the sewers below.

She just had to make it to the bridge. She had to get there.

Sophie knew the intricate pattern of the city's streets well enough to trust her instincts over her actual thoughts, and sure enough, she eventually stumbled across the tramlines and up under the Old Town Bridge Tower, its looming bulk a comforting sight in the darkness. Her phone had long ago run out of battery thanks to the almost incessant calls which she had mostly been pretending to answer for the past few days, but Sophie had the city's many clocks to help her keep track of the time. There were only a few hours left now until midnight – and then there would be just one choice left open to her.

As she made her way along the right-hand side of the bridge, her eyes searching the stone wall for the muted golden glow that would tell her that she was where she needed to be, Sophie saw the snow begin to fall around her.

45

'I still don't understand.' Megan stared at Ollie. The ashen look on his face was scaring her. She had never seen him so worried, or so clearly distraught.

'The poor duck's in denial,' Hope told her, close to tears. 'Prague is where they met, where they spent so much time together. My guess is she wanted to come here to feel close to him. Toby says she's barely spoken since it happened – not to anyone.'

'And Toby is?' Megan asked, still playing catch-up.

'Robin's older brother.' Hope pointed through the glass of the hotel doors, where a blond man in a sheepskin coat was pacing up and down, his phone clamped to his ear and a grim expression on his face.

'I knew there was something wrong,' Ollie said, shaking his head. 'I just knew it in my gut.'

Megan remembered what she'd said about knowing things in her gut, and blanched. This was not the time.

'I can't believe Robin's dead,' she stuttered. 'All those calls Sophie took. I even saw his picture flash up on her phone once. What was all that about?'

'She must have been lying,' Ollie said simply.

'And perhaps that photo was of Toby, not Robin,' suggested Hope. 'He's got the same blond hair, and he told us he's been trying to get hold of her non-stop over the past few days. She only let slip where she was yesterday, apparently, and he booked the first flight he could.'

Annette, who had been sitting quietly off to one side listening, finally asked the question that the three of them were avoiding.

'What is Toby so afraid of?'

At that moment Robin's brother came back in through the doors, his hair wet from the beginnings of snow. His skin had the weathered look of a man who spent much of his time outside, and Megan remembered what Sophie had told them about Robin's love of surfing.

'I've just spoken to her parents,' he said, addressing Ollie. He didn't even seem to notice Megan, so she stepped forward and offered her hand.

'I'm so sorry for your loss,' she whispered, her mouth set in a line as he squeezed her hand in response, a polite smile flashing up momentarily on his face.

'I'm afraid if I don't find Sophie, we could have another loss on our consciences,' he told them all, his voice unsteady. 'Sophie's mum said she found a note. It said that she'd be home with Robin, or she wouldn't be home at all.'

'But how could she . . . ?' Hope stopped mid-sentence, then brought her hand up to cover her mouth. 'Oh no.'

'I don't think she's been eating much these past few days,' Ollie added. Megan looked down and realised he was holding her hand. She hadn't even noticed him take it. 'I should have stayed with her after she fainted on the bridge. I'm so sorry.'

This, again, was directed towards Toby, but Robin's brother shook his head.

'It's not your fault. How were you to know?'

'I know,' Ollie stared at his feet. 'But I still feel dreadful. If something happens to her . . .'

Annette stood up. 'Come on,' she told them, reaching for her coat and shrugging it on. 'Let's go out and look for her.'

Megan, who'd only had the briefest of introductions to Annette and still had no idea where the hell Charlie had vanished off to, looked over at Hope's daughter with admiration.

'Annette's right,' she agreed, pulling her gloves on. 'The receptionist here has Toby's number, right?'

Toby and Ollie nodded.

'Well then, if Sophie comes back here then we'll know soon enough. I don't know about you lot, but I don't like the idea of her alone out there in the snow.'

'You're right.' Toby was already moving towards the doors. 'I have no idea where I'm going – can I come with you?'

'Of course.' Ollie touched his shoulder briefly. 'I'll lead the way. We can start in St Wenceslas Square and work our way from there through the Old Town.'

Outside it was eerily quiet, as it always seemed to be when the snow began to fall. Megan thought guiltily of the way she'd wished for it earlier in the day. Now all she could think of was Sophie, hunched over somewhere in the city, her grief eating away at her insides, the snow landing on her cheeks and eyelashes. She couldn't begin to imagine what must be going through her mind, what turmoil she must be in. It made her shudder just to think about it.

Toby and Ollie were walking side by side ahead of her, with Hope and Annette just behind, their hands clasped in each other's as they scanned either side of the near-deserted street. When Ollie described the rainbow-striped hat that Sophie always wore, Toby's mouth dropped open in a new horror.

'That's Robin's hat,' he told them, his voice cracking again. 'She knitted it for him years ago.'

Megan could hear Annette trying to comfort her mum. Hope had started crying almost as soon as they left the hotel. She wasn't demonstrative about it, and Megan guessed she must be trying not to upset Toby more than was necessary, but her face was a mess of tears. Annette looked so much like her, with her delicate features and her bright eyes. Megan would have liked to take a photograph of the two of them – but that would have to wait.

Prague's endless collection of souvenir shops, cafés, bars and restaurants had seemed so charming just a few hours ago, but now all they represented was another place to look, another dead end in their increasingly frantic search. Megan noticed that Toby kept wringing his hands and running them through his hair. He wore neither gloves nor a hat, and seemed outwardly unaffected by the cold, although Megan knew he must be feeling it. She could feel it even in her tiniest joints, and in the stinging of her lips and bare cheeks. The Prague winter wasn't taking any prisoners tonight, and this only made the hunt for Sophie all the more urgent.

'No sign of her in there,' Ollie called out, emerging from an Irish bar on the south side of the square. They'd already been walking for over an hour now, and Toby was beginning to stamp his feet with frustration. His phone was ringing every ten minutes, as well, and the last time he'd actually yelled into the handset, telling whoever it was to keep the line clear, for God's sake. Megan imagined what her mum and dad would be doing if they were trapped at home in the knowledge that she had potentially lost her mind and was alone in a snowy foreign city, and she shuddered violently.

They must find Sophie.

The clocks in the Old Town Square inched around towards midnight, and still there was no sign of her. They had been inside every bar and the girls had checked every single ladies' toilet this side of the city. Toby had found a photo of Sophie on his phone and was showing it to everyone who passed by, from locals to huge groups of tourists, but nobody seemed to have seen her.

Megan couldn't help thinking about how well Sophie knew the city in comparison to any of them. There were so many places she could be hiding out that were away from the centre, places that none of them would know how to find.

'Did she mention anywhere special to any of you?' she asked, as they came together at the base of the Astronomical Clock. 'A place she and Robin might have gone together?'

The others collectively shook their heads from side to side.

'Shit!' Megan threw up her arms in frustration. She was close to tears herself now. They were all exhausted and frozen, and they'd still only covered less than a third of the city. The music and laughter coming from the bars only served to remind them of how bleak their situation was beginning to look. It was getting so late, they were all silently thinking. Sophie should have come back by now.

'We'd better start searching in Mala Strana,' Ollie said, inclining his head in the direction of the Vltava. 'Perhaps she went up Petrin Hill.'

'But it will be so dark up there.' Megan wrapped her arms around herself. The snow was falling harder now, and she blinked as the flakes fell against her face. Ollie, sensing her mounting panic, moved to stand behind her, his hand a solid comfort in the small of her back.

'What about the castle?' Annette suggested. 'There are plenty of places to shelter up there, and it will be deserted at this time of night, surely?'

They all jumped as the clock above them began to chime, and Megan peered up through the falling snow just in time to see the figure of Death emerge and rattle his hourglass. A grasping unease made its way through her as she allowed herself to believe for the first time that Sophie's life could be in danger.

Hope was watching Death, too, but unlike Megan, she didn't look frightened. Instead, she looked thoughtful, her pretty head on one side as the succession of wooden apostles completed their little circuit high above them.

'What was it you said about that note Sophie left again?' Hope asked, turning to Toby.

He had been momentarily distracted by the clock, too – the heavy snow no match for the awe-inspiring power of its intricate beauty.

He took a deep breath, 'That she would be home with Robin, or she wouldn't be home at all.'

There was a weighty pause as they all digested the implications of his words, then Hope spoke again.

'She thinks he's going to come back to her,' she said slowly, as if the words were written on pieces of a shattered vase that she was painstakingly slotting back into place. 'It's why she's here.'

Megan squinted at her through the snow. 'What do you mean?'

'The bridge,' Hope said, a sudden look of triumph on her face. 'The Charles Bridge, that's where we'll find her – she'll be waiting for her wish to come true.'

Ollie got there faster than Megan, his teacher's brain reaching the end of the puzzle first, and she watched as his face registered relief, only for it to fill again immediately with dread as he looked up once more at the clock; the clock that had just struck midnight.

'But her wish isn't going to come true,' he said, urgency and fear distorting his features. 'And I think time may have just run out.'

There was a horrified and unified beat of silence, then Ollie turned and began to run.

46

Sophie's legs were shaking as she prepared to climb up on to the wall. Whether it was from cold or fear, she couldn't be sure, but it was becoming increasingly difficult to stay upright. She knew it was snowing, she could feel it on her cheeks and see it settling between the cobbles. Glancing left in the direction of Mala Strana, she could see it beginning to form little white mounds on the heads and shoulders of the many statues dotted along the bridge.

There had been so much death here already, so many fallen souls honoured by a stone likeness – what would it matter if there was one more?

Sophie didn't want to die, but she didn't want to live without Robin. This part was always going to be difficult, and she realised now that it was this fear that must have been gnawing away at her over the past few days. It had rendered her unable to eat, barely able to sleep; it had woken her up screaming in the hotel in the middle of the night and brought her literally to her knees – but now she was here, and in a few moments it would all be over. The pain, the loneliness, the agony of yearning for him – with just one step, one leap, she could wipe away all that intolerable suffering.

The city clocks had stopped chiming now, and the silence crept back along the bridge and wrapped its dark arms around her. The snow continued to fall soundlessly, and Sophie stared again over the side of the wall – down into the inviting blackness of the Vltava. The water shifted and swelled, a silent whisper of promised salvation rising up from its hidden depths.

The time had come. A year and a day ago she and Robin had stood here side by side and wished for a miracle. But their wish had not been granted. Robin was not going to be returned to her, and so she must go to him.

She stepped forward, her leg raised ready to climb, when all of a sudden there was a shout.

'Sophie!'

She turned and saw a figure approaching through the snow, his blond hair illuminated in the soft glow of the moon.

It was him, he had come.

Sophie returned her foot to the ground, her hands still gripping the wall of the bridge. The figure stopped a few metres away, his hand raised over his mouth to mask the sobs of what sounded like relief.

'Robin?' It was the smallest of whispers.

The figure stayed silent, and it was then that Sophie saw the other people behind him. Confused, she ran her eyes over them, counting four. Who were they? Was Robin not the only person to have been returned tonight?

'Robin, it's okay,' she said, her voice sounding far away from her. She squinted through the snow at him. Why wasn't he coming to her?

'It's okay,' she said again. 'I'm here. It's me. It's Sophie. I came back for you.'

The figure shook his head, bending forward to rest his hands on his knees. Sophie heard an anguished cry, and looked again at the other people on the bridge. There was something about them, a familiarity, but she couldn't feel her way through the thick brambles of twisted confusion in her mind. What was happening to her?

There was a harsh rasping sound in her ears, and Sophie realised with bewildered alarm that it was coming from her. She was gasping for breath and gripped the wall tighter, her fingernails bending as she drove them hard into the wet stone. Black spots began to merge with the relentlessly falling snow, and she was aware of a tight sensation in her chest.

'Sophie, are you okay?'

A different voice this time, a man, someone she knew.

'I can't . . .' she began, but there was no air to inflate her words, and they lay limp and useless in her throat.

She was aware of movement, of people approaching her, and she lurched forward and leaned right over the side of the wall, the bile burning the inside of her mouth as she heaved and spluttered.

'Sophie, let me help you.'

She looked up as the blond figure finally stepped towards her, felt the surge of love rattle its way through her, and got ready to throw herself into Robin's arms. But no. This man was not Robin.

'Don't touch me!' She shrank away from him, her voice restored by the shock of seeing him. He hesitated for a moment, then moved forward again, but Sophie was too quick for him. In just three swift movements she was standing up on the wall of the bridge, a single step between herself and the inky blackness below.

A woman started crying, and Sophie saw Hope emerge

through the snow, her hands outstretched and her face painted with fear.

'Please come down from there,' she whispered. 'You don't have to do this, love.'

Sophie blinked in response, and looked down again to where Toby was still standing, his eyes focused on her.

'I can't,' she said, her voice immediately cracking into a sob. 'I can't do it any more.'

Toby was crying now as he stared up at her. He looked so much like his younger brother, with his hair curling around his ears and his square jaw rigid. Sophie wanted to love him for it, but all she could feel was hatred that it was he and not Robin who had lived.

'We'll all help you,' Hope said now, her voice pleading. 'Come down from there and let us look after you.'

Sophie's legs were trembling. She felt so tired, so unbelievably tired. She wanted this to be over now. It was time.

'I'm sorry,' she whispered, not at the assembled group below her but into the air, so that her words might travel home and find her parents, her friends, those who would be angry with her for leaving them.

She took one more final breath, and stepped off the wall.

47

It all happened in what felt like a few seconds.

One moment Sophie was there in front of her on the edge of the wall, her tiny trembling form so like that of a baby bird, her eyes huge and frightened, and the next she was whipped out of the air by a pair of quick, strong arms. Ollie's arms.

Hope hadn't noticed him move silently around the bridge, but in the moments before Sophie went to jump, she saw him creeping soundlessly back towards them, his eyes never leaving the figure up on the wall.

Toby let out a roar at the same time as Ollie propelled himself up off the ground and into the empty air, snatching Sophie as she fell and staggering backwards on the cobbles. Beside Hope, Megan gasped out loud then immediately began to cry.

Reaching wordlessly for Annette's hand, Hope used the other to wipe away her own tears. Her heart was hammering against her chest, and she shivered violently. Ollie had put Sophie down, but kept his arms wrapped tightly around her, his mouth moving constantly as he soothed and reassured. Again she heard Megan's gentle weeping.

Sophie had fallen silent, her eyes wide and unblinking, and Hope watched as a stricken Toby moved towards her, beckoning her into his own arms, desperate to comfort her. There was a beat of silence as Sophie looked at him, and then she began to scream.

Unable to bear the sight of her anguish, Hope looked up instead at the sorrowful faces peering down at them through the gloom. The statues were motionless, their expressions forever pensive, carved as they were from stone but exuding such a sense of pity.

Sophie was still screaming. Long, drawn-out wails of utter despair and unimaginable pain. Hope felt as if her heart was splintering, and helplessness engulfed her. Agitated and disturbed, she clung to Annette, each leaning on the other for support. Megan had curled herself into a small, tight ball and was propped up against the wall, her cheeks wet and her hands clasped over her ears.

Hope could see that Ollie was beginning to struggle, too, his composure cracking as Sophie's anguished body rocked back and forth against him, her rasping cries bulldozing the silence with wretchedness.

'ROBIN!' she screamed, over and over, spittle flying from her mouth as her shouts turned into howls of misery.

Ollie let her continue until her words became whimpers, never releasing his grip. His glasses had fallen off and were lying in the snow by his feet, his woolly hat askew and his face flushed. Toby was kneeling in front of them, his hands still reaching out ready to catch Sophie, his face contorted with distress.

'Where is he?' Sophie suddenly cried. 'Where has he gone?'

Toby failed to disguise his own muffled sobs as he replied.

'I don't know, Soph. I don't know where he is.'

Sophie wailed again, her eyes closed and her mouth open. 'No,' she repeated, taking the word and drawing it out. And then again, over and over, 'I can't. I can't do it.'

'I'm so sorry,' Toby stuttered. 'I wish it had been me. I wish every day that I could take his place.'

Hope allowed herself to imagine how she would feel if Annette ever got ill. How she would do anything she could to take away the pain, to have it all for herself. Death was one thing, grief quite another. While one was so final and so certain, the other was a deadlier sort of enemy. Grief would lurk in the background, waiting to pounce; it would snatch you by the throat and leave you breathless. That burning sense of indignation, of something happening that was too horrible to fathom. Death became merely a kindly cousin to the raw, relentless and all-consuming emotion of grief.

'It hurts so much.' Sophie was sobbing. 'I can't bear it. I can't bear the pain. I can't.'

'I know it hurts,' Toby said, reaching out to touch her. 'It hurts me, too. I can't breathe with the pain of it sometimes.'

'I don't want to live without him.' She sounded so sure that Hope actually jerked as if she'd been struck.

Hope's eyes travelled to where Megan was still sitting against the wall, her head now against her knees, her arms wrapped around her legs. She hadn't spoken a word since Ollie had run away from the square and led them all here, and Hope wondered what was going through her mind. Was she, too, remembering an echo of a long-buried grief of her own? She thought about what Ollie had said back in the bar, and how matter-of-fact he'd been when discussing his feelings for her. It felt like it had happened a lifetime ago.

'I know you don't,' Toby was telling Sophie, her hand now in his. 'But you must. You have to – you have to do it for Robin. He wouldn't want you to give up on life, you know he wouldn't.'

Sophie opened her huge eyes even wider. The snow was at last beginning to disperse, and Hope could see the redness around her pupils.

'I know,' she said at last, quietly, nodding her head up and down against Ollie's chest. 'But I don't work without him. There's a part of me missing. I feel . . .' She searched for the word. 'I feel hopeless.'

She started to weep again as she said it, her own realisation catching her off guard. Grief wasn't hiding away on this bridge, on this night – it was dancing around them all with glee, rubbing its hands together at the promise of such a unified banquet of agony.

Very slowly, Ollie lifted up his arms and let Toby take his place on the wet ground. Sophie was hesitant at first, but then she wrapped her arms around Toby's back, her fingers entwined, and the two of them wept as they clung to one another.

Ollie stood and paused for a moment, looking first at Hope and Annette, and then towards Megan. He looked exhausted, and Hope watched as Megan shuffled to her feet and the two of them stared across at each other. Megan opened her mouth as if to speak, but Ollie shook his head, silencing her. There was nothing any of them could say, Hope thought. All they could do was be here for Sophie and for Toby, and be here for each other, too.

Looking up as the last of the flakes floated silently around them, Hope's eyes found the yellow pebble of the moon. How small they must all look from up there – how tiny and insignificant against the colourful tapestry of the ever-moving world. But this moment was anything but small, and nowhere close to being insignificant. They had all come to Prague wishing for answers, and the city had granted them in the only way it knew how – by bringing them together.

48

Megan couldn't remember ever feeling so cold.

Her fingers throbbed inside her gloves and her feet felt fragile in her boots, as if the slightest touch would cause them to shatter. Hunched against the wall on the bridge, she had been shivering, but now that they were on the move again, the shaking had been replaced by a numbness. The cold had got right into her bones and was freezing her now from the inside out, making her hunch over as she walked, her shoulders pulled up and her back aching.

Ollie was ahead of her, maintaining a discreet distance from Toby, who had Sophie in his arms. Hope and Annette walked just behind her, their arms wrapped around each other and their expressions stilled by the enormity of what they had all just witnessed. Megan kept replaying the moment over and over in her mind – how Ollie had caught Sophie as she jumped, and how awful it had felt for that split second when she feared that he may go over the side of the bridge, too. Losing Ollie was as abhorrent a thought to her now as any had ever been, and she couldn't believe how utterly stupid and short-sighted she'd been.

She felt a deep twisting in her stomach as she thought about Sophie, hearing the sound of those anguished wails replaying in her mind. She could only begin to guess at the pain the poor girl was going through, but in a strange way she was oddly grateful that she had been there to witness it. Sophie loved Robin more than anything, more than even herself, and she had lost him. How could Megan push Ollie out of her life, when he was right here, ready to be with her? How could she be so ignorant as to think that anything was more important than the love she now knew, without a flicker of a doubt, she felt for him?

She had almost told him back on the bridge; she had opened her mouth to tell him, to say, 'I love you.' But he had stopped her; he had shaken his head – and he was right, it wasn't the right moment. But surely any moment is a good moment when you're telling someone that you love them. Didn't everyone want to hear that? Even if you didn't love someone yourself, it was still a good thing to hear, wasn't it?

She knew Ollie loved her, even if she hadn't let him say it up in the park all those hours ago – and now, finally, she had worked her way through the chapters of confusion, fear and uncertainty, and reached the same page as him. If Sophie had taught her anything, it was that every moment is precious, and Megan wanted all her moments from now on to be with Ollie.

The hotel receptionist made a huge fuss of them as soon as they got back, calling someone down to fix them all a hot drink, conjure up blankets and bring out a platter of sandwiches. It was a kind gesture, but none of them could face food, and Megan felt her stomach churn as she stared hard at a thick piece of ham between two roughly cut slices of brown bread. Sophie was still curled up against Toby, her eyes closed and her cheeks wet from the tears that never seemed to stop. Megan wished she could do or say something to alleviate even a tiny bit of her pain, but she knew there was nothing worthy she could contribute.

Hope clutched a cup of hot wine with both her hands. She looked lost in thought, and Megan caught Annette's eye as they both stared at her. She still had no idea what had happened to Charlie, but she didn't feel able to ask. The room stayed quiet, unsaid words suffocating the empty spaces between them all.

'Shall we go up to bed?'

Annette spoke first, making everyone except Sophie jolt with surprise.

Toby nodded. 'I think she's asleep,' he whispered, inclining his head towards Sophie.

'I'll show you where her room is,' Ollie offered, keeping his voice low. 'Reception will have a spare key, I'm sure.'

He turned before leaving the room, glancing at Megan.

'I'll meet you upstairs,' she told him.

Hope drank the last of her wine and stood up.

'Shall we try for breakfast in the morning?' she asked. 'What time is your flight?'

'We have to leave by ten,' Megan told her, thinking as she did so how strange it was to be having a normal conversation again, as if the events of the past few hours had never happened, and all their lives had not been irretrievably altered.

Hope nodded. 'We're off at lunchtime – but I'll make sure I'm down here by nine.'

They took the stairs together, and when Hope reached the first floor she pulled Megan into a hug.

'Take care,' she said, her thumb brushing Megan's cheek. 'And take care of Ollie, too.'

Megan nodded. 'I will.'

Once in the room, she hung up her damp coat and peeled off her jeans, tossing them on top of her suitcase and reaching for her pyjamas. She'd ended up packing the least attractive pair she could find, which were made from a fleecy material and covered in pictures of snowmen. It seemed so absurd to her now that she had been trying to repel Ollie – and even more absurd that she'd believed a pair of festive pyjama bottoms would make the slightest bit of difference in how he felt about her.

Her hair was so matted and bedraggled that she couldn't face even running a comb through it, so instead she scooped it up into a bun, washing off the streaks of mascara from her tear-stained cheeks and cleaning her teeth. She'd just got under the covers when the door opened and Ollie came in. His glasses steamed up almost immediately thanks to the heat coming from the radiator, and he took them off, rubbing the inner corners of his eyes with a thumb and forefinger.

'Are you okay?'

He looked up, seeming to see her for the first time, but he didn't smile.

'Not really.'

'What you did, on the bridge,' she began, watching as he took off his coat and threw it over the back of a chair. 'You were amazing out there tonight – a real hero.'

Ollie let out a non-committal grunt.

'Don't be so modest,' she chided. 'You saved Sophie's life – we all saw it.'

He shrugged. 'I was just the closest. Any of us would have done the same thing.'

She shook her head. 'I think you're wrong. You were the only one really thinking out there tonight. If it had been just me, she would probably have gone over the side.'

'Don't say that.' He sounded weary, and Megan frowned. 'She's safe now,' he continued. 'That's all that matters for now.'

'I don't think she's okay, though,' Megan couldn't help but remark. 'I don't think she'll be okay for a very long time.'

Ollie rubbed at his eyes again, refusing to look at her. 'You may be right,' he said. 'But she's still here, she's still alive. Where there is life, there's hope – and I know Toby will look after her. I was just chatting to him a bit upstairs, and his whole family adores Sophie. All the stuff she told us about her and Robin, it was all true.'

'Just not the part about him still being alive.'

She knew it sounded cold, but she meant it to be sympathetic. Ollie looked at her, his expression unreadable.

'Yes. Just not that part.'

He went into the bathroom and shut the door, and Megan heard the sound of the shower running, then the toilet flushing, of Ollie spitting toothpaste then mouthwash into the basin. When he emerged, his hair was wet and flat against his head, and she could smell peppermint. Instead of the usual boxer shorts he always wore to bed, Ollie had put on a clean pair of jeans and a T-shirt.

'Why are you dressed?' she asked, aware of a creeping feeling of unease.

'I'm going to go down and sleep in the bar,' he told her, again avoiding her eyes.

'What on earth for?'

'I just need to be on my own.' He selected a jumper from his suitcase and pulled it over his head. Megan watched him, noticing as she did so that he'd tossed the flowers he'd bought her that morning into the bin. 'I'm not sure if I'll be able to sleep at all anyway,' he went on. 'Not with everything that's happened.'

'Please don't.' Megan could hear the fear in her own voice, and Ollie looked at her, surprised.

'You want me to stay here with you?' he guessed. 'Comfort you? Look after you?'

'I want—' She stopped, suddenly unable to finish. He seemed so angry with her still.

'That's just it, though, isn't it?' he said, folding his arms. 'It's always about what *you* want.'

She hadn't expected this.

'I'm sorry,' she started, but he interrupted her.

'You're always saying that,' he said. 'But do you actually know what it means? Have you ever actually felt sorry for the way you've treated me?'

'You know I have!'

'Do I?'

Megan pulled the covers up until they were right under her chin, a makeshift shield against the resentment he was throwing her way.

'I can't do this any longer,' he said, looking more upset than angry now. 'We all saw what heartbreak can do to a person tonight – I don't want to put myself through any more of this pain and bullshit.'

'I don't either,' she cried. What she meant was that she wanted to stop playing games and be with him properly – but Ollie flinched at her words.

'Before we came out here, I thought I could be your friend,' he went on. 'I didn't set out with a plan to fall for you like this, but I did, and now I can't take it back. But you've rejected me twice now, Megs. You can't just pick me up when you feel like it, to satisfy your own ego – I can't be that person in your life any more.'

'I don't want you to be,' she said. 'I want you to . . .' She stopped again, her cowardliness making her punch the mattress with frustration.

'You want me to what?' Ollie asked. He still had his arms folded across his chest, his chin jutting outwards defiantly. 'Want me to hang around you like some teenage girl around her favourite boy band member? Want me to tell you how great you are every day, so you can strut around the place? Want me to fall into bed with you whenever you click your fingers, then pretend I don't care when you run off the next morning?'

Megan opened her mouth, but all she could muster was an indignant snuffling noise. She wanted to tell him, the words were ready and waiting impatiently in the back of her throat, but with every snide comment he threw her way, she felt them recede back down into her chest. He had loved her, but she had ruined it with her dithering, and now he'd seen what happened to a person who really got their heart broken into pieces. It made sense that he would be afraid.

'I'm sorry I ran off,' she said instead, and he grunted again in response. 'I was confused. I just needed to think.'

'It's always about you,' he said. 'About what you want, what you need, what you feel – what about what I need and want? What about how I feel?'

'I'm an idiot,' she told him, attempting a smile. 'I know I'm a selfish cow and I've been awful to you. I am sorry, I really am. Please believe me.'

Ollie shook his head. 'It's too late,' he said. 'I can't be your emotional punchbag, Megs, I don't have the strength. I know you're scared of trusting people after what that bastard Andre did to you, but I'm not him. You know I'm not. I don't want to end up like poor little Sophie, broken almost beyond repair. I need to try and get over you, and to do that I need to stay away from you for a while.'

'You don't mean that?' she whispered, but she could tell by his face that he did. 'I don't want to lose you.'

For a second his face softened, and he walked across to the bed and put a hand on her head.

'I know you don't,' he said. 'But this is the way it has to be now. I have to put myself first this time around. I'm sorry.'

There was nothing left to say. Nothing except those three words that she could never quite manage to utter. And now it was too late. Even if she could find the strength to tell Ollie how she felt, she didn't think he would believe her now. And so she let him go, watching in silence as he walked towards the door and opened it. For a brief moment before he closed it again, Ollie looked right into her eyes, and then he turned away.

49

Five months later

Spring had rolled out late this year, the last guest to arrive at winter's annual leaving party, and though it was now May, the daffodils were still pushing their way determinedly through soft, wet ground that was littered with tree blossom.

Sophie leaned her head against the glass and watched the scenery speed past, a blur of greens, browns and yellows. The gentle rocking motion of the train had lulled her into a comfortable silence, her abandoned headphones lying untouched against the front of her jumper. The last time she had been on her way to London had been when she flew to Prague, and she had imagined that today's trip would be difficult. On the contrary, however, it felt good to be away from the trappings of home. Away from the fearfully concerned blanket of her parents' affection, so heartfelt yet so smothering in its intensity. This was the first time they had let her out of their sight in months, the first time she had felt as if they trusted her again, and that in itself was enough to keep a smile on her face.

Spring had always been her favourite season, dappled as it was in the positive light of rebirth, new beginnings and opportunity. In the winter, leaves fell and died on the ground, animals hid away in their burrows and dens, and birds took flight, searching for warmer branches to perch on and sing their daily song. Spring, on the other hand, welcomed everything back, its arms opening up to envelop those on the start of a new journey. Sophie knew she was at the start of a new life, a life without Robin by her side, only now it didn't feel like she was staring only into darkness. Now there was a faint light on the horizon of her pain.

Megan's exhibition had provided the perfect chance for her to test her newly acquired state of acceptance. She knew there was a long and bumpy road ahead of her, and she knew that she would probably never be able to let go of that perpetual ache of sadness and of loss, but this trip to London proved that she could still get out there and live her life. It was important that her parents trust her again, but it was even more important that she was able to trust herself.

Sophie reached inside her bag and withdrew the letter. She had read it so many times now that she could recite it word perfectly, but she still liked to see Robin's untidy scrawl. It was such a personal thing, so like him in its haphazard manner, and she found she could hear his voice in her head as she read.

Toby had given her the letter in Prague, explaining that it had been amongst a number of items that the hospital had given the family after Robin's death. In the aftermath of bewildered grief that had followed, the bag of belongings had been put to one side and forgotten about. It was only when Sophie's parents had called to say she had gone missing and they were all frantic, that Toby thought to check.

It was Robin, in the end, who saved her. His words that got her back on her feet.

Sophie slid the single sheet of paper out of the envelope and began to read.

Dearest Bug,

I know you hate it when I call you that, but there's not much you can do about it now, is there? Sorry, probably not the best time to make a joke, but you know me – an idiot first and foremost. And anyway, you really do look like a bug with those ridiculously big eyes of yours. A very beautiful bug, but a bug just the same.

The worst thing about writing this letter is that I know you'll be reading it without me there beside you. I think I've finally got used to the idea that I'm going, but I know you haven't. Sometimes when I wake up in the night and you're still here, curled up next to me on top of the covers, you look at me and I see such hope in your eyes. I want you to know that I didn't want to die. I wanted to live. I wanted the chance to grow old with you and watch those eyes of yours get even bigger as your head shrinks. (Again, sorry!)

I have to tell you something now, and you must promise not to be cross. Promise? Okay. When we went to Prague last year and made our wishes on the Charles Bridge, I lied to you. I didn't make a wish at all on that first day, I just pretended.

I waited a few days, then I slipped out while you were sleeping and went back to the bridge on my own. But even then, I didn't wish to be well again. I didn't even wish for a miracle. Instead, I wished with all my heart that you would find the strength to be happy, and that you would get what you needed to carry on without me.

Do you remember how it was in the beginning, when we would lie together in the darkness, sharing secrets? You would tell me that life without me wouldn't be worth living, and it always scared me, Bug, because you are so full of life. You have so much love in your heart, and you must try to find people to share that with. My story is coming to an end now, but you've still got so many chapters to get through. You've got marriage and motherhood, and hell, even grandmother-hood. I want you to have all those things. And I want you to live as if I am still by your side, spurring you on every step of the way, because believe me, I will be.

So, that's why, that early morning on the bridge – the very same place where I met you – I wished for my Bug, my Sophie, to be happy, to be loved, and to live. It is my dying wish, and selfishly I'm going to hold you to it. You were my life, and now you must use what we had to move forward. Use that love to do good, to yourself and to others. See more of the world, have new adventures. That is my wish.

I love you so very much, my beautiful Bug.

Now and forever.

Robin xxxx

A single tear rolled down Sophie's cheek and hit the back of her hand. She couldn't ever get to the end of Robin's letter without shedding at least one, but there was a hint of a smile on her lips. Being strong was what he had wanted, happiness a wish that he trusted her to grant – and she wasn't about to let him down. Not now, and not ever.

Strolling out of Waterloo Station an hour later, Sophie was greeted by the sunshine and a fresh May wind. It wasn't quite warm enough to ditch jumpers completely, but the winter coats had certainly been hung up for the final time until late autumn.

Megan's exhibition was taking place in a studio space overlooking the Thames, not far from Tate Modern. Sophie took her time meandering along the South Bank, watching as skateboarders pulled off impressive tricks in their concrete park tucked under the eaves, and children pulled on their mothers' arms, begging for an ice cream from a pop-up stall. The sunshine had drawn people out from their homes, as it always did, and the passing faces looked almost bewildered in the sunlight, as if they'd just come out of a long hibernation.

The river bank was a riot of noise and colour, of faces and shouts, of happiness and contentment, and for a time Sophie just strolled through the middle of it all, soaking up the atmosphere like lemonade through a straw. She wondered now why she'd had such a bad impression of this city, why she'd failed to embrace the beauty of the place. Well, now she had the chance.

Sophie fished in her bag for the invitation that Megan had posted out. Her exhibition was entitled 'Unlocked', the word in a bold black font, and below it a bright red padlock, much like the one she and Robin had left up on Petrin Hill. This one, however, wasn't fastened shut, but gaped open, its metal ring pulled out to the side. On the other side of the laminated card was a photo of the Charles Bridge at dawn, and Sophie felt her skin prickle with recognition. She hadn't seen Megan since that night on the bridge, the night she'd come so close to ending her life. Thinking about it now felt strange to Sophie, as if she was recalling a scene from a film rather than her own life. The details were still hazy, and her counsellor assured her that this was to be expected, that her mind was protecting her from reliving it and traumatising herself further. Toby had eventually told her what had transpired, and she had burned with mortification. But of course there was no need. Nobody who had been on the bridge with her that night felt anything other than relief that she was okay. They, like Robin, wanted nothing more than for her to be happy, but Sophie had never forgotten what they had done for her. She would never forget.

'Sophie, is that you?'

She turned to see Hope elbowing her way through the crowds to reach her, a huge smile on her face and a bunch of yellow roses in her hand.

'Hello!' Sophie ran to meet her and the two women hugged each other tightly. Hope had set her blonde hair into tight ringlets today, giving her the look of an excited Cupid. She looked fresh and bubbly and full of the joys of spring, and Sophie found that she couldn't stop smiling.

'You look so well!' Hope exclaimed, reaching up to ruffle Sophie's ear-length bob. She must have looked such a sight in Prague, thought Sophie, with her baggy clothes, shorn head and Robin's ridiculously tatty hat. When she'd offered to shave her head alongside his to show solidarity, he'd been appalled and begged her not to, but she'd done it anyway. One thing Sophie had learned about herself was that she usually did whatever she wanted – and it was one of the things she knew Robin had loved the most about her.

'So do you!' she told Hope, meaning it. Her friend seemed almost fit to burst with pleasure.

'This is my first weekend off since Christmas,' Hope

informed her. 'I've been at that B&B day and night, not that I'm complaining, obviously, but because I live there, too, it can feel a bit like I never leave the damn place.'

'It gets like that at the farm, too,' Sophie agreed. 'This is the first time I've left home since . . . since Prague.'

They exchanged a look loaded with so many unsaid words, and then Hope shook her head.

'How have you been? I mean, I know you said in your emails that you were okay, but people tend to always say that. How are you really?'

Sophie considered the question before she answered. 'I'm getting there,' she told her truthfully. 'Taking it a day at a time.'

Hope put a warm hand on her arm. 'That's all you can do, love. And I for one am very proud of you.'

Sophie grinned back at her, fighting tears once again.

'Come on.' Hope spoke first. 'Let's get ourselves to this party before all the free wine runs out. I've barely had a drink since Christmas either, and I fully intend to make up for lost time.'

It took them another ten minutes to reach the venue, by which time Hope had filled Sophie in on her exciting news: she was going to be a grandmother. Annette had apparently been planning to come down to London with her mother, but, Hope laughed as she told Sophie the story, Patrick was so obsessed with wrapping her up in cotton wool that he barely let her out of the house at the weekends, let alone all the way down here. Hope also told Sophie that she and her ex-husband Dave were on better terms, and that she was set to get some money from the sale of the house.

'I told him to keep it, but apparently he likes the idea of downsizing,' she said. 'Turns out keeping a three-bedroomed house clean and tidy is a lot more work than he realised. I wonder why?'

She didn't mention Charlie once, and Sophie resisted asking. If Hope wanted to broach the subject, she could do so in her own time.

'Do you know if Ollie is going to be here?' Sophie asked instead.

Hope shook her head. 'Megan says they haven't spoken since the day they flew back from Prague. I think she tried a few times, but he won't return her calls.'

'That's such a shame,' Sophie said. Ollie was a genuine hero in her eyes, and she had so been hoping to see him so she could say a proper thank you. Plus, she had seen him and Megan together and, even in the catatonic state of denial she had been in over in Prague, had realised the depth of their feelings for one another. That kiss she'd witnessed on the stairs of the hotel had reminded her of the ones she used to share with Robin. A kiss like that came from a place of love.

'Are you sure you're ready for this?' Hope asked as they reached the door. 'Seeing photos of Prague after, you know . . .'

Sophie shrugged. 'Who knows? But I'm willing to go in and see what happens.'

Hope looped an arm through hers. 'That's my girl!'

The first thing Sophie saw as they crossed the threshold was a huge photograph of her and Robin's padlock. Megan had edited it so that everything else in the photograph was a muted grey, meaning the red of the lock stood out all the more. She closed her eyes briefly, remembering the day she and Robin had drawn their initials on it, giggling to each other about how clever they were to hide it way up on the hill, away from the rest of the city's many padlocks. It had been in the time when their relationship felt invincible, and the memory still made her smile.

'Is that . . . ?' Hope gasped, staring at the initials in the photo.

Sophie nodded. 'Yes. I had no idea that Megan had found it.'

'I hope you don't mind?'

They both turned to find Megan standing behind them, her long blonde hair piled up in an extravagant chignon, red painted lips to match her clinging scarlet dress.

'Megan!' Hope stepped forward to embrace her, and Sophie smiled at her over Hope's shoulder.

'Of course I don't mind,' she replied, when Megan was free again, Hope's gift of yellow roses clutched in one hand. 'In fact, I'm flattered. And I'm sure Robin would be, too.'

Now it was Megan's turn to smile. 'You look so well,' she said, echoing Hope's earlier observation.

'So do you!' Sophie winked. 'I mean, swit-swoo! Check you out, lady.'

'Oh.' Megan blushed and smoothed down her skin-tight dress. 'This old thing?'

'Is Ollie coming?' Hope asked, presumably unable to help herself.

Megan frowned. 'I invited him, but I haven't heard anything back. I hope so. I texted and told him that you two were coming, so I'm sure he will if he can.'

She was careful to keep her tone vague, but Sophie detected a yearning in her eyes. It was clear what Megan was wishing for, and Sophie crossed her fingers behind her back in solidarity.

They chatted for a bit, then Sophie left Hope telling Megan all about Annette's pregnancy and wandered over to the bar, selecting herself a sparkling water. There were photographs of Prague on every wall, with more set on plinths at irregular intervals around the large, airy space. As Sophie peered closer, however, she began to realise that many of these photos had an additional subject. The same additional subject over and over.

'She loves him,' she said out loud, coming to a halt in front of an A3-sized photo of Ollie on the banks of the Vltava River, a smile on his face and a pigeon up on his shoulder. He looked happy and carefree, and peering closer, Sophie could just make out a reflection of the Charles Bridge in the lenses of his glasses.

'Who loves who?'

She turned to find a man standing next to her. He was tall, much taller than her, with dark, slightly floppy hair and a large nose. He was pulling a very serious face, but Sophie detected a playfulness behind his brown eyes.

'Megan loves Ollie,' she told him, gesturing at the photo. 'That's Ollie.'

'Ah, yes.' The man pretended to notice the photo for the first time. 'So it is. Mr Morris, as us lot at the school know him.'

'You're a teacher?' Sophie guessed.

'Guilty as charged.'

They exchanged a smile, but Sophie immediately felt a

prickle of guilt herself. Reaching up a practised hand, she picked up her locket from where it lay warm against her chest, and ran the chain through her fingers.

'How do you know Ollie?' he asked her now, unaware of just how difficult a question that was for her to answer.

'We met in Prague, actually,' she mumbled, sipping her drink.

There was a pause, and Sophie watched his face, registering first recognition, then immediate pity.

'Are you Sophie?' he guessed.

She nodded, again using her glass to hide behind.

He pulled his mouth into a line. 'I'm dreadfully sorry about your fiancé. Ollie and me, we're quite good mates. I hope you don't mind that he told me?'

She shook her head. 'Of course not. What he did for me . . . He's just . . . Well, he's amazing.'

The man looked again at the photo. 'Looks like you're not the only one who thinks so,' he said. 'I'm Adam, by the way. Adam Clarke.'

They shook hands, Sophie not needing to tell him who she was, then moved on to the next photo. This one had been taken on Petrin Hill, she recognised, and Ollie was running towards the camera, his face covered in dripping snow.

'What a great photo,' she exclaimed. The more she looked at it, the more she found she could almost hear Ollie and Megan's excited shrieks and feel the cold of that Prague winter wind on her cheeks. It was so alive, so bursting with vitality and with love. Ollie was on every wall of this exhibition – it was like one giant, visual love letter.

'Is Ollie coming today?' she asked Adam, who looked down at his wine glass and twisted it around in his hand.

'I'm not sure,' he admitted. 'He didn't seem very keen when I spoke to him about it, but that was a few days ago. Maybe he's changed his mind since then.'

'I hope so,' she said, stepping sideways to examine the next photo, this time of Ollie on the Charles Bridge, ducking to avoid the attentions of a seagull that was trying to steal his pretzel. 'It would be a real shame for him to miss seeing this.'

They continued making their way around the room, eventually being joined by a thoroughly overexcited Hope, who'd made good on her vow to take full advantage of the free bar. She was also far less shy about making conversation with Adam than Sophie was, and by the time they'd completed one circuit of the exhibition, they had learned that Adam was thirty-two, single, a keen tennis player and a closet Céline Dion fan.

'Have you travelled much?' Sophie eventually managed to ask. Hope was busy going into ecstasies over a photo of some children chasing bubbles in St Wenceslas Square.

Adam pulled a face. 'Not as much as I would have liked to – but it's funny you should ask. I'm actually going away this summer, to India.'

'Oh?' Sophie gave him her full attention. India had been on her mind lately, too.

'There's this charity over there that sponsors children from the most impoverished areas and helps them get a decent education. They're always looking for extra teachers, so I thought it would be a good thing to do.'

'That sounds amazing.' Sophie beamed at him. 'Really amazing.'

Adam was blushing now, and seemed to be momentarily lost for words.

'Can I get you another drink?' he asked, quickly draining what was left in his own glass.

She resisted the temptation to laugh, instead nodding at him. 'That would be nice. And go on, I'll have a white wine.'

She watched him lope across the room, easily a head taller than anyone else. It felt strange talking to a man she'd never met before, but there was no real reason not to. Sophie knew she was still a very long way away from feeling ready to even consider a date with someone new, but it was nice to be reminded that if and when she felt like taking that step, there were some perfectly acceptable candidates.

'You met Adam, then?'

It was Megan, looking slightly more flushed than she had an hour ago, her lipstick long ago transferred off her lips and on to the cheeks of all her guests as they arrived.

Sophie nodded. 'He seems nice.'

'He is. In fact, he's the only one of Ollie's friends who messaged me after we got back from Prague to see if I was okay. Not even my own mother did that.'

'Is she here?' Hope asked, joining them.

Megan pointed across the room to where a slim, Bohemian-looking woman was laughing with a handsome male companion.

'She's an artist,' she told them, as if that explained everything. 'I think she's bemused by what I do. She thinks art must be painted or sculpted. I imagine she secretly thinks that using a camera is cheating, but she would never admit it to me.'

'I'm sure she's very proud of you,' Hope argued.

Megan grinned. 'Maybe.'

'So . . .' Sophie gave her a light dig with her elbow. 'All these photos of Ollie – is there something you're not telling us?'

Megan took a deep breath and looked around. There was Ollie with a cat sitting on his shoulder, a cup of coffee in one hand and a bemused expression on his face; there he was peering down from his perch atop the horrible bronze baby sculpture, the snow on the ground lending such a brightness to the scene; and there he was beside her in the Mirror Maze, both their faces ridiculously contorted, but not so much that you couldn't almost hear their shared laughter leaking out through the glass frame.

'Yes,' she said finally, dropping her eyes. 'I love Ollie. I bloody love him. I love him more than anyone and anything I've ever loved.'

Hope squealed and clapped her hands together.

'But what does it matter?' Megan groaned, swinging an arm round at all her assembled guests. 'Now the whole world knows it except him.'

Sophie put up a hand to silence her.

'I wouldn't be so sure about that,' she said.

50

Ollie had stopped just inside the entrance, his eyes scanning the room from behind his glasses and an expression of pure bewilderment on his face as he took in the endless photos of himself framed on every wall. He'd had his hair cut, Megan noted, and put on a shirt for the occasion. It was dark blue, with those crisp creases along the sleeves that suggested it had not long been out of a packet. Seeing him standing there, looking so completely and brilliantly like the man she had been dreaming of for months, made a huge smile break out across her face. He had come after all.

Hope was still beside her, and Megan heard her let out an audible gasp of pleasure as she realised who Ollie had brought with him. Charlie looked nervous, she thought, like the newest fish in a well-established tank, his eyes darting from face to face until he found the one he was looking for. When he did, Megan heard Hope murmur something unintelligible, something that sounded a lot like joy.

'They came.' This time it was Sophie who had spoken, and it was she who raised a hand in the direction of the new arrivals and beckoned them over. Megan, who had been watching the door like a cat next to a mouse hole all afternoon waiting for this exact moment, suddenly found herself overcome with shyness, and headed swiftly towards the bar.

'Red wine, please,' she told the barman, who was actually the eldest son of her boss at the gallery. She'd promised him thirty quid and an endless supply of pretty female guests if he gave up a few hours to help her out, and he'd jumped at the chance. But as he tried to make small talk with her now, Megan found herself unable to concentrate. She couldn't take her eyes off Ollie, who had made his way across the room and was hugging Sophie, the pleasure on his face at the sight of her looking so well causing Megan's insides to squidge together like a marshmallow sandwich.

Sophie said something to him and he laughed, so easily and with such affection, but when she gestured behind her to a photo on the wall of Ollie standing in front of the merry-go-round in the Old Town Square of Prague, the colours streaming out behind him, he seemed to freeze. Megan watched as he pushed his glasses up on to his nose – something she knew he did when he was nervous or uncomfortable – and fiddled with the invitation he was holding in his hands. She wondered if he'd worked it out yet – what she'd meant by calling her event 'Unlocked'. Would she be forced to explain it to him, and if she did, would he even want to hear it?

She was distracted from her thoughts by the arrival of a reporter from the *Evening Standard*, who was keen to interview her about the exhibition and take some photos for an upcoming piece on travel photography. Glad of the excuse to hide from Ollie for a while, she let herself be led away into the far corner of the room.

All the fears she'd had about the turnout for this event had proved to be unfounded, and loads of her old friends from the photography circuit had arrived en masse to support her. A huge stir had been caused by the arrival of Clara Flynn, a model that Megan had met on a shoot over ten years ago who was now one of the most famous catwalk stars on the planet. She had sashayed straight over to Megan as soon as she crossed the threshold, wrapping her long, slim arms around her back and telling her in that gorgeous Irish lilt just how proud she was of her. She was going to be an auntie, she told her, adding as she did so that Megan must make the Greek island of Zakynthos her next project. Her older brother lived there with his girlfriend, and Clara assured her there were no better tour guides than the two of them.

And why not? Megan had thought. Wasn't exploring the world next on her to-do list? And Greece was as good a place to start as any. At least it would be warm there, after all. She still shivered when she thought about how cold it had been in Prague.

The exhibition was scheduled to close at six, and by the time Megan had talked the newspaper reporter through two thirds of her work, carefully avoiding his increasingly probing questions about her main human subject, the room was beginning to clear. She hadn't seen Ollie for at least half an hour now, and was starting to panic that he'd already left. Perhaps she'd been a fool to include quite so many images of him – especially that candid shot she'd blown up to almost wall-size and hung in a prominent spot at the back of the studio. It was her favourite of all the photos, and it showed Ollie with his head bent at the top of the Observational Tower in Prague, talking to the old couple he'd met who had told them about the Mirror Maze.

She'd bleached out the colour to give the image added

depth, and there was something so mesmerising about the scene – the frozen laughter caught on lips, the hand raised, mid-gesture, the faint dusting of snow on Ollie's hat, left over from their snowball fight on Petrin Hill, and below them the city of Prague was spread out, a blur of spires and towers, of bridges and water. Megan loved it not only because it reminded her of such a nice moment, but also because it represented to her the very essence of Prague, of its different generations coming together, of its history and its beauty and, for her in particular, its magic. She hadn't even known what it was she was wishing for when she arrived in the city, but Prague had shown her very clearly that all she really needed to inspire her was one thing. One person.

Megan made her way towards the door, thanking people as they left, kissing cheeks and shaking hands. Her pub quiz teammates Magda and Neil stopped to chat for a while, as she had suspected they would, given that they had also spotted Ollie, and she did her best to reassure them that yes, she did plan to talk to him. Her mum and dad promised to call in the morning and told her how proud they were, and Megan had to blink hard to mask ridiculous tears. Her mum had somehow resisted the temptation to mention the subject of Ollie, even though Megan knew it must have been burning the end of her tongue off, and she was grateful that her family knew her well enough to recognise what this exhibition meant.

People had left empty wine glasses on every available surface, and Megan began to wander around and collect them, inserting a finger into the top of each one so she could carry four in each hand. She'd just deposited a second lot on the bar when she spotted him. He had his back to her, but she could see that his arms were folded, his head to one side as he examined a collection of photos she'd taken of the John Lennon Wall. They were some of the few that didn't feature him. Taking a deep breath, she walked over and stood behind him.

'"Bob loves Bug – now and forever",' she read aloud. 'It still makes me smile.'

'Robin wrote it,' Ollie said, his eyes never leaving the image of colourful graffiti in front of them. 'Sophie just told me. He used to call her Bug because of her big eyes.'

'Is that so?' Megan was instantly captivated. 'I had no idea.'

'Some might say you just had an eye for this sort of thing,' he went on, still not looking at her.

'These photos are two hundred pounds each, if you're interested?' she said. 'But I know the artist. I reckon I can get you a discount.'

Ollie turned a fraction then, but didn't meet her eyes.

'I should hope so, too,' he said. 'Given that I'm in most of them.'

'That one over there.' She pointed towards her favourite. 'It isn't for sale, I'm afraid.'

'Oh?'

'Yeah, sorry. The artist is too attached to it.'

She braved another step so she was standing right beside him. She could smell the familiar scent of his aftershave and the slightly cloying aroma of the gel he'd plastered into his hair.

'Thank you for coming,' she said. The room was still

bustling with the sound of chatter, but there was nobody else within earshot. Megan imagined a bubble around them – an invisible force field that whispered a plea of Do Not Disturb.

Ollie shuffled his feet on the tiled floor. 'I almost didn't.'

Her heart dropped as if tugged like the string of a balloon.

'But then I got a call from Charlie. He'd come all the way down from Manchester and was too scared to come in on his own. I think Hope invited him, but they haven't seen each other since Prague.'

'Really?' Megan was surprised.

'I know.' Ollie glanced across at her. 'A grown man too scared to face a woman. Sounds ridiculous, doesn't it?'

Realising as he said it that he'd clearly been scared to come today, too, Megan swallowed her next comment and coughed instead.

'Not ridiculous at all,' she said. 'No more ridiculous than a grown woman being too scared to face a relationship with a man who is clearly the most amazing person in the world.'

Ollie nodded slowly, his focus never leaving the photos on the wall. She watched as his eyes roved over the prints, seeking out the phrases he recognised and the things they had laughed about together. There was the wolf pack's message of 'Don't stop believing' and the black-and-white face of John Lennon. And those words she had so loved: 'May the best of your past be the worst of your future.' Was it too much to hope that they might come true?

Finally, Ollie replied. 'You're right,' he said. 'That really *is* ridiculous.'

There was a pause as Megan tried in vain to pluck the right words out of the nest of mangled confusion that had inexplicably become her brain.

'I've missed you,' Ollie said, again not looking at her. 'I thought it would be easier if I didn't see you, but actually it's been really tough. Every day things happen that I want to tell you, that I know would make you laugh. You're with me all the time, Megs.'

He stopped, taking a deep breath. Beside him, Megan watched her hand move out towards his, so desperate to touch him but so afraid, even now, to assume he would want her to.

'I miss you so much,' she told him, feeling him shift. 'All that time, I thought I couldn't be inspired if I was with you. I thought you affected my ability to take photos, to create all this.' She gestured at the walls. 'I thought you were a distraction. I wanted to go out there and achieve my dreams without needing a man by my side.'

'What changed?' Ollie asked, his voice small.

'When we were in Prague, it was you who was inspiring me. The city was so beautiful and I knew I was capturing something special, but the most magical images I took were all of you. You were my inspiration.' She stopped as her voice cracked, and Ollie finally turned around to face her.

'Are you sure this is what you want?' he asked, his eyes serious. 'Us, I mean.'

'I'm more sure than I ever have been about anything.' She smiled. 'I wanted to show you how much you mean to me, hence all this.'

'This is certainly something.' He raised an eyebrow and

she laughed, relieved to see him relax. 'But couldn't you just have sent me an email?'

She pulled a face at him, but he wasn't laughing.

'I wanted to do something romantic,' she mumbled, barely getting the words out through the humiliation chainmail.

'I just worry that this whole thing . . .' He gestured towards the photos again. 'That it's just part of some big show you've created in your mind. What if tomorrow, you wake up and realise that you don't want me after all?'

Megan considered the question. 'All I know is,' she said, hearing the near-desperation in her voice, 'I've woken up every day since we got back from Prague wanting you to be beside me, and feeling absolutely gutted when you're not. I know I hurt you before when I rejected you, and believe me, I've been bitterly regretting it ever since. I was just scared and confused. I thought I had it all worked out, but of course I had no idea.'

'I don't know, Meg.' He shook his head slowly. 'I'm not sure I have it in me to be hurt by you.'

'The padlock, on the invitation,' she said suddenly. They both looked down at the card in his hands. 'It's supposed to signify—' She stopped again.

'Signify what?' Ollie moved a step closer and put a single finger under her chin, raising her head up until she had no choice but to look into his eyes. It felt so nice to be touched by him.

'All those locks we saw in Prague, the ones with initials on them,' she said.

He nodded. 'I remember.'

'Well, they were all shut, just like I was. I had shut

myself off from feeling anything for you. I had told myself that I didn't want to be in love, that I couldn't be if I wanted to achieve what I'd always tried to with my work. I thought I couldn't have both – but I was so wrong and so bloody stupid.'

Ollie's eyes widened behind his glasses, so wise and full of hope. Megan had missed those eyes so much; she had missed his eyes and his hands and his lips and his smell and his ability to make her feel like the most treasured person on the planet. And more than that, she had missed who she was when she was with him.

'That's why the padlock on the invitation is open,' she said. 'Because so is my heart.'

Ollie didn't need to hear any more; he was already running his hands from her chin around the back of her neck, his mouth inches from her own. When he kissed her, Megan felt every part of her begin to sing, and she pulled him against her. There was nothing in her gut now but warmth, nothing in her heart but love. This was where she was meant to be, where she would flourish – she knew it with an instinct that almost overwhelmed her with its sweet simplicity. The future was no longer a dark passage but an open meadow of possibility, one filled with happiness, laughter, companionship and maybe, just maybe, some children of their own one day. She and Ollie belonged to each other, they always had.

There was a polite cough, and Megan pulled away from Ollie, blushing as she turned to find three figures standing a few feet away. Hope's hand was clasped firmly in Charlie's, who was gazing at them both with unbridled satisfaction, while Sophie was smiling next to them, a hand pressed against her own heart as if she could sense how close Megan's was to bursting.

'Glad to see you two are getting along,' teased Hope, her eyes shining.

'I could say the same to you,' Megan replied, catching the older woman's eye and grinning.

Hope let go of Charlie and came closer, beckoning to Sophie as she did so. With a superhuman effort, Megan relinquished Ollie's hand and let herself be drawn into a corner with the two women.

'Can you believe they came?' Hope whispered, delight making her cheeks glow bright pink.

'I knew Ollie would,' said Sophie, glancing over her shoulder at a large framed photo of the man in question examining a sculpture in Kampa Park. 'He couldn't really have missed seeing this, could he?'

'I suppose not.' Megan laughed in relief, before turning to Hope. 'What's happening with you and Charlie?'

Hope blushed an even darker shade of puce. 'I never thought he'd actually turn up,' she admitted. 'I don't think I ever really explained to him what was going on in my head, and then I let him walk away from me in Prague. I didn't handle the situation well at all.'

'He's here, though, isn't he?' Sophie pointed out happily.

Hope beamed, looking across with affection to where Charlie and Ollie were now standing by the bar with a bottle of beer each. 'I just had to learn how to take my own advice,' she continued. 'Do you remember me telling you, Megan, that you had to do what made you happy and put yourself first?'

Megan nodded in agreement.

'Well, I finally realised that what I needed to do in order to be happy was to find out who I really was. All I ever knew how to do was be a mum and a wife, but I wanted more than that – I wanted my own life. Taking over the B&B has been such an eye-opener, I can tell you. I've never worked harder in my life, but I'm actually really good at it.'

'Well done you!' Megan was thrilled.

'But even with my work and having a grandchild on the way, there was still something missing,' Hope said. 'I almost didn't dare hope that Charlie would agree to see me again – let alone that he still loved me.'

'And does he?' Sophie asked, even though they all knew the answer.

'He does,' Hope smiled, her eyes bright. 'He really does. And I love him, too.'

It was such a lovely moment that even Megan didn't baulk when Hope pulled them into a group hug, kissing each of their cheeks and wiping her eyes with the back of her hand.

'What did you think of Adam?' Megan asked Sophie as they broke apart, careful to keep her tone light.

'He's nice.' Sophie hesitated. 'He gave me his number, actually, just because I've been to India before and he's going there. I probably won't use it, but . . .' She trailed off.

'It's okay.' Megan gave her shoulders a squeeze. 'All in good time.'

The three women looked at each other in turn, each one celebrating an individual victory in their shared moment of friendship. Then Hope peered up at the ceiling.

'They've started turning the lights off,' she said. 'Do you think that's our cue to leave?'

'So they have.' Megan glanced around at the rapidly dimming room. 'I didn't even notice.'

They made their way back across the studio to join the others, and Megan's insides turned to liquid yet again as Ollie slid his arm around her shoulder.

'I still can't believe you came,' Hope said, leaning happily against Charlie. 'I honestly thought I'd lost you for good.'

'He still needed me to hold his hand, though,' Ollie put in, and Hope cackled.

'Oh really?' she said. 'And here was me thinking that it was you who was too chicken to come on your own.'

Ollie opened his mouth, but Charlie spoke across him.

'This beautiful lady here has offered to take me on a date,' he told them. 'But only if we let you lot come along, too. We thought it would be nice to grab a bit of dinner along the river.' His cheeks flushed as he added, 'That's if you two don't have other plans?'

Megan blushed as she pictured the plans she and Ollie would almost certainly have in a few hours' time. For now, though, she was content to simply bask in the glow of their shared feelings – and what better way to do that than with friends?

'I'm in!' She turned to Ollie.

'Me too,' he said, smiling at the group and then down at her, leaning over to kiss her again until Hope started clapping her hands.

'Come on,' she said, stepping forward and linking arms with Megan. 'I think we've kept these boys waiting for us long enough, don't you?'

The sun was just beginning to dip as they set off along

the bank of the Thames, each remarking in turn how beautiful London looked when it was bathed in such flattering light. Waterloo Bridge lay ahead of them, its cream arches turned grey with the promise of approaching darkness. Beyond the bridge, Big Ben stood tall and proud above the Houses of Parliament, its round clock face so reminiscent of the city where they had all come together.

The London Eye was lit up in an array of pinks and blues, and Megan knew that if she were to lift up her camera, she would be able to capture the excitement and awe on the faces pressed up against the glass, as people of every age and nationality garnered their own mental snapshot of London, unaware that they were each adding their moment to a tapestry of history that was already so rich.

But she didn't feel that need tonight, and for once it didn't worry her. All she had needed to inspire her was love – it had just taken her a while to figure it out.

Back along the river, behind the locked doors of the studio, a single spotlight flickered into life. From its position high above the cityscape of photos, it was almost like a moon – a neat yellow pebble, so clear and true in the darkness. A passing couple paused to peer through the glass, their eyes following the beam of light right down to the image at its end – the image of a gold cross set in stone, a star on each of its five arms.

As they stared, each one transfixed by an unknown allure they could feel deep within their chests, the spotlight flickered again and went out. There was no light in the room now, but they could still see the cross. It glowed golden and bright, as if lit from within, just as it always had.